Arcadia

Arcadia

EMMANUELLE BAYAMACK-TAM

Translated by Ruth Diver

SEVEN STORIES PRESS UK
London

Copyright © 2018, Emmanuelle Bayamack-Tam
Original title: *Arcadie*, initially published by Editions POL, Paris, France, 2018.
English translation © 2021, Ruth Diver.

This work received support from the French Ministry of Foreign Affairs and the Cultural Services of the French Embassy in the United States through their publishing assistance program.

Cet ouvrage a bénéficié du soutien des Programmes d'aide à la publication de l'Institut français.

All rights reserved.
No part of this book may be reproduced, stored in a retrieval system, or transmitted in any form or by any means, including mechanical, electronic, photocopying, recording, or otherwise, without the prior written permission of the publisher.

Seven Stories Press UK
8 Blackstock Mews, Islington
London N4 2BT
United Kingdom

ISBN: 978-0-9955807-4-9 (paperback)

Printed and bound by CPI Group (UK) Ltd, Croydon, CR0 4YY

9 8 7 6 5 4 3 2 1

For Célia, Céline, Geneviève, and Philippe,
the members of the only club worth belonging to.

A real community is the product of an inner law, and the most profound, the simplest, the most perfect and the first law is that of love.

—ROBERT MUSIL
The Man Without Qualities

1.

And There Was Evening and There Was Morning, One Day

We arrive in the middle of the night, after an exhausting trip in my grandmother's Toyota hybrid: of course we had to drive halfway across France, avoiding high-voltage lines or cell-phone towers, and enduring my mother's wailing, even though she was swaddled in shielding fabric. I don't remember much about the welcome we received that night or my first impressions of the place. It was late and dark, and I had to share my parents' bed because a room wasn't ready for me yet. But I do remember everything about my first morning at Liberty House, about the moment dawn slipped through the weighted curtains without really pulling me out of my slumber.

Sleeping on their backs, their hands loosely crossed on their laps, with satin masks on their wax faces, my parents are lying on either side of me like two peaceful funeral effigies. This peace is something I've never felt with them before. Day and night, I've had to live with my mother's suffering and my father's tortured worrying, their permanent and sterile unrest, their convulsed faces, and anxious discussions. And so, although I'm impatient to get up and discover my new home, I stay here, listening to their breathing, making myself small, so I can bask in their warmth and luxuriously share their bed.

Cheery trills come in from outside, as if the invisible sparrows in their nests shared my joy at being alive. This is the first morning, and I am new too. I finally get up, quietly get dressed, go down the marble staircase, and notice in passing how the steps are worn in the middle, as if the stone had melted. I respectfully clutch the oak handrail, itself polished and darkened by the thousands of moist hands that grasped it, to say nothing of the thousands of young thighs that triumphantly straddled it for an express launch down to the entrance hall. As I touch the varnished wood, I am assailed by suggestive visions: *Mädchen in Uniform*, kilts hiked up over legs sheathed in opaque woolen stockings, braided hair, girls' high-pitched giggles. There is something here—connected to the place itself and its impregnation with a century of pubertal hysteria and Sapphic friendships—but I will understand the reason for this only later, when I learn the original purpose of the building I've just moved into. For now, I'm happy to tiptoe down the staircase and inhale the smell of something like religion in the wide hall with its checkerboard floor. Yes, it smells like wood polish, parchment, melted wax, and devotion, but I couldn't care less: I'm outa here, into freedom, the invigorating fresh air and evaporating dew, the early morning all for me.

Arcady suddenly appears on the majestic front steps, with their intricate cast-iron awning, and finds me immobile, dumbstruck by so much beauty: the soft slope of the pine woods, the blueberry bushes, the powdery rays of sunshine filtering through the trees, the veiled call of a cuckoo, the furtive scamper of a squirrel over a bed of moss and leaves.

"Do you like it?"

"Yeah! It's so cool!"

"Take it, it's yours."

I don't have to be told twice, and scamper off too, towards the magic pulverulent light under the huge trees, looking for that invisible bird whose cooing echoes my own feelings so well. But then it isn't long before I run into my grandmother, plunged into perplexed contemplation of a mound of crumbly earth at the foot of a pine tree. She hardly even glances in my direction:

"What do you think this is? A grave? It looks like someone dug it recently. I'm not at all sure about all this, that house, that Arcady..."

I would be happy to play along with my grandmother's gruesome speculations if she weren't naked as a jaybird in the greenery. A nudist to her very soul, she doesn't miss a chance to strip off, still I was hoping she might have waited a little longer before dropping her sequin dress. As for me, I'm used to seeing Kirsten wander around in her birthday suit. One of my first memories is finding myself face to face with her vulva when I was coming out of my bedroom. My eyes were at about the same height as the industrial-grade piercing on one of her outer labia, a kind of golden rivet, which was so attractive I couldn't stop myself from yanking it firmly, thereby causing an understandable howl:

"Let go, Farah, it's not a toy!"

Since I must have been about three years old, I pulled even

harder on that fascinating object. Bang, first memory, first slap. I howled too, causing my panic-stricken parents to rush in. Immediately assessing the scope of the drama that had just played out, Marqui hauled me up into his arms with dignified reprobation:

"Kirsten, for pity's sake, go put some clothes on, I dunno, some panties, a T-shirt, something! You're just impossible!"

"We're all family here! I don't have to cover up for my own family, do I? And she really hurt me, the silly goose!"

"Serves you right: next time, try to avoid provoking little children with your hardware!"

My grandmother retreated, full of contrition, but the lesson didn't stick; she persists in exhibiting her skeletal and dilapidated anatomy, which clearly has nothing obscene about it, for the simple reason that it no longer has anything human about it. It takes a lot of imagination to figure how that mangy pubis, those ochre teguments, that pallid sagging flesh, that network of veins with their scaly serpent-like appearance once belonged not only to a woman but to one of the beauties of her generation. And her bust. . . . Having always proclaimed that bras were lethal for breasts, she doesn't seem to realize that hers now flow parallel to her torso, with her nipples at the end of their tethers twelve inches away from their birthplace and swinging from side to side with her every move.

It's no use chiding my unruly grandmother, so I squat down meekly in front of the freshly dug grave and crumble up some clumps of soil before formulating a hypothesis:

"Maybe it was an animal that did this?"

"What kind of animal, then? A giant mole?"

"I'll go ask Arcady."

"Yeah, you do that. Go ask your guru."

I hardly know what a mole is, and even less what a guru is, so I hold my tongue, as I often do with Kirsten, who has ideas about everything and is constantly lashing out with her firmly held opinions. Regarding Arcady, my own opinion isn't quite formed yet, but since he has just saved my mother from certain death—a slow-burning extinction in the terrible suffering of electromagnetic hypersensitivity—I'd like Kirsten to give him a break, so I hazard to ask her:

"Well, why d'you come then, if you don't like Arcady?"

"I'm keeping a weather eye open."

She turns on her heel towards Liberty House. The passing years have taken nothing away from her majestic poise—she still walks like she's on a catwalk, no doubt unaware of the spectacle offered by her lumpy wobbling triceps and melting buttocks. Once she gets within sight of the house, she vaguely drapes her sequin dress around her body, but it won't be long before I realize that I needn't worry about the impression created by my grandmother's nudity within the walls of Liberty House—its inhabitants all live in nostalgia for Paradise before the Fall.

I'm left alone with the unresolved mystery of the earth mound and that other great mystery, for me, of this stretch of Mediterranean forest, with its scaly tree trunks, rustling foliage, scents of resin, and fauna on high alert at my slightest movements. This forest is mine, Arcady gave it to me. The fact that it is nothing more than the grounds of a large country estate doesn't even cross my mind: for me, it's an unexplored jungle, whose administration I take very seriously. I signpost my paths, mark my trees, and take a census of my subjects: the pipistrelle bats, the longhorn beetles, the wood-boring beetles, the chickadees, the caterpillars, the slowworms, the foxes.... Not a day goes by without my making another magical discovery: red toadstools with white spots, startled rabbits standing stock-still, wild blueberries and strawberries, clouds of midges in midair above a path, a jay's feather with perfect black and blue stripes, which I tuck into my pocket as a talisman.

As for the mystery of the earth mound, it is solved a few days later, when my family and I are invited to the setting of a headstone at the foot of the great cedar, for the dogs of Liberty House are entitled to their own funeral rites. What a pity, I wish I could have led an investigation, taken charge of a midnight exhumation, dug up human bones or at least a buried treasure of doubloons and pistoles. But there are too many mysteries left unsolved at Liberty House for me to waste my time feeling sorry that the key to this one was given to me. My childhood has just taken a new, unexpected, and enchanting turn, and I can feel it, as I stand over the tomb of this unknown dog, this sense of jubilation and happy expectation rising up inside me. All I have to do is look at my mother's face, free at last of its beekeeper's veils and spasms of pain, to feel sure that my great expectations will be justified.

2.

Be Not Afraid

It was about time: my mother suffered from migraines, memory loss, concentration lapses, and chronic fatigue. My father was in the best of health, but empathy being what it is, he was just as affected as his Birdie and had actively searched for a safe haven, a healthcare center, a cave, anywhere she might shield her legendary hypersensitivity from radiation. I know all about the contempt this diagnosis is usually met with, and I can sometimes appear to be ironic myself about the symptoms my mother presented, but I can testify that before her first stay in a quiet zone, her life was a living hell.

In my memories of that distressing period, she is constantly wearing a kind of beekeeper's outfit, a protective cape, an anti-radiation scarf, and gloves woven with copper thread. This attire means she is the object of suspicion, whereas I am the object of tender compassionate glances, me, whose mother has converted to such a strict form of Islam that she doesn't unveil a square inch of her reassuring flesh or hair. And who's to know whether she won't get radicalized and blow herself up, loaded with TATP and screws ready to perforate the infidels, who are legion in the neighborhood? Needless to say the few times we went out for a walk always turned into psychodramas, with a hasty return to home base for Birdie, weeping under her niqab. And so now she never goes out: she reclines on the cushions of her Mahjong couch, talks with a wavering voice and flaps her feeble hands at her staff: Marqui, Kirsten, and me, respectively husband, mother, and daughter of this elegant shipwreck.

We live isolated from the world. Metal blinds have replaced our beautiful velvet curtains: they are supposed to deflect the waves and cut the electromagnetic field down to a third of its strength, but Birdie still feels a strong burning sensation whenever she goes near the windows. To give Marqui his due, I must say he went all out to insulate our home, starting with the master bedroom: shielding wallpaper, bio switches, vital-field amplifiers that are supposed to convert electromagnetic pollution into beneficial effects, detoxifying indoor plants—everything has been done so that Birdie can get a little rest. But it's hopeless: she sleeps only three hours a night, generally in the bathtub, deserting the conjugal bed even though it is enclosed in an anti-radiation curtain. Needless to say we don't have computers anymore, or cell phones, or an induction stove. Even the electric coffee machine was deemed undesirable. We're back with a fixed-line phone, a stainless-steel Italian espresso pot, and LED lightbulbs. But here's the thing, six of our ten neighbors have Wi-Fi. Not to mention the obvious fact that we live near a cell-phone tower. Marqui did everything he could to turn our apartment into a sanctuary, but Birdie is still wasting away, and the list of her symptoms is growing longer and longer: headaches, joint pain, tinnitus, vertigo, nausea, loss of muscle tone, pruritus, tired eyes, irritability, cognitive impairment, intractable anxiety—to name but a few.

But then it seems to me that I've never known my mother to be anything except neurasthenic and abulic. The doctors she consulted didn't hold back in suggesting that her motor deficits and the decline in her mental faculties might have more to do with depression than with any sensitivity to electromagnetic pollution. Except that depression is a diagnosis Birdie considers insulting, so she shoots the medic her withered-lily look. My mother is not Lillian Gish's doppelgänger for nothing, and although hardly anyone remembers that star of the silent screen, you can count on my mother to perpetuate her memory. It's worth noting that Lillian Gish lived to a hundred and that Birdie will no doubt do the same, like many a fragile and overprotected princess. I say this with no acrimony at all, for I love my mother deeply and she totally deserves to be loved, since she is as kind as she is beautiful. She would even be funny and cheerful if her depression, or EHS, take your pick, gave her a half a chance. Yes, you might as well get used to all those acronyms that invaded our family, because on top of electromagnetic hypersensitivity, my mother suffers from MCS, multiple chemical sensitivity, and ICEP, idiopathic chronic eosinophilic pneumonia, not to mention IBS, irritable bowel syndrome—but then, of course, all those conditions are really only one and the same pathology: an intolerance to everything. God knows she doesn't get that from her mother, the unsinkable Kirsten, who freely admits that she has never known a minute of low spirits in her seventy-two years of existence and has absolutely no understanding of what is happening to her Birdie. And you might as well get used to nicknames too, because on entering Liberty House, everyone is expected to abandon their birth names.

"That's right," Arcady bellows, "it's like the Foreign Legion here: no one cares who you were before. What matters is what Liberty House will make of you!"

Arcady has therefore de-baptized just about everybody, inventing more and more monikers and diminutives. My father became Marqui, which he persists in writing without the *s* because of his severe dysorthographia, my mother is Birdie, Fiorentina is Mrs. Danvers, Dolores and Teresa are Dos and Tres, Daniel is Nello, Victor is either Mr. Bitch or Mr. Mirror, Jewell is Lazuli, and so on. I was not entitled to this initiation ritual, no doubt because my very young age made this symbolic rebirth superfluous. However, honesty compels me to mention that Arcady generally tags on incomprehensible words to my name: Farah Faucet, Farah Diba, Princess Farah, Empress Farah, et cetera. And, of course, all these titles are flattering, but I can't quite figure out what it is about me that suggests even the slightest notion of nobility or supremacy.

In any case, we were happy at Liberty House. We led precisely the pastoral existence that Arcady promised, with Arcady himself in the role of his life, the good shepherd leading his innocent flock. I say this with all the more conviction now that our happiness is under threat, if not irremediably compromised. But fifteen years ago, when we were setting that absurd headstone under the blue June sky, we felt light, delivered from our anxieties, confident in the future for the first time in a long while—and in my case, for the first time ever, since I had always seen my parents timorously withdrawn into their preoccupations and incapable of dealing with the outside world. At the age of six, I was already the pillar of my little nuclear family, the one who was sent out to slalom between real and imaginary dangers: collect the mail, take out the trash, buy bread or the newspaper. Kirsten was in charge of the weekly shopping as well as administrative tasks, and it was pretty clear that she greeted our decision to move to Liberty House with some circumspection:

"Quiet zones are all very well, but sooner or later they'll build cell-phone towers in the area. And who knows, there are probably high-voltage lines there already, or a nuclear-power plant nearby, and you don't even realize it! And that house must be at least a hundred fifty years old: it'll be full of lead, asbestos, and mold—I say you won't last more than three years there, tops."

Three years, in my grandmother's mind, was about the life expectancy those volatile organic compounds would give us. For although she didn't completely share all her daughter and son-in-law's phobias, she still agreed that, as a species, we were facing extinction. We were afraid, and our fears were as varied and insidious as the threats themselves. We were afraid of new technologies, global warming, electro-smog, parabens, sulfates, digital surveillance, prepackaged salad leaves, mercury levels in the oceans, gluten, aluminum salts, polluted aquifers, glyphosate, deforestation, milk products, bird flu, diesel fuel, pesticides, refined sugar, endocrine disruptors, arboviruses, smart electricity meters, and the rest. As for me, while I didn't quite understand who was out to get us, I knew that their name was Legion and that we were contaminated. I took on a sense of dread that was not mine but which readily played into my own childhood terrors. Without Arcady we would all be dead sooner rather than later, because our anxiety was stronger than our capacity to handle it. He offered us a miraculous alternative to illness, madness, and suicide. He gave us shelter. He said: "Be not afraid."

3.

The Perpetual Adoration

I was made for adoration. It is the climate in which I thrive. And no one deserves adoration more than Arcady. If I hadn't met him, I might have spent my whole life idolizing mediocre people, and what a waste that would have been. I was immeasurably lucky that our savior was also an extraordinary man, worthy a thousand times over of the worship I immediately and irrevocably rendered him. Before meeting him, I already had a notable tendency towards veneration, but it had found no outlet: I felt pity for my parents and a strong desire to protect them, and as for my grandmother, I loved her dearly, even though I couldn't stand her. Arcady immediately crystallized my fervor, my fanatical desire to follow and to serve, so that I could forget myself in that servitude. He found me at his heels in the very first days of our life at Liberty House.

"What you up to, Farah Faucet?"

"I'm coming with you."

"Oh, OK, if you like."

He soon got used to my company—bestowing on me the same distracted pats as his pack of dogs and cats—which didn't stop him from being attentive to my personal development in a way nobody had been until then, neither my poor parents nor my grandmother nor even my kindergarten and elementary school teachers, who had contented themselves with noticing my physical unsightliness and the ostracism my peers inflicted on me, which my teachers seemed to consider inevitable, if not in the order of things: they probably thought no one is that ugly without deserving it just a little.

So, yes, my birth put an end to a long lineage of remarkably beautiful, flawless individuals. In my mother's family, beauty is the only inheritance that is passed down, for lack of other qualities or resources. On my father's side, it's less striking, but over three generations of yellowed photographs, I've been able to find only harmonious figures and appealing faces, nothing like the spectacle of my spinal hyperkyphosis, drooping eyes, squashed nose, badly defined lips, and simian hairline. Puberty only made things worse: I became massive and bony, my pilosity took an exuberant turn, and instead of growing with the expected boldness, my breasts spread over my chest in a kind of hesitant jelly, with barely salmon-colored nipples. In any sexual competition, I don't stand a chance, I'm disqualified in advance. Luckily for me, Liberty House essentially welcomes the losers in life's great beauty parade and removes them from the pitiless rigors of the social world. Of all Arcady's guests, I'm not even the worst off: alongside those who are obese, depigmented, bipolar, hypersensitive, seriously depressed, multiple drug users, cancer or senile dementia sufferers, I can even hold my own. At least I have my youth and good mental health on my side. That's the gist of what Arcady tells me, the day I approach him to sort this all out once and for all:

"Do you think I'm pretty?"

I imagine that's the kind of question girls ask their mothers, but how could I ask mine, whose incontestable splendor has been celebrated since her most tender childhood? When Kirsten was close to forty and could foresee the decline of her own career as a model, she decided to monetize the charms of her only child, whom she turned into a prize pony, a kind of mini-Miss ahead of her time. Of course my mother now has too many problems to deal with to be able to make much of her enchanting features, or for them to inspire any kind of vanity in her, but if what I'm looking for is an assessment of my physique, I still prefer to ask Arcady, who is less intimidating in these matters. I must say he takes my question very seriously, and we position ourselves side by side in front of a rust-speckled cheval mirror. He makes me spin around, so that he can examine me front on, then in profile and from a three-quarter angle, and I almost start to feel hopeful: Arcady is a magician who can make my flaws disappear or transform them into unexpected assets—but that would be forgetting his pitiless honesty and frankness:

"You're a bit . . . chunky. And your eyes look like they are running away from each other. And your hairline is too low, it makes you look dense. Open your mouth. Yeah, your teeth could be OK, they're healthy anyway. It's just a pity your incisors . . ."

"What about my incisors?"

"They overlap each other. And your jaw is slightly prognathous."

"What?"

"Oh, well, it's not serious. I prefer that to all those hyper-correct bites: everyone with the same smile? That's not for me!"

I know that Arcady is against orthodontics, but I would be very happy to have a retainer, just like everyone else. And even a corset, I wouldn't even mind that either, since, as Arcady points out, I am hunchbacked—and no one has seen any hunchbacks in France for decades.

"I mean, really, your teeth, they're fine, but that thing there, your back, your parents really should have . . ."

He doesn't finish his sentence, so as not to cast any blame on Birdie and Marqui, and also so as not to forswear himself, since he professes that we should accept ourselves as we are, with all our flaws—big noses, wrinkles, cellulite, buck teeth, flappy ears, all those conditions that a certain kind of surgery is determined to correct, repair, align. Between my birth parents' negligence and my spiritual father's dogmatism, there's no chance I'll ever have a straight back, and I despairingly examine myself in the mirror, which is flattering only because it's so dilapidated.

"I'm a mess."

There again, I'm waiting for Arcady to contradict me, but it's no use: he agrees.

"Yeah, they slightly blew it with you. Slightly, right, don't make me sound like I've said something else!"

I've got enough to deal with from what he already has said without putting even more insulting words into his mouth, so I content myself with pushing my heavy bangs back from my forehead and offering my face to Arcady for an unbiased evaluation. I can't really disagree with him: something does seem to have screwed up my embryogenesis, sending my right eye too far away from my left, flattening out my nose, weighing down my jaw. I've come within an inch, if not half an inch, of pathological ugliness. Just as I let out a sigh and am about to leave, he grabs my arm and pulls me towards him:

"How old are you?"

"Fourteen."

"Have you got your period?"

"No."

"OK, well, let's wait a little while, but in two or three years' time, if you don't find a boyfriend and you want to take the plunge, come see me."

"To do what?"

"I dunno: you tell me."

"Do you wanna be my boyfriend?"

"Why not?"

"But you already have a boyfriend . . ."

That's an objection I make only as a matter of principle, for I can see nothing wrong with Arcady two-timing the hideous Victor, especially if it's with me. And anyway, Victor or no Victor, the very idea that Arcady and I might have sex someday drives me wild. He is still holding me in his arms and looking at me with something like tender puzzlement:

"Do you have a problem with me already having an official lover?"

"No, no, of course not!"

For pity's sake, I don't want him to go away thinking that I have scruples or to renege on the almost promise he is making right now! I'm fourteen years old, but I already know that I love him and want him, even though he is fifty and not much better physically endowed than I am: short, pudgy, with light-blue eyes popping out of his head and a sort of simian swelling between his nose and upper lip—Arcady is far from a paragon of beauty. He hugs me harder and whispers into my ear:

"Farah, I'll always be here, OK? And we'll do whatever you want: we'll have sex if you want us to have sex, but we don't have to."

"Do you think I'm attractive?"

He shrugs, and opens his eyes wide, as if my question was futile or the answer was obvious:

"Yes, of course!"

"So why did you say I was a screw-up?"

"Because you have a strange head and body. But you know, it might improve with time. And even if it doesn't, I couldn't give a shit: I think you're sexy."

"Well, then why don't we do it right now?"

"I'd prefer you to do it with someone you really love. To start with."

"But you're the one I love!"

He laughs and grabs my hair with both hands, pulling and twisting it like he's going to put it up in a bun. There's no tenderness in his eyes now, but what I do read in them gives me so much pleasure that I try to put all my powers of persuasion into mine. Why wait? I'll never feel this way about anyone else. I'd like to say something but I don't trust myself, and anything I could say would never do justice to the feelings I have for him anyway. How do you convince the man you love, when you're fourteen years old, to give you the priceless gift of deflowering you with due ceremony? For it seems to me that he just about offered to do so, although he's postponing the event into the hazy far-off future. And so I gather my words together again, a little laboriously:

"I'll never find a boyfriend! I know it.... And I want to... take the plunge. Right now."

"But you haven't even reached legal age! Do you want me to go to prison or what?"

He can say what he likes—I can see he's tempted, and I push my pelvis into his a little harder. He pulls away from me with a jolt, but it feels like he doesn't really want to.

"Farah, darling, we'll talk about it later, OK? You really are too young."

"I'm not too young! I'm too ugly!"

Of course, I've known Arcady and have been fervently drinking his gospel for nine years now, so that's how I know that the best way to titillate him is to claim to be ugly, which he doesn't believe is possible, not for me or anyone else. With Arcady, everyone is in with a chance, whether they're hunchbacked, obese, cross-eyed, decrepit old ladies or handsome old men. He sighs:

"You are perfect. Just give yourself some time to think about it instead of throwing yourself at just anybody."

"But you're not just anybody! I know you!"

"That's a pity too: it might be better with someone you don't know, it would be more of a turn on for you."

"But you're the one who turns me on!"

"What on earth do you know about being turned on?"

How can I tell him that besides shame and panic, being turned on is my most familiar feeling? And why does he insist on pushing me away when he has slept with just about everyone else here, including my parents—mind you, they're so easy to harpoon that it doesn't really count: all you have to do is talk to them a bit firmly and they'll say yes to anything. But even with the exception of my dear parents, Arcady's list of conquests is still impressive. Only my grandmother isn't on there, but then Arcady really isn't her type. What is my grandmother's type?

Women with issues, usually younger than her by fifteen or twenty years. Kirsten got married only to procreate. Once she had fulfilled that objective, she stuck to what she liked best, and I watched a long parade of Laurens and Valeries and Roxanes and Malikas, all flouncing creatures smelling of vanilla or mimosa.

It's weird how quickly most people specialize—like it's all over when they hit twenty: not only do they love men to the exclusion of women, or the other way around, but then they also like brown hair more than blond, sporty types more than intellectuals, Black people more than Arabs, and so on and so forth. I know from a credible source that Arcady tried it on with my grandmother and from an equally credible source that she sent him packing in the name of those ridiculously specific tastes I've just mentioned. For reasons that escape me, she can't stand virility. Manly women like me haven't got a chance with her. But poodles do, judging by her predilection for little curly things, of which Malika is the best example so far—as well as a personal best for my grandmother, since they've been living together for nearly three years, when the others lasted barely three months. Anyway, Arcady would have quite happily banged my grandmother, but now he's being sniffy about the youthful assets I am putting at his disposal with such an open heart. It's a worry, no matter which way I look at it. I feel like crying, but I restrain myself. I'm too horsey for tears. So instead of letting my sadness out, I try to obtain guarantees:

"OK, but when I'm fifteen, you'll be OK with it?"

"Sure, as long as I'm not your first."

"Oh, no, that's a crappy condition! What I actually want is for it to be you, and that we make it a kind of party, you know, like a ceremony."

I think I've got him here: no one likes parties more than Arcady. There's always one being organized at Liberty House. The only drawback is that I don't want to give my deflowering too much publicity, but then, I'll do whatever it takes. Only eight more months to go. In the meantime, I'll get rid of the hair on my upper lip, get my teeth straightened, and sort out my back: I will be the fairest one of all. Arcady catches me looking mournfully in the mirror:

"Stop looking at yourself like that! Don't you remember what I told you all about mirrors?"

If it's anything to do with him, I remember everything, and his sermon on mirrors was one I had listened to enthusiastically. I should say that Arcady gets us all together once a month to harangue us on all sorts of subjects. By "us" I mean the residents of Liberty House, of which there are generally about thirty, with very marginal fluctuations, more frequently connected with deaths than with voluntary departures. What person in their right mind would choose to leave this safe haven of their own volition, this place so devoid of everything that makes the outside world a permanent pit trap, an open hole in the ground we fall into and where we spend our whole life in agony, if you can call that a life? Arcady keeps telling us that life as most people understand it only distantly resembles a fully self-actualized human destiny: people live from day to day, people vegetate, people die waiting for the moment when their life will begin, but that moment never comes. To start living, they should first try staying away from all the things that are quietly killing them, but they don't even realize these things are harmful, and even if they did, they wouldn't have the strength to stay away.

I can see I'm not sticking to my topic here—namely, Arcady's sermon on mirrors, but to get back to it, I need to step away again, to broach a chapter I find difficult, which is about the love of Arcady and Victor—for although I wish it wasn't so, I am forced to admit that the love of my life has several lives, and in one of them he is the lover of Victor Ravannas, who doesn't deserve him but is still entitled to him, while I pine away.

4.

The Mirror of Simple Souls

I'd like to describe Victor in a way that does justice to all his repugnant characteristics. Am I objective? Certainly not, but subjectivity is the only way to go, unless you want to get lost in oratory precautions and lukewarm circumlocutions: Victor is a vile human being, and putting it any other way is a travesty of the truth. The fact that he manages to hoodwink Arcady about his deepest self is a source of surprise and affliction to me. Unless, in fact, Arcady is hoodwinking himself, incapable as he is of imagining the existence of an evil soul. That's always the risk with superior beings: they have trouble imagining that anyone can be base or have abject motivations.

I must admit that Victor Ravannas has a certain poise and urbanity that can make him agreeable company. To begin with, he is physically impressive: tall and fat, he never goes anywhere without a walking stick, whose utility is debatable, but which has the advantage of capturing attention. Its octagonal ivory pommel is part of a wider and much more carefully considered strategy than might first appear—but I know all about appearances, because they work strongly enough against me for me to get all caught up in them, and it hasn't escaped me that what Victor is trying to create around himself is an atmosphere of nobility and the illusion of a fine lineage: nothing is said, but everything is there to suggest it, from his cane to his carefully arranged silver ringlets, the puffy sleeves on his shirts, and the fake casualness of his babouches. I could forgive him his little vanities if he made up for them with qualities of the heart, but he doesn't have a heart, or rather, his is only an organ smothered in fat that persists in beating despite my daily prayers. After all, obesity does significantly reduce life expectancy, and there's nothing wrong with wishing for the inevitable to occur. Unfortunately, all these prognoses are thwarted, and Victor makes his perky and theatrical appearance at the dining table every day, to offer a spectacle of gluttony that dares not speak its name. At Liberty House meals are taken together in the dining room, Victor's favorite room by far, for he appreciates its majesty, especially of the ogival ceiling vaults under which he stuffs himself with mind-boggling quantities of food—not without delicately padding his hideous lips with a monogrammed handkerchief, for everything is a pose with him, everything is a planned and affected contortion.

Before it became a refuge for freaks, Liberty House was a girls' boarding school, and the house retains multiple traces of that original vocation: the dining hall, the chapel, the study rooms, the dormitories, and especially the countless portraits of the Sisters of the Sacred Heart of Jesus, a whole series of blessed and venerable nuns—blessed in name only, judging from their tubercular complexions and baleful looks. I don't know what gaggle of bishops, theologians, and doctors ruled on their cases, but they clearly confused martyrdom with bitterness and frustration. Luckily I'm not as easy to intimidate as I used to be—when I first came here, I found all those edifying chromolithographs rather demoralizing. I particularly dreaded a member of the order who came from Kerala, whose yellow cheeks and crazed eyes spied on me from a hallway on the second floor. In order to pass in front of her, I would slither along the opposite wall and hold my breath, but I could still sense the remanence of her bitterness and the exhalations of all the vile fevers she burned with between these very walls. Unlike me, Victor adores Marie-Eulalie of the Divine Heart, and he has long been planning to paint a fresco of her with her arms open wide, an ecstatic smile, and her eyes raised towards the heart crowned with thorns to which she devoted all her pathetic existence. Luckily when the members of Liberty House were consulted about the proposal that they should all take their meals under her saintly aegis—for obviously it was the dining room that was to receive the dubious honor of the mural of the beatific sister of Kerala—it was defeated by one vote.

In fact, it's not enough for Victor to be vain and hypocritical, he is also a zealot of the worst sort. I must say, however, that his devotion to Marie-Eulalie is nothing compared to the cult he renders his most famous homonym, Victor Hugo. Yes, indeed, Victor the Small idolizes Victor the Great. It's even thanks to the author of *Les Châtiments* that he and Arcady met—if thanks are even an appropriate response to that event. In any case, it was love at first sight, while they were both admiring a bust of Victor Hugo in his Paris apartment on the Place des Vosges. While I deplore the fact that they fell in love, I can only celebrate the happy consequences of that meeting and their relationship: this phalanstery that the two of them planned and set up, feeding off each other's megalomania, under the patronage of their illustrious master, himself an expert in delusions of grandeur. For whereas Liberty House once sheltered residents wearing braids and ribbons, herded by nuns steeped in devotion, Arcady and Victor have made it into a place inspired by Victor Hugo, closer to Hauteville House than the Convent of the Birds—if only in terms of its décor.

The least you can say is that they didn't nickel-and-dime about anything. Gothic cabinets and armchairs were brought in to replace the plain furniture of the Sisters of the Sacred Heart, while Savonnerie carpets and damask tapestries appeared all over the place. And antique or secondhand mirrors are, of course, Victor's little obsession: he collects every kind he can find with the obstinacy of one possessed. They come in all sorts of shapes and sizes: trumeau mirrors, cheval mirrors, barbers' triptychs, witches' mirrors, sunburst mirrors from the seventies, full-length mirrors, gilded mirrors, inlaid marquetry mirrors, mirrors framed in wicker, rope, bamboo, brass, whitewashed wood, or cast iron, asymmetric mirrors, ovoid, octagonal, rectangular, beveled mirrors: one can't take a single step anywhere in Liberty House without coming face to face with one's own dismayed reflection. I say dismayed, though that's just my reaction, because Victor always seems delighted to admire himself. He has turned the large living room into a real hall of mirrors, where he prances around for ages, just checking and adjusting his little touches: his walking stick with its ivory knob, his crimson pocket square, his cuff links, the precise piles of his snowy curls. Unfortunately for him, all these sartorial efforts are ruined by his shapeless drawstring pants, the only kind that can fit around his belly, which is collapsing to his knees. I know how tolerant Arcady is of physical monstrosity, but I still do wonder about their sex life. In any case, Victor's nickname at Liberty House is "Mr. Mirror." So I could be forgiven for thinking that Arcady's diatribe against those very mirrors was a way to condemn his lover's runaway narcissism. And I must say he was rarely as virulent and convincing as that day he gathered us all together in the chapel to forbid us to look at ourselves in any reflective surface of any kind. His voice vibrated with passion, his cheeks turned purple, his fist flew up to the skies or fell down on the solid oak pulpit to hammer out his indignation:

"Not only do mirrors contribute to your psychological suffering but I can't even imagine what you're trying to learn or to confirm in there! Mirrors teach us nothing. Nothing! If only because they have their own geometrical reality! Just try raising your left hand in front of a mirror, you'll see your reflection raising a right hand!"

Arcady's gaze sweeps over the audience, all those gaping mouths and unsteady heads aspiring to only one thing: reassurance about their place in the beauty stakes. They've probably forgotten that Liberty House principally recruits ugly people. With the notable exception of my mother, who is gorgeous, and my father, whose charm and regular features everyone admires, all the others, including me, are hideous, and can indeed expect no consolation from spending time before mirrors. Arcady continues:

"Not to mention the fact that nothing is colder or flatter than a mirror! What can a mirror tell you about your warmth, your particularities, your inner life—in other words, precisely what makes you *you* and not someone else? You know what?"

The audience shudders, holding their breath along with him, in anticipation of what they are about to know. Arcady wrinkles his forehead, bringing his eyebrows together, and takes on that imperious air that makes him absolutely irresistible in my eyes:

"We are going to veil or turn around all the mirrors in the house! All of them! Including those you have in your bedrooms and bathrooms, is that understood? Let's make Liberty House an MFZ! A mirror-free zone!"

His flock nods in unison, but Arcady hasn't finished:

"I hear that some people even have magnifying mirrors! That's really taking things too far, don't you think? Because tell me, honestly, what is it about you that deserves magnifying? Seriously?"

A few chairs away from me, I can sense incipient unrest, rustling fabric, huffing and puffing: Dadah is getting ready to say something, and it always takes her a little while, as if her shriveled brain and body needed a warm-up or a good shake to become operational. Her furious groan resounds, her flounces flutter, her teeth gnash, her hand taps impatiently on the armrest, here goes, she's ready:

"Arcady..."

Made more virile by almost a century of smoking, her voice rises up to the Gothic arches in the ceiling, startling everyone—except Arcady, who is never upset by anything. I have to say that Dadah, whose real name is Dalila Dahman, has always spoken to be feared and obeyed—and if obedience and fear were not her goals, then she got them anyway without even demanding anything, just like she got everything else she was entitled to since birth. Born into a mega-rich family of art dealers, Dadah found nothing better to do with herself than to get even richer, rich beyond reason—and even beyond imagination, for what human intelligence is capable of understanding the scope of a fortune counted in millions? Needless to say, Dadah also knew how to spend her money, and contrary to that inept popular motto, it did bring her quite a lot of happiness. And if the tribulations of old age didn't keep her stuck in a wheelchair, she would continue to be as happy as possible and just as indifferent to the unhappiness of others. Now that arthritis and emphysema no longer allow her to leap into her private jet, her world has shrunk to the dimensions of Liberty House, of which she is the principal benefactress. But while she could sponsor dozens of charitable institutions like ours with her munificence, she is as stingy with her donations as she is generous with her recriminations about our ingratitude—and she makes us pay a high price for every euro she spends on heating or garden maintenance. Let's not forget that rich people can be tightfisted, and Dadah is actually the only person I know who reuses aluminum foil and suggests using the water from cooking potatoes to water the plants or wash the dishes. Anyway, she's off, and I have no doubt she will have a word to say about Arcady's magnificent sermon about mirrors:

"Arcady, magnifying mirrors are actually quite useful for putting on makeup, especially at our age!"

At ninety-six, Dadah is the doyenne of the phalanstery by a wide margin, but she can't help herself from talking about Liberty House as if it was an old people's home. Whereas in fact, apart from my grandmother, who is only seventy-two, and Victor, who pretends to be fifty, most of the residents are in their prime. But it suits Dadah to pretend that everybody is close to senility. At the pulpit, Arcady gathers up his notes, a pile of yellowing papers that probably have very little to do with today's theme—he just likes to provide visual aids to give his eloquence more substance, and to impose ostentatious signs of his erudition upon us all. Dalila Dahman better watch out.

"What is the point of makeup? Have you ever seen anyone who is more beautiful with foundation or lipstick? It's just the opposite: with every stroke of the brush, with every drop of varnish, with every dab of the powder puff, you move farther and farther away from the truth and from beauty, believe me!"

Clutching the armrests of her seven-thousand-euro electric wheelchair, Dadah shivers at the offence, but also with the anticipated pleasure of jousting with her life coach—since that is the role she assigns Arcady. When she came here, she delivered her soul into his hands, abandoning its governance with relief to his care. That doesn't stop her from kicking up a fuss over trivialities, just to remind him that she can reclaim her freedom—and her money—at any time, so she launches into a spirited defense of mascara and blush, which she insists on calling Rimmel and rouge, but you can understand what she means, especially since she uses both excessively, and is a living illustration of the artifice that Arcady is condemning: asymmetric cheekbones daubed in saffron, a turgescent, glossy mouth, plastered wrinkles, gummy eyelashes. Next to her—figuratively speaking, of course, since they hate each other and keep their distances—my grandmother looks as fresh and clean as a round of reblochon. Of course, Kirsten didn't wait for Arcady to be suspicious of the cosmetics industry, and she prefers to display the rosacea on her cheeks and the creases on her décolleté without having recourse to creams or potions of any kind, to say nothing of scalpels or silicone.

Arcady is listening to Dadah with only a distracted, if not impatient, ear. No matter how much affection he professes for the elderly, he is quickly exasperated by her customary senile ramblings. Unfortunately for him, she is on top of her subject and not about to give up. Unlike Arcady, who has a platform and a captive audience whenever he might feel the need to express himself, Dadah no longer finds the same indulgent listeners as in her glory days. Yes, she is still frightening and rich, but she now has such frequent and enduring lapses in lucidity that even her most fawning courtiers accord her only minimal attention. But even if Dadah is losing her marbles, she still has enough neuronal connections to realize that her words have been devalued. And so, as soon as she gets the chance to hold forth, she makes the most of it and superbly ignores any interruptions or signs of irritation. On the contrary, boosted by adversity, she voluptuously sways in her wheelchair and modulates the dramatic inflections of her contralto:

"For goodness' sake, it's unbelievable that we shouldn't be allowed to pretty ourselves up while we still can! Erasing tiny imperfections seems like the least little courtesy! And you can get really incredible antiaging foundations! No, it's true, I assure you!"

As strange as it may seem, Dadah still believes that her skin has only a few little flaws, a liver spot here, a dilated vein or a smile line there, nothing that can't be disguised with an eye cream or an illuminating concealer pen. Here she is now, raising a trembling finger to her ravaged features, as if presenting evidence of the miracles accomplished by cosmetology on her person—when she is in fact the living proof of its ineffectiveness. While she allows thirty seconds of triumphant silence to pass, Arcady hastens to take up the thread of his speech again, to arrive at the "only mirror worth looking into." As a good orator, he waffles for a while to build suspense, just so all of us can search our minds and wonder what that might be. I have the opportunity of considering all sorts of saccharine hypotheses: our eyes, our consciences, fountains, springs, puddles, the sky, whatever. But it turns out I got it all wrong, for now Arcady is straightening himself up behind the pulpit to his full and diminutive height and proclaiming that *The Mirror of Simple Souls Who Are Annihilated and Remain Only in Will and Desire of Love* will be our mirror from now on. A respectful silence obviously follows this declaration, but a few glances to right and left allow me to confirm that no one has understood a word of this, except for Victor, whose satisfied and smug air makes me believe that he is the inspiration behind this bookish reference. Because, if it's a book, you can be sure that the idea didn't come from Arcady—he hates reading.

It took me a while to understand this, given that he professes to love literature in general and the works of Victor the Great in particular, given also that he has liberally furnished Liberty House with bookcases and shelving able to house hundreds of fine gold-stamped leather bindings. I've spent hours leafing through them myself, sitting in a patch of sunlight on the Aubusson rug in the library, a perfect allegory of youthful erudition but also a living image of perplexity—for most of them are old arithmetic or agronomy treatises, bought by the yard, Arcady being more concerned about matching the bindings to the armchairs than providing real books to quench our thirst for knowledge. Decorative spell books came to be added to the hagiographic collection of the Sisters of the Sacred Heart, but literature has only a small place here—one shelf, no more. No, I'm exaggerating, for Victor may be a terrible poseur, but in fact he is well versed in the art of poetry and has a library of his own. Alas, not only is it in the room he shares with Arcady but it's in a magnificent neo-Gothic vitrine with a triple door he takes great care to padlock, which means I've never had access to it, despite my secret incursions into their nuptial suite.

I love Arcady, and I think he's the paragon of a great soul, but I must admit that he and Victor have allotted themselves the most sumptuous rooms in Liberty House, while the other members are lodged in quasi-monastic cells or alcoves, resulting from the subdivision of the dormitories. I myself have only a cubbyhole of fifty square feet, and my parents are hardly better off. Having said that, I couldn't care less. On the contrary, I love the idea of my modest quarters, and I feel safe in my cozy nook with its tiny window. Especially since the tiny window in question looks out onto the branches of an Atlas cedar, whose very proximity makes me happy, as do the smell exhaled by its kernels and the insistent brush of its branches against the outer wall and the cheerful racket of the birds nesting there, which wakes me up every morning—every morning like the first morning. Before coming to Liberty House I had lived in a state of sensory deprivation I wasn't even aware of. Parents should be severely punished for raising a child more than a hundred yards away from a nest of warblers or a rockrose bush. Mine committed that error, and I almost grew up not knowing the pleasure of unfurling my petals in the sunshine, of pressing my cheek against a tree trunk all sticky with resin, or of running before a storm.

Arcady launches into a vibrant exegesis of the best pages of *The Mirror of Simple Souls Who Are Annihilated and Remain Only in Will and Desire of Love*, but I've stopped listening to him, struck by this obvious thought: the simple and annihilated soul is me; the desire for love is my only desire—and I could never really tell the difference between love and annihilation anyway. While the only man for me jubilantly discusses Marguerite de Porète and the Confraternity of the Free Spirit, I let my own free spirit make full use of its freedom and wander down the scented paths of my domain. That is where, in the lyrical screeching of the cicadas, I delight in annihilating myself and feeling my whole being disperse itself on the wind like a dandelion head.

"No one can be a more annulled man!"

Arcady looks at me as if he was guessing my thoughts, and that definitive sentence was meant for me, no doubt a citation from the remarkable Marguerite Porète, whose complete works I decide to acquire ASAP—unless she already figures in the two volumes of the *Seraphic Palm Tree*, a book that presents the advantage of combining Arcady's taste for half-Morocco-leather bindings with the spiritual aspirations of the Sisters of the Sacred Heart. I love the title of the *Seraphic Palm Tree*, and I have started it several times, but each time I try, there's nothing I can do, the book just falls out of my hands as soon as I get to the part about the edifying life of Jean Parent, nicknamed the "Master of Tears," which should have given me the hint long ago: there's nothing more boring than people who cry. In short, I am also annulled, completely abandoned to my bucolic contemplations, a dandelion seed of no substance; or completely consumed in the exclusive adoration of Arcady, a zealous disciple, a groupie, almost a soubrette—whatever he wants. And yet, I can feel it, something inside me is resisting dislocation, something is hanging in there. It's tiny but tenacious, like the promise of resurgence after the ardors of summer or the rigors of winter, like a fragile season with no name, besides mine, perhaps.

Arcady has finished his sermon and sends us off to our own occupations. Everyone shakes with relief as they get off their chairs. Only Victor stays put on his, but then he needs help to extract himself from it, and there is no question of my doing him this favor, of enduring his moans of effort and his belly flap swaying from side to side, and so off I go, even though his eyes are seeking me out and his signet ring is knocking against the knob of his cane as I slip away. He can sort himself out: I've made a vow of servitude, but he is not my master.

5.

Dilly Dilly

At Liberty House, all able-bodied adults work—which means very few people do, precisely because the place welcomes all kinds of invalids. My mother, for example, is dispensed of all activities because she is easily fatigued and prone to migraines. Yep, without electromagnetic radiation, her fragility had to find some other way to express itself. Her body had become accustomed to certain symptoms: to deprive her of them would be almost as cruel as leaving her exposed to technological pollution. So although she is doing much better, she still suffers from panic attacks, headaches, and episodes of low blood pressure. My father, on the other hand, has started growing and selling flowers, having discovered within himself a limitless patience and interest for this activity.

Well before our arrival, and on Arcady's impetus, Liberty House had set itself up as a productive unit for organic fruit and vegetables. We therefore have an orchard and a vegetable garden, over which I feel I have certain rights, even though they were not part of the domain expressly handed over to my administration. The orchard doesn't interest me enough to fight the wasps' claim to it—with all the rotting apples and pears they become fearless, if not downright aggressive—but the vegetable garden is a delicious place, with rows of cabbages going to seed, Belrubi strawberry plants, heavy squashes, and the smell of tomato leaves, exalted by the sunshine as well as the rain.

My father started timidly, with nasturtiums and dahlias, then, giddy with the success of his bouquets at the local markets, he diversified—gladioli, irises, tulips, carnations, jonquils, marigolds, daisies—and has now become quite the expert on seeds, sowing, natural fertilizers, and pesticides. He used to come in from the garden and the greenhouses, dazzled, overwhelmed, unstoppable in describing the buds of Japanese anemones, unstoppable about the scent of lilies or freesias too. It turns out flowers are an excellent topic of conversation: try this out, everybody has something to say about them; everybody has their favorite flower, or one they can't stand because of its heady smell or its superior airs. It's true! There's always someone to say that heliotropes are too pretentious or peonies too full of their scruffy little selves. My father, having been painfully aware of his lack of conversational skills until then, had finally found an audience along with a topic, people who would listen to him at last. One day when he was holding forth a bit at the lunch table, blushing and speaking too quickly, Marqui—whom no one had ever seen like this—attracted the attention of Victor the Small, who was busy gulping down his cream of squash soup. When the meal was over, he led my father into the library and took down two books bound in blue percaline, the legacy of a certain Odette Garnier to the community of the Sacred Heart, as shown by the ex libris carefully glued into each of them: *Botany for Ladies*, volumes I and II.

"Since you seem to find it interesting, here, take a look at this! Flowers have a language, you know!"

Language was precisely something my father sorely lacked, which means that he went against his well-established habits of intellectual laziness and read the books Victor recommended from cover to cover—and he was never the same man again.

In order to understand the scale of this metamorphosis, I should go back into the scholastic past of poor little Eros Marchesi—namely, my father. He retained only vague memories of his kindergarten years, but as far as he knows he did very well and was full of enthusiasm for group singing, throwing balls around, and jumping through hoops. He was perfectly behaved most of the time, sticking out his tongue only when he painstakingly wrote the four wobbly letters of his name. It was in the first year of elementary school that things started going wrong. Little Eros had gone in with his confident smile, his unrelenting goodwill, and his conviction that they would be enough for him to do well. But, in fact, they weren't. No matter how hard he tried, he did everything badly. Or more accurately, he failed at what appeared to be precisely the main goal of his first year at school: learning to read. As long as no one had asked him to put them together, he'd had no problems with letters. He recited the alphabet like a little parrot, and had no difficulty pointing at the *X* or the *M* on a cross-stitched alphabet sampler made by his maternal grandmother. Words were another story, to say nothing of sentences—and that was just it, no matter how wide he opened his terrified eyes, all anyone ever talked about was that: letters-making-words-making-sentences, for everyone but not for him. No, I'm exaggerating. By January there were three children in the class of thirty who didn't yet get it: my father, a little immigrant girl who spoke only Comorian, and a strange child whose sugarloaf-shaped skull had little chance of containing a brain.

Every morning, my father prepared himself to receive the instruction dispensed by Mrs. Isnardon. He methodically set out all his school things on his little desk, crossed his arms, and opened his ears wide. It was a waste of time. The letters would immediately start moving on the page and Mrs. Isnardon's strident explanations would only add to his panic. Daniel led the donkey to the stable, the maid put a steaming roast and mandarins on the table, Valerie cut herself with a flint, the geese waddled to the pond, and there was never an end to any of it. Luckily the sepia vignettes in the reading book gave him some clues about Daniel and Valerie's bucolic life, for otherwise he would have burst into tears. When he was called on to answer a question, he took his chances, using the pictures to help him, identifying a word here and there, getting it right once in a thousand times, attracting the pitying glances of Mrs. Isnardon and the less charitable sniggers of his classmates. In April, even the little Comorian girl had understood what it was all about and looked at him triumphantly as she chanted along: "Daniel hits the rat with a paddle and kills it," for Daniel was cruel, but then so was she.

My father had all kinds of difficulties to contend with. The first one was that, for him, some letters had colors, and no one ever mentioned this at all. When he had tried to talk about *a* as the red letter, Mrs. Isnardon had made a face with big round eyes and continued her patient speech as if nothing had happened: "*r-a*, ra, like in rat, *p-a*, pa, like in paddle, don't you see?" No, he didn't see anything except that that awful Daniel had squashed the rat with the blows from his paddle. For that was another of his problems: he wasn't sure how much credence to give to those sentences that everyone was busy trumpeting all around him. After a while, he formed an attachment to Valerie, her blond braid, her doll, her little dresses; the donkey, the goat, and the geese also seemed worthy of affection, and he shuddered to see them stupidly going to the river, where they were at risk of drowning— especially since Daniel was there with his pitiless paddle. Everything on the page in the reading book ended up getting all jumbled, Valerie's inoffensive games, the waddling flock of geese, dreadful Daniel's deeds. He concentrated, opened his eyes wide, licked his index finger to follow the line, but at the end of his finger, the words started looking like processionary caterpillars, with only the confusing blinking of a vowel here and there: the blue of *e*, the orange of *o*. . . . He stopped and raised a discouraged eye towards Mrs. Isnardon. He felt like something had swooped down on him, that there was a system there, a giant magmatic system—except that the others managed it, found shapes in shapelessness, decoded the encrypted messages sent by Daniel and Valerie from their little farm, and rendered their secret meanings.

Alerted by the teacher, my grandparents finally realized how severe their son's difficulties were and did their best to remedy them, giving him additional reading lessons at home, with the little boy on their laps and the reading book open on the living-room table. Alas, Eros failed just as miserably at home as he did at school. "What's wrong with this child? Is he thick?" That was the question my grandparents anxiously asked themselves after those sessions, which were distressing for all concerned. And my father probably was thick, even though his IQ was normal and allowed him to do mental arithmetic or memorize three verses of a poem—as long as someone had read it to him first, obviously. Normal IQ or not, he had to repeat his first year of school the following year, while the cohort of his classmates flew straight into second year. The child with the sugarloaf skull was there too, in his usual place at the back of the class, and with an imperceptible blink of his lizard eyes, he had given a sign of connivance and commiseration to his companion in misfortune. Mortified by this companionship, Eros had decided to give it all he had, but the nature of what he needed to swallow still escaped him. Luckily for him, the child with the pointy head died in November of that year, suddenly, sitting up straight on his chair in class, without it being noticed. His heart, no doubt as atrophied as his brain, had refused to go for another spin of the wheel and put an end to the little life of Jean-Louis, for that was his name. Eros was the only one to notice that Jean-Louis was suddenly abnormally rigid and that his lizard eyes had grown opaque. What to do? Overcoming his timidity, he had sidled up to Mrs. Isnardon's desk and whispered:

"Teacher, Jean-Louis is dead!"

Contrary to his expectations or even his fears, Mrs. Isnardon had burst into a cheerful laugh, thinking that this was a joke, and mostly because she was incapable of imagining that a seven-year-old could abruptly pass away in such an inappropriate place:

"Oh, no, come now, of course he's not dead! You know very well he's always like that: Jean-Louis is always well behaved and quiet! Not like some of you!"

She had taken the opportunity to give the little group of impenitent chatterboxes her death stare—for it wasn't often that poor Jean-Louis could be held up as a model for the rest of the class. But at that very moment, the unfortunate boy had finally fallen off his chair, scattering a variety of disturbing objects: a pair of secateurs, some locknuts, a smoke bomb, and some miniature rum bottles. What his untimely death revealed was that Jean-Louis had undoubtedly had an inner life of his own, and that he was even preparing his own little version of the Columbine shooting, sickened as he was by months of failure and humiliation at school. And who knows, maybe the stress of the preparations was what had hastened his demise? In any event, his death had the same effect on Eros as a blow from a giant paddle by the awful Daniel. Where no lesson, no method, no handbook had succeeded, Jean-Louis's death was a complete success: the letters stopped blinking, the syllables stopped reversing themselves, the words stopped sliding into each other. His eyes were brutally and tragically opened, and he could read. In the meantime, his parents had benefitted from the informed diagnosis of their family doctor: their little boy was dyslexic and dysorthographic to the highest degree. He might just get away with not being completely illiterate, but language would always remain a giant pitfall for him.

So you can understand why, forty years later, he jumps at the idea of being able to do without words, and to use flowers to communicate instead. Painfully decoded, the two volumes of *Botany for Ladies* turn out to be a gold mine of precious information. He's fully aware that cyclamens and geraniums limit him to expressing only sentiments and emotions, but that's a good start, and he doesn't despair of one day devising a more elaborate floral code than the one he enthusiastically discovered thanks to Odette Garnier, Victor Ravannas, and the aptly named Roselyne Saniette, the author of his new bible.

At the markets he now sells ready-made bouquets to which, despite his difficulties, he ties a rectangle of card with his own painstaking calligraphy. A bunch of red amaryllises, white hydrangeas, and blue anemones will mean: *you are too flirtatious and your whims aggrieve me, but I retain my trust in you*, whereas fire-colored irises and wallflowers overflow with the happiness of love—*today more than yesterday and far less than tomorrow.*

My father is also capable of adapting to the complicated love lives of his clients and proposing personalized floral arrangements. Requests for forgiveness or a rendezvous, calls for caution, regrets for an indiscretion or an insult: flowers can say everything and do so willingly. Quite quickly he is a little overwhelmed, since his clients don't stop at ordering flowers, they also confide in him.

"You see, Mr. Marchesi, I'm just unlucky: I always fall for straight guys who only want to see what it's like to sleep with a guy, you know, just once, on a whim. But then I get attached—you can't stop yourself from getting attached, can you?"

"No, you're quite right. You can't."

"So I fall apart every time it happens."

"I'll put in some bellflowers for you. And some yellow gentians."

In the end, the bouquet tends to look like a prescription rather than an attempt at communication with the beloved: pink chamomiles for the misunderstood lover, yellow coreopsis for the unhappy rival, multicolored snapdragons so the beloved comes soon. My father's gentleness and patience work wonders with these tortured souls, and there are crowds at his stall every Sunday. As his second-in-command, I make one bouquet after another, tying the little simultaneous interpretations to the stalks of the arum lilies, the nasturtiums, or the hyacinths: *listen to your soul, you can no longer love, the hope you give me is enchanting.* Meanwhile my father is holding a weeping client's hand and imploring him to use flowers as therapy. He finally found his calling and a new source of revenue for Liberty House: with all the encoded bouquets and the shrink sessions, my father contributes ever more significant sums of money to the community. Of course, it's nowhere near enough, as we shall see. As our spiritual leader keeps harping on, not everyone is capable of working, but everyone is capable of earning money—and I can see that I need to relate another one of Arcady's memorable sermons.

6.

Love Squads

In the chapel that day, the cast-iron radiators with their floral motifs are busy keeping us warm, lustily grumbling and bubbling away. My grandmother is just back from a trip to Formentera and in dazzling form. Next to her, my mother is more emaciated than ever, but let's get this straight: she is doing better and better and will bury us all, including me, since she is now spared any effort or worry. Arcady goes up into the pulpit with a preoccupied expression I find a little alarming, given his usually carefree and cheerful nature. Instead of a pile of yellowed pseudo-notes, he is holding a sort of large register, which he sets down on the lectern with the same serious air.

"The accounts are not good, frankly. If we keep going like this, I don't see how we can keep going."

The incongruity of his statement escapes him, as it escapes the audience, which is according him its usual free-floating attention. I am the only one who is actually worried. My grandmother is scratching a scab on her suntanned shin, Victor is polishing the knob of his cane, Dadah's hoary head is already bobbing, and Daniel is yawning to the sky. Daniel? Yep, he's here, armed with his paddle and ready to squash all the rats in the world. Except there are no rats at Liberty House, and our Daniel is not the same one as the one in the reading book, the one from the farm, with the donkey, the geese, and little Valerie. No, this is Victor's godson, a tall sullen gangly boy. I never quite figured out what Victor put into his role, probably erotic practices rather than purely educational goals. In any case, Daniel follows at his godfather's heels with a sort of lascivious and ostentatious languor, as if he had just risen from their nuptial bed. I find that rather insulting for Arcady, but it would never even cross Arcady's mind to claim exclusivity in matters of love. I'll get back to love, which was actually my topic, or rather, Arcady's topic on this December morning. For the moment, he is dealing with the balance sheet, but it's obvious this bores the shit out of him and he would rather get to the point. Here goes: his eyes lock into mine, but I barely have time to rejoice at this before he shoots daggers at Dadah from his pale-blue irises, then sets them on Birdie, Gladys, Epifanio, Daniel, Kinbote, Coco, Jewell, Salo, and all the others, all his sheep nestled in the same woolly torpor:

"*Omnia vincit amor!*"

None of us know any Latin, but Virgil's motto is familiar to us, since Arcady has it tattooed between his shoulder blades and never stops crowing it. Love conquers all, of course, but Arcady appears to have decided to turn it into a war machine, a nonlethal weapon, but still a weapon, to bring society to our enlightened views.

At Liberty House, we bathe in love: the love Arcady gives us and we gladly return to him, but also the love we feel for each other despite the exasperation that communal living inevitably causes. *We* . . . I think I can say this without fear of ridicule, without that pronoun referring to an anemic and atrophied structure like a couple or a family. I even think I can say that my start in life has made me a specialist in *we*, contrary to most people who don't have a clue, and spend their whole lives never imagining that they could be anything more than themselves. I have been *we* since childhood: it helps. Not only did I share board and lodging with over thirty people of all ages and backgrounds but I also had to give up my special relationship with my parents and grandmother, who were soon in the grip of new emotional relationships and delighted with the sudden deregulation of their sexual lives—to say nothing of how I had to get used to the idea that Arcady belonged to everyone. That's why I can say *we* without any presumption or incongruity. That's why Arcady's new sermon doesn't surprise me at all. For what is he proposing, in fact, if not for us to practice outside our colony's walls what we are already experimenting with inside them—namely, the gift of oneself, pleasure with no inhibitions or conditions, love that can only be completely free and absolutely mad? Having let my mind wander, I focus my attention again on the orator—who is also the only man I will ever love, even though he refuses to accept it and even though that expression has no meaning for him. Arcady is talking about the ways of the world, and indeed the world is in a bad way, only because it doesn't understand that all it needs is to love, to be somewhat attentive and benevolent, and to spread the irresistible strength of desire everywhere possible in order to annihilate barbarity forever.

"When I think about all those poor people killing each other..."

His eyes drift off into the distance, his voice sounds distracted, his words evasive. We will never know whether he is thinking about the recent terrorist attacks or the war in Syria, where he is originally from. Unless it's just where he was born, since he hardly ever talks about it, and lets the details of his genealogy and personal history remain rather vague, as if they had started only with Victor and Liberty House. Before that: nothing, or not much. He was born in Syria, lived in Lebanon, Switzerland, and Poland—in other words, nowhere, or rather, in countries about which no one has any opinions. His homeland, in any case, is love, is Liberty House, is us. That's why my heart beats so hard when I look at him and listen to him: it beats in unison with his emotions, his indignation, his pity, his infinite sadness about the inept laws that rule our existence. I am inside him, just as he is inside me, just as all the members of our little libertarian confraternity are. Love conquers all, I know this full well since I saw it conquer my parents' madness, sociopathy, abulia, suicidal moods, depressive states, polymorphic phobias, and inability to raise a child or to project themselves into any kind of future. Loved by Arcady, and guided by him, they smoothed out their little balled-up, crumpled souls until I saw them become companionable adults—their maturity still leaves much to be desired, but still, I'm used to it now and I have enough maturity for all three of us.

Although we live sheltered from new technologies, that doesn't mean that the news of the world doesn't reach us: it comes to die in waves at the foot of the drystone walls enclosing the property. Victor has an eclectic selection of newspapers delivered every day, and spends his mornings reading

Le Monde, *La Croix*, and *Le Figaro*—yes, his eclecticism stops at those three titles, of which we are allowed to avail ourselves after Mr. Mirror has conscientiously read them, not without creasing and staining the pages. Not that he's particularly messy or that he forgets to wipe his hands, but he permanently exudes a kind of greasy vapor. If only for that reason, I am sometimes happy enough to let the others' comments inform me of the day's news. Especially since I have easy access to the internet at school, and I often go online there. After all, I'm not hypersensitive to anything at all, and even though I would never admit this to my coreligionists and especially not to my poor parents, I'm not exactly thrilled to live in a quiet zone and would give my right arm for an iPhone. But then, living at Liberty House offers so many compensations that I won't moan and groan about not having easy access to social media. I have my own networks. They snake underneath the ash trees and the beeches, they crisscross with the starlings' and squirrels' paths, they run alongside the meadows and the coppices, with their autumn crocuses innocently unfurling their toxic stamens, and the blackberry bushes just as innocently setting traps with their black thorns. I am happy: I don't need Periscope, WhatsApp, or Snapchat.

While I let my thoughts wander once again, Arcady formulates our assignment: we are instructed to go out into the world and to flood with love all the souls in torment we are sure to find. Although it sounds simple and generous, this campaign is actually a recruitment drive, and the rich are our prime target. Of course, one can be undiscriminating in love, and Arcady is just that, screwing everybody with no distinction of gender or age, but if we wish to preserve our collective hotel and our little bucolic lifestyle, we need to learn to be slightly selective. The ideal would be to rally to our cause super-wealthy widowers or disgraced heirs, who could then find a useful outlet for their immense wealth. It could be argued that we have Dadah, but Dadah contributes only a tiny proportion of her fortune to the community, and obstinately refuses to include Arcady in her will—to say nothing of the fact that she is constantly threatening to abandon us and go bestow her largesse on some ungrateful venal nephew or other. The continued existence and prosperity of the phalanstery must rely on the diversification of its sources of revenue, and each of us, in our own way, can help with this diversification.

"You are my love squads," Arcady bellows. "Go, charge! Spread yourselves throughout the streets and squares, talk to people, tell them about what we are trying to do here! That's all they're waiting for: to talk about love, to have someone take an interest in their soul, to be reminded that they have one! Maybe they've even forgotten they do!"

He's not wrong there. In the outside world, at school, at the market, no one talks to me about their soul or mine, ever. Sitting next to me, Daniel is wriggling, sighing, and making a show of impatience: "What is this, mass or something?" he whispers into my obliging ear. Well, yes, it is a bit like mass, but so what? Although I've never been to church, what with all the reliquaries and lives of saints and photographs of beatific nuns, I've ended up steeped in Catholic liturgy. Sixty years after being decommissioned by the Sisters of the Sacred Heart, the walls of Liberty House still exhale devotion, and Arcady himself was raised in the Syriac Orthodox Church. Although he rarely mentions it, he has retained a certain fondness for gold leaf, beards with ringlets, purple chasubles, and conjuring tricks: try to get rid of religion, it comes back at a gallop. Last year, after an invasion of aphids in our vegetable garden, Arcady even pronounced an exorcism taken straight out of a bilingual Greco-Arabic manuscript, bound in black shagreen stamped with gold, which came to him from a Cycladic great-aunt. In the name of all the cherubim and seraphim, twenty species of pests were enjoined to flee the eggplants and the Chinese cabbages, and I must say that the creepy-crawlies decamped pronto, no doubt terrified by the power of Arcady's oratory—unless our black laundry-soap spray also helped.

In any case, I had received my marching orders, just like the others: if I meet a rich person, I am instructed to seduce them and take them to Liberty House, where Arcady will be the one to close the deal. Given my flagrant lack of charisma, it is clearly for the best that someone else finishes the job for me. I notice that Daniel is just as full of doubt about his own charms as I am about mine. I must say we look quite similar and that we are often taken to be brother and sister: we're both tall, horsey, bony, and dark, and also share an androgynous appearance that others find rather unsettling. To increase our chances, we decide to hit on people together. With my wrestler's body and my nascent mustache, I look like I'm twenty, though I'm not yet fifteen—the age at which I decided Arcady and I would celebrate my deflowering with great pomp and circumstance—that is, unless Arcady declines the active role that I have offered him on this occasion, in which case I will put off losing my virginity until later and make do with a birthday party. On the other hand, Daniel is sixteen but completely lacks any teenage freshness. Quite the opposite—with his shambling gait, his furrowed brow, his sullen complexion, and his dying eyes, he easily looks ten years older. Never mind, he can come with me to the market on Sunday. While Marqui sells flowers and personal-development advice, we will attract the customers—as long as they show some exterior signs of wealth. We have something to sell too: our youth, of course, but also our little libertarian gospel. The Jehovah's Witnesses, who are also everywhere to be seen between the market stalls, better watch out, with their outdated flyers and their promises of the Kingdom. The Kingdom is where we live, Daniel and I: it is here, it exists, a few miles away from this Mediterranean market; we don't need to promise it, we can lead our consenting prey to it, all those idle retirees who don't know what to do with their money, their time, their life. Blessed are the rich, for they will have everything, if only they take the trouble of lending their ears to our good news, our incandescent message, our fiery words, which tell them we are ready to love them passionately if only they hand over the dough—that vital element of the war we are waging against the injustices and aberrations of this world.

And it works: on the very first Sunday, we gather a few subscriptions. Daniel and I must somehow form an irresistible couple, despite our lack of grace. But then Arcady had also supplied us with the required convincing phrases: the end of the world, the vanity of all things, the seven mirrors of the soul, the magnificent idea of love. When I don't know what to say, Daniel flies to my rescue with unheard-of vigor. I have never seen him like that, and I must say I am completely flabbergasted. Where does he get that teasing jokiness and that flirtatious glint in his eye, when he ordinarily has such a weary and cynical gaze? That day we return to Liberty House in my father's truck, feeling tipsy with our success: one Nelly Consolat, who is apparently the granddaughter of an astronomer, but more importantly is a self-proclaimed millionaire, declared that she was highly interested in our propositions. As blonde as Dadah is brunette, but in significantly better shape despite their similar ages, this Nelly seems to all of us to be a choice recruit, and Arcady suggests we go all out to welcome her:

"Let's make her our tofu in flaky pastry with truffle sauce, and our beet tart with mascarpone foam, OK? And our sage-and-butternut ravioli: she'll love it!"

We're talking about food, so Victor has something to say, as always:

"What about tempeh slices with mint and cranberries as well? And a jasmine-raspberry zabaglione for dessert!"

Food is like flowers: an ideal topic of conversation for people who have no ideas of their own and nothing to say to each other, which probably go hand in hand. And here again, I suggest you experiment with introducing the topic, just like that, for no particular reason. You'll be surprised to see faces light up, tongues become unbound, and even the quasi-autistic speak up to share their chocolate-cake recipe or to explain their preference for meat or fish—a preference that is meaningless in our case, since we are strictly vegetarian, hence the tempeh and the tofu. We managed to escape veganism, but only just, following stormy arguments and a no less turbulent vote. If Fiorentina hadn't kept a weather eye open, the consultation might even have ended with the victory of the gluten free, a very active little lobby group in our midst. But then Fiorentina put all her weight on the scales, and I am just about to make up for the wrong I have done her by giving her the homage she deserves.

7.

The Torture Garden

If I wasn't already in love with Arcady, I would certainly be in love with Fiorentina, despite her advanced age—even though it's difficult to determine precisely. She was here before anyone else, of that at least one can be sure. It even seems that she was one of the pupils of the Sacred Heart, back when Liberty House was a girls' boarding school. Arcady and Victor found her here and bought her along with the house and the grounds she managed in her spectral fashion. In accordance with the unwritten laws that govern our life at Liberty House, she was assigned a moniker that is just as puzzling as mine: Mrs. Danvers. She puts up with it, just as she puts up with all the rest—Arcady's whims, Victor's fancies, the vegans' activism, the carelessness of some and the failings of others. She puts up with everything all the better by doing precisely as she pleases. She looks like an allegory of docility, with her apron and her sweet expression, so everyone takes a while to detect her strength of character, but as far as docility is concerned, Fiorentina mostly appreciates that quality in others. You only need to see her at work in her kitchen, where she accepts help solely on the express condition that her assistants know their place, as simple executors of her sovereign decisions. Faced with such a well-tempered character, the gluten free didn't stand a chance. No, I'm wrong, I can see that love is blinding me—which is in the very nature of love. I am wrong because, despite her autocratic tendencies and her heart of bronze, Fiorentina suffered a terrible defeat the day she was forced to renounce her *vitello tonnato*. I should add that Fiorentina comes from Piedmont: for her, a meal must be organized around wild-boar stew, with carpaccio as a starter and polenta as a side dish—or at least pan-fried boletus mushrooms. She cannot understand the point of desserts, and she prepares them without pleasure or zeal, which doesn't stop her *crostata di castagne*, her *semifreddo al torroncino*, or her *sbriciolata fragole e panna* from being worthy of the most luxurious tables.

When it was just starting out, Liberty House had only a handful of members and was seeking its inspiration, modus operandi, and house rules all at the same time. Those were the days when Fiorentina could go wild in the kitchen and subject everyone to her carnivore diet, alternating *arrosticini*, Venetian liver, meatloaf, and pulled beef cheeks—along with her famous wild-boar stew, of course. I wasn't there and I regret it, for Daniel, who has tasted her *fritto misto* of veal offal, talks about it with tears in his eyes. But then, kaboom, after two or three years of absolute authority, Fiorentina had to submit. Not that anyone came to lay claim to her title and functions—no, she remained the uncontested queen of our kitchen, but since

Arcady had made equality between humans and animals one of the seven pillars of his wisdom, we were deprived forever more of *osso buco* and rabbit in mustard sauce. As for me, I eat meat at the school cafeteria, even though my parents send countless anti-speciesist letters to the catering service. And as for Fiorentina, I suspect she breaks the rules too and melancholically consumes her *vitello tonnato* in the privacy of her giant medieval kitchen.

And yet Arcady is never so eloquent as when he is talking about animals, and I would find it difficult to refer to a single one of his sermons on the topic, since he has given dozens of them—and also since I don't want to change my subject, which is Fiorentina. But anyway, what more can I say about this Italian sphynx? Daniel calls her Metallica, a nickname that has the advantage of clarity and perfectly accounts for the indestructible armor she hides under her placid outward appearance, her waxy complexion, her Piedmontese warbling. Fiorentina has a daughter and a granddaughter, but no husband or son-in-law. You'd almost think that women from the Maira Valley reproduce with each other. The daughter and granddaughter sometimes appear within our walls to hold long confabulations in Italian. Where do they come from, and where do they live when they are not making their ghostly apparitions at Liberty House? It's a mystery, another mystery in a life that is made up of closely guarded secrets and a duty of confidentiality in all circumstances. You could clamber over Fiorentina's dead body before she would surrender the keys to the ramparts of her soul.

Her bedroom is next to mine, in the most isolated wing of the house, but I can count on my fingers and thumbs the number of times in ten years that I've seen her velvet-chenille bedspread, her dark wooden wardrobe, and the photograph of

Pope Benedict XVI—either she hasn't yet moved on to Francis or she is harboring a grievance against him that is as obscure as the rest of her inner life. In short, beside the crucifix and the little branch of boxwood, only Benedict smiles widely, raising his pontifical hand. Fiorentina never smiles, and laughs even less. No, I'm exaggerating and letting myself get carried away by my love of fine phrases, for she does have moments of cheerfulness—but then you have to be right there to see them. They arise at unexpected times and for impenetrable reasons, although I've been able to figure out a few constants over time: animals make her laugh until she cries, especially when they are young and foolish—for being a carnivore has never stopped anyone from appreciating the clumsy grace of a kitten or a calf.

Unfortunately for Fiorentina, our love of animals is of a different quality from hers and forbids us to eat them. Fiorentina understands this perfectly and refrains from expressing her disapproval, but I can feel it even in her way of beating eggs, of chopping up celery, or of stirring her cornmeal, all procedures that she masters to perfection, but which don't allow her to express the full scope of her talents. For want of anything better, she serves us borage tarts, eggplant tians, minestrone, arugula pesto, or fricassee of girolle mushrooms, but her heart isn't really in these dishes. If she wasn't so attached to the property, or maybe even incapable of living anywhere else as it's been so long, she would no doubt have offered her services to less unreasonable people. Unfortunately for her, the members of Liberty House are firmly committed to anti-speciesism, and the reintroduction of meat to our diet would lead to Fiorentina's being banished for life—in other words, condemned to death, given her age and her ignorance of the modern world. Unless her ironclad mind is what allows her to survive in a hostile environment? And who knows, maybe she has already survived the worst? When you think of the miserable valley of her birth and the militant folly of the Sisters of the Sacred Heart, it's clear that she can't have had an easy childhood. Adulthood must have come as a relief, and I can understand that she feels little compassion for the fate of hens and pigs whose living conditions she no doubt shared: chestnut pottage in a shack made of mismatched boards. The other inhabitants of the house do not have this same hardness of heart, and animal suffering is unbearable to them. I'd say I'm mostly on Fiorentina's side in thinking that the destiny of a hare is to finish in a stew. I've learned to pretend that the animals are my brothers and sisters, but I keep my thoughts to myself.

I don't know when Arcady and Victor's conversion to vegetarianism took place. When my family arrived at the phalanstery, it was already an accepted fact that no meat or fish would be eaten. There were ongoing discussions about eggs and dairy products, but as I mentioned earlier, Fiorentina triumphed over the members' vegan fundamentalism and orthorexic fantasies.

At Liberty House, we live happily together with all sorts of animals: cats and dogs, of course, but also a whole flock of winged creatures, and even a modest herd of cows and goats, which we take turns milking, trying to avoid their brutal shoves and nauseating farts. I completely understand that we don't have the right to kill them just for the pleasure of consuming their hocks or ribs, but taking it a step further and according them the same consideration as human beings is not a line I'm prepared to cross, and my acquaintance with our degenerate farm animals has only reinforced my conviction of my superiority. Apart from laying eggs and screeching, hens and guinea fowl have no special skills and are not even particularly likable. At least dogs are friendly, and I completely understand that one shouldn't eat one's friends, but a chicken? God knows I love Arcady, but when he takes to his pulpit to defend animal rights, my eyes glaze over, my ears buzz, and I escape into my thoughts, I scramble down the hills, I climb the trees, I roll in the grass studded with crocuses, I wait for the end of his regurgitation of Claudelian claptrap. Yep, Arcady hardly reads but considers himself a lover of literature, and claims Victor Hugo, Marguerite Porète, and Paul Claudel as his favorite authors, gaily ransacking their work for citations to pad out his foggy sermons, instead of counting on his own intellectual resources, which are in fact considerable—as if his fine intelligence had a blind spot, an inaccessible corner which his powers of reasoning couldn't reach but where his madness about animals and his promotion of absurd and mortifying nutritional interdicts could thrive.

I suggest anyone protesting against the force-feeding of geese spends half an hour in their company. After you've been bitten a couple of times, you'll feel fewer scruples about eating their *foie gras*. Not to mention that geese are horrible animals, with their yellow-rimmed eyes, their squamous feet, and their necks that stretch like they are trying to beat the record held by the swan or the ostrich—which are just as ugly and nasty animals. To top it all off, our menagerie includes a couple of peacocks. The peahen is OK, and doesn't make a big deal of her dull plumage, but the male is insufferable with his hideous squawks, his ruffled crop, and the angry show of his fancy-dress tail feathers. As one might expect, Victor has made the peacock his totemic animal: it figures as a line drawing on his personal cards and even on his signet ring, a jewel he flaunts like an ancestral heirloom, but which was made by melting down some mismatched earrings and his infant name bracelet. But then, isn't the peacock's special attribute to show off its looks and parade about? A useless animal if there ever was one, apart from its ornamental function.

The more time I spend in the animal kingdom, the less I understand why Arcady would relinquish his supremacy over inferior creatures and not seek to benefit from them as much as possible. I say this all the more serenely since I love animals, and I'm never happier than when a hedgehog crosses my path, or I surprise a fox cub or a wild-eyed buzzard. And, of course, I'm passionate about our pack of lame dogs and cats. For it's not enough for Liberty House to welcome the socially maladjusted, it is also an animal refuge, since Arcady and Victor spend their time rescuing laboratory rabbits, ewes destined for the knacker's yard, or mongrels abandoned on the roadside. Of course our cats and dogs are fed vegetarian kibbles, although the cats ensure they have their daily allowance of animal protein by decimating the population of field mice on the property, after first dissecting them alive at length. And there again, all you need to do is spend time in the company of a cat to discover that it is the most cruel and careless vivisector, cruelty being the one thing that is most widely shared in the animal kingdom, including among humans of course, but not exclusively.

Before anyone starts whimpering about the injustice done to our animal friends, I suggest they have an internship in the world of the jungle, which, of course, starts at our very doors. In any of our suburban gardens, in any of our city parks, there are whole populations of little feathered or hairy torturers. And don't get me started about insects, they deserve a whole chapter of their own in the universal history of cruelty. All gardens are mostly torture gardens, in the secret of their humus or the simple rustling of their leaves. And let's not forget crustaceans. If you think they are harmless and fit only to end up on your plate with a dollop of mayonnaise, that's because you haven't heard of the *Cymothoa exigua*, which gradually devours the snapper's tongue until it replaces it completely, gripping on to the stub with its clawed feet. And what about the sacculina, another crustacean, well known for its sadistic behavior towards the green crab, whose genital organs it crushes, among other similar abuses? When anti-speciesists say that the worst things happen at sea, they have no idea how right they are, even if they are thinking only of the misdeeds of trawling and completely ignore what marine animals inflict on each other. So Arcady can spout as much as he likes about the octopus's remarkable brain, or monkeys' sense of community, I couldn't care less: I know what I know, and I will continue to eat my cheeseburgers, unlike my extended family and without their knowledge, and come home every day with the open expression and languid eyes of a staunch vegetarian—for I am a serpent, and in our Garden of Eden, that is no small thing. Never mind. I take responsibility for my crimes, my perjury, and their dissimulation, if that is what it takes to lead a quiet life in what my nearest and dearest are obstinate enough to call the garden of delights, incapable as they are of reading the pages of blood and murder that are being written here every day.

8.

I Am Fifteen and I Do Not Want to Die

When I arrived here I shared my parents' irrational fears, but with the passing years my own fears have taken over. I'm about to turn fifteen, I'm not frightened anymore by stories of phthalates or electromagnetic radiation—not that I'm disputing their noxious effects, but to tell you the truth I'm more concerned about what humans inflict on each other than endocrine disruptors or carcinogenic substances. If I have to die of something, I'd just as soon it was from a long illness rather than a bullet from a Kalashnikov: with a long illness, I'd have time to prepare, time to get used to the idea, time to choose the friends I want around me, and time to find the precise spot where I would wait for death. In the heart of the heart of my kingdom, I know a little hollow, not even a hollow, just a little depression in the ground, carpeted with soft grass and sheltered by a copse of hazelnut trees, which will be just perfect. That is, of course, if I don't die before then, struck down by a volley of bullets from an automatic weapon or the explosion of a TATP bomb. And even though the probability of a violent death is extremely low in my case, I can't stop thinking about it as soon as I step outside the garden walls of Liberty House, which don't provide much of an obstacle to invasion but do have the merit of materializing what separates us from those who haven't chosen the seven-step path to wisdom.

What separates us hits me like a slap in the face every day of the week. All I have to do is climb aboard the school bus that picks up children along the river whose name shall not pass my lips. Even though I sit at the front and glue my forehead to the window, in less than half an hour, I garner enough stupid or insulting remarks to last a lifetime. Not that I am even the target—not me or anyone. They get passed around almost mechanically from one middle schooler to another, along with all the rest: sneers, gobs of spit, down jackets with fake fur trim on the hoods, backpacks with the same black and red label, the same ugliness for everyone—I'm the only one with my own version. It's not just that I have to put up with the pettiness and crudeness of my peers every morning: if all I had to do was to get through my middle school years, I'd find a way, especially since they are nearly over. No, what really worries me is that I don't sense any more kindness in adults than I do in children—to say nothing of teenagers, for whom nastiness is second nature. Outside my little secret confraternity, people don't want to be good, and don't want to grow, to elevate themselves, to enlighten themselves either. Their crass ignorance suits them very nicely. And if they get the chance to shoot me, they will. No need for a reason to do it: madness is enough. In the outside world, it's everyone for themselves and against everyone else. No, it's not even that: they'll all shoot themselves first, because you have to be already dead to go to war.

My upbringing didn't prepare me to understand or submit to violence—and even less to inflict it. It takes more than observing how cats put mice to death, or taking a school bus, to become an expert in barbarity, and the problem with all the people around me, starting with my parents, is that their kindness makes them weak. Under attack, they would be incapable of an effective response. Fortunately the house is difficult to access: only one road leads here, so we would be able to see the enemy coming from a long way off—that would give us time to retrench, if not to take up arms. After that, come what may: there are enough provisions in the cellars to get us through several months of siege, and it's a well-known fact that patience is not the main quality of terrorists.

Terror doesn't stop me from venturing to the closest town, whose name shall not pass my lips either. Let's just say it's a human-sized border town, and that there are enough streets, boutiques, cafés, and lively sidewalks for a young woman of almost fifteen years to get lost in, and to find joy in doing so, brushing past strangers who might become friends. It seems I haven't completely lost faith in human nature, since I still believe in the miracle that will allow me to distinguish one face among many, an opening of light in the opaque crowd, an unknown friend whose memory I will take back to my castle in the air. That's the thing too: I was spoon-fed the notion of impassioned love, I have heard the ardent language of desire, so now that's all I can think about. That's why, despite my panicky fears about assaults or attacks, I continue to look for my soulmate in the midst of the city lights, even though I always rush back to find refuge in my bedroom under the eaves, or to curl up in my secret hollow or the fork of a walnut tree, or to join my father in the greenhouse full of the scent of freesias, where nothing can happen to me. Except that's just it: I do want something to happen to me. So actually I don't know if I really want the tenderness of my family, the panes of glass misty with the breath of flowers, Fiorentina's Italian warbling in her kitchen, Victor's grotesque but inoffensive waddling, the ooze of hardened resin on the trunks of my pine trees, the heady scent of summer, the patch of blue sky between the metallic storm clouds, the invisible but tinkling cattle, the obstinacy of a cat following me on my secret paths—my zone to defend against all threats, including my own desire to lose myself. For I can tell that the inevitable convulsions of my youth are threatening Liberty House from the inside.

I am fifteen and I do not want to die, that's for sure—not under a hail of bullets or the rubble of an airport destroyed by a bomb, in any case. But I don't want to be completely and perpetually spared either, or to put it another way: I am fifteen and I don't mind dying, but not before being loved, not before a thumb rubs my cheekbone. Yes, I know, that sounds pretty strange, and you'd have to be there to see what I mean, you'd have to see Arcady stroke Victor's face with an inquiring and tender thumb to understand that, yes, it's true, love does conquer all, and I can say that out loud because I've been the witness to that victory, to that rescue *in extremis* of everything that was going to collapse, to fall into the abyss, to be lost forever. But now it's my turn to be saved and to make sure certain promises are kept:

"I'll be fifteen next week. Do you remember what you said?"
"Not at all."
"That you would have sex with me when I was fifteen."

"I said that?"

"Yes."

"Have you got your period?"

"What is this, an obsession, this periods business? No, I haven't got it, so what?"

"You're really special, Farah Faucet, but I'd just as soon have sex with a real woman."

"But you said we just needed to wait until I reached legal age!"

"Well, of course, that's best, but then, if your body is still a child's body, the legal age doesn't mean much."

"But I have breasts, look!"

Of course, he's seen me in the buff often enough that I don't need to show him anything: we have communal showers, and our house rules stipulate that the community is nudist. But between those who go around naked all the time, like my LGBTQ grandmother, and those who wear stockings in high summer, like Fiorentina, all sorts of practices are present in the bosom of our community. I myself wander around in shorts or underpants as soon as the weather permits it, neglecting to hide my modest bust. On the contrary, I like to expose it to the sun, so that it loses its nasty winter colors, pallid globes and purplish nipples.

"And I have pubes too!"

Arcady glances skeptically at the elastic of my pajama bottoms, but abstains from verification. That's a mistake. My pubic hair is my most luxuriant asset.

"No periods at fifteen, it might be worth getting that checked out. Not that I know much about puberty in girls. . . . Do the girls in your class have them?"

The girls in my class have not been girls for a long time. All of them have been buxom and menstruating like clockwork since they were twelve. I am the only one whose body is still hesitating. We agree that Arcady will take me to a gynecologist sometime soon, but that doesn't sort out my issue, which is still to find love. Well, no, not exactly, since love is standing in front of me, in a tricolor sweat suit that would make anyone ugly, but not him—for he professes a complete indifference to physical appearance in general and to sartorial codes in particular. Arcady, my love. . . . Things would be so much simpler if you accepted to pay your respects to my burgeoning femininity instead of proposing substitutes:

"Why don't you do it with Nello? He's cute, isn't he?"

Nello—in other words, Daniel—is not bad, but he makes no effort to be desirable and is always dragging himself around as if he was suffering a thousand cuts. Before trying anything out with him, I'd have to make him lose that pained expression.

"Or Salo? Why not Salo?"

Salomon is our resident bipolar, so I'm not quite sure how I should take Arcady's suggestion. Do I really want an obsessive man? Because that's what Salo is: he has his little fixations and can talk about them for hours, indifferent to his interlocutors' signs of exasperation or attempts at escape. He actually seems to have very little awareness of the existence of others. Of course, that's how it is even with lots of people who are of sound mind, but I can't help wishing my first lover might pay a little attention to me, just for a change. Community living and open relationships, that's all very well, but I would like a little exclusivity. But at Liberty House, love is diffuse and undifferentiated: everyone gets their share and everyone gets all of it—which suits me better in theory than in practice. Since my arrival here, I've shared everything with everyone: showers, meals, household chores, fireside evenings, sun salutations. Even my parents no longer belong to me, and I sometimes catch them gazing at me with a puzzled look in their eyes, as if they had completely forgotten about my existence, absorbed as they are by their own. As for their parental authority, they completely delegated it to Arcady, just as they relinquished all the rest, all their adult responsibilities and preoccupations. When I run into them in the corridors or on the pathways in the vegetable garden, they respond to my panting puppy-dog cuddles with good grace, but always with a touch of astonishment, as if they were wondering what they did to deserve such a display of tenderness.

Which is why I wish I could inspire someone with more passionate feelings and a more pronounced liking than the lukewarm affection I receive from the members of my confraternity, parents and guardian included. I wouldn't mind trying dating sites, but my school library blocks access to them, as if it was unthinkable that a teenager would want to look for love. No, if Arcady persists in not wanting me, my only chance to find a partner who might fulfill my aspirations is to continue to wander the streets of my little town, those streets that twinkle in the rain as if they were telling me not to despair: be patient, love will come.

9.

Love Will Come with Your Eyes

Some promises are easier to keep than others. Arcady takes me to the gynecologist, as he said he would. But if he thinks this dispenses him from deflowering me, he's kidding himself, and I'll get him sooner or later. The gynecologist is called Mrs. Scampi, and although I suspect that her name has some secret connection to her specialty, I'm too stressed to figure out what it might be. I don't know what to expect, but I'm anxious about her examining my genital organs and kneading my hypotrophied mammary glands. It turns out I had no need to worry, since Mrs. Scampi is charming and shows no surprise at the fact that I am accompanied by my spiritual director. That said, he introduces himself as my father, and waves his health insurance card under the good doctor's nose.

"So what brings you here, Farah?"

"Well, I haven't got my period."

"Oh, really? Since when?"

"What d'you mean, since when?"

She looks at me with weary patience:

"Your period? How long since your last period? You're afraid you're pregnant, right?"

"No chance of that: I'm a virgin!"

I can't help checking with the corner of one eye the effect this proclamation has on Arcady, but he retains his paternal and smug demeanor, while Mrs. Scampi trots out her spiel about the irregularities of the menstrual cycle in very young women.

"There's really no need to worry. Especially since you've never had sexual intercourse."

It's her turn to glance at Arcady obliquely. No doubt she's wondering how much of the truth I can tell in front of my father. He puts a protective hand on my shoulder blade and is quick to resolve the misunderstanding:

"Farah has never had a period. At all. That's why we came to see you. At fifteen, usually . . ."

Mrs. Scampi reassures us enthusiastically:

"In France, the average age for first periods is twelve and a half! But there are girls who have them at eight, others at sixteen, and that's just the way it is!"

"Yes, but the other girls in my class . . ."

"Tsk tsk, I'll examine you anyway, but I'm absolutely positive: not having periods at fifteen is perfectly normal. Take your clothes off. Do you want me to ask your dad to leave?"

It's out of the question that I remain alone with Mrs. Scampi. She does seem nice but you never know, or in fact, you do know only too well. In any case, I know from experience that I have the knack of bringing out the worst in people: sadist urges and delirious rushes. Dad will stay where he is.

My feet in the stirrups, I silently endure Mrs. Scampi inserting a metallic object into my vagina and rummaging around in there unceremoniously, but less and less vigorously. It feels like it will never end, but then at last she removes her torture instrument and throws away her powdered latex gloves. Arcady coughs diplomatically:

"Is a speculum really indicated, for a virgin?"

She gives him an offended look.

"Sir, there's nothing better that a speculum to examine the vagina and the cervix. And it allows us to take all kinds of samples too. That said, in your daughter's case . . ."

She stops, allowing him to imagine how his daughter's case might be infinitely more difficult than those of her everyday gynecological consultations:

"I'm going to do an ultrasound. Do you know what that is?"

I see that everything is now happening between Arcady and Mrs. Scampi, as if I was not lying in a dorsal decubitus position in the middle of the room, naked as the day I was born. Don't ask me how, but Arcady seems to know all about medical imaging, so he and the gyno are there talking wavelengths, echography, and piezoelectric effects, while she slops her transducer around on my slimy gelled-up tummy, and the bluish pulsatile images send us their enigmatic signals. I almost expect to see a 3D fetus show up on the screen, but no, of course not. Time passes. Mrs. Scampi seems to be taking more and more snapshots and measurements, slashing the images with dotted lines as mysterious as all the rest of it, those funnels of light where dark ill-defined masses float.

"Well . . ."

All is not well, clearly, but I quickly wipe my tummy and get dressed, just so I'm not surprised by the diagnosis with my four limbs in the air. But I might as well stay stark naked, since the gyno doesn't even look at me. When she is not staring at her images, she's fiddling with her Montblanc pen or addressing Arcady with little embarrassed beginnings of sentences:

"It's quite strange, because usually.... I mean, I'm not saying.... But still, I would have expected.... Anyway, we'll have to see if.... What we need to do is...."

Even the beginnings of sentences come to an end, as she runs out of rhetorical precautions, then points her pen in my direction:

"It looks like Farah doesn't have a uterus. And not much of a vagina either."

I'm well placed to know that I have a vagina, and she herself stuck her nose and even a speculum in there for a good ten minutes, so what the hell is she talking about?

"Well, in fact, she only has a vaginal cupule three centimeters long. Basically she's missing the top two thirds of her vagina. It looks to me like we're dealing with a case of MRKH, or Rokitansky syndrome, if you prefer."

I don't prefer anything at all, and I couldn't give a shit about labels: I just want to have my uterus and the missing two thirds of my vagina back. Because I can't stop thinking that before entering Mrs. Scampi's consulting room I still had them, or at least I was living with the idea that I had them, which amounts to exactly the same thing, given the lack of use that a fifteen-year-old girl makes of either of them. Sure, I had already put a finger into my vaginal cavity and found that the exploration came to a rather sudden end, but not knowing anything about other people's vaginas, I had made do with clitoral stimulation without asking myself any further questions. Mrs. Scampi is now hitting her stride. Visibly giddy with the thrill of this diagnosis, she is now talking enthusiastically about the deformities that are associated with my utero-vaginal aplasia:

"Do you have good hearing?"

"Um, yeah."

"You're quite sure, right? And you don't have back problems do you? No deformity of the spine? No scoliosis?"

"I have dorsal hyperkyphosis."

"There you are, then! There you are! There's the whole picture! MRKHs often have problems with bone growth. You'll have to go get your kidneys looked at too, and get an MRI done."

"When will I get my periods?"

"Never. Your ovaries look functional, but you will never have periods."

Arcady pulls himself out of the stupor into which the diagnosis of my incurable condition had plunged him—since that is what it is, as well as the first case of Rokitansky syndrome that Mrs. Scampi has ever seen in her cozy little practice, which up until now had dealt with nothing more than contraception methods, pregnancy care, and hormone replacement therapy, maybe a case of breast cancer from time to time, and even then. . . .

"Will she be able to have children?"

"Without a uterus or a cervix? Impossible. It would be quite something if she could even have sex!"

"How's that?"

"Your daughter is impenetrable. Three centimeters of vagina—do you understand?"

At that point in the consultation, she finally seems to realize the cruelty of her words. Her face turns purple and she can't wait to get rid of us, scribbling letters for her colleagues who are better acquainted with MRKH as fast as she can and blurting out one comforting phrase after another:

"You can live very well without a uterus, you know. And periods are much more of a nuisance than anything else. I have patients who would pay good money not to have them anymore."

As she shows us to the door, loaded with collegial correspondence and various prescriptions, she is suddenly possessed by the demon of diagnosis again and grabs my jaw with an inquisitorial hand to turn it this way and that under the light:

"No, you see, what surprises me is her hirsutism. Normally MRKHs have a feminine phenotype. Externally, they're normal, with breasts and not much body hair: pubic hair, armpits, that's all. But it looks like Farah is starting to grow a mustache..."

Arcady pushes me outside before Mrs. Scampi declares straight up that I am in the process of virilization on the outside as well as the inside, but the harm has already been done, and we despondently shuffle back to the car.

"Do you want us to go for a drive? To the harbor, maybe?"

Unlike my parents, who know nothing of my life outside Liberty House, Arcady is perfectly aware of my urban escapades.

"No. I wanna go home."

"Come on, Farah, let's go have a drink. There's a really nice café in Les Sablettes. I know the waitress, and they have an amazing prosecco. You'll love it."

I have no doubt that he knows the waitress at that café and many others, given his proclivity to socialize with anyone anywhere, but I don't want to drown my sorrows in *spumante*, no matter how exceptional it might be. No, I want to feel my sadness, to explore all its nooks and crannies, before forcing it to surrender. Except that Arcady doesn't see it that way.

"Let's go."

Bad luck, it's the beginning of December and his really nice café is shut for the season, just like all the others along the beach. We end up like two shitheads kicking the sand and soaking up the ambient desolation.

"Farah, who gives a fuck if you don't have a uterus. I don't have one either."

"Yeah, but you're a man. I thought I was a girl, you know. Until today."

"But you are a girl!"

"No, I'm not! I don't have a uterus and I don't have a vagina."

"But that's all bullshit! Look at Daniel!"

"What about Daniel?"

"He doesn't have any body hair or an Adam's apple, but he's still a boy!"

"I'm sorry but Daniel is a really bad example."

"Why?"

"Because Daniel is just like me, neither a boy nor a girl!"

We sit down on a drift of damp sand, facing the gray, white-capped, charmless sea—a thousand miles from what it can be when the sun turns it into a mirror of its glory.

"What difference does it make that you don't have a uterus?"

"I don't have a vagina either."

"Let's take these problems one at a time. What good is a uterus?"

I don't know what idiot defined health as the silence of the organs, but I'm positive: health is first and foremost their presence, no matter how noisy and painful. I don't have a uterus, and I have a condition called Rokitansky syndrome. There it is.

That's my illness. It may be incurable, but it defines me completely. Arcady listens to me rant and rave, his eyes open wide:

"Come on, you can't be serious!"

"I'm totally serious. See, you were right when you said that my parents screwed up with me. Something did turn to shit in my embryogenesis."

"Something always turns to shit anyway. If it doesn't happen during embryogenesis, then it'll happen later."

"Yeah, but I still don't have a uterus. And to answer your question, a uterus is what you need to have children."

"You're not even fifteen yet! Do you want to have a child? You're a child yourself!"

"I don't want one now, but what will I do when I do want one?"

"You can get a grafted uterus. Your mom can hand over hers: she's not using it anymore."

"And what about my vagina? What do we do about that?"

"But the vagina is no use for anything either!"

"Speak for yourself!"

"Well, yeah, that's just it, I am speaking for myself and I know what I'm talking about: it's not like sex is just about vaginal penetration, you know."

"Arcady, did you even hear what Mrs. Scampi said? I have a vaginal cupule. A cupule!"

"What did you just say?"

"A cupule."

"No, the gyno's name!"

"Mrs. Scampi?"

"Mrs. Campi, not Mrs. Scampi, for goodness' sake! Do you know what scampi are anyway? Hey, how about we go have a seafood platter by the harbor?"

"Aren't you vegetarian?"

"Yeah, but if it will cheer you up, I'm ready to demolish as many scampi, sea snails, and crabs as it takes."

I appreciate the effort he's making to change the subject; I also appreciate the fact that he is prepared to transgress his own food doctrines, which he promulgates in the bosom of our little community, but it seems to me that my anatomical deformities warrant more attention.

"Do you know what a cupule is? The only cupule I know about is an acorn's cupule: you know what that looks like, right, an acorn's cupule?"

He knows full well since he was the one who taught me how to make a whistle with one, teaching me the word and the technique at the same time: you close your fist, you put the cupule between your thumb and your index finger, and you blow. It produces an incredibly high-pitched and loud noise, capable of waking up all the animals in the forest and very useful in case of emergency. An emergency is what I see on his face as I furiously draw up a detailed list of everything I will miss out on because of my utero-vaginal aplasia:

"I mean, I'm already not a hottie, right? So can you imagine how guys will react when they discover they can't penetrate me? And if I do manage to find a guy who doesn't run a mile when he finds out and it starts getting serious between us, what am I supposed to tell him? Honey, if you want kids it can't be with me, because I can never get pregnant, even if you go at it for hours in my cupule? Because, if I'm getting this right, not only is my vagina just three centimeters long but it's a dead end too, right? Geez, that's just gross."

"Farah, I assure you, all this stuff about uteruses and vaginas doesn't matter. You'll get heaps of guys. Or girls! Among them—

selves, girls don't tend to mind all that much, and anyway, they don't give a shit about the vagina, they stop before they get there."

"That's bullshit! Go tell that to Kirsten, that women don't care about vaginas!"

I've always heard my LGBTQ grandmother boasting about the satisfaction she derives from her own vagina, and the pleasure she takes in penetrating her lovers', in feeling their elasticity and innervation. Arcady is speechless, so I keep going:

"What, don't you think the vagina is an erogenous zone?"

"That's not at all certain, Farah: it varies from one woman to another, I think. Some women are strictly clitoral."

"Yeah, well, I better be one of them."

"Listen, you know what? Let's organize a great big party for your fifteenth birthday, next week. A *quinceañera*, just like in Mexico. How would you like that?"

"You can go rub your *quinceañera* on your balls for all I care."

Of course, sooner or later, thanks to medical progress, they'll probably find I have balls too. Maybe they're already hiding in my abdomen, waiting for the opportune moment to drop down into my outer labia and to transform them into a dangling wrinkly red scrotum—given the male propensity for exhibitionism, I know all about scrotums, and those at Liberty House are no more of a secret to me than the caruncles on our turkeys, to which they look very similar. Only Victor keeps his shirttail over his reproductive organs, which is one of his rare good qualities. Anyway, my abdomen may look normal and all, but I now know that I can't rely on that normality, and that it probably holds other disagreeable surprises for me, other missing or supernumerary organs. That's the gist of what I vent to Arcady.

"You can never rely on normality, Farah. You should know that by now. You can be sure that the more a person presents outward signs of health and normality, the more they are eaten up inside by disease. It's better to have a pathology that is obvious and out in the world and not trying to pretend anything. And isn't that exactly what we're aiming to do at Liberty House?"

He's right. Our phalanstery is the perfect place for all sorts of patients waiting for treatment for their syndromes—Lyell, Asperger, Cyriax, Alezzandrini, Down, and now Rokitansky—wandering through the corridors, taking their meals in the dining room, and doing their asanas on the lawn dappled in sunlight. As I ruminate darkly, Arcady forces me to lie down, with my head in his lap.

"Can you feel it?"

"What?"

"I have a hard-on. You're making me hard."

"Oh, really?"

Indeed, I can distinctly feel the bulge of his penis against the back of my neck. So what? Does that even mean anything? Arcady gets a hard-on for everyone and everything, he's notorious. His erection doesn't prove a thing, and especially not my capacity to arouse desire in others, who are all less well endowed with libido—I may be just turning fifteen, but I can tell that most individuals go through life without even knowing what it's all about. For example, no one can make me believe that Fiorentina has ever held her belly with both hands because she wanted to fuck so bad. And it's the same for Vadim or Palmyre, those creatures whom nothing perturbs; same for my mother, who endures sex to give pleasure, but who freely admits that she never wants it herself. And let's not even talk about Salo, who considers coitus as both an ingenious and perverse invention:

"I mean, it's incredible! You couldn't make it up, right? Going and poking your, your thingy, you know, into a woman's thingy! Or a man's, right? It's the same with guys, right, just as disgusting! I mean if you really wanted penetration, it seems to me there are less bizarre options, I dunno, like: a tongue in the ear, a finger in the mouth! Why choose our excretory organs? Especially since God had all eternity to think about it, right, it's not like he had to improvise, to cobble something together at the last minute so that the human race could reproduce!"

I remember Salo staring at me while he talked, shivering with disgust, as if I had just suggested he penetrate me, something that will never happen, even if I did have anything more than a cupule, because I never found him attractive. Not only is he mentally deficient but his genital organs are just as atrophied as mine—which doesn't stop him from being an Adamite, just like all the other members. Adamism is one of the many streams of thought that our congregation brings together in its synthesis of ideas—well, mostly Arcady and Victor actually, since I couldn't care less about the theoretical underpinnings of our little sheltered lifestyle. I content myself with the knowledge of the Edenic principles that mean that Salo wanders around stark naked as soon as the weather allows it, while manifesting the most profound disgust for everyone else's genitalia and for sexuality in general.

A ray of sunshine finally finds its anemic way through the clouds, and under my neck, Arcady continues to be hard as a rock. He starts again:

"All bodies are part of nature! Can't you get that into your skull once and for all? You're no worse off than anyone else.

Look at Victor: would you like to have Victor's body? He's my guy, right, I'm crazy about him, but you know, he has to heave all that flab around: he can hardly walk and he has all kinds of dermatoses, because of all the flaps, the sweat, and so on. . . . Would you like to be him?"

"And you still want him?"

He stares at me with stupefaction, as if I was really talking nonsense:

"For fuck's sake, Farah, how long have you been living with me, since you were, what, six, seven . . . ?"

"Six."

"Do you even listen to me when I talk to you?"

"Always. I'm all ears."

I don't think it would be useful to tell him that my attention strays as soon as he starts his sermons about animals. Especially since I've now found out that his anti-speciesism is not rock solid, and that it doesn't take much for him to go and stuff himself with a plate of sea snails. But maybe he makes an exception for gastropods, who, you must admit, don't do much to generate empathy.

"I keep killing myself telling you, telling all of you, that desire bloweth where it will! And that you especially shouldn't let anyone else dictate your own desire! So, sure, that takes a little attention: it's easier to go for an Adonis than to feel you might be attracted to an obese person, a victim of third-degree burns, or an old man!"

"A third-degree-burn victim? Are you serious?"

I sometimes wonder to what extent he is the hostage of his own exhausting theories and how honest he is about his tastes. But then again I shouldn't really need to ask myself that question: after all, I have sufficient proof of the frenetic character of his sexual activity, and I've lost count of the times that I've found Arcady having his way with Victor in the shrubbery—and when it wasn't Victor, then it was perfect strangers, men and women, who all had nothing special about them, or were even decidedly ugly—in other words, completely matched Arcady's ideal of beauty (i.e., none at all).

He sighs, and I can tell he's sad that I'm incapable of agreeing with his views. He gets up, brushes off his jacket, and reaches out to me:

"Come on, let's go home."

When I get into the car, I lose myself in the contemplation of his hands on the steering wheel, his concentrated look, his sure movements. Maybe it's because I don't yet have my license, but I'm always attracted to people who can drive—especially since I'm always attracted to Arcady, no matter what he's doing or wearing. It's crazy. And yet, he's not exactly looking his best today, in his old Sonia Rykiel orange quilted-velvet jacket, a present from my grandmother, who dresses the entire household with her stocks of vintage clothes leftover from her years as a fashion model. I myself have suit blazers, bustier dresses, sweaters with ruff collars, and safari jackets, which I would never be seen dead in outside Liberty House—but Arcady is happy to pull on any old rag as long as it doesn't come from a store.

While driving, he often shoots me worried glances, and eventually puts his right hand on my thigh, which he starts kneading with his usual energy.

"Just you wait, I'm gonna give you a really good time!"

I'm not sure whether he's talking about my *quinceañera* or the pleasure he intends to give me, but all of a sudden I'm not there anymore, I have one of my episodes of lightning-flash disintegration, the kind I usually have when I've stayed too long in the fork of a tree, in the sunshine and the wind, too long losing myself in the contemplation of flowers or birds. Except that these are usually happy trances, whereas now I just feel horribly and irrevocably emptied of myself, just like my empty pelvic cavity, which appears not to contain much at all in fact, if I am to believe the images I was given by Mrs. Campi—to call her by her real name.

"Who am I, really?"

The question escapes me, and it takes us both by surprise, Arcady and me. It makes him let go of my thigh and the steering wheel too, which he grabs again just in time to avoid a fatal swerve. That might have put a happy end to my existential woes, but I'm not asking for that much: an answer would do just fine. And I can see how that answer has always been connected with my femininity. A fragile and dubious femininity, but one that I believed in with all my heart, before being confronted with Mrs. Campi's cruel diagnosis. Don't get me wrong: I know what I look like, and my classmates never held back in reminding me, calling me "dude" or "Farès," which is the name of a boy at school, who is just mortified by the similarity in our names. I'm five foot ten, burly, buff, and, lately, mustachioed: that's a lot to claim to be a girl. But that's the thing, I kept telling myself that femininity was still within reach. That all it would take would be for me to grow my hair long, remove the hair on my upper lip, resign myself to lip gloss, mascara, bright and light colors, to be able to join the cool girls' gang. Not that said gang is particularly interesting, but it always seemed my inevitable destination, after a deliciously indeterminate childhood, a floaty, floral, elemental childhood.

Under my very eyes, the road is crumbling away, that very

road winding through the river gorges whose name shall not pass my lips, that road I know so well from taking it every weekday in my school bus. Arcady's voice reaches me, but from a long way off.

"Farah, stop this bullshit! If you don't know who you are, I can tell you!"

I don't want him to tell me. Actually, I want him to be quiet. Who I am is an issue between me and me. And I'm suspicious of his talent for talking endlessly on any given subject. Yes, of course, he'll be able to find an identity for me and to convince me that gender is a social and cultural construct, a trap, an affectation for ordinary suckers. So what? What if I still want to be a girl despite my mustache and my atrophied vagina? What if I always believed I was one? While Arcady is rolling out all his brilliant rhetorical tricks, my cells are scattering along the road's tar surface, along the rocky walls or the tumultuous flow of the river; a residual shred of consciousness flies up into the tormented clouds and melds into their whorls. If I couldn't distinctly feel the blood pulsing in my ears and my guts peacefully gurgling, I would be annihilated, purely and simply. But pulsations and gurgling are perhaps just as illusory as the rest; maybe I am only the vehicle of these illusions, an arrangement my body has made with the world, without my having anything to do with it.

The river is in flood. It drowned its banks and is rising and roiling, threatening to submerge the road—but I need to hold firm against this tempestuous swirling, I need to gather together enough integrity to be rock solid, to be a retaining wall, to resist the temptation to overflow, which would be a great relief from myself, since comfort is not an option. Arcady is talking and I let his words come to me.

"Let's do it, OK? A great big party for your fifteenth birthday, and then a little intimate party, just for you and me, for your first time?"

I say yes. After all, if I am nothing, I can agree to everything.

10.

Baile Sorpresa

Even though I want to do this just about as much as I want to hang myself, Arcady is hell bent on celebrating my fifteenth birthday with great ceremony and is mobilizing the whole community towards this goal. As luck would have it, one of our members is a certain Epifanio, born in Mexicali, a fine connoisseur of the *quinceañera*, who is determined to respect the tedious protocol of the ceremony to the letter. I had hoped to get away with a nice meal, a cake, and a bit of music, but I never even had a chance. Not only does my *quinceañera* require active participation on my part, it also calls for a whole series of blingy accessories: a dress, a tiara, a Venetian mask, a pair of high heels, and all sorts of other stuff I could well do without. Or at least I would like to do without, but that's not possible, because as soon as I suggest we diverge slightly from tradition, Epifanio's eyes almost pop out of their sockets. Some reasonable person should make him understand that no one is less suited to frilly stuff than I am—but reason seems to have completely deserted our extended family, to the point you'd think that everyone was turning fifteen and hoping to get smashed out of their brains with all sorts of lascivious dances and syrupy cocktails, which—you couldn't make this stuff up—have to match the color of my dress. When this information reached my grandmother, she was suddenly completely galvanized and has been spending hours extracting grenadine red, or crème-de-menthe green, or curaçao blue outfits from her dressing room.

"There's no way I'm wearing that!"

"Why not? I was always a hit in that dress!"

"Kirsten, you are a size four, size six max!"

My grandmother strikes a pose and hangs a shift dress up against her emaciated hips:

"Sure, but you know, you're not obese either."

"I'm a size twelve."

"Ah. Well, in that case, you'll need floaty things, a tunic, an A-line. . . . Let me see what I have here. Hang on, have a look at this!"

And presto, she exhumes a crumpled rag, which, once unfolded, turns out to be a golden-yellow silk dress that flows from the waist—in other words, exactly what I need, according to Kirsten. I do try to protest:

"But what are we supposed to drink that's that color?"

"Whatever you like, lemonade, pastis!"

"Pastis isn't yellow! And I'm warning you, there's no way I'm wearing a dress the color of sperm!"

I don't know if she's following my train of thought, but the very idea of sperm makes her groan with retrospective disgust. Luckily for her, her rare encounters with penises soon resulted in the birth of my mother, so that she didn't have to reoffend very often.

"We'll put some food coloring in the cocktails, I imagine, so don't worry about that: try it on at least."

The dress fits, which is already a great relief. I can't say it flatters my complexion, but at least it doesn't make me look like an overdressed monkey. Now all I need are two pairs of shoes—yes, two, because I'm supposed to arrive in ballerina flats and swap them during the evening for a grown woman's heels. Since I live in sneakers most of the time and am barefoot the rest, ballerinas are already a challenge, to say nothing of the vertiginous four inches on which my grandmother wants me to perch. *Non, nyet*, no way.

"But sweetheart, it's tradition!"

"What tradition? We're not Mexican as far as I know!"

"You could make a bit of an effort for Epifanio!"

Send help! Who's celebrating their fifteenth birthday here? Epifanio, that decrepit forty-year-old, or me? My grandmother can't find an answer to objective reality, but is an expert in surrealist non sequiturs, just like everyone else in our madhouse:

"He has vitiligo, poor thing!"

Yes, indeed, Epifanio's skin has been losing its pigment at warp speed lately, and although I can't see what this has to do with my birthday party, my grandmother continues in the same vein:

"It's stress! If you let him organize your *quinceañera*, it will give him a goal and calm him down."

Just about nothing is known about vitiligo, but I can't see how playing the master of ceremonies is going to remedy a long-standing melanocytic deficit—what I can see, though, is that my refusal to follow this ridiculous Aztec protocol will only cause me trouble. I'll be labeled a horribly selfish person, who thinks only about her own pleasure, when she could be saving one of her coreligionists from depression and albinism, since that is all poor Epifanio can look forward to, as his patches converge to form a uniformly pale mask, instead of the geographical contours we are used to seeing on his face.

I've barely gotten away from my grandmother to find a little respite among the pine trees when I hear Epifanio panting at my heels:

"Farah, Farah! I had an idea for the *baile sorpresa*!"

"What?"

"Yes, your special dance!"

"Pardon me?"

This comes as a complete surprise: I had just about resigned myself to waltzing with Arcady, especially since we both enjoy ballroom dancing, but it is out of the question that I swing my hips in a solo routine to Kanye West or Shakira!

"But it won't be a solo, you'll do it with your girlfriends!"

Epifanio has his heart in the right place, but where does he get the idea that I have girlfriends? I mean, really, he's lived alongside me for years, when has he ever seen me with a girl my own age? My only friend is Daniel, and even though he can make a very convincing girl, I can't imagine us doing a street-dance routine together, since this is what Epifanio seems to be suggesting. He's even miming what he has in mind, which seems to involve much waving and enthusiastic stamping. If it wasn't so pathetic it would be hilarious, this flabby forty-something shimmying on a carpet of pine needles, admired only by me and a chicken—one of our Wyandottes, a splendid specimen with round eyes and gold feathers edged in blue, standing with one foot in the air three yards away from us, frozen in terror at this demonstration. All of a sudden, she scuttles away as fast as her legs can carry her. But instead of seeing this desperate flustered escape as a learning moment, Epifanio gets right down to teaching me a few basic steps, so that I can look the part on my big day. Except that I'm not having any of it, and I leave him standing there and skitter away like a Wyandotte chicken into the underbrush until I find the lower branches of an oak, which I scramble up to escape from my tormentor. As I heave myself up onto a comfortable perch three yards up from the ground, Epifanio hugs the rugged trunk and lifts his pleading eyes to mine:

"Farah, you want the party to be a success, don't you? For it to be an unforgettable memory?"

If the party is a catastrophe, it's unlikely I'll ever forget it, but I don't think there's much point discussing this with Epifanio, who persists in talking me through his insane program:

"You have to serve flaming cocktails to your guests: you'll see, it's really pretty. And then Teresa will give you a doll: your last doll."

Epifanio arrived at Liberty House a few years before us, and already had a severe skin problem, which was probably the motivation for his desire to avoid social interaction, but he also had Teresa and Dolores in his luggage, his twin daughters, who go to middle school with me, but are two years below me. Dolores is a lily-white redhead, with diaphanous skin and pale eyelashes. Teresa, endowed with a fierier version of redness, has dark eyes and an ideally golden complexion that doesn't need to be protected from the sun—whereas poor Dolores is condemned to parasols, hats, and SPF 85 sunscreen. Their father obviously takes their dermatological development very seriously, and it's not an infrequent sight to find him inspecting their childish cheeks, their fluttering eyelids, or their knuckles, which are the zones that are first affected by depigmentation from vitiligo.

From the height of my great oak, I look at poor Epifanio, who has a white clown's mask from his illness:

"And there's the cake. You are OK with having a cake, right? You have to nibble it . . ."

"What's that supposed to mean?"

"Well, you're not supposed to really eat it, you see. You're just supposed to taste it, a bit like a child, and then hand it round to your guests. Is that OK?"

Raised by weaklings, I don't know how to say no. And so, instead of sending Epifanio packing to his madness, his depigmentation, and his daughters, I acquiesce and let myself slide to the bottom of the tree. I go home, and the coup de grâce is given to me by Fiorentina, who informs me, her eyes shining in eager anticipation, that my birthday will be the occasion of a sort of charity gala dinner, a fundraising event for our phalanstery, with Nelly Consolat as the guest of honor. I imagine that what Fiorentina finds so delightful is that she will have an opportunity to express her extraordinary talents: ragout of heritage vegetables, deep-fried zucchini flowers, polenta with porcini mushrooms, Swiss chard and Sorrento tomato pies, oyster-mushroom flans, tagliatelle with truffles, ravioli with arugula pesto, angel cream with mandarins, chestnut mousse with praline rubble—she'll have the time of her life despite the significant limitations imposed by our committed vegetarianism. Everyone is happy in the end, apart from me, so it would be wrong for me to start complaining. What I have in mind actually is not so much to complain as to escape. Except that of course I won't do that, because then I would miss the second part of the festivities, the one that involves Arcady bravely burrowing into my cupule, so that I can accede to adulthood in some other way besides bullshit high heels and nibbled cake.

At school, those two pests Dolores and Teresa have spread the news that I'm having a big party for my fifteenth birthday, and now my so-called school friends are assiduously and hypocritically courting my favor so they can make it onto the guest list.

"Come on, Farah, be nice!"

All of a sudden, no one is calling me Farès or Farouk, no one is running their finger along their upper lip to make fun of my mustache—no, I am now someone that needs to be cajoled and flattered. I know exactly what's motivating them, and that they've heard about both our luxuries and our weirdness, just like everyone else. From their point of view, we are probably what comes closest to the castes of wealth or even nobility, the two of them being slightly muddled in their minds. They want to be part of the celebration, to drink our champagne and eat our caviar, unaware as they are of our frugal lifestyle—the polenta will be such a disappointment. Not to mention the fact that they will be asked at the door, not to abandon hope, but to turn off their cell phones and hand them over to Arcady or Victor. So much the better: that way there won't be any viral videos of my *quinceañera* all over the internet.

11.

The Queen of the Party

On D-Day, I'm in a sullen but resigned mood. Of course, I'd prefer to skip the surprise dance part, but just in case, I've put together a routine inspired by *Modern Times*, for which I will get rid of my yellow dress and my pumps and put on a pair of oversized pants, an undersized jacket, and a pair of Dr. Martens. I've convinced myself that the only way to escape ridicule is to dive right in. If there's going to be a cringe-worthy video going round, I can always say I was impersonating Charlie Chaplin, whose films I was bottle-fed from age zero to six—before my parents started weaning themselves from technology. In fact, I continue to watch them on streaming sites, as soon as I can get a connection. Even though I wholeheartedly agree with the principles regulating our libertarian and self-managed existence, I'm hungry for images, hungry for music. And even though I despise my classmates and think we're light-years apart, I am well aware that I need to maintain a certain level of familiarity with the media and social networks if I don't want my school life to be a nightmare. Teresa and Dolores agree with me too, and as soon as we get back to our quiet zone, we solemnly exchange the information we have acquired with regard to iPhone applications, YouTube influencers, and music. We will always be three beats behind, but that's better than nothing, and since Daniel also has access to precious information, I'm less lost than I should be—even though I am completely lost anyway.

In any case, here I am all dressed up in golden yellow. Nothing can be done about my hair, but Malika, who has made a spectacular return into my grandmother's favor, has done my makeup so that the outline of my lips is defined, my jawbones softened, the plaintive droop of my eyes corrected—contouring, she calls it. And, of course, my upper-lip hair has disappeared with a strip of depilatory wax. I am at the peak of my beauty—in other words, absolutely hideous, but then, why does the queen of the party have to be beautiful anyway? It's a well-known fact that members of royal families are generally deformed by consanguinity and afflicted with prognathism or macroglossia, when they're not mad as a box of frogs. I was spared from mental illness, but judging by my prizefighter's physiognomy, my dorsal hyperkyphosis, and my Rokitansky syndrome, I'm a direct descendant of the Habsburgs. I would prefer the Romanovs, who were just as rotten on the inside, although much nicer to look at, but no one asked for my opinion.

In any case, I may be the *quinceañera*, the sweet fifteen whose entrance into adult life we are now celebrating, but the real queen of the party is Nelly, not me. You just have to see all the solicitude she is surrounded with, while I wander around, spectral and disillusioned, in my flimsy dress. As soon as she arrives, Nelly Consolat is given a guided tour of the house and the maintained part of the property—and I have to admit that she merrily follows along on her little robin legs, cheerful, curious, indefatigable:

"Oh, you grow rutabaga? That's incredible! I don't think I've had any since I was a child. . . . Just like Jerusalem artichokes: oh, I see you have those too!"

She admits to being seventy, but if she remembers the vegetables from rationing, she must be closer to eighty. Which still makes her a decade younger than poor Dadah, whom we left on the porch, frightened that her wheelchair would get bogged down in the ruts and fulminating at seeing herself thus dethroned. And what am I supposed to say now? I was promised all sorts of wonderful things for this special day, and now my only role is as an extra behind this dowager.

The evening inexorably progresses, and I have all the time I need to meditate on the irony of fate when Arcady opens the dance with Nelly instead of holding me tight for a languorous waltz. It's my birthday, but everyone seems to have forgotten it except for Epifanio, who is nagging me to go get changed for my *baile sorpresa*. Can't he see that no one gives a shit about my *baile sorpresa*, my tiara, my high heels, my contouring, and all the efforts I've made to look like a fifteen-year-old girl?

In our dining room, transformed for the occasion into a formal reception room, I'm still accorded the honor of sitting at the top table, whose average age I fortunately and brutally slash. Stuck between Dadah, who's still angry, Victor, who's fawning, and Nelly, who's simpering, I am bored stiff. Well, I am bored until I feel a foot slide in between my thighs. Looking up, my eyes lock with Arcady's, which are sparkling with mischief and lust. The party is getting started at last.

Fiorentina shepherds the children of the house to help with the table service. I mean, the children, there aren't many: just the twins, Djilali, who is Malika's son, and Daniel, who is not quite a child anymore either. If I wasn't the *quinceañera*, I would be roped in too, and I am quite happy to be able to stay seated with Arcady's wriggling toes just finding my clit—for even though I don't have a vagina, I have a perfectly formed vulva, with all the necessary folds and circumvolutions. Needless to say, I did some research after my visit to the gyno. Our library includes an eighteen-volume women's and family encyclopedia, bound in leather with gold titles and volume numbers: the last two volumes are all about body hygiene and care, so there were plenty of anatomical plates for me to find out what I needed to know.

On the table, the food keeps appearing: after the little *clafoutis* of morel mushrooms and the polenta cakes with microgreens, it's time for the smoked leeks with goats' cheese, immediately followed by radicchio ravioli with a port wine sauce, and eggs cocotte with white truffles. We barely have time to draw breath before the pitiless Fiorentina launches a second attack: stuffed boletus mushrooms, celery mousse with cranberries, Treviso risotto, Jerusalem artichokes with truffle butter—and she doesn't need to hold back with the truffles, since they grow on the property and we have a truffle pig called Edo. The only problem with Edo is that he likes truffles too, and aspires only to gobbling them down himself on the sly. We should really have trained a dog, but it's too late now, and apart from yapping and running around like lunatics, ours have no talents at all. That said, having spent so much time hanging out with Edo, I've learned how to find the fairy rings which are often the markers for truffle trees, and how to follow the flights of the truffle flies, their obstinate circuits around the same square inch of soil. If Fiorentina would take the trouble of putting a leash around my neck, I would make a very competent truffle sow, especially since females are much better at that game than males, because truffles exude a pheromone that is very close to the sexual hormones of hogs—but to what extent am I still a female?

As far as Nelly is concerned, however, there is no room for doubt: she seems as sensitive as a sow to the aphrodisiac emanations of the white truffles, and at each new dish she breaks into equivocal cries and shudders of ecstasy. She all but joins her hands and lifts her gaze to the skies, just like the blessed sister of Kerala on the engravings on the second floor. And so, when we finally get to dessert, she has exhausted her stock of expressive mimicry, unless it's because she's now incapable of swallowing another morsel after that uninterrupted gorging. In any case, the green-tea tiramisu and the charlotte with candied mandarins raise only a wan smile, as opposed to her exalted moaning at the start of the meal.

Fifteen candles were added to the charlotte *in extremis*, but you can see straight away that it wasn't planned: the candles are mismatched and already half-melted from a previous birthday. I can't see how I can graciously cut the cake and offer pieces to our guests, as is the tradition in good Mexican families. In the end, my *quinceañera* will be one in name only, and all the better for it. At the table next to mine, Epifanio is champing at the bit. Every once in a while he turns his sad clown face towards me and emits a guttural whistle to attract my attention:

"Farah!"

"What?"
"The *baile sorpresa*!"
"I said I'm not doing it!"
"But why?"
"It's too late now: we've almost finished eating!"
"No, it's not! You can still do it after dinner!"
"I don't want to!"
"What about the doll? What am I supposed to do with it now?"
"Give it to Dolores or Teresa!"
"But it's for you! It's your last doll!"
"I never played with dolls anyway, I'm not gonna start now that I'm fifteen!"

He dips his spoon into his green-tea tiramisu, but you can tell it's with no conviction or appetite. The party is a disappointment for him. It is for me too. I wasn't expecting much, but I was still hoping to be accorded a little more attention on the day I step from childhood to adulthood. What presents have I received, apart from Arcady's big toe, now positioned inside my cupule? My *quinceañera* is going to end without my person attracting any more attention than it usually does. But I've spoken too soon, for Dolores and Teresa are sidestepping across the dining room each holding a tray of flaming glasses, which they ceremoniously present to me. What am I supposed to do? Arcady precipitously removes his foot from between my thighs, while Epifanio rushes to our table to whisper in my ear:

"Take one!"
"What for?"
"Go serve your guests!"

I cheerlessly grab the tray that Dolores is holding out to me with a beaming smile—and she has so few opportunities to smile, poor Dolores, whose implausible red hair unleashes even more mockery and teasing than my masculine looks and sailor-on-a-bar-crawl clothes. Teresa is just as much of a redhead, but gets a better deal because of her darker skin, and one can only hope that she didn't inherit her father's defective genes, in which case her lovely gold and rose satin will soon start losing its color in splotches. Anyway, here I am in the middle of the room my father decorated with bunches of lilies, arrangements of ferns and hydrangeas, and garlands of purple vine shoots draping over all the tables. The tray is solid silver and weighs a ton. I just have time to see my face reflected in it between the dangerously wobbling glasses, before one of them spills its flaming contents on me. By virtue of a law that means that light fabrics are more flammable than heavy ones, my silk dress catches fire immediately—if I had been wearing my tramp's jacket, I wouldn't have turned myself into a living torch, but it's a bit late for regrets—and that's precisely the moment Epifanio chooses to start the music for *Modern Times*. To give him his due, I must say he hadn't noticed my combustion—for which he is completely responsible, with his bullshit traditions. And now I've won, I am the queen of the party, the main event: everybody is looking at me and rushing towards me with their glass of water, or damask napkin, or bottle of champagne. In a flash, I'm doused and soaking wet. The remains of my silk dress are sticking to my massive form—not to mention the fact that it burned from the bottom up and now no longer hides much of my exuberant pubic hair, a black fleece that, to my great shame, spreads all the way down to mid-thigh. I can only hope that the technological embargo has been respected and that no one has immortalized this horrible moment.

After a moment of hesitation, the party starts up again, but since it was already coming to an end, the guests start leaving one after the other. Into the urn set up for this very purpose, Nelly drops an eye-watering check and swears on everything holy that she now wishes to join our confraternity, even if that means she will have to abandon her luxury retirement home to do so. All those efforts we made will therefore not be in vain, and I won't have sacrificed my thighs and my dignity for nothing. For I do have a bit of a sense of having been the turkey in this farce—which is ironic at our vegetarian table.

When Arcady at last bursts into the kitchen, after saying goodbye to all our distinguished guests, he finds me there with Fiorentina. While she is soaking the dishes that she considers too delicate to go in the dishwasher, I'm applying slices of raw potato onto my burns—that's supposed to be the best thing to do in such cases. He crouches down to see the extent of the damage, remarks that little blisters are already forming on my seeping red skin, and heaves a sigh of pity.

"Does it hurt?"

"Yes, lots."

In fact, it's excruciating and I can't imagine anything inserting itself between my thighs on this first night of my sixteenth year. My deflowering will have to wait.

"You're sure?"

"Quite sure."

"I was thinking of doing it from behind, you know."

"Fine, but even my behind is burned."

He looks at me, and in his eyes I see all the compassion and love in the world. Maybe that's what I was waiting for, that look, that tender whisper:

"Farah Faucet . . ."

"I wanted to ask you: who is this Farah Faucet?"

"What? Don't you know who she is?"

"No, I have no idea."

"Then there's something missing in your education."

That's what I thought too, but since he is involved in my education I keep my trap shut.

"Farrah Fawcett was the most beautiful woman in the world: I'll show you some pictures of her."

He stands up and reaches out to me, pulling me against him, putting his arms around me, kissing me passionately:

"And you are the most beautiful woman in the world too, Farah Diba."

"Who's she, then?"

"There's no way you would know her: I'll show you pictures of her too."

It would be nice if these old people would just quit it, with all their references to bygone days: I've had it up to here with not understanding what they're talking about. Especially since, thanks to the quiet zone, I don't understand much of what young people are talking about either. Yay! It's a fact: my education is an epic fail! That's the gist of what I try to explain to Arcady, but it's no use trying to discuss grievances and sadness with him: they are just not part of how he functions.

"But I'm here, Farah, I'm here to explain everything you don't understand!"

"Oh, yeah? So who is Sylvester Stallone then?"

"Why are you asking me that?"

"Because Nelly spent the whole evening telling me I looked like him."

Sylvester Stallone must have a particularly repulsive physique, for Arcady looks a bit embarrassed. Instead of answering, he squeezes me even tighter and starts singing the song that

Charlie Chaplin massacres in *Modern Times* into my ear:

"I'm looking for Titina, Titina my Titina . . ."

And hey, presto, he drags me along in a kind of passionate mazurka, while continuing to sing—for, unlike Charlie Chaplin, he knows the lyrics. Fiorentina is observing us from the corner of her eye, but doesn't show any more concern about our dance than she did about my burns. In fact, she is lovingly wiping one of our cocktail coupes, the same as the one that emptied itself all over my dress and thighs, and is all but humming along herself. What is wrong with all these people, well, almost all of them, who idolize objects and give them more care and attention than to human beings? Victor is the same, with all his mirrors and books, his ivory-pommeled canes and monogrammed shirts—but for Fiorentina, it's reached the stage of an obsessive mania, and I can't be sure she pampered her daughter with as much tenderness as that crystal glass, whose every facet she inspects at length, to make sure that there's not a single trace of humidity left on it, not a speck of dust, before putting it away into the cupboard, next to its equally immaculate sisters.

After promenading me around the whole kitchen, Arcady at last releases me onto a straw-bottomed chair, but not without first whispering in my ear that there's a present waiting for me in my bedroom. So I rush up the stairs four at a time to my attic room, indifferent to the painful rubbing of my thighs against each other. On my bed, a marquetry box, obviously an antique. I have the time to imagine all sorts of things: a diamond necklace, which I would never wear, but which would be touching anyway; a set of Japanese knives, gems in their felted box, or an assortment of ink pens. . . . Nope: the box contains candles, arranged in increasing size. Candles with no wick, mind you.

Weird. Someone scratches at my door, and it's Arcady, looking excited.

"And so? Do you like it?"

"Well, yeah . . . but what are they?"

"Vaginal candles!"

And off he goes. It turns out that vaginal candles are candles only in name, luckily, since I feel charred enough as it is: in fact, they are dilators of different diameters, which I will insert into my vagina to progressively stretch it to a respectable size. Arcady looks so happy that I don't dare show my disappointment. I even force myself to push away the unwelcome memory of a gift I received for my seventh birthday, a box of craft activities that allowed me to make my own scented and sparkly candles.

"You have to take it easy to begin with, just move them back and forth a little. And in circles too. And you'll see, in a few months, your vagina will be just like all the other girls'! I'll help you if you like!"

My birthday may have been a catastrophe, but I fall asleep with this erotic promise, my thighs covered in second-degree burns, but my spirit at peace.

12.

The Other Name for Childhood

Before he went crazy, Salo was a documentary filmmaker, and we owe to him a collection of little home movies showing our community's lifestyle. We spend winter evenings watching interminable projections, sequences put end to end along a mysterious thematic line. Salo knows where it's heading, the rest of us not so much, but at least some traces will remain of our utopia, images that we can send into space, along with a poem by Emily Dickinson and an aria by Schubert.

Last December, as I was almost falling asleep to the purr of the projector, I was surprised to see myself on the screen. I should say that Salo's camera generally avoids me, skirts around me—unless I'm edited out, who knows. Anyhow, the result is that I'm always absent from our cinematic archives. Well, I thought I was, but it turns out I did manage to make an impression on three minutes of film, from a movie that is at least ten years old.

I'm six. We've been living at Liberty House for a few weeks. My parents are just starting to lift their heads. My grandmother is there, but she is still dithering between her beautiful Paris apartment and life in a community of social misfits. As for me, it didn't take long to go along with everything, to adopt it all holus-bolus: being a vegetarian, walking around naked, saluting the sun, living among the senescent, the crippled, and people with all kinds of syndromes. Perched on the railing surrounding the terrace, I'm observing the adults talking among themselves or picking at food from the buffet. The music playing softly in the background suddenly becomes identifiable and insistent, greeted with exclamations of pleasure. The camera lingers on smiling faces, bodies swaying to the pulsing base. My grandmother hurls herself into an incongruous and brutal jitterbug, manhandling one of her lovers, whose name I can't remember, dislocating her arm each time she twirls her around, while my parents timidly wiggle their hips. Everyone gradually joins the dance—Arcady, of course, but also Jewell, Orlando, Palmyre, Richard, and Vadim, and even Dadah, who is not yet stuck in her wheelchair and dances just as ferociously as my grandmother.

On my railing, I'm bursting with enthusiasm, and ten years later I can perfectly remember the feeling I had at the sight of all those bodies joyfully forgetting themselves as they entered a spaced-out trance—usually to whatever music Richard had brought back to us from the Balearic Islands. My memories are especially clear since my first encounter not only with dancing but also with music occurred on that day: having spent my first six years in a soundproof catafalque, I had heard nothing more musical than the soundtrack to *Modern Times*, so, of course, the techno music from Ibiza blew my mind.

Abandoning my perch, I sidle into the midst of the adults. I had never danced before, or even imagined it was possible. At first, I'm happy just to jump up and down on the spot while energetically swinging my arms, then I launch myself into an inspired and frenetic pantomime, as if I am attempting to reclaim my body, my sensations, desire, pleasure—everything that I had been deprived of since birth. I turn red very quickly, my hair is a mess, my dress hiked up on my plump little thighs. I remember that dress very well too: short, white, sprinkled with sequins, and edged with fringes—it suited me as badly as can be, but was probably one of Kirsten's efforts to make me look prettier.

Galvanized by the throbbing synth pads, the other dancers seem to be floating in midair. Even my grandmother finally lets go of poor Odile—yep, I remember her name now—to sway rather gracefully. My mother is sublime, Arcady is doing OK, but Richard, the old warhorse of Amnesia and the Pacha Club, is simply sensational, and Salo didn't miss immortalizing me standing in front of him, staring at his footwork with my mouth gaping and a trickle of saliva sparkling on my chin. In turn, I try out a few more daring steps, some *glissés* inspired by Richard's, my face lifted up, looking for signs of approval and encouragement. I've never forgotten my happiness and overexcitement, cruelly fixed on film by our own Stanley Kubrick—for where other children might have been cute, and their efforts endearing, I was a painful sight to behold, and the looks the adults give me, as I see them now ten years later, leave no doubt on the matter: pity, affliction, even faint embarrassment, that's what you can see in my parents' and grandmother's eyes. Even Richard, who finally notices my existence, throws a compassionate wink in the direction of the camera.

The film finishes with a close-up on me, my hair stuck to my sweaty temples, my arrhythmic jumps, my little cries of pleasure, my big gap-toothed smile. It's so sad, this joy. What a waste of the mad desire to join in and do the right thing, all that love forlornly shining its light on those adults who wanted nothing to do with it. And what am I supposed to do with my memory, now that Salo's film has furnished this stinging refutation, this cinematic proof that I was wrong to be happy, or rather, that I was happy only through a miraculous lack of awareness and understanding that is perhaps the other name for childhood? What value should I accord to these images and what credit should I give to my memory, which preserved them intact in their shell of fake accuracy, intact in their radiance, blazing all the way to today and responsible for my being set alight?

It was hot, the music was beating inside me like an extra heart, Richard was moving languidly, a weary forty-something, but handsome as a movie star to my adoring eyes, with his Ibiza tan, his faded blond hair, his tropical smell made stronger by the dancing. He wasn't the only one that was beautiful; everyone was, even Dadah, with her ebony bouffant hairdo, her bewitching hands moving in oriental fashion, and the ruby-red arc of her lips, stretched over her sparkling dentures; even Epifanio, laughing, a redheaded twin on each hip; even Jewell, not as damaged as she is now, and lost in her own personal choreography; even and especially Arcady, whose tender eyes followed our movements. Everyone was beautiful, smelled wonderful, danced gracefully—except me. And if I hadn't seen that film, I would have dated the start of love, happiness, and freedom to that day.

13.

The Sermon on the Mount

No sooner said than done, Nelly has moved in with us—but still, without giving up her thousand square feet in Nice, with sea views, laundry, and meal services. She can always fall back there if the living conditions at Liberty House don't suit her. I should mention that the rooms here are monastic, and that except for Arcady and Victor, no one has a private bathroom. Dadah couldn't care less, she has a urinary catheter and an ileoanal pouch, but Nelly will have to get used to it. For the time being, carried along by the excitement of this change of pasture, she seems to think everything is fine and pays no heed to trivial practical inconveniences.

With Nelly Consolat, a real geomagnetic storm is blowing through our phalanstery—but without causing any particular symptoms for our EMS folks. For while Nelly is happy to renounce all technology as well as the luxurious comfort of her retirement home, she arrives with a trunk full of marvelous objects, inherited from her illustrious ancestor: a spherical astrolabe, a telescope on its mahogany tripod, an assortment of brass and wooden spyglasses, multiple volumes of celestial atlases, and a reproduction of Apianus's planisphere, which she immediately hangs above her little nun's bed. Also from her great-great-grandfather, who was a pioneer of the observation of comets, she has a hanging inspired by the Bayeux tapestry: Halley's comet, though clumsily embroidered, is nevertheless easily recognizable and accompanied with a little Latin phrase that Nelly translates with great pomp for all her visitors:

"*Isti mirant stella!* They admire the star!"

We are also invited to join in the admiration, and we make all the right noises, especially me, but of course admiration comes naturally to me and Nelly enthralls me with her prolix cheerfulness, her enthusiasms, her memories of cruising round the world in a cargo ship, her photographs of the aurora borealis and archaeological sites, and her collection of space rocks: chondrite, siderolite, regmaglypts.... I can't get enough of handling them under her tender gaze:

"Unbelievable, right? The one you're holding is a fragment of the 2008 TC3 asteroid, or Almahata Sitta, if you prefer. Its impact was followed live! It's ureilite, it's very rare! I can't tell you what I had to go through to get hold of it!"

She laughs heartily, letting me imagine all kinds of things, including indecent propositions—for although Nelly is seventy-nine years old, she still looks great, and I can easily imagine astronomers letting themselves be corrupted by her blond hair and beautiful smile.

"Actually, I just had to shell out: it cost me an arm and a leg, that tiny little thing! But when you love something, you don't count the cost!"

Indeed, the love she feels for our little cross-border utopia was quickly translated into a more than generous donation. So now Arcady is planning to build an additional greenhouse and fix the roof of the west wing. Nelly loves us and we love Nelly.

Victor is the only one being persnickety. I find him one morning sitting on the roots of an oak tree—even though he rarely drags himself outside the maintained parts of the garden. I barely have time to wonder how he got here, and especially how he's going to get back, given his weight and bulk, before he asks me:

"Ah, it's you. What are you doing here?"

He's the one who should be answering that question. As far as I'm concerned, I'm at home here, on this land that Arcady gave to me on my arrival at Liberty House. Four months have passed since my calamitous *quinceañera*, spring is on its way, and I feel like inspecting my dominion, just to check up on how the squirrels, jays, and rabbits have spent the winter. Not to mention that I intend to expose my thighs to the April sun, to complete the healing of the scars from the fire.

"Uh, just going for a walk."

I know from experience that when people stare off into the distance with that preoccupied look in their eyes, they couldn't care less about what you might have to say. They just want to talk themselves, to spout out their little self-centered soliloquy, and it doesn't matter whether you listen to them or not, you're there to tell them what they want to hear, in a simulacrum of conversation of which millions are held every day. I'm preparing myself to be bored senseless, since Victor is an unstoppable showoff.

"You know what? I'm not sure Nelly is such a great recruit for our confraternity."

"Oh, yeah?"

Onomatopoeias, one-syllable words, nominal phrases, I have my stock of noncommittal, mechanical responses ready. While pretending to listen, I rummage in the tunnel of a dung beetle, although as far as I know, dung beetles go through a hibernation phase. In any case, you see them only when the weather is fine. If we had an internet connection, I could do some research, but since that's not the case, I will have to remain ignorant. Unless the library at Liberty House has an entomology handbook, which is highly likely, but I'll need to check.

"We have enough old people as it is. I don't think it's good for morale that there are so many old people among us. We don't want to transform Liberty House into a hospice!"

He has some nerve, talking as if he was in the first blush of youth, and I decide not to let poor Nelly be accused of all evils.

"But she looks young, doesn't she?"

"Are you joking?"

"Not at all. And besides, she's really . . . into life."

For the moment, I'm humoring him and taking care not to say that he's the one who looks like a crumbly old man, with his silver curls, his cane, his signet ring, and his straitlaced manners. That said, I don't know any adults who see themselves as looking their age: all of them are convinced they look ten years younger. Since he doesn't deem it necessary to respond, I decide to go for it:

"Yeah, she's incredible! Do you know she's traveled around the world? And in a boat!"

"Are you sure she's not making it up?"

"She showed me photos!"

He annoys me with his sedentary skepticism, but I must admit Nelly doesn't have the profile of an adventurer—I could never have imagined that she would open up such wide vistas to me, with her shriveled-up body, her narrow head, her slender limbs, and her incessant birdlike chirping. In any case, it wasn't Nelly that Victor was thinking about—that was just a preamble, a pretext to spit out what is really bothering him. I thought so, and I concentrate even harder on my entomological dig.

"If she has shown you photographs, there's nothing I can say. And anyway, you're right, Nelly is not a bad horse. I'd just like there to be some new blood at Liberty House, you see. It's a shame you're still a bit too young to have children . . ."

Well, at least Arcady didn't divulge my repulsive little secret. For once he held his tongue, even though he professes that the truth needs to be told in all circumstances, and that there is nothing to hide and no one to spare.

"As for me . . ."

It has taken him less than two minutes to get to his favorite subject: me, I mean, him, for not all selves are created equal in Victor's eyes—any more than they are in anyone else's. I must be the only person I know to consider myself a negligible quantity.

"As for me, I would have loved to reproduce, but given my sexual orientation, that would be, shall we say, less simple than for a straight person. . . . Maybe it's easier nowadays, but nowadays I'm no longer a young man."

"Well, men can have children until they die, can't they? Take Charlie Chaplin: he had his last child when he was seventy-three."

Charlie Chaplin is my idol, I don't miss an opportunity to talk about him—after all, each to their own subject. One day I'll have to try to understand this predilection, but unlike Victor, I have all the time I need ahead of me to do that.

"Good for him."

"Well, you could too, with Arcady, all you'd have to do is find a woman to consent to it."

"Yes, thank you, Farah, I know how human beings reproduce. It's just that it's too late for me, I wouldn't have the energy, the stamina you need for a small child. . . . You see, that's why I can't stand Nelly's arrival: she reminds me too much of my own fragility. We are all fragile enough as it is. Or at least I am."

I let him pontificate about his fragility: if it gives him pleasure to see himself as a pitiful little thing, when he is afflicted with a spherical paunch and the dewlaps of a draft ox. Maybe he can read my mind, for he continues with a note of self-derision—but it will be the only one:

"Yes, I know, I don't look it, but I assure you that I am fragile. You just can't understand . . ."

Why does he persist in talking to me if I can't understand? No doubt because in his eyes, I simply don't exist. It just so happens that I was passing by at the very moment when he needed to vent. He might just as well be talking to the dung beetle I have just exhumed, which is emerging from the friable soil waving its circumspect antennae. Perfect timing: dung beetles are accustomed to shit, and Victor persists in pouring out all of his, his obesity, his type II diabetes, his functional colopathy. . . . Time is ticking by, the dung beetle has long since scuttled off to find the first tender shoots and fresh droppings. With a bit of luck he'll find some foxes' scat. Tan, grainy, tapered, it is a thousand times less repulsive than city dogs' poop, the mere sight of which makes me retch. I share this observation with Victor, in an effort to cut him off.

Against all hope, it works. He stops speaking and looks at me in astonishment:

"What? Why are you talking to me about dog shit? That's disgusting!"

I could retort that his health issues are just as disgusting, but I would rather let him arrive at that conclusion all by himself. I needn't have bothered, he contents himself with a shrug and a purely rhetorical question.

"Am I boring you? Do tell me if I'm boring you!"

My protestation is equally shallow, and in any case he takes up his sermon on the mount again—for indeed, he is perched on the little hillock that the oak's roots have raised over time. Just at the moment when I am ready to abandon him on his tumulus, the gong sounds, sparing me from finding a pretext for my flight. At Liberty House, a Tibetan gong made of seven different metals marks the important times in our community life—and particularly the meditation and group listening sessions. We also have Nepali singing bowls, from which Arcady draws soothing and purifying harmonics, which are highly effective in cases of epidemics or conflicts. I'm just about to bound away from dear Victor's debilitating orbit, forgetting that he is incapable of getting up unassisted. I reluctantly hold out a hand to him, but once he's vertical, he clutches on to his cane and takes an incredibly long time to stabilize his enormous belly, panting like a seal the whole time. Save me! Give me beauty and lightness, give me some way to make up for the cartloads of filth that Victor felt entitled to spew out all over me. Especially since I'm about to experience another episode of disintegration—I've learned to recognize the warning signs, that slight iridescence in the air, that buzzing in my ears, that volatilization of everything except the dancing particles inside and all around me, that brutal collision between interior and exterior space. Here we go, it's happened, I am no longer myself—and so much the better, since I've never benefitted in any way from being myself.

The gong booms again, propagating its vibrations into the pine woods, infiltrating into the tunnels of the dung beetles, the jays' and squirrels' nests, and into my own sternum. I slip back into my disappointing corporeal envelope, the vehicle of my illusions, the seat of my insane fantasies. I am me, since I have to be, and I grudgingly make my way back to Liberty House, with Victor at my heels, to hear Arcady's sermon on the vitrified city of Hodeida.

14.

Hodeida

The idea of vitrified cities is one of Nelly's, who is the great-granddaughter of an astronomer, of course, but also the granddaughter of a navigator and the daughter of an archaeologist. In fact, she is now standing beside Arcady behind the solid oak pulpit. Wearing a metallic-pink down jacket and a felted-wool beanie, she looks like she's about to embark on a polar-exploration ship, or to go trekking into the Himalayan valleys where her father made his major discoveries: bodies buried in jars—or was it engraved steatite seals, I can't remember, especially since it's easy to drown in the flow of Nelly's information and adventurous anecdotes. Arcady is wearing his eternal Sonia Rykiel orange quilted jacket: they clash as badly as possible but seem to be moved by the same vital energy and the same desire to galvanize the congregation. While Arcady speaks, Nelly holds up enlarged photographs.

Neither electric projectors nor PowerPoint presentations are allowed at Liberty House. No, everything is old style, to the great delight of the members, who hold on to their archaistic ways as a source of pride and morose delectation. But, in fact, the real reason for this is that in their previous lives they were completely defeated by digitization and social networks—not only defeated but submerged and terrified, starting with my parents whose odyssey out of the electromagnetic grid, in search of a territory safe from radiation, technology, and progress I have already recounted. Arcady is quivering at the pulpit, and I even let go of my own sources of morose delectation and let myself be penetrated by his lyricism and slowly won over by his enthusiasm:

"We now know for certain that civilizations at least as advanced as ours, and maybe even more so, existed in the past! The vitrified cities and fortresses of the Valley of Death or those in northern Syria are the irrefutable proof of this! And in central Africa, they've found things like crystal flagstones and zones of molten glass that can be explained only by atomic destruction! For that kind of vitrification to take place, temperatures infinitely higher than lightning are required! And the radioactivity levels there are still very high: whether it was a war or nuclear accident, nobody knows, but it has to be one or the other!"

On Nelly's photos, the turrets and minarets sparkle, as if covered in frost or a mentholated glaze.

"Look at these cities! They surprise the traveler like a mirage, but they are actually real! And guess what you'll find, not far from these glass cities? Uranium mines that show all the signs of having been exploited millions of years ago!"

Arcady barely gives us enough time to digest this information before launching out again onto the dazzling, crystallized path of his chimeras:

"The end of the world has already happened! It happens every time mankind reaches a critical level of civilization and technology! Bang! And every time, it's round we go again! Every time, to our great misfortune, we come out of the caves, domesticate fire, invent the wheel, printing, electricity, nuclear power, and then . . . catastrophe, chariots of fire, the apocalypse! Man dies at his own hand, and takes millennia to recover, to rise again here and there, first in scattered tribes—separated by shadowy forests, stretches of desert, unexplored oceans—then in unlivable megalopolises: that's the ultimate stage, the one we have now reached and that is unsustainable for life. The end of the world has already happened, but it will happen again, it is even imminent and I can see the signs of it everywhere!"

He is preaching to the converted: apart from me, all the members are declinist and convinced that humanity is heading for extinction. Liberty House is their last refuge, but in the case of a nuclear war, no hillside, no row of ash trees, no drystone wall will protect them. According to Arcady and Nelly, we need to prepare ourselves for annihilation. What this preparation should consist of exactly is not very clear, but as far as I'm concerned, I'd like to be dispensed from all school obligations, so that I have the time to complete all our purification and propitiation rites—not to mention that if the end of the world is nigh, maybe I don't need to acquire all that knowledge. And while we're at it, maybe I'll stop using my vaginal candles: what's the point of dilating an orifice that will never be put to any good use?

In front of me, Epifanio nervously puts his arms around his two daughters. It seems his vitiligo didn't make him lose all his paternal instincts then—whereas my parents, faithful to their little egotistic couple's agenda, haven't even turned to look at me, reserving their manifestations of solicitude, their embraces and distressed whispers only for each other. Hodeida, Lop Nur, the Euphrates valley, the Thar desert, Pierrelatte in Gabon: Nelly gives more and more examples of the sites where mute millennial traces have been found of worlds as advanced as ours that have mysteriously disappeared. She moves on to aeronautical technology in ancient India, as evidenced both in carved steles and epic cycles: it seems that the Mahabharata relates the details of wars fought with spherical bombs, reactive devices, toxic gases, and interstellar spacecraft that compare favorably to our modern arsenal. I have some trouble seeing the connection between the prowess of the vimanas and vitrified cities, forever sunk under their green jasper paving, but all I need to register is that their disappearance foretells our own.

A new strike of the gong signals our dispersion, and we come together again on the wide terrace that Arcady and Victor have had restored in Lecce stone, for its incomparable golden sheen. All around me I see disconsolate faces and red eyes, as if news of the apocalypse had taken the members of my little millenarian confraternity by surprise. But, of course, Arcady has never talked to us about anything else besides the end of the world. It was even with this in mind that he gathered us all together under his protection in the reassuring enclosure of Liberty House. And so? It seems that Nelly and her prehistoric nuclear wars, her radiation levels, and her Mahabharata have given some kind of scientific confirmation to Arcady's farfetched eschatology. Not to mention that he usually concludes his remarks with a luminous and comforting peroration on how we will survive the worst because we are the best. We have been nursed with this fable for years: to abruptly deprive us of it is to throw us into the sufferings of weaning and withdrawal. Even Malika, who has as little brain as the lapdogs she so closely resembles, seems overwhelmed, sheltering under my grandmother's martial shoulder and affectionately kneading the back of Djilali's neck.

Since we still have to live while waiting for death, we all end up sitting down to eat Fiorentina's butternut and rosemary risotto. Contrary to her guests, she doesn't seem particularly upset, but I do notice that she serves us floating islands for dessert, which could be interpreted as an allusion, an encrypted message of reassurance: the world may be heading for self-destruction, but Liberty House is an autarchic island.

In the evening I go have a little visit with Nelly, and find her as animated and cheerful as usual. I suppose, after seventy, the apocalypse is no big deal. Having found something to occupy her old age, Nelly couldn't care less that I haven't yet done anything with my life: the end of the world would be a catastrophe for me, but only an explosive epilogue for her, a glorious finale. Nelly is busy unpacking a new delivery of books and various funerary objects, paying only distracted attention to me. She barely even stops to show me a piece of pottery or a solid gold fibula. She seems so happy to be opening her boxes—drawing up an inventory of her possessions, finding just the right place and lighting where they will look their best—that I make sure I don't become a killjoy by talking to her about the effect of her clanging prophecies on our little community. The room Arcady allocated to her is one of the most spacious in the house, but it is still too small to contain all her treasures, and Nelly finally offloads an earthenware jar in my direction:

"Here, put this in your room: I'll get it back from you later. Or not..."

"What is it? Where does it come from?"

"From Anatolia. There's a child inside."

"What?"

"Yes, yes! Inhumed vertically, with folded legs."

"Is that allowed?"

"Is what allowed?"

"Is it OK to keep dead people, you know, just . . ."

"No. It's perfectly illegal. But what am I supposed to do with it? I inherited it. From my father. I can't just throw it in the trash!"

"No, but you could give it to a museum."

"That's out of the question! If you don't want it, I'll keep it!"

"No, no, that's OK."

In fact, the idea of having a long-dead Turkish child as a roommate doesn't really worry me. On the contrary, then I'll have some company. Apart from Arcady, occasionally, no one ever comes into my little room under the eaves. That very evening, I install the jar by my bedside and timidly caress its scaly glaze, feeling the softness of the ancient clay.

"Are you asleep?"

Stupid question, of course he's asleep! I'm the one having trouble nodding off. It wouldn't take much for me to swap places with my little friend: it must be nice to snuggle with your head on your knees and your arms wrapped around your shins, in the dark, the warmth, the silence. It might even be a good way to escape Armageddon, as long as I had a slightly more spacious jar and a few survival rations. Then again, if I emerge from my amphora after the end of the world to find only lunar landscapes, polluted water, and swarming scorpions, I really can't see the point. Trust my bum luck to be born when humankind had only a few years left! As I squash a few tears of frustration on my cheeks, someone knocks at the door: it's Nelly, just as impetuous as earlier on—you'd think she has no idea of the time, which is quite possible in fact:

"Farah, I forgot to give you something. Here! It's a photo of Sylvester Stallone!"

She trots away again, leaving me with a slightly crumpled page from a magazine. Since Stallone had a great career with that face of his, I shouldn't be offended by people thinking we look alike, but I still find this latest slur difficult to swallow. Luckily Fiorentina has started her deep sleep cycle in the room next door. I can hear her snoring, as loudly and regularly as usual, and I squeeze against the wall to hear her better, so the peace in her soul can come over me at last.

15.

Dreams of the End

Custom has it that the members of Liberty House tell each other their dreams over breakfast. I generally keep my mouth shut and listen only distractedly to the accounts, which hold meaning and magic only for the dreamer. Not to mention that I suspect some people of pure fabrication—Malika, for example, who invariably tells of dreams of abduction and sequestration:

". . . and then, he tied me to the foot of the bed, and then he got a kind of . . . like, a mallet, you know, but with pointy bits, like a meat tenderizer, you know?"

"How would you know what a meat tenderizer looks like? You're a vegetarian!"

My grandmother's voice vibrates with suspicion, while the rest of us remain unaffected by Malika's latest nightmare, since we're all used to hearing her childlike voice describing the abuse inflicted on her night after night.

"And then he spread my thighs, and I was terrified, and then . . ."

"What did he look like? You say 'he,' but are you sure it was a guy this time? You said he was wearing a ski mask! And that he didn't speak!"

Malika turns to her lover with the nth variation of her beautifully wounded look:

"Yes, Kirsten, it really was a guy."

I imagine that this is precisely what aggrieves my grandmother: despite their passionate and sexually satisfying relationship, Malika continues to dream about a man penetrating her with blunt instruments. Worse still, this man seems to recur from one dream to the next, never quite the same but never totally different either, which means Kirsten is leading a dogged investigation to unmask him—especially since her prime suspect is José, Malika's ex-husband and the father of little Djilali. Of course, Malika manages to leave clues, talking about a familiar smell, a sense of déjà vu, a Portuguese swear word, or whatever: Kirsten is the only one who doesn't see what's going on and keeps frothing with rage.

For once, I have a dream to tell, and I interrupt Epifanio before he launches into the monotone story of his latest nightmare. Because dreams, just like intestinal gurgles and body odors, carry the mark of their owner: whereas Malika fantasizes about assaults, Epifanio dreams that he's taking the bus for Èze or Menton, that he's lost his glasses, or that he's helping his daughters study for their physics test. What's the point of dreaming, I ask you, if your dreams are the carbon copy of your boring life? And so, I start:

"We were all in the house and we heard a noise outside, like explosions. We went out and saw there was a storm coming:

the sky was all black, but in the distance, way up high in the hills. We thought that's what the noise was. And then, all of a sudden, we saw thousands of people sliding towards us, like an avalanche or a mudslide. And then we understood, I don't know how, the way you do in dreams, that in fact there was a terrorist attack, up there in the villages, and that the people were running away. But we knew there were thousands of casualties and it would go on and on. So we all went inside and Arcady told us to close the shutters and doors and not to make any noise, to pretend that the house was uninhabited, because that was our only chance of survival. So that's what we did, but we could hear the people arriving, and they started banging on the doors and windows for us to open up and save them, but we stayed absolutely silent, and then I woke up because I was so afraid we'd be killed. That's all."

It's strange, but my dream does not evoke any response or lively exegesis. No one could give a shit. Only a wasp ventures a cautious mandible in the direction of my tahini toast. What is going on with me? Why is it that everyone has something to say when it's Malika or Epifanio's turn, but they shut up as soon as I open my mouth? Is it because of my physical appearance? I do look more and more disturbing, I must admit. Since my visit to Mrs. Campi, things have gotten even worse: not only my pilosity but also the timbre of my voice and my muscle mass have now gotten out of control.

"Your shoulders are bigger, aren't they?"

Yes, my shoulders are bigger and my tits are smaller: there's no more room for doubt about my galloping virilization, Rokitansky syndrome or not. I am one of nature's mistakes, a complex of symptoms that will make my life very difficult without offering any explanation or hope of an adequate cure.

The more time goes by, the farther away I get from the position I was aiming for in matters of femininity: having always been aware of my scarce assets, I was just hoping to be a good friend, a girl with fresh cheeks and a kind of honest charm, without any of the affected artifices of most women. Alas, I won't even fit into that modest niche: the only one left to me is transgender, shemale, or the third sex. I have nothing against them, but this wasn't my idea, and I always come back to the question that almost drove Arcady and me into a ditch: who am I?

I meet Arcady's eyes across the breakfast table, which we set up on the terrace as soon as the weather is fine—his beautiful, perplexed but still loving eyes. It's impossible to guess whether he is wondering about my dream or just realizing, like me, that I don't look like anything anymore. His lips articulate a sentence directed at me, but at that moment I have trouble seeing through the tears welling in my eyes, and I quickly look down. Plop: the damask tablecloth is splattered with a dark stain, immediately followed by another one. I'd like not to burst into tears, but what can I do? What kind of life can I construct for myself with this face and this body?

If I didn't live in a quiet zone, I could at least go on social media sites about intersexuality: I could talk with my peers and draw a little comfort from the comparative observation of our dysmorphia. I tried to do a few sneaky searches at the school and public libraries, but there's always someone looking over my shoulder just when I get to photos of Thai kathoeys or Indian hijras. I'm left with my own cogitations and intimate reckonings—and other dreams too, no doubt impossible to tell, that have me endowed with a penis or, conversely, eight months pregnant, proudly carrying a restless belly before me, flapping like a sail full of wind.

When I decide to look up and hold Arcady's gaze, I can see that he has caught my sadness and that he is close to tears himself. Everybody cries a lot at Liberty House. Arcady and Victor have even set up crying sessions, which are supposed to drain our personal and collective grief. I never go, but my parents are very diligent attenders and swear that they come out of them feeling refreshed and purged. Good for them.

It's Palmyre's turn to tell her dream: the river is flooding and even threatening to inundate our eagle's nest. While distractedly dipping into the basket of homemade croissants and pastries, she describes the rising waters, their slow and inexorable suction, the iridescent splats of oil on the surface, and the smell of the pallid sludge—not the foaming eddies one might expect. And, of course, everybody has a comment to make. I must say that the river whose name shall not pass my lips does in fact flow at the bottom of the hill and is subject to spectacular flooding. From our position up on the slope above, it always seemed that we were out of danger, but unlike my tale of a terrorist attack in the mountains, which is just as plausible, Palmyre's dream seems to be affecting everybody.

Above our heads, a flock of swifts starts a strident round, the first of the season. It seems to me that they are early this year in the ornithological calendar, but I wouldn't dare share this impression with the others, who would of course start saying that there are no seasons anymore and everything is out of kilter. Breakfast goes on and on, as it often does on Sundays, which we scrupulously observe as the day of rest. Across from me, my mother is squashing her banana in honey before drowning it in spelt milk and chopped hazelnuts. Her dream was about a swarm of unidentified insects, but she retained only a few images from it, and the commentators quickly dispatched it.

A pause. The sun is already high in the sky, and the pine wood is exhaling its resinous scents. I'm keen to get up, to shake myself off in the limpid air and to escape these old fogies' brooding. For Victor is right to say that Nelly, despite her aggressive vitality, has vertiginously raised our average age. Even my parents' early forties seem washed out compared to the new growth all around us and my own hormonal turmoil.

Taken together, our dreams all say the same thing: that we are afraid of the end—even me, although I'm just getting started. An unsteady start, but a start nevertheless. As I get ready to clear the table, giving the signal for our dominical dispersion, I again meet Arcady's gaze, and I read so much tenderness and concupiscence there that I forget that I belong to the third gender and that the end is nigh. I bounce up, leaving the remains of the meal, the damask tablecloth, the senile rehashing and interpretation of dreams. My legs are shaking with impatience and desire, which I can subdue only by running away. I scramble down the steps of our majestic porch, sprint past the greenhouses, leaving behind the blossoming orchard, the pond, the raked walkways, and civilization itself, to reach the wild part of my dominion. I jump between the torches of the broom bushes, over muddy ditches, pull myself up on the branches of a knotty pine, and yep, do a couple of pull-ups, just so my boyish muscles are put to use; I pivot around a chestnut tree, embracing its trunk with one hand, and after a few more leaps and skips, I reach my secret hollow, my hideaway in the long grass. I don't need to turn around to know that Arcady has followed me, and that our time has come at last.

16.

Come Sit on My Mouth

Yes, he is here, my beloved, breathless and sweating in his beige linen tunic and maroon velvet harem pants. And as if his outfit wasn't hideous enough, he's also wearing a long Amerindian pendant that bounces to the rhythm of his panting as he tries to catch his breath. I don't really care, especially since if things go my way, it won't be long before he takes it all off and is naked in my arms and thighs. I can barely contain the excited roar rising to my lips as I lie down in the grass in what I hope is an attractive lascivious pose. But with Arcady you don't even need to pose, there's no point trying to look sexy: he needs no incentives to desire endlessly. Leaning on an elbow, he is contemplating me as if I were the eighth wonder of the world, and starts singing an antiphon of praise such as I had never heard in all my life and will probably never hear again—and I wish everyone could be lucky enough to hear one someday, because everyone should be desired as I was that day between the fennel parasols and golden fescues:

"You are so beautiful, Farah! It's amazing, last year I thought you were cute but kinda drab, but now, now you drive me crazy! You know that you drive me crazy, don't you? I was looking at you just now, when we were having breakfast, and I was wondering, shit, when am I gonna be able to get it on with her? I couldn't cope anymore! And when Palmyre started telling her dream, wow, I thought it would never end!"

Without wasting any time, he pulls down my sweatpants and pulls up my top, revealing the tight curves of my tummy and thighs. Without bothering to undress me more, he buries his adoring face in my pubic fleece.

"And you smell good! Oh, you smell so good, Farah! If you only knew how good you smell!"

I had vaguely worried that, because I hadn't foreseen this intimate moment, I'd only had a hasty wash this morning, but I clearly didn't even need to bother. As the turquoises of the Comanche necklace dig into my tender flesh, Arcady is sighing convulsively and taking up his ecstatic chant again:

"My darling . . . you looked so sad just now! What is it that makes you so sad, my love? I don't want you to be sad, ever! I want you to be happy and proud to be yourself, I want you to go out into the world like a beautiful sailing ship, and drive all the guys crazy! And the girls too! You're so hot!"

Since this is the second time he's said that, I start to believe him, especially because, to illustrate his claims, he extracts his quivering penis from the velvety fold of his pants, glistening and darting at me like a little snake. Not so little either. He's going to have some trouble inserting it into my cupule, even though I've been working assiduously at stretching it over the last few months, with the help of all the vaginal dilators. I might start feeling discouraged, but Arcady doesn't give me the time for that: licking my thighs with his tongue, which is both hard and soft, he brings me to such a state of arousal that I lose the thread of my sadness and worry. He stops only to sing even more praises of my beauty and his mad desire:

"I want you, Farah! What about you? Do you want me? Do you want me as much as I want you? Coz I can wait, you know? I can wait for you to be ready. It's just that you are so sexy . . ."

He better not make another play about how I'm too young and how it would be better for me to do it with someone I love before doing it with him, et cetera. The right time is now. And, of course, with all those candles I've been shoving up my pussy, I can hardly even call myself a pure virgin anyway, so he can take his scruples and stick them where the sun don't shine. I whisper, in unison with the wind in the long grass and the tops of the ash trees:

"I want you!"

And it's true: I have never wanted anyone but him—even though a stranger sometimes slips into my dreams and inspires my perambulations in the city whose name shall not pass my lips, because it is much too close to our haven of peace, our snow globe with no snow and no globe.

Arcady's face lights up above my palpitating stomach:

"Well, then, if you want me . . ."

He crawls towards me and grabs my chin with fervent tenderness:

"My princess . . ."

He bursts into a brutal laugh, as if he realized the incongruity of what he just said:

"Or my prince?"

I might feel humiliated by his hesitation, but I share it myself, and I know that I will have to live with these doubts my whole life. And so I'm happy to make love in the midst of his indecision and mine, not knowing what I am or even what that says about him and me. I accept being nothing, except a torrent of love, at last free to be unleashed, to flood everything on my path, a rising river just like Palmyre described it, but more tumultuous and implacable. Watch out, I'm surging: Arcady better look out.

He kisses me. He laughs against my lips, our teeth clack together, our saliva blends. He smells good too. One of his rare indulgences, the only one perhaps, is to wear the same rich and penetrating cologne in all circumstances. Any time of the day or night, he smells of palm trees, resin, musk—a Byzantine sacristy.

Without my noticing it, he has taken off his tunic and harem pants, and I try to do the same with what I wear as pajamas. At last, we're both naked, and it seems to me that I've been waiting for this moment all my life. He eyes lock with mine, happy and triumphant. He tirelessly caresses and smells me, puts his fingers into my mouth and on my eyelids, pushes back my hair to blow onto my lips or the nape of my neck or around my ears, always with his tender and persistent chant to which my song of songs replies, I love you, I want you, my love, my one, my only love. He turns me over and bursts out laughing at the sight of my buttocks:

"You really do have a guy's ass! And I know what I'm talking about!"

Thanks to nudism, I also know the difference between a boy's and a girl's ass, and I have to agree with him: solid, firm, muscly, with hollows in their sides, my buttocks have none of the soft heft of Malika's, Jewell's, or Birdie's. To say nothing of the pocked sacks of cellulite that most women drag around.

"Come sit on my mouth!"

I do as I'm told, shivering with the joy of being understood. I mean, it's true, right? I would not have appreciated him penetrating me with no further ado. I do know that Arcady is easy to please, but I remain skeptical about my ability to make anyone cum in my vagina. Even though the candles have enlarged it, it's still too small to contain a normally proportioned penis. I kneel down in the grass and settle my groin above my beloved's ecstatic face. Arcady's tongue goes in search of my clit, and I lean back to enjoy his passionate assaults. He sucks, licks, inspires, nibbles, and expires his hot breath on the only organ I am more or less sure about—but for how long? How long before it betrays me too, and is subjected to its own ignominious metamorphosis?

"Lick your fingers!"

His command comes to me, choppy and wet, and I obey without understanding why.

"Done?"

"Yes."

"Stick them up your ass!"

"What?"

"Put your fingers up your ass!"

It's too late for obedience, for at that moment I feel pleasure arriving, first as a very localized annoyance, something that I would almost want to stop by sending Arcady and his tongue packing, but then like a strike on a gong, immediately followed by voluptuous harmonics from one end of my body to the other. Pulling himself out of the embrace of my thighs, Arcady observes me with satisfaction:

"It's great, right?"

"Yes!"

"But you'd already cum though, right? That's not the first time, is it?"

"No, it's not the first time, but it's better with you than by myself."

"Ah, yes, my darling, you've discovered one of the great truths: sex is better with two people. Or three, or four, or more. What do you think about a threesome with Daniel?"

"No."

"Because you really look alike: it could be quite exciting. To see you doing it together, giving each other pleasure, and giving me pleasure too . . ."

"Well, I really don't feel like it."

He heaves a sigh of regret before pushing me back onto the grass, which is already rather crushed by the throes of our lovemaking. In my green hollow, the heat of the sun is strong, as we are sheltered from even a breath of wind. After my orgasm, I'm covered in sweat, but Arcady is too, his red face covered in my secretions. Without any further delay, he presses his body against mine and starts caressing me again, with his fingers, his lips, his cock, which stayed hard during his inspired cunnilingus. I have a passing thought for poor Victor, who has to deal with so much vigor every day while his is in constant decline—but I don't have time to waste on compassion. I have time only for me and Arcady.

"Our time has come!"

Arcady just pronounced this sentence, as if he could read my mind and was way ahead of me on the path of impatience. From his penetrating tone, I can tell it's a quotation, and I ask him who the author is:

"I can't remember. A poet, I think."

"Victor Hugo?"

"No, not Victor Hugo. He's not the only poet, you know! It's just that I can't remember right now: you got me too excited! And you know, Victor is the one who reads a lot, whereas literature, for me . . . to tell you the truth, it actually sort of breaks my balls. But, like, don't tell anyone."

My jubilation is boundless: it's only with me that he dares show himself as he really is, ignorant, vulgar, and keen to eat sea snails. I am in his confidence and my own goes up a notch. I return his kisses and caresses, and even dare to grab his frisky cock. It's the first time I've touched a penis, and I should probably make a wish, but everything is going too fast for me, with the swifts cheeping and swirling above us, Arcady's cologne blending with the scent of the nearby pine trees, the back-and-forth movement he makes my hand do with his, so wide and warm, his racing breath, and the delight I see in his eyes.

"Where do you want me to come?"

"What?"

"Yes, where do you want me to come?"

No matter how many times he repeats his question, I still don't understand it.

"On your stomach? Between your breasts? In your mouth?"

Light dawns on me, but I barely have time to react before the salvo is launched, not on my stomach or between my breasts, but somewhere between my epigastrium and solar plexus—in other words, an indeterminate zone of no interest, and not even slightly erogenous. This is also my first encounter with sperm, and this time I have all the time I need to think about my wish. Arcady interrupts my thoughts by pointing at the sky:

"You know they never land?"

"Who?"

"The swifts: they can fly for months and months without having to land."

What a good idea. I take it as my own at once, and wordlessly formulate the mad, fervent wish to continue to fly—without stopping or slowing down, with no period of despondency or doubt. I carefully pick up a bit of sperm and bring my fingers to my nose. Arcady's resin and amber scent has given way to a softer and actually more familiar smell:

"It smells like chestnut trees, doesn't it?"

My little woodland kingdom includes enough of them for me to be sure of my facts, but out of politeness, I let Arcady decide on the relationship his sperm has with the floral emanations I never really liked that much—I much prefer my father's lilies and freesias.

"Oh, really?"

He knows just as much about flowers as he does about literature, I can tell, but I forgive him because his specialty is humankind. Or love. Or the love of humankind, which is even more rare and more commendable than any old certification in botany.

17.

Happy Days

The arrival of summer having temporarily dispensed me of all school obligations, I have nothing else to do besides be myself—full time. Luckily, full time has a few black holes, those moments of absence I've already talked about and that are tending to occur more and more frequently. Maybe I should be worried: after all, my mother is not a model of good mental health, and my grandmother is bonkers, judging by the erotic fury she unleashes on poor Malika. Who knows, maybe I have a bipolar disorder or a neurological condition—on top of all my other malfunctions.

I don't care: never have I been more in tune with the summer and all its rustlings and screeches, its corridors of heat between the pine trees, its blasts of mineral air and blue horizons. Every morning, when the dew is still shivering, I run to my nest, my hideaway, the harp of long grass where Arcady joins me, if he isn't already there waiting for me, stretched out with a teasing yet impatient expression. In less time than it takes to say it, we are both naked in our Eden, and we unleash our raging need for pleasure on each other. I was right to wait and to start with him: no one else would have been the right one. I tell him that's what I think, but he denies it lightly, nonchalant and unaware as he is:

"No, of course not! I know heaps of guys who do it just as well as I do! It's just that I'm your first and you don't yet have any points of comparison!"

"I want you to be my first, my last, my only one."

"Don't get too carried away, Farah Faucet."

"You still haven't showed me any photos."

"Photos?'

"Of Farah Faucet! You said you'd show me some photos!"

"Oh, right, that's true. But where am I gonna be able to find any?"

"On the internet!"

He turns to me with a pained and suspicious look.

"Let me remind you of the rules of the confraternity, which forbid us from using the internet. You don't go online at school, do you?"

I have rules too, which forbid me to tell untruths. You have to despise people to lie to them, and contempt is not in my nature.

"I do sometimes. But remember we have to! For study. The teachers expect it."

"We asked the school to dispense the children of Liberty House from using it: you, Dos, Tres, Djilali . . ."

"Well, they couldn't give a shit. And I don't know about Djilali, but in middle school they treat us the same as everyone else."

Of course, I don't tell him anything about my own little online research project on trans people: there are limits to my frankness, and, to be quite honest, a little dissimulation suits me. Arcady sighs, but he doesn't seem scandalized by my confession. He snuggles against me, puts his arms around me, squashes his nose into my neck—his nose that I love, meaty, turned up, and always a little cold. An ecstatic groan rises in his throat, he rolls the *r* of my name until it becomes a sumptuous, imperial, munificent consonant: farrrrah, farrrah, farrrrah. . . .

We roll in the grass, and everything starts all over again, the confused tangling of our ardent flesh, the panting, the moaning, the adjustments, his hands grabbing me, lifting me, turning me over, his voice directing me, and my delight in obeying. My worries about my cupule didn't last long, as he made it his launching pad, a zone of friction that magnifies our energy, but to which we would be foolish to confine ourselves. I've taken on Arcady's philosophy: it's not like sex is just about vaginal penetration. Anyway, as an erogenous zone, the vagina is wildly overrated, considering the pleasure I get from all the extra-vaginal practices into which my spiritual director initiates me—for even having taken over my sexual education, he is still concerned with my spiritual education. He is concerned with it more than ever, since he claims that the spirit is everywhere, in each of the cells of my body, from my unruly hair to the calluses on my heels, and, of course, in my atrophied genital organs—the spirit doesn't discriminate.

Over time, my secret hollow has become a real casemate, protected with a canvas canopy that clacks in the wind and shelters us from the sun. I have laid in stores of water, peaches from our orchard, and provisions that I steal from the cellar whenever Fiorentina is not there. But she must have a sixth sense for larceny, or maybe she just perfectly remembers her stock levels. In any case, she complained that her reserves of Pavesini biscuits were dwindling, those Piedmont biscuits that are the only ones she ever uses to make tiramisu. That's odd, because I actually got into the dried fruit. In any case, Arcady says that fucking is better on an empty stomach.

"And a full bladder. At least for girls, coz for guys it's a bit more complicated."

And so I arrive at our rendezvous without having eaten or pissed. I do it afterwards, and then it's an added pleasure: pissing behind the hazelnut trees or eating stale bread and overripe peaches, while Arcady caresses me with his loving eyes, waiting for the moment to taste the dried fruit on my tongue and the sharpness of urine between my thighs.

"You taste good, Farah, you taste so good!"

Sometimes we spend the day under the shivering canopy, but most of the time, we go home in time for lunch, so that Arcady can see his flock and manage daily business. Our idyll has not gone unnoticed, but at Liberty House everybody has sex with everybody without getting into a stew about it. Of course, there are a few exceptions, like Fiorentina, but as far as I know, even the other older women continue to be sexually active or at least go to a lot of trouble to pretend they are. And I'm not even talking about the older men, Kinbote, Orlando, who are convinced they have found the ultimate brothel here—I mean, ultimate for them, those moribund valetudinarians. In other words, it would never even cross anyone's mind to be upset about our activities. I even wonder whether Victor, far from being jealous, is actually secretly relieved to see me redirecting some of Arcady's torrential energy and making good use of it. In any case, he is showing me a new kind of respect and offering me little signs of affection, which are quite surprising when you know the old man. For example, he dug up a photo of Farrah Fawcett that I had been pestering Arcady about. Obviously torn out of a book, it is now stuck alongside Sylvester Stallone on the whitewashed bedroom wall that my predecessors had covered with olive boughs, crucifixes, and views of Lourdes, Fatima, or Castel Gandolfo. My eyes flit from the animal magnetism of the one to the canonical beauty of the other, with the disillusioned melancholy of the missing link. Maybe in a pinch I do look something like Sylvester Stallone, but there is unfortunately nothing of Farrah Fawcett in me. Except that maybe I didn't miss by much. You just have to look at my mother to convince yourself that I just didn't luck out in the draw. Or with the scratch tickets either: even if I didn't get Birdie's delicate features, I could at least have been granted her light-blue eyes, her perfect skin, her full round breasts, or her delicate ankles, just the scrappy leftovers of her splendor, but no, nothing. Nothing from my father either: neither his light-brown curls nor his long eyelashes nor his shapely mouth. You'd think I went and delved somewhere else in my lineage, into a capital of genes that had been dormant for millennia, from a prehistoric era when women didn't need to distinguish themselves all that much from the men in the tribe—but no, I'm dreaming, even in the Pleistocene I would have been expected to have normal genitals for my sex. But then I suddenly wonder how far our ancestors took their explorations into female anatomy. Did they open up the innards, or did they content themselves with what fingers could inspect, the moist opening of the vulva, the elastic tightening of the vagina, and for the lucky ones, a proper cervix—in which case, my lack of a uterus would never even have been noticed? People are always going on about the progress of medical imaging, but they're wrong, or at least they don't give enough thought to people like us, who would be much better off without all those humiliating investigations.

All this is going off topic—namely, my mother's resemblance to Farrah Fawcett, but less athletic, less radiant, and less American. Their smiles have the same sparkling perfection, their hair is the same silvery blond. But I should mention that my mother's is so tightly curled that it's impossible to do anything with it, and so she has long since opted for a nebulous afro look. Since the fine mother-of-pearl of her skin tans easily and well, one might well wonder how faithful Kirsten was to her husband, who is just as pink and blond as she is. Kirsten, of course, swears to God that there was only ever one man in her life and that he was one too many anyway, but still: Birdie has the hair of a Black woman and a complexion that leaves room for doubt. But since she protects herself from UV rays just like everything else—electromagnetic stress, parabens, phthalates, and the rest—she is whiter than many white women, starting with her mother and daughter, who both let themselves get kippered by the sunshine.

For it's in the sunshine that I meet my lover, and in the sunshine that we make love, as long as the heat is bearable. Afterwards we fall back under the baldachin he set up for me, stretched over the wild oat grass, making the most of the stiff trunks of the hazelnut trees to hook up its twisted silk cords. Here begins the short happiness of my life. . . . No, that's wrong: happiness began earlier. It was only later that it all went bad. But from my arrival at Liberty House to the summer I turned fifteen, I was happy, of course. Happy to grow up in a community of loving adults; happy to live in a palazzo that is a little run-down but so much more romantic than other people's houses or apartments; happy to be the undisputed ruler of my acres of pine woods, my chestnut trees, my meadows, my shadowy lanes, my population of hens, cats, and jays—to say nothing of the ponds swarming with newts, the fox cubs' burrows, the tree forts up in the forks of branches, the cowbells ringing from one valley to the next, which bring me sometimes peace, and sometimes exaltation—in other words, just what a child's soul needs.

Arcady's great perspicacity allowed him to seize the exact moment when my kingdom might not be enough for me anymore and to unleash the storm I had been waiting so long for, my orgiastic passion, my great transformation. I am insatiable, but so is he, and it's so good to feel his love, his desire, his appreciation for what I am, in spite of my intersexuality, my Stallone looks, my Farrah Fawcett dreams. My mother must also have felt love and desire, in the same way as they float around me when I climb out of my hollow, breathless, sweaty, and with all the tender zones of my body irritated by Arcady's nibbling and the chafing of his stubbly beard, his sperm drying in splotches on my neck or between my thighs. She looks at me with a new curiosity and asks me with abrupt frankness:

"Is it nice with Arcady? Do you like what he does to you?"

I'm used to frankness and abruptness, especially from my poor parents, who have a mental age of twenty between the two of them; I'm also used to not keeping any secrets from anyone, and for them not keeping any from me, in the great glass house in which I grew up, but that doesn't mean that I want my sex life to be a topic of conversation. Especially with my mother, whose sexuality consists in submitting herself to my father's, enduring his spirited onslaughts, his passionate kisses, and the furtive insertion, conceded at the very last, of his impatient member. For life is full of mistakes, and couples are mismatched: my mother, who would manage quite nicely with a partner like Victor, with his rare and softening erections, is burdened by my father, who is always pressuring and harassing her to open her thighs to him. It's the only shadow in their life, for they agree on everything else and are almost consanguineous in their shared views—and maybe that's the explanation of my physical flaws: they were too alike to reproduce.

Perched on one of our boundary walls, a low affair all in dry stone and scampering lizards, my mother is taking a drag on a little crumpled cigarette. I don't know what she's smoking and I suspect she doesn't either: my father rolls her cigs and slips in a mixture of a few herbs he grows himself. Recently he's planted a little aromatic herb garden alongside his greenhouses and vegetable garden, in which he's been furiously conducting experiments. As other people search for the philosopher's stone, maybe he is attempting to find the supreme aphrodisiac substance, the one that will finally turn his wife into a wild unrestrained lover. In the meantime, my mother seems to be constantly in an altered state, a kind of dreamy, amiable perplexity, not very different from her normal state, but a couple of notches higher on the detachment scale.

"You see, Farah, I'd like to tell you something . . ."

I look at her hopefully, this mother of mine who never says anything, this mother who needs protection from everything, this mother whose only knowledge of desire is that she has always inspired it, because she is ideally beautiful.

"Yes?"

She's finding it difficult to go on, and drags on her cigarette while looking about, as if the lavender and rosemary bushes might inspire a little maternal lecture. The landscape all around us is buzzing like a beehive under the implacable midday sun. Soon the gong will ring, inviting us to the table set on the terrace. My mother is quite capable of using this as a pretext to get away, to jump off her little drystone wall before she can deliver her message. But I actually need a little maternal wisdom more than ever now, some incentive to grow up, some advice on finding my path, a path I can expect to be narrower and steeper than it is for most people.

"I was thinking it was about time I had a talk with you . . ."

Yes, I totally agree, it's more than about time, since she has never spoken to me in her whole life, and I'm not making this up. As much as my father and grandmother were always taking me to one side to share their ideas about everything, my mother has always kept well away from anything resembling my education. She declared herself forfeit from the moment I was born, delegating to others the task of feeding, washing, dressing, distracting, or educating me. But I would feel bad about painting her as the baddie in this picture, for she was always there, a guardian angel in the background, levitating into the powdery azure sky, holding her tutelary boughs aloft and smiling benignly.

Time passes. Smells of food come to us: butter, sage. Fiorentina must have made her gnocchi. My mother stubs out her cigarette between two stones and carefully picks up the butt. A gust of wind lifts up the marvelous cloud of her ash-blond hair and a melancholic smile settles into the dimples on her downy cheeks. She probably doesn't care that she has no conversation skills, even on the most trivial topics. Except that this is anything but trivial: at last, my mother is going to tell me how to find my way on the winding road of adolescence. After all, she must have found her own way, right? I even remember hearing that it wasn't all that easy for her, with my LGBTQ grandmother trying to foist her on to her girlfriends, while taking her to one audition after another to monetize her incredible beauty. No surprise then, that she took refuge in my father's love as soon as possible, the moment they met at a summer camp where they were both supposed to be learning English and making friends with other rich kids.

My mother sighs, stretches, and slips off her wall, just as I feared. Her eyes, slightly milky opals under the fringe of her long, astoundingly dense black eyelashes, seek mine:

"See, I'm trying to think, but I still can't quite figure out what I could say to you. Believe me, I'd love to . . . you know, talk, and stuff, but nothing seems to come to me . . ."

From her disappointment I draw the courage to face my own. It's true, of course, I can see that she is sorry for me, and I'm sure that she racked her brains to find something or other to pass on to me. Did I mention that my mother is really dumb? No? Well, it's a well-known fact. She and my father are simple souls, all but half-wits. She found it just as difficult as he did to learn even the simplest things and owed her passing up through the grades only to her kindness and silence. The teachers were grateful she never made waves and was serious, docile, and diligent—even if she gained absolutely nothing from their instruction. She failed her final high school exams twice before throwing in the towel. After all, she was already earning a sumptuous living as a model, compensating for the modesty of her five feet and six inches with her uncommon grace, the perfection of her features, and the subtlety of her coloring: lavender blue, oyster or almond green, mother-of-pearl from the ocean depths, soft mushroom from the forest's edge.

How could anyone want to harm Birdie, in word or deed? I hold back my frustration and follow her, reflecting on this little interlude. I was wrong to expect anything from a mother who doesn't have the slightest idea of who she really is. Not that she is alone in this. From what I can tell, it even seems to me that humankind can be divided into two groups: those who know themselves, and the others. Into this latter category I'm obviously and incontestably putting my parents, but also my grandmother, and Malika, Salo, Epifanio, and Teresa—Dolores seems somehow better endowed with critical judgment and lucidity than her twin sister is. Djilali is still too young for me to evaluate how he sees himself, but something tells me that he will be one of those individuals who direct their own life instead of submitting to it, strong in the wisdom acquired by living in the midst of the madness of others, which is children's lot in general, and Djilali's in particular. You can see what I'm getting at: there's nothing like a complicated childhood to make you want to avoid complications.

While I take a second helping of gnocchi, I evaluate my companions and try to fill the other column of my imaginary table. While Arcady and Fiorentina require no hesitation, I am much less sure about Victor, Dadah, Nelly, or Daniel, whose common sense is sometimes lost in an eclipse, if not in a permanent shadow zone. One might deduce from my little evaluation that the majority of people have no idea who they are, but I will need to apply some variable coefficients to these demoralizing figures, for one of the perverse effects of our collective utopia is that it concentrates failings and incompetence. Perhaps the rest of humankind does a lot better.

Arcady's hand finds my thighs, his fingers follow the ridged traces of my burns, climb up to the hem of my shorts, furtively caress my fleece, before coming back to fumble on the table, looking for a ramekin of Parmesan—even though Fiorentina considers it sinful to put cheese on her butter and sage gnocchi. It's a pity I'm sitting next to him and not across from him: I like to see him doing things, being busy with others, conversing with his neighbors, but throwing me conniving looks from time to time. Worse luck, Victor is the one sitting across from me, faded, leonine, his appetite not at all reduced by his lover's infidelities. Stuffing his face is probably his way of telling me that I am just small fry in their long love story.

Grabbing a grissino myself now, I start eating it in a suggestive manner, sucking in my cheeks, making little squelching noises, licking my lips, just to remind Victor how good it is to take a tumescent hard penis into one's mouth, even though the caliber of the grissino has nothing to do with the girth of Arcady's cock. Everybody is looking at me, but I persist with my pantomime, until the grissino vanishes completely into my tender mouth. And then I swallow it all in one go, with a sigh of satisfaction. There, done. Until next time. Until dawn finds us, Arcady and me, stretched out under the baldachin shuddering in the gusts of wind, his cock on my tongue, his fingers in my cupule, and our hearts beating in unison—in unison too with the pulsations of summer in the white-hot stones, the parched dead grass, and the heights of the heavens, amen.

18.

An Anguish with No Remedy

My rendezvous under the canopy and Arcady's tender attentions must not divert me from my purpose. It's all very well getting fondled, but I won't always be lucky enough to find omnivorous and undiscriminating lovers: if I want a sequel to this beautiful summer, I need to determine if I am a girl or a boy, instead of staying in the state of indetermination towards which my body is irresistibly tending.

When I ask my LGBTQ grandmother about it, she is categorical: 15 percent of the world population presents some level of intersexuality. OK, sure, but this is my grandmother, right? She always tends to bend reality in favor of her own communitarian interests, so I decide not to rely too much on her assertions or resign myself to my in-between status just yet. Mind you, if I compare her numbers with my own personal statistics, and my two imaginary columns of figures, that makes a lot of people living in confusion and ignorance of their profound nature—and there's no way I'm going to join their ranks. Especially since I continue to feel like a girl, even though I get called "young man," or even "sir," more and more often. The fact is, my budding breasts have inexplicably receded after their promising start, and from the outside only my clothing choices signal my belonging to the female gender. And since I live in jeans, shorts, T-shirts, and sneakers, that doesn't help much in making the distinction.

I could accept being a boy if I had even the faintest idea of what that meant, but I just don't. But since I need to make a crucial choice and I have all this summer to do so, I decide to start a full-scale investigation. After all, Liberty House has an exceptional library, is haunted by young ladies in uniform, and is home to people of both genders, who are all quite happy to fill in my survey—since that shall be my research methodology. In the hottest hours of the day, I therefore retire to the library, which is also the smaller living room—only relatively small, of course, since the room is around 970 square feet—in other words, the average size of French homes. But before anyone starts requisition procedures against us, let them remember that there are around thirty permanent residents at Liberty House, and that's what it takes to provide housing for them all. That said, apart from Victor, Djilali, and I, no one ever goes into the library. So much the better: I can conduct my research in peace and quiet.

A summary inventory of our shelves brings me to a first observation: our *Encyclopédie de la femme et de la famille* does not cover the question of men. You could argue that given its title I should have expected that, but, in fact, no: eighteen volumes should theoretically provide enough latitude to cover the topic, if only as part of the chapter devoted to reproduction. In fact, there is nothing at all about them in there, and since I've already spent many hours darkly contemplating sagittal-plane drawings of female reproductive organs, I think I can put the eighteen leather-bound volumes back in their usual place next to Buffon's *L'Histoire naturelle*, whose entomological and ornithological plates I've gotten into the habit of consulting, to distinguish one songbird from another and to identify butterflies without fear of error. I had great hopes for the *Natural History of Man*, and a treatise on lovers called the *Traité de l'amant*—except it turned out that their binding in red Morocco with three-line gold fillets didn't contain any more useful information than the women's encyclopedia. Not to mention the fact that the *Traité de l'amant* is actually a *Traité de l'aimant*—a treatise on magnets—and I have no interest at all in magnetite or iron oxides. Anyway, I can stay here for the pleasure of being in one of the most comfortable rooms in the house, but if I want to get on with my research, I would do better to start my fieldwork, notebook in hand.

Since I've decided to temporarily exclude dykes and gays from my study, that doesn't leave many people in my immediate circle of acquaintance. Don't get me wrong, gays undoubtedly have things to say about sex and gender, but they might distort my inquiry. I start with Fiorentina in her kitchen. Something tells me that she must have a clear idea about her own femininity, all the more so since she hasn't been sexually active for a long time. No wisp of romantic smoke will come between her and the truth. She greets me in her usual fashion, a tea towel thrown over her shoulder and her hands locked around a wire salad basket full of green beans.

"They're for the minestrone. Give me a hand?"

While we both top and tail the beans picked that very morning, I go for it:

"What does it mean to you, to be a woman?"

I had thought of more subtle questions, but subtlety is not what is called for with Fiorentina.

"*Lavorare. Sempre lavorare.*"

Huh. That's a strange response. Strange that she says it in Italian too, since she usually saves her warbling for her Piedmont family. Her pile of tailed beans is already three times the size of mine, so I concentrate on my task and keep my objections to myself: with Fiorentina it's best to be diligent and quiet. But, really, that's nonsense. Dadah, Malika, and Birdie, to stick with the women I know best, never did a day's work in their lives. With a sigh of impatience, Fiorentina slides some of my beans over to her side and starts decapitating them at magical speed. Once her job is dispatched, she goes and drains the borlotti beans that have been soaking since last night, while pointing at a bunch of fresh basil. It smells so good in her kitchen, and an atmosphere of serene efficiency reigns, which I have come to associate with happiness.

"You dreaming?"

Yes, that's exactly what I'm doing, half-steeped in my postcoital languor and the aromatic vapors of the minestrone. If only I could stay here. Never leave this kitchen. Never leave the people who know who they are and what they have to do—but not expect a miracle either: Fiorentina has nothing to teach me about femininity. And so I move on to Jewell—who I haven't said much about until now, but who richly deserves her own little character development, even though there's not much about her to cause a stir. Jewell is between thirty-five and fifty years old, with blond hair, graying in spite of the chamomile decoctions she conscientiously rinses it with, black eyeliner, and ex-junkie's arms sprinkled with old scars and punctiform wounds that will never heal. Although she's more discreet than the other members about her sex life, she still has regular lovers who make her unhappy on a regular basis.

Jewell defines herself as a freelance artist, but as far as I know she has never sold a single drawing or a single painting, despite their unique beauty. Victor doesn't have harsh enough words to describe her production, but that harshness says more about him than it does about her: he is simply incapable of recognizing a talent that hasn't been ennobled or burnished by time, incapable of being delighted, as I am, by her powdery pastels, her obsessional India inks, and her striking self-portraits; he sticks to his antiquated tastes, and that's too bad for him. I seek Jewell out at the antipodes of Fiorentina's kitchen, in her little workshop under the eaves, at the antipodes of Fiorentina's kitchen, which opens onto the large living room, the cellar, and the gardens.

"How are you?"

"OK, and you?"

"What are you painting?"

"Geese."

"Really? Our geese?"

"Yeah, why not?"

Jewell certainly had not led us to expect animal paintings. Her drawings are a mixture of multicolored corpuscles, stylized skulls and syringes, enigmatic gradations, and raging scribbles, usually names of meds one after the other, *noctamidpimoziderivotrilmirtazapine*, or short and cryptic reminders, *tak a shower, call samia bak, shit cok, get im, do not kil.* . . . Jewell's oeuvre smells of schizophrenia from a mile off, but the geese seem to indicate a fragile return to mental health. In any case, they really are ours, I recognize them, crossing our gravel walkways heading for the orchard, and I don't have to force myself to make appreciative remarks:

"I like them a lot. They're different."

"Oh, really?"

"Yes, really, they're so beautiful."

But since I'm not here to pretend I'm an art critic, I get started on my topic:

"What does being a woman mean to you?"

Jewell turns a tragic gaze towards me and I catch a fleeting glimpse of her trashed beauty, the exoticism of her cheekbones under her swollen face, the voluptuous line of her lips in spite of their sagging, the distant glint of her golden eyes under her withered eyelids. She answers with a kind of savage fervor, as if my question had wrenched her out of her usual stupor:

"Women are all about generosity, about giving! No man is capable of giving as much as a woman!"

She's almost shaking from providing this response—her vision of the world where adoring women madly share their love, their time, their body, their money. . . . I've apparently raised a sensitive and inspiring subject, for now she's launching into a bitter *lamento*:

"You can't imagine everything I did, everything I sacrificed, for men! Everything—I gave them everything, every time! And every time, they betrayed me! Each as bad as the last! And when I was in the shit, well, then . . . !"

She leaves her sentence unfinished, I can imagine very well. Shit is something she knows all about, at least as much as masculine ingratitude. But this isn't really getting me anywhere: I would be quite happy to allow that being a woman is about generosity, if I wasn't surrounded by living counterexamples, starting with my grandmother, who is a first-rate egotist—and if it weren't for Arcady.

"What about Arcady?"

"What *about* Arcady?"

"Well, he's a man, and he's generous, isn't he?"

It's even thanks to Arcady's generosity that Jewell has a roof over her head, for there is no way that she could survive on her handicapped-adult benefit. Contrary to the wishes of Victor, who excoriates parasites and intends for Liberty House to be a home only for dowagers, magnates, and the independently wealthy, Arcady maintains his little quota of economically vulnerable social misfits within our walls, come what may. Jewell cannot object to my objection, and her fervor abates, as does my interest: she doesn't hold the key to femininity any more than Fiorentina in her kitchen does. It's enough to discourage anyone from conducting surveys.

And so I leave her to her geese and go back to the library, so that I can rethink my modus operandi. I clearly need to sharpen my questions if I don't want people to tell me their life stories. I need criteria, distinctive signs, not just everyone's lamentations. That's as far as I get in my thinking when Victor comes into the little living room. Waddling, puffing, stabbing the Aubusson carpets with his ivory-pommeled cane, he finally reaches me:

"Are you looking for something to read?"

Yes, that's exactly what I'm doing: if my contemporaries cannot enlighten me, then I can always go back in time, in search of more ancient lights—which doesn't mean they are now irrelevant. After all, men and women are a very old story—I should know, living as I do in the Garden of Eden, surrounded by adults who claim to believe in Adamism, among other age-old doctrines. I mutter a vague discouraging response to Victor, but he stays put with his floppy paunch, bracing himself on his wobbly legs and his ebony cane, observing my slightest movements. As if he had nothing else to do—and that's probably true: he can rage all he likes against parasites, he's a fine example himself of masculine idleness and unproductivity.

"If you don't know what to read, I can give you some advice."

Yes, well, he's never one to hold back in giving advice. In fact, that's the mode in which he expresses himself most willingly, as if he could boast of some existential success that would confer the right to direct other people's lives with his judgments and pontificating suggestions. Well, no, sorry: Victor has never inspired me with the desire to be like him or to do as he does. To get rid of him, I finally spit out that I'd like to know more about men and women, but our encyclopedias don't have much about the subject. What have I done! Slumping down into an armchair facing me and padding his wide moist forehead with his emblazoned pocket square, he launches into another one of his rants. I can't stand it. Just shut up. I came here to have some quiet time to think and to pick out a few books about gender, not to listen to his oration number 167.

"If you want to understand the differences between men and women, you should definitely not read nonfiction on the question, no, definitely not! Go straight to the source! Read men's and women's literature! Penetrate their psyches, conduct a comparative study! Novels, poetry, drama, they're actually a really good way of getting to know heaps of people, the authors, most intimately, and without all the social folderol that just confuses things."

I sigh, without much conviction, discouraged in advance by the size of the task. I enjoy reading, of course, but at the moment

I have other things to do. Fucking, for instance. But since my lover is also my interlocutor's, I can't really offer this objection and so I have to listen to him developing his thesis. According to him, at the end of my studious summer, as long as I've chosen a sufficiently representative sample of world literature, I will know what makes men and women of all epochs and countries tick; I will know their respective tastes, obsessions, and anxieties. I can tell anyway that for Victor the case is closed: men and women neither write nor think in the same way. Delighted with himself and his idea, he heaves himself out of his chair and guides me towards a stretch of shelves that has been spared the decorative bindings that Arcady buys by the yard. He dislodges some of the books with his cane, and lets them fall onto the carpet, where they land with an appealing felted thud.

"Here! Take this, and this too, that'll give you an idea! Ah! *War and Peace*, perfect, *War and Peace*! Just read *War and Peace*, and then *Sense and Sensibility* after that. Where is it? We have it, I'm sure: we have all Jane Austen! Look, even just the titles are an education: only a man could have written *War and Peace*, and only a woman could have written *Sense and Sensibility*!"

I think I can detect a trace of malevolence in his satisfied laugh, but I meekly pile up the books that Victor's cane has selected for me. *Les Châtiments, The Skin, The Sound and the Fury, The Man Without Qualities, The Odyssey, The Magic Mountain, Journey to the End of the Night, The Flowers of Evil.* . . . Very quickly, the men's pile seems about to topple, whereas the women's pile rises only with difficulty, which Victor doesn't fail to comment on, with another snigger:

"Well, yes, that's sort of the problem: women are infinitely less creative than men. You'll find it difficult to get any good books written by women authors."

"*The Princess of Cleves?*"

"No interest at all. No life. It's nothing more than an etiquette handbook."

Oh. It's always been sold to me as a masterpiece, but I've learned to be cautious about teachers' enthusiasms: if you follow them, you only end up reading stuff about women who marry badly and then die, those Madames de Tourvel, those Emmas, those Gervaises, those Jeannes.... I did read them, because I was a serious student, but you won't catch me at it again. I reluctantly tuck *The Man Without Qualities* and *The Charterhouse of Parma* under my right arm, *Sense and Sensibility* and *The Voyage Out* under my left. That'll be enough for now—although I'm not giving up on my grand sociological survey.

That very day, I give a little progress report to Daniel. I should have said that I involved Daniel in my research right from the start, despite, or perhaps because of, the fact that he is just as intersex as I am. Over time, I've come to see him as an informed and reliable discussion partner, and even a sort of friend. Not to mention the fact that he recently introduced me to the world of the night, and I can feel that there might be a place for my androgyny there, a niche that no one will try to haul me out of on the pretext that my case is indecipherable.

For the moment, I'm reading *The Man Without Qualities*, which I don't understand much of, but I like anyway. As a worthy godson of Victor, whatever that might mean, Daniel is a good reader too, but he doesn't have much to say about Musil.

"Isn't it boring as shit?"

"Absolutely not. You just have to skip a few pages and keep going. And look, I've found a passage that talks about us:

'Imagine a squirrel that doesn't know whether it's a squirrel or a chipmunk, a creature with no concept of itself, and you will understand that in some circumstances it will be thrown into an anguish with no remedy by catching sight of its own tail.'"

"An anguish with no remedy. You're right: that's us."

As if to confirm that he is right, one of our cats jumps up to perch on the little wall we've come to sit behind to smoke my father's aromatic and therapeutic cigarettes. It's Blinky, a one-eyed tomcat who must be at least a hundred years old, counting in cat years. Although his fur is ragged and mangy in places, his mustache at half-mast, his bad eye permanently shut under a sticky white spot, Blinky still exudes a sense of satisfaction in being himself, a thousand miles from the doubts that torture hybrid creatures such as Daniel and me. Neither of us knows quite what we are, and that's where the problem lies.

"I mean, seriously, whaddya think I'm supposed to be: a girl or a boy?"

"I think you look more and more like a boy, actually."

"I don't have a dick, you know."

"That can be fixed."

"And I have ovaries."

"Wow, are ovaries actually a thing?"

"Of course they are! Just because you can't see something doesn't mean it doesn't exist!"

"Hey, I'm just saying this to help you, right: you look more like a guy than a chick."

"OK, but I prefer chicks."

"That's another reason to be a guy: you can bang chicks."

"I don't want to bang chicks: I want to be one!"

"Well, you know, you say you're asking my advice, but you've actually already made up your mind."

He's not wrong. Even though I have muscles, body hair, and the beginnings of an Adam's apple, I still think of myself as a girl, and dream of making a U-turn, whoosh, turn the handlebars the other way and backpedal through puberty—involuting hair follicles, wasting muscle mass, eroding maxillary bones, so that I have a softer shape, more velvety skin, a higher voice—a process that will, of course, be accompanied by subtle sartorial changes, nothing too over the top, let's not go crazy, but still. Voluptuously stretched out, Blinky keeps his monarchical eye on us and waves a floppy, indulgent paw in our direction, to let us know that we may continue to chatter as we please, as long as we don't disturb the heliotherapy session he has at this time, on this wall, on a daily basis. Having not gotten any useful information from anyone, living or dead, not from Fiorentina or Virginia Woolf, not from Daniel or Robert Musil, I lie down in the grass that the summer has already mostly dried and thinned out.

"Do you wanna go out?"

"Tonight?"

"Yeah. We could go to Les Tamaris: they're having a lesbian night."

"One thing I'm quite sure of is that I'm not a lesbian. Either I'm a guy and I'm gay, or I'm a girl and I'm straight."

"Why are you so binary? You're such a pain."

"Oh, yeah, like lesbian nights aren't binary? Sure."

All of a sudden, I'm sick of Daniel, and I conspicuously pick up *The Man Without Qualities* again—nine hundred dog-eared pages, warped by the dew in several places—just to show him I'd rather be left alone. But instead of leaving, he lies down himself, his head on my stomach, and asks again:

"OK, so you go and pretty yourself up, and we'll go?"

"Aren't I allowed to be ugly?"

"Farah . . ."

"OK, I'll go to your lesbian night. But I'm staying as I am."

"You'll get bounced if you're not dressed right."

"Last time I sailed in."

"Last time you were wearing a super-miniskirt and a crazy bra top. No wonder you sailed in."

"Yeah, well, this time I'm not wearing a skirt."

Daniel and I usually spend a crazy amount of time talking clothes and discussing our respective outfits, but now, all of a sudden, sorry, I don't want to do anything at all, I just want to be left alone under the high patronage of Musil and Blinky. Daniel finally gets it and goes away on the promise that I'll come to his Wet for Me Night—as if I'd be wet for anyone besides Arcady, and anyway girls don't turn me on all that much, that's what I keep trying to explain to Daniel: I like them, and given the choice, I'd like to be one, but I don't want them. Or maybe my desire just stays stuck behind my eyeballs and doesn't go down any farther, not into my mouth or my breasts, and even less into my belly or between my thighs.

That evening, I put on a tuxedo that used to be Kirsten's, just like 80 percent of my clothes. On Malika's advice, I try putting on some eyeliner, but then furiously rub it off. There are girls, and no doubt also boys, who look better with makeup. I'm not one of them: eyeliner just makes my eyes look sadder and more clown-like. For want of anything better, I smooth my hair back with gel, which means I look even more like Sylvester Stallone.

I zoom down three floors on the polished banister, just so my thighs collect some of the remanent energy from all the girls that have preceded me, some of their hormonal effervescence, some of their impatience to mount creatures other than this dark varnished wood. The banister catapults me into the wide hall, to an astounded-looking Daniel, who gets a serious rebuke from me:

"You're such a fuckwad!"

"Why?"

"You said to get dressed up, but you . . ."

"What, me? Aren't I handsome?"

"That's not it, you just haven't really made an effort, have you? And now I look overdressed."

He is wearing shorts and a T-shirt—two-tone shorts, like a slice of Neapolitan ice cream: one green leg and one pink leg. OK, so there's a color missing for a Neapolitan slice, but since he's also wearing lemon-yellow fingerless gloves, that makes up for it. In spite of his ridiculous outfit, he stares at me triumphantly:

"Do you recognize it?"

"Should I be recognizing something?"

"Um . . . no, not really. But I'll show you."

We ride through the warm night, until we see the lights of the town. Daniel parks his 125 cc motorbike in an almost deserted parking lot, and extracts from his pocket a rectangular object, which I soon identify as a cell phone.

"You've gotten one? But we're not allowed to!"

"I know that, duh! But you know, it's not like I was the one who chose not to have one! It's not my fault I came to live with Victor and Arcady. I'm not saying I don't like them, they're great, and I love the house, and everything, it's just that not having a cell is going way too far, right? Everybody has one except us!"

"Is it a smartphone?"

"Yep. Hang on, lemme get online."

In less time than it takes to say it, he shoves the screen under my nose and his earbuds in my ears, which means that I am immediately submerged: clapping hands, snapping fingers, white-clad shapes moving in the backlit background, guitars, voices, keyboards—and then, "boom-boom into my heart, into my brain, bang-bang, yeah-yeah," all I can do is watch the singer surrounded by his adoring fans, and I'm a fan myself, instantly and for life: "Take me dancing tonight," oh, yes . . . after the white pants and "Choose Life" T-shirts at the start, everyone is suddenly in pastel outfits, actually very close to what Daniel is wearing: from the shorts to the bandanas, everything is pink and baby blue—except for the delicate yellow of the fingerless gloves. Two thirds of the way through the video, when I'm almost in a trance myself, the singer with the blow wave joins his backup singers behind a mike for a few seconds of pure frenzy—with an ecstatic face, open lips, alternating raised arms, golden, fuzzy, irresistible thighs offered up and shaking to the rhythm. . . .

"Shit, who is this guy?"

Daniel is beaming:

"Isn't he gorgeous?"

"Yeah, but who is it?"

"George Michael, 'Wake Me Up Before You Go-Go,' Wham! Doesn't that ring a bell? Guess not, we weren't even born then."

"Oh, really? Then how old is he?"

"He died. 'Last Christmas . . .'"

That's what you get, or rather, what you lose, from living in a quiet zone, with no technological contact with the outside world: George Michael died before I could meet him, love him, be loved by him, maybe even save him, since according to Daniel he died of sadness, of excess, and who knows, maybe of the exhaustion of being himself, or of regret at being who he was.

"Apparently, he got super fat."

Daniel and I glumly view those few torrid seconds over and over again: George Michael in two-tone hot pants and a candy-pink sweatshirt, rolling his eyes to the heavens, putting his yellow-gloved hand to his forehead. As we get back on the bike, I realize I'm wet, which is probably a good omen for a Wet for Me Night—and a good indicator of the posthumous sex appeal of George Michael.

19.

Who's That Chick?

At Les Tamaris we get in with no trouble at all, despite our mismatched outfits. All I can see on the dance floor are butches with low foreheads, baby queens like Daniel, or intersex creatures like me. I order a Leffe Ruby, just so I can take the pulse of the evening and observe what's going on, while Daniel launches into a very personal imitation of George Michael, whose existence and demise I discovered at the same time. I'm still inconsolable, but it's not long before a little blonde with shaved temples and big breasts comes up to me:

"Hi. Has anyone ever told you that you look like Kristen Stewart?"

I've been told I look like Sylvester Stallone, but Kristen Stewart, no, never, and who is Kristen Stewart anyway?

"Who's that?"

"You've never heard of Kristen Stewart? Where are you from? Mars?"

No, but I might was well be: I come from a place where Kristen Stewart has no right to exist, a place where cultural references reach us light-years after first being emitted, which means that I'm still stuck with Farrah Fawcett, Sylvester Stallone, and George Michael, while everyone else apparently knows who Kristen Stewart is.

"And she's a lesbian too! And super gorgeous!"

I'd be very surprised if I looked like a super-gorgeous chick, even if she is a lesbian. And, in fact, the little blonde immediately qualifies what she first said:

"It's not that you really look like her, but you have the same hairstyle, short and pushed back. I mean, she doesn't always wear her hair like that, but you know . . ."

This lookalike business doesn't seem to add up, except as an attempt to socialize by my new friend, whose name turns out to be Maureen.

"Yeah, I know, it's not great, but my friends call me Mor."

Mor doesn't sound a lot better than Maureen to me, but anyway, I tell her my name:

"I'm Farah."

"Oh, are you an Arab?"

"No, not at all."

"Isn't Farah an Arab name?"

"I don't know, but anyway, I'm not Arab. And, in fact, my grandmother is Danish. And guess what? Her name is Kirsten. Funny, right?"

"Kristen?"

"Kirsten."

"Oh, yeah, same thing. But you don't look Danish."

I know exactly what she means by that, and what she imagines Danish women to be: tall blonde things with Baltic eyes, the opposite of my kind of beauty.

"Well, my grandmother does look Danish. She was even a model. And she's gay too."

Maureen's face breaks into a wide smile, which scrunches up her tiny nose and makes her pretty blue eyes even more almond shaped.

"You should take her to the Wet for Me Nights."

Oh, no, spare me, my grandmother is already such a looming and intrusive presence in my little life as it is, without getting lumbered with her at the club as well. Not that I have any doubts about her capacity to set the dance floor on fire, but I have no desire to see her make a spectacle of herself in her Versace sheath dress, with Malika at her side stinking of Shalimar and waving her ruffles. There's half an inch of Leffe at the bottom of my glass when Maureen clearly launches the offensive, sliding a decisive hand between my tux jacket and my skin, and immediately finding my right breast. I have to say that I stupidly didn't put anything on underneath, not a shirt or a T-shirt, not even a bra, since my breasts don't really need any textile support.

"Woah, you're naked!"

"No, I'm not!"

"Feels like you don't have big boobs. That's great, I hate them."

She lays a sorrowful hand on her own bust, of which I'd already noticed the astonishing volume, even under the formless top with which she hides it.

"I'm gonna get breast-reduction surgery."

We're getting to the heart of the matter. Great. I can ask her about the sexual characteristics of women and men.

"How could you tell I was a chick?"

"Why? Is there any doubt?"

"Well, yeah, actually."

Maureen puffs herself up:

"I know how to recognize a babe, babe!"

"You don't think I look like a guy?"

"I swear to God, you, like, totally look like a chick! What's your problem anyway?"

"I don't have a uterus."

"Wow! You're so fucking lucky!"

"You think so?"

"Well, yeah, it means you don't get periods!"

"Yep, that's a fact."

"Well, you're not missing out on anything. Periods are just a pain in the ass. And they stink too."

"If you say so."

"And does that mean you can't get pregnant either?"

"Unless the embryo goes and implants itself in my pancreas, no, I won't ever get pregnant."

Mor doesn't seem to get my sense of humor, or maybe she's just never heard of a pancreas, which is entirely possible: only children raised in quiet zones have the leisure to dive into anatomy treatises as I did assiduously between the ages of six and fifteen. In any case, what she seems to be interested in is twiddling my nipples, which sort of leaves me cold. Not to be discouraged, she ends up dragging me onto the dance floor, yelling into my ear that "Who's That Chick?" is just the song for me. Well, maybe she isn't completely lacking in a sense of humor after all, or at least psychological insight: the question is indeed to determine who this chick is, or rather, whether she really is one—except that while dancing with Maureen I forget all my identity issues, "Feel the adrenaline moving under my skin. . . . Sound is my remedy, feeding me energy, music is all I need," yes, of course, I should have done this ages ago, dancing like my life depends on it, "Baby, I just wanna dance, I don't really care!" Actually, why should I give a shit about knowing who I am, or even what I am: I am this organism flooded with adrenaline and pulsing with energy, from the music, of course, but also from Maureen, whose exuberance is so contagious. Just seeing her luminous smile, her lovely red flushed cheeks, and her big breasts bouncing away under her shapeless T-shirt, I'm almost getting wet. What is going on? Didn't I just swear on my life to Daniel that there was no way I was a lesbian? And aren't I supposed to be passionately and exclusively in love with my spiritual director, my sentimental educator, the only man who could understand me and see beauty where others constantly balked at my strangeness—or worse! One shouldn't swear anything, and especially not about the object of one's desire.

After "Who's That Chick?" comes "Fade," and even though I live in a nature reserve, surrounded by noble savages, one-eyed cats, and Wyandotte chickens, I've still heard of Kanye West. I should also say I've found an observation post—or a supply point, as you will—a café downtown connected 24-7 to NRG Hits, which allows me to get my hit of forbidden images, polluting lyrics, and toxic radiation. I'm out of touch, but not as badly as I would be if I followed our iron-cast law to the letter.

With "Fade," the dance floor is instantly invaded by Black girls who dance like Teyana Taylor, and are gorgeous like her too. With a sullen groan, Maureen falls back onto the synthetic-leather benches:

"The Black chicks have taken over: that's, like, such unfair competition."

Competition never bothered me. Unless it's just the opposite:

since I'm not serious competition, or even any competition at all, no one gives a shit whether I'm dancing or not. I've learned to live with universal indifference, to not feel judged, or threatened, or anything really. And so I'm more than happy to sit back and watch the performance of these girls waving their wet hair and swaying their toned thighs—especially since they're showing off their breasts, which are just as big as the ones Maureen keeps hidden. As for Daniel, not in the least discouraged by the influx of Black goddesses onto the dance floor, he's following his own lead, doing his own little return to the future of the eighties: sent into orbit by George Michael, he sees nothing and nobody, which is a good way to spend the evening—but what's the point of going clubbing if that's what you're going to do? Poor Maureen, on the other hand, is finding it hard to recover her self-assurance, since the song after "Fade" consists of shooting commands, which the dancers seem to take extremely seriously: "Shake that booty nonstop . . . percolate anything you want to, oscillate your hip and don't take pity." And, in fact, there is no pity at Les Tamaris tonight: I've never seen such a display of oiled abs and triceps. And don't even get me started on the infernal rotation of all those sublime asses. No one can make me believe that it's just Afro-Caribbean genes that explain those asses—no, no, asses like that come from at least ten hours a week working out and a sugar-free diet. Maureen is fuming:

"Sean Paul now: what's the deal here? This totally sucks."

"Are you racist, or what?"

"No, I'm not, that's bullshit! It's just that this is a Wet for Me Night, not a Shake That Booty, Bitch, Night!"

"Do they have those?"

"I don't know and I don't care."

And, no doubt to forget her disappointment, she shoves her hand down my cleavage again.

"Shit, you actually have pecs!"

"No, I don't! They're breasts! They're just small, that's all. It's a family thing."

"Don't talk shit to me, babe: you have pecs!"

It's my turn to be sullen now. It's true, right, she's a real pain: it started with I'm a real girl, no two ways about it, then it's I have pecs—make up your mind. On the dance floor, Daniel is looking at me with big round eyes and making frenetic hand signals. He must have noticed that Maureen's hand has disappeared down the front of my tux.

"Do you know that guy?"

"Yeah, we live together."

"Is he your roommate?"

"No."

How do I explain this to Maureen in between Sean Paul and Drake? That Daniel is not a roommate, not a brother, not even really a friend?

"Is he your guy?"

He could have been. If I had followed Arcady's directives, we would have had sex, Nello and me. First by ourselves, then with Arcady. That was the idea. Well, at least one of the multitude of ideas to sprout from my mentor's fertile mind.

"No, he's not my guy, can't you see he's gay?"

"Yeah, that's what I thought. But then, since you don't seem so sure about what's going on . . ."

"What do you mean, what's going on?"

"Well, with you, right! Whether you're a girl or a guy!"

"You can talk!"

"What?"

"Well, yeah, did you take a look at yourself? Your weird haircut, your shoes, your pants—you're showing your underwear! You look like a guy too!"

She instantly beams:

"Oh, really? Do you think so? My boobs aren't too big?"

"Well, yeah, they're big. But I know guys who have ones just as big, so that doesn't mean a thing."

I'm not going to say anything, not about Victor. Victor, who I reckon is about a 52B. Of course, 52" is his chest size, but he has at least six inches more for the cups, which he could easily fill with the two flaccid sacks dangling from his thorax. The main thing is that Maureen is happy, especially since the music is back to something she feels she can dance to, with her narrow-minded little white lesbo tastes. She drags me back onto the dance floor, with her beaming smile, her cargo pants, her hiking boots, and her mind-blowing tits. That's how the night passes, between rounds of Leffe Ruby, Maureen's obstinate attempts at seduction, "Music is all I need, sound is my remedy," and other platitudes of the same caliber. Did I mention that I love the night? This is something I have in common with Daniel, the desire to gain extra time in life, to not waste it on useless sleep; that desire to break out from daytime hours with their regulated schedule. When we don't go out together at night, I escape from my hutch as soon as midnight strikes, out into my kingdom: I run beneath the starry skies, I breathe in the insistent, faintly muddy smell coming from the thickets—with the soundtrack of the crickets softly stridulating, and sometimes a sigh, an exhalation, no, an inhalation, a breath that catches me for a few seconds before I give in to other intimate palpitations.

When at last we leave Les Tamaris, Maureen, Daniel, and I, the night has already packed up and gone home, and you can hear the first songbirds gossiping. With the heavy insistence of a drunkard, Maureen is pestering me to get my number:

"Come on, Farah, gimme your cell."

How can I tell her that I'm not technologically connected? That I don't have a cell phone, or an email, or WhatsApp, or Facebook, or anything?

"Hmph! Whatever! If you don't want to see me again, just say so, OK? You don't have to gimme that shit!"

Daniel makes a diplomatic intervention:

"It's true, I swear, we live in a quiet zone, me and Farah: our parents are against cell phones, the internet, all that stuff."

Maureen scrunches up her nose incredulously in the first rays of morning sunshine:

"Fuck, I don't believe this."

"Well, OK then, bye!"

Leaving her standing there, I straddle Daniel's motorbike again for our triumphant return in the early hours of the morning. The road winds under our wheels, the river flows down the slope below us, and we ride back to our retrenched hillside, our Eden preserved from evil—and too bad for those who don't understand.

20.

Free Instinctive Flow

War, peace, magic mountain, sense, sensibility, punishment, devil's pool, and sea wall, my summer reading is progressing, but I still haven't found anything that might dissipate my gender trouble. As for my grand sociological survey, I simply gave up on it after so many salvos of wretched and inapplicable answers. I've just settled into the shade to start *The Voyage Out*, when Epifanio comes to find me, more distraught and panting than ever. I notice in passing that he has nothing but a few scattered spots of brown left on his forehead by which to remember his original color: the rest of it is now Circassian white.

"Farah, I need you!"

The twins hurtle up behind him, with grumpy faces that do not bode well—they know all about their dad's enthusiasms.

"Dolores and Teresa . . ."

"Yes?"

"They have their . . . their thing, you know, like, their business."

No, I don't know, and I wish he would make up his mind and use the right word instead of waffling on.

"Of course you do! You know what I mean! They . . . they got it!"

Dolores breaks the standoff with a whisper:

"We got our periods."

Relieved, their father suddenly becomes dangerously garrulous:

"Yes, can you believe it? The same day! This morning, both of them, at the same time! Can you believe it? I'm completely bowled over, because, you know, I don't know anything about it, and then, usually, it's mothers that talk to their daughters about these things. Right? Am I right? But my daughters, poor things, don't have a mother, and so here we are, I thought you could help. Just you girls together, right, you can talk about stuff. You can tell them, like, what to do, what happens, and all that, right? And then, what they should buy, you know, diapers, pads, what they should use when it happens, I mean, you know . . . because, like, I don't want them to make a mess of their clothes. This morning, right, we didn't have what we needed, but from now on, I want them to have what they need . . . and maybe they also need, I dunno, like, some medicine, you know, just in case . . ."

In fact, Dos and Tres do have a mother, except she took off shortly after they were born. Apparently two babies were just too much for her—and Epifanio was probably too much too. He attributes the onset of his vitiligo to the emotional shock of waking up one morning, alone, with two babies howling with hunger and their mother vanished with no explanation.

Embarrassed by their father's logorrhea, the twins are avoiding eye contact with me: Dolores's orange eyelashes drop onto her translucent cheeks, while Teresa pretends to be insatiably interested by her freshly polished nails. Epifanio, having finally shut up, is standing in front of me with crossed arms. He's probably expecting me to remedy thirteen years of maternal deprivation just like that, thinking I'm richly endowed with the knowledge that Birdie has passed on to me, and fortified by my own experience of menstruation. How can I tell him that I'm not the right person to enlighten teenagers, never having had much more of a mother than his daughters did, and when my own puberty is more akin to a gender mutation than to anything else? Since it is out of the question for me to reveal my nasty little secret to Epifanio, I say yes to everything, and he leaves the three of us under the noxious shade of the walnut tree—if one is to believe Fiorentina, who consents to collecting its nuts, but avoids it like the plague at any other time.

"Yeah, well, I don't quite know what to tell you girls about periods."

"Well, what do you do when you have them? Do you use pads or tampons?"

"And how long does it usually last?"

"Do you bleed a lot? Coz we're not bleeding much."

"And it's not even red."

"More like brown, actually. Gross."

"But maybe that's because it's the first time."

"And do you get cramps?"

"Coz we don't have cramps."

I have no answers for any of these questions, and to be quite honest, I always thought that periods were painful, and that there was lots of red blood. So much for all that . . .

"I think you should ask Birdie. Coz, like, being on the rag is not really my thing."

Without giving them the time to ponder that enigmatic assertion, I take them both to the gloriette, where we are pretty sure to find my mother at this hour of the day. We also have a bioclimatic pergola with movable slats, a gift to the community from Nelly, but my mother prefers the charms of wrought iron crumbling under the weight of the roses and wisteria, the to-and-fro of the bees, the view over the ponds below, and the proximity to the greenhouses where my father works most of the time.

"Mom, the twins would like to ask you something."

"Yes?"

"They got their periods today. So they'd like you to give them some advice, to explain it all to them."

I have a hankering to turn on my heel and leave them to it but I stay, out of curiosity, and also to have, by proxy, that famous mother-daughter conversation that could never happen between Birdie and me.

"Well, why don't you just tell them?"

My mother's innocent eyes make me feel even more unworthy than ever, and completely incapable of informing her of my utero-vaginal aplasia. Putting off the moment of truth until some later date, I mumble that I have an irregular cycle, and that I feel embarrassed to talk about it. My mother, however, seems delighted to have been asked about something, which almost never happens, given her ignorance and incompetence at everything—not to mention her lack of intellectual resources. She launches into a longwinded, confused, and predictable lyrical spiel, about how today is a great day, and the presence of blood in their underwear is going to propel Dos and Tres into the magnificent and enchanted world of femininity.

Since I'm not counting on my mother to enlighten me on the enchantments in question, I content myself with glumly observing the ravishing scene of the three of them under the arbor, in the dappled light streaming through the climbers: my blonde mother, the redheaded twins—so different in their ways of being redheads, Teresa tan as a fox, and Dolores as milky as the wisteria blossoms framing her delicate face. I would so love to be beautiful too, and it's so unfair that I'm not, that I have this massive figure, this brutal jawline, this flat nose, these droopy eyes, and this dull complexion—not to mention the hint of a mustache, which I decided to shave after trying to bleach it with peroxide.

Make no mistake, it's not out of narcissism or flirtatiousness that I wish I was beautiful, or even because I want to be desired and courted more than I am, since Arcady spoils me in that department; no, it's just that in moments like these, I wish I wasn't the odd one out, I'd like to harmonize with all this grace: Teresa's fruity cheeks, Dolores's pulsing temples, the ashen blue of my mother's eyes, the exuberant invasion of the arbor by the perennial flowers, the delicate leaves and green tendrils. The world is beautiful, but I'm not. The twins, completely unaware of my woes, and indifferent to their own juvenile perfection, start their little interview again:

"How many days do periods last?"

"Our friend Lauren has them for a week!"

"And do they hurt?"

"Coz Lauren gets cramps that are so bad she has to stay lying down. Well, for the first day, at least."

"And does it smell gross?"

"Someone said it did."

"And that you had to wash three times as much."

"What do we need to buy? Sanitary pads?"

"Can we use tampons?"

"Even if we're virgins?"

My mother has an answer for everything, and I was right to send the twins to her, but when we get to the worrisome question of sanitary protection, her exaltation knows no bounds:

"No, not sanitary pads, and especially not tampons! With tampons, you run the risk of toxic shock, you poor dears!"

"Well, what are we supposed to do, then?"

"Yeah, what should we use?"

My mother beams—obviously the topic is important to her.

"Nothing, you use nothing!"

"But it's going to go everywhere!"

"That's disgusting!"

"We'll get dirty!"

"Have you never heard of free instinctive flow?"

The twins and I have never heard of anything at all, but *free* and *instinctive* belong to the community's basic vocabulary, so we are not surprised.

"Well, what you have to do is retain your flow. You contract your pelvic floor and you don't use any intimate protection. You manage your period just like you manage your need to go to the toilet: you learn to know when you need to go 'empty' yourself to avoid stains and leaks. And then, you're not dependent on pads and tampons. It's economical, ecological, and super convenient. Especially when you have an irregular cycle: you're never caught short. The free instinctive flow method has only benefits, in fact. You listen to your body, you feel free, you're in control, it's amazing! And of course, girls, you wouldn't believe all the toxic ingredients that go into tampons and disposable pads! Aluminum, alcohol, fragrances, hydrocarbons, pesticides, dioxin residues! And since the vagina wall is very absorbent, the chemicals get into your system and accumulate. It's super dangerous for your health!"

She's delighted to have delivered her little public health warning, and looks at us for a reaction. But if she expects an immediate and enthusiastic agreement, she'll be disappointed, for the twins take off after saying perfunctory thank-yous, and I follow in their stride—short and hesitant strides, in fact: I can tell they're afraid of unexpected leaks. We head for one of our many secret hideaways: one of the low drystone walls in the terraced fields, hidden by tall grass.

"I don't like the sound of this free instinctive flow thing."

Dolores agrees and sighs, echoing her twin's disillusioned statement. It's weird, because I do like the sound of it. It even seems to me that it perfectly summarizes what I aspire to be, what I sometimes am, in my moments of depersonalization: an instinctive flow, free to dance in the light, to float in the blue, or to flow in the impetuous current of the nameless river, delivered from the obligation to look after myself and to create a life.

Since Dos and Tres seem worried, I spare them my desire to be nothing, and give them my own informed advice:

"Let's buy you some sanitary pads, that's safer."

"Yeah, right! They'll never agree!"

"We're already not allowed to use Kleenex and cotton pads . . ."

"That's going too far."

"They'll force us to make our own tampons, just you wait and see."

"Yeah, with sticks covered with old rags..."

"Or your dad will make something for us out of leaves."

"It's so gross, I can't stand it."

"Yeah, neither can I."

I share their disgust of course, since I know all about the community's propensity to impose insane ecological diktats. I've already mentioned the vegetarian kibble for the cats and dogs, but there's an infinite number of other examples I could give.

"I'll talk to Arcady about it."

"Oh, no, please! Don't do that!"

"Why not? He'll understand that you don't want to stuff leaves into your vaginas."

"He won't understand a thing! And he's going to come and drive us crazy because now we got our period, we're, like, women now, and so we have to have sex with him, and so on..."

"That's nonsense! Arcady never forced anyone to do anything!"

"Yeah, well, you're in love with him, so of course he doesn't force you, but he'll insist with us."

"You're out of your minds! Arcady isn't a pedophile."

"Well, what about you?"

"I'm nearly sixteen. We waited until I reached the legal age, you know!"

"Yeah, well, don't talk to Arcady, that's all we're saying."

In the end I do talk to him, I tell him everything, the twins' first periods, their reticence to use the free-instinctive-flow method, and also their fears regarding him.

"But, you know, I told them you'd never do such a thing."

"What? Rape them?"

"Yes."

He shrugs in scorn and disbelief:

"One of these days I'll explain to the twins that what really excites me is the desire and the pleasure of the other person."

"OK, but what do they do about sanitary pads?"

"Well, there are washable and reusable pads, you know . . ."

No, I don't know, since sanitary protection is not my problem. But the fact that Arcady knows about them, although he has even less use for them than I do, doesn't actually surprise me. I snuggle up to his chest, bury my nose in his armpit, get high on his Byzantine smell, rub my pelvis against his powerful thigh, to make him want me. Slipping a finger under my chin, he brings my mouth to his and passionately kisses me, before bursting into laughter, suddenly remembering what I had confided in him:

"You say Birdie does what when she has her period? She holds it in? She controls her flow? All that so as not to pollute her pussy with tampons?"

He laughs, he can't stop laughing, and stops only momentarily to whisper all sorts of lascivious promises into my ear:

"You're gonna have a party, Farah: I'll give you a free instinctive flow! I'll take care of your pussy, you're gonna love it!"

21.

Au Revoir Les Enfants

The episode with their first period has only tightened the bonds between me and the twins. Strangely enough, they don't hold it against me that I talked to Arcady about their sickening fantasies, even though that didn't stop him from giving them a good scolding:

"If you didn't know me, I could understand! But girls, I've known you almost since you were born! You were six months old when you came here! How could you believe for a second that I would force you to have sex with me?"

"You did it with Daniel, didn't you?"

"And Farah!"

"They both gave their consent. And neither of them was thirteen."

"You had sex with Dadah!"

"And Nelly!"

"What does that have to do with anything?"

"You're a gerontophile!"

"Well, yeah, then, that should put your minds at rest!"

I can see in their unsettled gaze that they have lost the thread of their own argument and that they're not all that sure they want to find it again. All they want is to get this embarrassing conversation over and done with and to get away as quickly as possible, to go cuddle together somewhere, forehead against forehead, in total silence under the tent of their red hair. They do this constantly, anytime and anywhere: in the garden, in the living room, in a hallway, mute, absorbed in each other, alone in the world.

"Stop doing that, it makes you look like morons."

No response. They come back to normal life only when they have drawn enough comfort from their ritual: they unstick their foreheads, take back their own hair—slowly, regretfully, and with looks of reproach for any outside observers. They can be extremely annoying, but our insular childhood has taught us to stick together and tolerate each other's little quirks: it was either that or be reduced to the company of adults, who were even more exasperating and incapable of accepting our views or joining our games.

Until then, the twins and I had been the stable core of the population of children, alongside other temporary members, such as Violette, Tamara, Lucien, Clarisse, or Arlindo, who stayed with us for only a few months before going back to the outside world, shunted hither and yon by their irresolute parents. As for Daniel, he was always our gang leader, strategist, and inspiration, a miniature Arcady for our personal use, before he irrevocably departed from our green paradise, beset by desires that could not be communicated to our innocent minds—and in this cruel summer, I can sense that my own defection is imminent, and the twins' is not far off either. Djilali seems to realize this too, and prowls around us without quite understanding anything, no longer daring to demand that we participate in activities that were once part of our daily routine: building huts or irrigation canals, treasure hunts, tracking imaginary game, pilfering, acrobatics, and breakneck chases.

Poor Djilali, I wish I could say something, find the right words to help him hang on until puberty—but everything is drawing us apart, our age difference, my putative gender, and my grand personal exploration of sexuality. All I can do is make sure he is included in our confabs and aimless wanderings—from the house to the garden, along the enormous ornamental pond where we vaguely look for carps and frogs—but my heart isn't in it and he can acutely sense that. I'm all the sorrier for him in that he has spent the school year being called a whale or a porker by his little classmates, all because of a couple of extra pounds he owes to Fiorentina's good cooking.

Did I mention that she loves him? Fiorentina who loves nothing and no one? Of course, when he arrived within out walls, Djilali could inspire only tenderness, with his gap-toothed smile, his hesitant lisp, and the frightened naiveté in his eyes. All the members, and our valetudinarians in particular, warmed themselves at his innocence, feasted on his young flesh. I was a child myself, but faced with Djilali, I felt a shiver of almost sacred joy and terror, discovering both that purity existed and that it could be annihilated—yes, purity, and I'm measuring my words, for Djilali, at age six, never appeared to have a single petty thought or dissimulation reflex. Tender and luminous, he would spontaneously go towards adults, put his little hand in their lap, and look up at them with confident eyes, never repulsed by their bulbous noses or withered dewlaps, never discouraged by their indifference, impatience, or incoherence.

Confidence and spontaneity are a thing of the past for him now: today Djilali is as enigmatic, dark, and velvety as a night butterfly, and I don't even dare think about the causes that produced these effects. I look at him and I feel like crying, because I can no longer be of any help to him, because all I can do is say goodbye and let him work out the difficulties that inevitably come to a little overweight boy living in a sect that resists new technologies—especially since he never sees his father, and his mother is too busy flaming with passion to raise him properly. Malika is no good at anything except covering him with kisses. Luckily Fiorentina is there, with her *gnocchi alla romana*, her panna cottas, and her well-seasoned common sense. She thinks he is sublime, with his puffy cheeks and fat tummy: he is a perfect example of her Italian ideal of what a child in good health should be.

Goodbye, children, I'm OK with the four of us still climbing trees, setting up a theater troupe, making perfume with lavender and pond water, setting fire to an anthill, and teaching class to stupid geese and Wyandotte chickens, but my heart isn't in it anymore. My heart now beats between my thighs, at the exact place where Arcady will soon poke his indefatigable tongue. I may not have a vagina, but that doesn't stop me from feeling pleasure.

22.

After the Storm

The first days of August have fallen upon us, with their spectacular storms: lightning slashing the low and heavy skies, the mountains shuddering under the roars of thunder, brief torrential showers—and then, a patch of blue widening between the golden cotton wool of the clouds, until the world is nothing but steaming meadows, smoking tree trunks, cowbells tinkling on the animals' necks, radiant powdery sunshine, the pure happiness of being and alive and being young.

As I am gamboling off to my grassy hollow allegretto that day, the whole valley is exhaling its psalm of thanksgiving, all in gleeful cooing, wet stalks, dripping leaves, and crickets gradually gaining assurance as the storm moves off into the distance. I leave our little nature reserve behind, leap over a low wall, scamper along the edges of the fields. The cows raise their damp muzzles and worried eyes as I pass, as if they had never seen me before in their lives, which must really be the proof that they are stupid and deserve to be eaten, for I walk past here every day God makes. I even buried a time capsule under their watering trough, no later than last year. I must say in their defense that they were in the next paddock over and paid no attention to the burial ceremony, contrary to Djilali and the twins, who were invited to the occasion. You can put whatever you like into a time capsule: the idea is that it will be exhumed one day and bear witness to your singular short passage on this earth. Mine contains a jay feather, some seashells, a Bakelite cicada, a sample of Arcady's cologne, and a letter addressed to my human brothers who will live after us—although I don't rule out digging it up myself in twenty or thirty years, to read the message I sent myself from the wild era of my adolescence.

The idea of the time capsule generated so much enthusiasm that the others quickly emulated it. Dolores, Teresa, and Djilali made up their own capsules, and we carried out three solemn inhumations in succession. Even though they didn't confer, the twins collected identical objects: locks of their flaming hair, candies, nail-polish bottles, pictures of themselves, and letters scattered with exclamation points. Djilali made sure we didn't see the contents of his capsule, and I can't quite imagine what a little boy might deem worthy of traveling through time. Marbles? Pictures of Pokémon? A baby tooth? Or else, who knows, the cadaver of a field mouse, a snake's skin, a bloody blade, strips of skin taken from his own tender thigh, all the macabre paraphernalia of a disturbed child. . . .

I obviously told Nelly about our respective treasure chests. I knew that, as a worthy daughter of an archaeologist, she would be sure to be interested, and I was dead right.

"Oh, what a good idea! Do you realize, maybe, in two hundred years, someone will find one or another of your capsules!"

"Well, yeah, that's the deal. I just hope that it's not a guy building gross apartment blocks a mile away from the house! You know what I mean? Like, when he's digging where the cows are now, and cutting down all the trees, bang, he finds my box!"

"We'll both be dead, Farah! Who cares?"

"Well, yeah, but so what? I don't want all this to be destroyed! Can you imagine all this without the pine trees, the chestnut trees, the animals? Even after I'm dead, there's no way that can happen!"

Contrary to hers, my death seems highly improbable, or at least as distant as an archaeological dig in the year 2200. But then, why would I say that to an octogenarian who has one statistical foot in the grave—unless I wanted to shove her into it, which is really not my intention.

One last leap and I'm at my hideaway under its canopy heavy with rain, which I immediately take down and set out in the sun to dry. A scrunched-up package of Pavesini biscuits attracts my attention: whoever is stealing Fiorentina's biscuits came this way. I don't care: Arcady won't be long, and I lie down in the still damp but already warm grass. As I stretch out voluptuously, my eyelids closed on an incandescent kaleidoscope—I sense a rustle in the hazelnut trees, then a shadow interposed between the sun and me. I open my eyes: a stranger is staring at me, an apparition against the depths of the blue air. As the glare dissipates, I distinguish, no, I am struck in my very heart and in no particular order by the splendor of his dark skin, the unstable and frizzy mass of his hair, the flash of silver at his fine wrist, his sullen mouth, and his Eritrean cheekbones. A migrant.

There are lots of them in the valley. You see them walking along the roads, climbing up into the mountains in shorts and flip-flops, unaware of the climatic conditions that await them there—not to mention the fact that after three French villages, they'll be back in Italy, the very place they were trying to escape from. They also cluster together on the banks of the nameless river, under canvases that protect them from nothing at all, and especially not from the rising waters. While migrants are not a topic of conversation at Liberty House, at school there are constant brawls breaking out between baby fascists, who want to send all those things back to the wars, and the children of No Border activists. The kids also whisper among themselves that the migrants who die here—carried off by floods, or mowed down on the highways or in the tunnels—later come back to haunt the valley. Mine looks alive, in any case, with ardent eyes and his chin moving in mastication. I barely have time to wonder whether he's eating one of Fiorentina's Pavesinis before he spits out a peach stone, dark and gleaming. Then he volatilizes, confirming the ghost hypothesis—except that ghosts don't eat.

Arcady arrives at this juncture:

"Ah, you're here! Good: I was scared the storm might discourage you . . ."

"There was a guy, here, two seconds ago! A Black guy!"

"A what?"

"A migrant!"

"Oh, really? That's odd. Usually they don't make it this far."

He doesn't seem to be particularly interested in my stories of refugee peach-and-biscuit thieves: all he wants is to fuck, and that's just as well, since I'm as hot and wet as the grass around us. Once we've finished our little business, he leaves me with a last passionate embrace and saunters off with that spritely gait that is all his, his figure soon swallowed up by the nearest copse of trees.

I stay there, vaguely fiddling with myself, enjoying the last tremors of pleasure inside me, then I stretch the canopy out over our love bed again, take a bilingual edition of the poems of Emily Dickinson out of my basket, and settle myself down to read. Nelly affirms that in the late 1970s, the Voyager probe was launched into space with an Emily Dickinson poem on board—among other samples of terrestrial life. I love this idea, despite the fact that I haven't been able to confirm this through a forbidden internet search. As a time capsule, a spatial probe is much more impressive than a tin box buried under cowpats. Who knows, maybe I'm reading "How dreary—to be—Somebody!" at the same time as an extraterrestrial creature light-years away from my verdant hollow.

Just as I am preparing myself to attempt telepathic communication with sidereal space, a noise of broken branches attracts my attention. Here he is again, my feral migrant, the Friday in my Robinsonade—and from his frankly lewd expression, I understand that he witnessed Arcady's and my activities. Just so there's no doubt in the matter, he points to me and bursts out laughing. Adjusting my shorts and my tank top, I try to preserve a semblance of dignity, while wondering all the time what has led to this crazed hilarity in him. Quick, quick, I go through the film of the last half hour: oral stimulation, a quasi-penetration of my atrophied vagina, and a finish splashing all over my belly, vibrating like the skin of a djembe—nothing but classic moves, not even any haram sodomy or hardcore face jack—in other words, I don't get it. Unless he is simply laughing at me and my dysmorphic features? On the shores of the Red Sea, people might be backward, but they still know what a sixteen-year-old girl is supposed to look like. Just as I'm about to turn on my heel, he puts a light hand on my shoulder and forces me to turn round. It's my turn to stare at him and to notice his dazzling youth, the gleaming knots of his muscles, and especially the taught silk of his skin and the delicate bone structure of his face. God exists, who produces such creatures.

Sticking out an exaggeratedly pink tongue, Friday wiggles it outside his buccal cavity, while sticking his middle finger straight into the ring made by the index and thumb of his other hand, in a universal gesture of obscene derision. I skedaddle. They might be fast sprinters in eastern Africa, but I'll always be faster than him. Not only have I always run everywhere but I know the terrain and I'm wearing sneakers. With his shitty flip-flops, he won't last long on the stones of a dry riverbed or on the steep slopes of the chestnut wood, so I'm already zipping way ahead. When I get within sight of the house, I look back: nobody there. However, Daniel, Djilali, and the twins have spread a picnic blanket on the drystone wall and are equitably sharing the remains of a Mexican *pan de muerto*.

"Shit, you know what?"

"No, but I'm sure you're about to tell us."

"We have a migrant!"

"A migrant?"

"Yes, he's the one who's been stealing Fiorentina's supplies, I'm sure of it!"

"Well, where is he?"

"I dunno, but anyway, he knows where my hideout is."

"We know where it is too! Everybody does!"

I turn to Djilali with a furious expression: as much as I don't keep any secrets from Nello, I would still prefer the little kids not to know where I have my rendezvous with the man I love.

"You don't know a thing, you fucktard!"

"Yes, I do! And so do Dolores and Teresa! We saw you!"

"You saw nothing! Shut the fuck up!"

Djilali immediately shuts down, as touchy as an oyster. I should know better, really, than to speak harshly to him. Daniel takes things in hand again.

"Everyone calm down! What's the deal with this migrant?"

"He's Black. Young. He was near the hazelnut trees, past the cows, just where I set up my hideout: I have water, books, a shade sail . . ."

The twins snigger lasciviously with an air of understanding, while Djilali digs into the loose soil with a flint. Silence. Arcady's shadow floats for a moment over the scruffy blanket. If I want to conduct my love life as I please, I really need to leave the community.

"What did he say to you?"

"Nothing. Maybe he doesn't speak French."

"What's he like? Blue-black?"

Dolores's question might seem strange, or even straight out racist, but one must take into account that everything to do with melanin is of crucial importance to Epifanio's daughters—to say nothing of the fact that, for middle school children, there are several ways of being Black, a whole color chart that I don't really know that much about, but about which the twins are well informed. And as far as I know, it's not a good thing to be black as coal in the pitiless world of eleven- to fifteen-year-olds. Any more than it's a good thing to be red-haired or intersex. I hope, for the twins' sake as much as for mine, that things get better in high school. Anyway, my migrant is not blue-black.

"Is he nice?"

"I didn't see him for long. But no, he didn't look especially nice. He made fun of me."

"You said he didn't talk."

"Yeah, but he laughed."

I keep his nasty gesture to myself, the ring of the index finger and thumb, the back-and-forth of the middle finger, the libidinous wiggling tongue, all the sign language he used to express both his arousal and his contempt. I need time to think about them before I throw them to the feeding frenzy of my famous five club members. I kneel down onto the blanket myself and rip the last share of soft bread from Djilali's hands.

"Why are you eating this? It's August!"

I'm not a specialist of *pan de muerto*, but as its name suggests, it is usually eaten on the Day of the Dead. I even think that in their macabre madness, the Mexicans put it on tombs, as offerings to their dear departed.

"It's Dad. He can't stop making it."

"Oh, yeah? What got into him?"

"He's depressed."

I don't feel like finding out anything more about this latest depressive episode of Epifanio's. As long as he keeps to baking his death bread with orange-blossom water, that's OK. But he really should watch out, because Fiorentina is a stickler about rituals—especially since she makes her own variation of death bread, which is infinitely richer and more varied in its dried and candied fruit than the Mexican version. She would take it very badly if she knew we were eating it just like that, out of season, without any kind of cultural prescription.

The conversation dwindles a little, but we finally agree that, migrant or no migrant, the intruder must be placed under close surveillance, perhaps even kicked out of our kingdom. We can't allow ourselves to be invaded, to have hordes of refugees coming to camp on our land, stealing our food, leaving their litter everywhere, soiling our Garden of Eden, violating our tranquility. Of the five of us, Djilali is clearly the most bellicose. He's already suggesting whittling hazelnut branches to sharp points and hardening them over a fire. Of course, Djilali's bible is a survivalist guide from the 1970s, which he found in our inexhaustible library: the fashioning of a bow or a slingshot holds no more secrets for him, and I suspect he has been training on our flock of chickens, whose blue and gold feathers decorate his arrows and his quiver. Anyway, two of our Wyandottes have disappeared.

"I know, but it's not me. I just took the feathers from the coop!"

"Maybe it's him, maybe it's the migrant!"

"Well, yeah, of course it's him: he has to eat, right?"

"But he has no right to do that: they're our chickens!"

"And anyway, we don't even eat them!"

A soft sigh ripples through out little gathering, barely a wave, a snicker, about the vegetarian principles inculcated in us. It's all very well for the grown-ups to have chosen for us, but they have completely underestimated the attraction that a fricasseed chicken drumstick might hold for young stomachs. We go our separate ways with the solemn promise to keep our eyes open. Inspection of the arsenal, surveillance mapping of our kingdom, daily rounds, night watches, we're warming up to the challenge and loving it: there's nothing quite like a common enemy to awaken the spirit of the clan—and also, let's be honest, nothing like it to allow us to be children again while we still can, in this late summer that will see four of us set sail for other shores, shores with no charm or mystery, those of adult life.

23.

The Beginning of Terror

The very next day, a thorough survey of our territory allows us to collect new evidence of the occupation: carbonized remains of our chickens, human excrement, cigarette butts, and all sorts of detritus. The enemy obviously does not subscribe to our environmental charter, and Nello is furious:

"I mean, really, where does he think he is? What would he do if we went and made that kind of mess at his place?"

Methinks our migrant and his compatriots may have other concerns "at his place" besides the ecological emergency, but I don't pipe up. Especially since Friday did more than profane our woodland and pilfer our peaches: in a bundle hidden in the fork of an oak tree, we find blankets embroidered with the Sacred Heart of Jesus and an opened bottle of Barolo.

It doesn't take much for Djilali to set his capacity for deduction in motion:

"The blankets are from the laundry in the attic. And the bottle, he took it from the cellar: that means he's been going all through the house! Maybe even into our rooms when we're not there!"

"If Fiorentina finds out, she'll tear his eyes out!"

"Maybe there's more of them: Farah saw only one, but that doesn't mean a thing!"

"Maybe he has his whole family with him, his wife and kids!"

"Yeah, and Blacks have lots of wives and heaps of children!"

At the very idea of this uncontrollable family reunification, our indignation rises up a notch, and we agree that we need to act quickly:

"It won't be long before school starts, and we won't have as much time and won't see each other as often. Especially Daniel and Farah, you'll have heaps of homework at high school! And exams!"

Daniel obviously does not share the little ones' sacred terror: having already had a year at high school, he knows that it doesn't require any inordinate efforts—and since the adults at Liberty House don't expect much of us and couldn't give a shit about our education anyway, there's probably some way of continuing to cruise peacefully along. At the same time, it would set all our minds at rest if we could get rid of Friday and his imaginary tribe before classes start. Unfortunately he has volatilized and seems to be having fun planting unsettling clues all over our acres of fields and forests. For while the scrunched-up Pavesini packages and the turds whitened by the sun are easy to interpret, what are we to make of the composite amulets swaying from the branches of our ash and chestnut trees? Feathers, string, bark, lavender, gobbets of resin, lizards' tails, cicada chrysalises, or snakes' skins, Friday is speaking the language of the Indian summer to us, but we are finding it hard to translate. One day, however, we come across a watermelon erected on a drystone cairn—an intact watermelon, except for a cylindrical excavation. While the little ones are floundering in conjectures, Daniel takes me to one side, suddenly in a dark mood:

"Jeez, what an asshole! He's screwing watermelons!"

"What?"

"Yeah! He puts his joystick in the hole, and away he goes!"

"How do you know that?"

"Have a good look inside it."

I'm boggled by the fact that one can have sexual intercourse with a fruit, but I don't completely disapprove. Quite the opposite, actually—it opens up new vistas—but before exploring them, I stop Djilali and the twins from examining the innards of the watermelon too scrupulously. It stays on its pile of stones, like a milepost or a totem, and when at last I dare to have a look inside, the sperm, if there ever was any, has disappeared, as if infused into the grainy pink flesh. I insert a prudent finger into the cylinder, but bring back only a single black seed, gleaming, maleficent, a bad omen that I quickly flick into the dust.

Galvanized by the presence of a serpent in our Garden of Eden, Djilali is on the war path and flaunting some disturbing facial paint, to say nothing of his feathered headgear. When he isn't patrolling the pine wood, he's in the library, perusing books on anthropophagy.

"Do you want to eat human flesh?"

He looks up at me, his soft eyes fringed with implausible eyelashes:

"No, yuck, never! No, I'm just doing some research in case Friday is a cannibal."

"What makes you think he's a cannibal?"

"I don't think he's a cannibal, but I know there are heaps of Blacks who are."

Sensing my skepticism, he adds with conviction:

"Fiorentina told me so!"

"I doubt it!"

"Yes, she did! She said that Africans ate human beings: just ask her!"

Fiorentina doesn't like Blacks, we all know this, but to go and fantasize and spread those kinds of inanities is to take it a step further than I could ever imagine:

"Well, I'm telling you they don't. So who would you prefer to believe, me or Fiorentina?"

He pretends not to have heard me:

"So what do you think human flesh tastes like?"

"How should I know?"

"I read that it tastes like chicken! But then, I've never eaten chicken, so . . ."

That doesn't surprise me since his mother is one of the community's most rabid vegans.

"You never had a McChicken?"

"No."

"You never went to KFC?"

"We're not allowed."

"No, but we all went there at least once."

"Did you go?"

"Yes."

"And Daniel and the twins too?"

"Yes, I'm telling you."

"You're so lucky!"

"I can take you if you want."

A smile fleetingly lights up his face, before he pulls himself together again, looks down, and mutters a polite refusal. I really need to take Djilali's education in hand: having endured all those hysterical romances and communitarian fads, he's decided he'll be the reasonable one, and it's never a good idea to be reasonable to that degree. He's sitting quietly in a ray of dancing light, his big book on his lap, his index on an ancient engraving of an explorer hacked to pieces by a tribe of savages. He's living in the twenty-first century, but you wouldn't know it. That's the whole point of raising children in quiet zones: they acquire the habits of another era, of reading and contemplation in particular. I'm the first one to congratulate myself about this, and to think it gives us a decisive advantage over our contemporaries, but that doesn't stop me from worrying. When I consult Daniel about it, he is reassuring:

"Well, I think he's doing OK, actually. He's a pretty calm sort of kid, so like, where's the problem?"

"You think it's normal to be obsessed with cannibals?"

"All little boys have obsessions: dinosaurs, extraterrestrials, sharks . . ."

"What was your obsession when you were nine years old?"

"Dicks."

"What? Age nine?"

"Yes, and even before that. I mean I was always obsessed by my own dick, because it was so ridiculously small and I didn't have any pubes. You see, I saw the grown-ups' ones and I wondered why mine didn't look like theirs. No one explained it to me, you know, puberty and all that. And then I used to think about the dicks of the boys in my class. I couldn't stop myself. I imagined them, tucked up nice and warm in their tighty-whities; I wanted to see them, to touch them, to take them into my mouth. I was always hard as a rock and I thought it was the same for them. This may seem weird to you, but up until the age of eleven or twelve, I thought it was heteros that were the minority, not gays!"

"What?"

"Well, yeah! Remember, apart from your parents, there's not a single straight couple at Liberty House."

"You mean there are no couples at all!"

"There's Arcady and Victor, for one. Then Malika and your grandmother. You see: all gay."

"What about Epifanio? And Jewell?"

"Epifanio and Jewell are both single! There's no way you can tell if they prefer men or women!"

"Well, Epifanio has two daughters!"

"That doesn't mean a thing. You have no idea of the number of dads I've had!"

We're both hanging around Fiorentina's kitchen. There's no risk that she'll be upset by what we're talking about: "dicks," "hard-ons," "gays," "heteros" are all words that have no place in her vocabulary or her mental universe. The very idea of a penis probably never even crossed her mind. So being obsessed with one would probably make her burst out laughing, with that wild and young laugh she usually reserves for the shenanigans of baby animals. And in any case, she's not interested in what people say. In order to find its way into her ear canal, our conversation would have to be about household management and be extremely prosaic. You gain her attention only by talking about provolone or borlotti beans, and you conquer her respect only by being a workhorse just like she is: hanging up laundry, polishing the skirting boards, drying mushrooms, sorting lentils, collecting eggs, mowing the lawns, beating the carpets—that's how Fiorentina spends her days and that's what she enlists anyone within earshot of her contralto voice to do. And in fact, that's just what happens: seeing that we seem to have time on our hands, she sends us out into the vegetable garden.

"Tomatoes, mint, zucchini flowers. *Subito!*"

It's eleven in the morning, the heat is already oppressive, but we shouldn't dawdle. And guess who we find in the middle of our strawberry plants? Friday, of course—stopped in midgesture, tracked look, open mouth, he stares at us for three poignant seconds before running away in zigzags, like a hare.

"Shit, he's fucking gorgeous! Why didn't you say so?"

It's true. I kept the secret of his beauty to myself: the bluish white of his eyes, his sharp teeth, the fine arrow of his nose, the shadow of his eyelashes on his majestic cheekbones, the tangled ringlets in his hair, like a crown, a tiara, an emblem.

"To think that he's screwing watermelons, when I'm right here!"

With a moan of desperate covetousness, Daniel collapses under the pyrethrum bushes, which my father planted there for their insecticidal properties. I certainly don't tell him that the object of his desire let me know of his own desire with a suggestive wiggling of his pink tongue and the back-and-forth of his slender fingers—for, on reflection, I've chosen to see Friday's pantomime as an invitation rather than an insult to my anatomy or my virtue.

"I wanna fuck so bad, I swear!"

"What?"

"I really wanna do him! It's all his fault: he's made me so fucking hard! We need to find him, quick!"

"Even if we do find him, who's to say he'll want to have sex with you?"

Ripping up a bunch of flowers, Daniel sprinkles the leaves and petals into his gleaming locks, pouts alluringly, and strikes a pose:

"He'll want to, believe me . . ."

"You're such a shithead."

"OK, come on: if we don't bring back her tomatoes, Metallica is gonna kill us. But tonight, we're not sleeping, OK? We're gonna find him, we're gonna find his hideout! And then . . ."

He walks in front of me down the paths of the potager, rolling his hips ostentatiously and throwing lascivious glances over his bony shoulders. He bobs down to pick some zucchini flowers, not without shimmying so that his ass enticingly stretches his two-tone shorts—his George Michael ones. I hate it when he does his baby-queen act, but he's still my friend despite his annoying habits, because he also has other endearing qualities—besides I can't be too picky about friends, given the solitude to which my own oddities confine me. That night under cover of darkness, we meet at the foot of the big oak tree where Friday had tried to hide his bundle of blankets. He's not there.

"He must be asleep somewhere else. We need to keep a lookout."

Despite our precautions, the branches crack under our feet and the insects suddenly stop singing their night songs. If he's anywhere near, Friday will have heard us from a long way off and had the time to scarper. After two fruitless hours beating the area, we turn back, and just as we come in sight of Liberty House, a suspicious sound of lapping water comes to our ears. I would like it to be noted at this point that we owe it to Dadah that our old ornamental pool was restored last spring. Since it was a question of gaining the upper hand over Nelly,

Dadah had high ambitions: the old pool, narrow and cracked, was transformed into a wildly romantic pond, surrounded with rustling bulrushes, scattered with water lilies, and fed by a series of little waterfalls tripping over mossy steps. Djilali and the twins spend most of their days there, paddling about and tracking our sturgeons and multicolored koi. May I also add, in passing, that the battle to the death that our two old ladies are engaged in is of incontestable value to the community: not only have the rooves and pools been restored but also rare species of trees now shade the front garden, while the north wall of the building is now graced with a bay window with amber-stained glass. I also believe that Fiorentina's food budget was doubled. We swim in opulence, and our carps do too: fat and gleaming, they undulate in a milky moonbeam while Daniel and I stealthily move towards the pool.

He's there. On the calm dark water where the stars are sleeping, he's floating, like a black lily, one of those that my father cultivates at great expense thanks to Dadah's largesse, as it's her favorite flower, even her emblem. Nelly, on the other hand, claims to love the rustic simplicity of asters, just to mark her difference, and my father had better make sure that our greenhouses are not lacking in either. Anyway, our noble savage is there, shamelessly enjoying our lustral water and performing his ablutions between the water-lily stems and the bulrushes. All around us, the night is stirring, sighing; an invisible bird sends out an intermittent coo-coo, like a worried question. Pushing himself under with his whole body, Friday disappears completely beneath the silvery operculum of the pond. Next to me, Daniel is holding his breath and shoving his hand into his two-tone shorts, looking for his dick, I suppose. I tut-tut in exasperation, without distracting him for a second from what he's up to: of course he's jerking off, the fuckwit! Whoosh, Friday comes up to the surface, reaching his ecstatic face to the moon and shaking the black stamens of his heavy soaking hair in all directions. Now he's getting out of the water, naked as on the first day, and Daniel's hand movements become frenetic while he whispers in my ear:

"Fuck, see how buff he is?"

Yes, I see, and it's a change from Arcady's pudgy morphology, that's for sure, those long, firm thighs, that belly hammered like an iron breastplate, those sumptuous shoulders, those high, full buttocks, those narrow hips.... As if to salute this apparition, the frogs' song goes up a notch in its fervent passion. Sensing that Daniel is moments away from bounding towards the intruder, I grab the elastic of his two-tone shorts:

"Stay here!"

Unaware of our presence, Friday crouches down on the edge of the pool, rummages in a little pile of clothes that he left there, then rolls himself a cigarette, or more accurately, a joint, judging from the exhalations that come our way.

"That's your dad's weed!"

I can confirm that: the intruder obviously has access to the little medicinal garden, even though Marqui had fenced it with split logs to signify its highly private status—and for good reason, since between the sage and the St. John's wort, he planted opiates whose effectiveness he has been testing on his wife. I would recognize that rich, exotic scent anywhere, as it constantly surrounds my mother, like a little cloud of personal happiness above her head.

"He looks like Bob Marley, don't you think?"

He's not wrong. What with the clouds of smoke he's voluptuously exhaling, the charcoal locks of his hair, and the mahogany veneer of his Eritrean skin, Friday is just the picture of the mythical Natty Dread from Trenchtown. I nod silently, but Daniel couldn't care less since he is about to squirt into the pampa grass, without a second thought for their soft, rustling feather dusters. As we both hold back, him from moaning, and me from laughing, our migrant stands up, nonchalantly flicks his roach into the pond, inspects his surroundings with a cursory look, gets dressed again, and goes back to the edge of the woods, where he is swallowed up by the tree population.

"Shit, he's a slob, isn't he?"

But Daniel has lost all objectivity, and now takes an indulgent view of everything that yesterday seemed unbearable—namely, Friday's thoughtless littering.

"He's not a slob! Quite the opposite: he just had a bath!"

"He throws his cigs in the water!"

"I couldn't give a fuck if he throws his cigs in the water! Did you see how gorgeous he is?"

Yes, I did see, of course I did, but no one can convince me that this is not the beginning of terror, and the end of innocence.

24.

Mental Health Is a Fragile Thing

Visibly disoriented by the birth of his Black Venus, Daniel went at dawn to wake up our club members, to gather the five of us in an extraordinary council meeting on the drystone wall—there's nothing like a secret rendezvous in the tall grass to raise the morale of the troops. The over-excitable twins had put together a whole collection of detective equipment: a magnifying glass, compass, Swiss army knife, whistle, survival rations, even a bottle of invisible ink, whose usefulness escapes me, but which Djilali seems to find fascinating. He is wearing a complete Sioux chief's outfit: bow and quiver, fierce look, feather stuck in his thick black hair—that's if it's not stuck straight into his skull. Save me! I'm apparently the only one who has any common sense left. The little kids are firmly committed to kicking the demon out, but they're about to find out that Daniel has passed into the enemy camp with all the fervor of an apostate.

"Me and Farah saw the migrant: he goes swimming in the pool at night."

Without a word, Djilali throws his bow at our feet, which must be the equivalent of a declaration of war in Indian language. Daniel immediately sets him straight:

"Wait a sec, what are you gonna do? Shoot him? He's allowed to have a bath, isn't he? What about the right to hygiene? Let me remind you he's a migrant: he doesn't have a home, a bathroom, or anything! And maybe he's all alone here, with no family, no friends!"

"You said he probably had heaps of wives and children!"

"Dolores said that, not me. No, I think he's as lonely as a rat."

"Yeah, he's a rat! Rats are disgusting!"

"Only racists compare foreigners to rats! Since when are we racists?"

Contrite and disconcerted, the little ones lower their noses and don't even dare look at each other anymore. Make up your mind though! Yesterday, Friday was on the hit list, and today we're finding any excuse to welcome him with open arms? And, of course, Daniel is hiding the libidinous motivations of his U-turn. In short, Djilali and the twins are ordered to track down our chicken thief but are forbidden to shoot him.

"If you see him, you don't say anything, right? You don't try to talk to him, you just come and get me, OK?"

"What if he sees us?"

"You can't let him see you! If he sees you, he'll go away! If there are two of you, one stays there to keep an eye on him, and the other one comes to tell me—me or Farah."

No sooner have they received their marching orders than the little ones scatter to the four corners of the kingdom, leaving

Daniel and me with our languor and regrets. We should have made our move last night: everybody knows that in the wild, the best place to track animals is at the watering holes, when they are vulnerable, their vigilance lowered in the deceiving peace of the backwater, their legs spread wide so they can drink.... That's why, even though it's the middle of the day, we are dawdling around the pool, but only Epifanio is there, plunged into contemplation of the koi, especially one of them, which he points at with a trembling finger:

"Look! It's getting depigmented too!"

We look, just in time to see a fat carp burying its blotchy flanks in the mud—but neither Daniel nor I have enough headspace available for empathy and commiseration: Epifanio will have to work out his own obsessions, and leave us to the searing shadows of our own. For, in my case at least, it really is an obsession, visions impossible to remove from my mental background, images both unbearable and pleasurable: a peach stone spat out in the dust, soaked hair whipping the night air, majestic cheekbones, hollowed-out buttocks, an emerald trail of waterweed stuck on a thigh.

Our feet dangling in the cool water, our heads shaded by an acanthus palm, we glumly discuss our respective chances. Daniel is no longer so full of bravado, and a lot less sure of himself than he was the previous day.

"Do you think he's straight? Coz if he's straight, that gives you an advantage as a girl. Especially if he's Islamic."

"Even if he is straight, there's not much of a chance that he'll find me attractive. And are you sure people are Muslim where he comes from? Aren't they actually Jewish?"

"But, of course, if he hasn't had sex in a long time, maybe he'll jump at the chance. I mean, he did screw a watermelon . . ."

Djilali and the twins return at this juncture, as empty-handed as one might expect, cutting our rambling erotic musings short. They're so hot, they're fed up with looking for the migrant, they want to have a swim and play something else. Same for me, really, except it's the opposite: what I mean is, for the first time in six months, there's something else for me to think about besides my voyage out, my bumpy passage through appearances, from one gender to another. Even Arcady is suddenly relegated to the background, which goes to show that true love never lasts. Or else, that I had been deluded from the beginning in imagining I loved him. What a pity there's no one I can ask about the difference between true love and the desire that is torturing me on this searing August day. Arcady surely knows, but I'm not going to let the cat out of the bag with my questions: I'd just as soon he didn't know I'm being unfaithful to him. OK, so he does preach free love, and, of course, I haven't cheated on him yet, but maybe that makes it worse because I'm dying to do so, and I no longer have a second to myself to think about anything else.

Evening falls and things haven't become any clearer. I'm even past the point of no return in the clouding of my intellectual faculties. Mental health is a fragile thing. It doesn't take much to derail it, and then there are no more short supply chains between ideas: mine are galloping behind each other, without ever catching up to the slightest clear formulation or producing the slightest hope of implementation.

Dinner brings us together around pizzas with marinated artichokes, followed by a sublime molten-chocolate and raspberry cake, but neither Daniel nor I am in the mood to enjoy it: our legs are restless under the table, our fingers drum on the tablecloth, and we can't stand any of the conversations, none of which seem to fit with our obsession and our desire to honor our tacit rendezvous—for although he doesn't know this yet, Friday has a date with us.

As the clock strikes midnight, we are back within sight of the pool, hiding behind a curtain of rattling bamboo. We placed a basket of carefully chosen propitiatory offerings on the edge of the pool: a slice of pizza, a piece of provolone, some leftover quince paste, some olives stuffed with red peppers, a bottle of Barolo, some Pavesini biscuits, three joints of my father's grass, a lighter, some coffee-flavored candy, and a box of condoms. The idea is to let him know that we not only wish him no harm but also know what he likes, and that we like him.

He nonchalantly saunters up at about one in the morning. Without seeing our basket, he strips off his Barça soccer jersey and his ragged shorts before entering the pond, which is more lactescent than ever under the lace of the mastic trees. Like last night, he disappears under the water, but unlike last night, he doesn't reappear. He drowned: he got caught in the lily-pad stems, then held in the slime at the bottom by rotting logs—end of story, deliverance, I'll be able to return to normal life, even though normalcy means nothing in our open-air asylum, our hill station for varied defectives.

"Shit, where is he? We have to go look for him: maybe he's passed out . . ."

Leaving the cover of the bamboo thicket, Daniel goes into the water up to his thighs and searches the surface. Nothing. Just a string of desperate bubbles which I take care not to point out to him. It's not like we should be rescuing the one who will destroy us anyway. We might as well let him do battle in the deep. I barely have time to believe my story and to be invaded by horror and guilt, before Friday rises up behind us: far from drowning, he apparently swam from one end of the pond to the other and came around the side to surprise us. Daniel falls stunned to his knees in the green water, and ends up rolling his eyes above the glazed bowl of a lily pad, his head cut off already, offered on a platter, all Friday has to do is serve himself—and I have no doubt that he will do so, since he all but carried out the decapitation himself. I know what I know. The source of this knowledge—between hope and terror, between survival reflex and desire for the worst—does not matter.

Naked as the day he was born, his arms crossed between his silver navel and his pectoral shield, Friday is staring at us severely and I feel myself weaken under his gaze: I'm very sensitive to reprobation. Still on his knees in the pond, Daniel timidly greets our nighttime visitor:

"Hi. Do you speak French? English? I am Daniel."

Here it goes again: my dissociation trouble ambushes me, and now I'm petrified on the edge of the pond, not knowing how to introduce myself anymore: "Hello, I am Farah?" But no, that's the thing, I'm not Farah, I am the whole universe, a twelve-volume encyclopedia all on my own. It's a pity this is happening just as I am desperately trying to present myself to good advantage and to correct the disastrous impression I must have made the first time. One is not necessarily at one's best during lovemaking, if one lets oneself go: who knows what kinds of grimaces, noises, and unflattering positions Friday might have seen. If I wish to establish contact, I absolutely need to come to my senses, to repatriate my soul into its earthly body, otherwise Daniel will be the one to get his clutches on our migrant, and that will be the end of my dreams of a loving encounter.

To be honest, more than love, it's the encounter I'm dreaming of. I already have love, but I've never met anyone. Don't get me wrong, I know a heap of people, but most of them I grew up with, and was under their aegis: I've never had any kind of flash, or convulsive instant, or miraculous first look—just a peach pit spat into the dust and forever gleaming. That encounter could take place right here and right now, but I'm not actually here, and Daniel will be the one to make the most of this wildly romantic situation, "Love at first sight under the cherry moon." For the moon is indeed cherry red, and that might be the reason of this untimely orbit, this rapture that has deprived me of all my faculties and temporarily extracted me from the world.

Time passes. When I get back to reality, Daniel and Friday are crouched down face to face and plunged into an animated conversation, in a mixture of French and sign language. Daniel turns to me with a stupidly happy face:

"His name is actually Angosom!"

"Are you sure? That's a pretty weird name."

"Totally sure: look, he wrote it down for me."

Indeed, seven capital letters are engraved in the clay soil of the edge of the pond: ANGOSOM. I can't help thinking that it looks a lot like the start of "and go somewhere," which seems to confirm my state just now.

"Maybe it's his last name."

"No, his last name is something else: he told me but I didn't get it."

All the same, I couldn't care less about his last name: when he takes me in the pine woods or under my nuptial canopy, it will be "Angosom" that will rise to my lips, "Angosom" that I will scream to the starry heavens. I kneel down and write my own name next to his, and all but draw a love heart around them, "Farah + Angosom = True Love." I know, it feels like I'm going mad, and it's true, I am going mad, I want everything and nothing, for Angosom to die and to fuck me, but not in that order of course.

From what I can tell from their pantomime, the two boys are already making great oaths of friendship: hand on heart, solemn looks, a brief embrace under the foliage. I count for nothing. No one gives a shit whether I'm there or not, which is normally just fine with me, but not here, not now: I exist.

"Where you sleep? Bed?"

Palms together under his cheek, eyes shut, Daniel pretends to sleep then points to Angosom before spreading his hands and raising his eyes to the sky in sign of uncertainty. With a pitiful little smile, Angosom shows the edge of the woods and the rows of vertical trunks that have offered him shelter. Daniel quickly takes things in hand:

"Tonight, this night, you sleep in real bed. Bed: you know, bed? Come with me."

Come with us might have been more tactful, but the two lovebirds are alone in the world. Still as naked as ever, Angosom eyes the basket overflowing with victuals, which causes Daniel to break out into enthusiastic braying:

"Yeah, for you! Food! Wine! You want?"

No sooner said than done. Daniel opens the bottle, tears open the packet of Pavesinis, and brandishes a floppy slice of artichoke pizza in the direction of his protégé, who makes no fuss about accepting it. We clink the amber stackable glasses, vestiges of Liberty House's boarding school years. My lips touch them with a shiver, since whenever I drink from them I get flashbacks of Sapphic friendships. If they were only of Sapphic friendships, that would be OK, but I have to tolerate more alarming visions of greenish halos, ghostly starched headdresses, pursed lips, and hands clutching rosaries—to say nothing of the supplicating whispers, moans, and sobs suffocated in pillows for more than a century. I don't know why it happens to me or whether it happens to everyone. Maybe that's part of my spectrum of symptoms, along with all the rest, my ascensions, my intermittent consciousness, but also my gradual sexual reassignment—how should I know? I'm not a doctor, and those who are want nothing to do with cases like mine, which defy their understanding and don't fit into their little scientific baggage.

Once we finish the Barolo, the three of us go back to the house. It is agreed that Angosom will sleep in the attic, in an unoccupied room two steps away from mine. As long as he is discreet in his comings and goings, Daniel and I will keep watch. Without any further ado, we shove our basket under his bed: the olives, the quince paste, the three intact joints. . . . The toilets are at the end of the corridor. Best not to think about a nocturnal collision with a sleepy Fiorentina, who would still be capable of recognizing a clandestine resident.

I go to bed, and against all expectations, I fall asleep and dream of swans embracing with their sinuous necks, illuminating the pond with a heart of lustrous white feathers and black beaks: it must mean something, but what?

25.

Hermaphrodite Anadyomene

Up at dawn, I decide to conduct a thorough inspection of each part of my anatomy. What do I have to offer the world—and by world, I mostly mean Angosom—besides the fixed circus of my thoughts? In the large living room that Victor has so lavishly furnished with mirrors, I examine every inch of myself, raising my arms, spreading my legs, unscrewing my neck. After a full ten minutes of contortions, I am forced to admit that my metamorphosis is following its ineluctable course. My neck is even thicker, a crown of coarse hair surrounds each of my nipples, my superciliary arches are more prominent, and any tender swellings I might have had—breasts, hips, pubis—have shriveled into the mineral block of my new body. The involution of my female secondary sexual characteristics has been accompanied by a contrary movement and a still timid but incontestable tumescence of a pair of testicles in my outer labia.

Their color is somewhere between bister and verdigris, but fortunately I've seen dangling testicles all my life and I know they come in all sorts of strange shades without that being a sign of decay. In short, let us not hide from the truth, I am now a monster and the R. syndrome has nothing to do with it: I've been cursed, that's the only explanation, and unless I find a counter-curse, I will never have a normal appearance. In the meantime, my lovers will have to have a strong stomach—or be equipped with an ultra-sensitive radar to detect my powers of seduction.

All this to say that with Angosom, it's not going to be a sure thing. Looking into the eighteenth-century trumeau mirror with the painting above it—a scene of gallantry framed in gilded wooden moldings—I conduct a critical audit of the extent of the damage and an assessment of my chances. The former is considerable and the latter slim, but never mind: one must be courageous in love. And since I have courage to spare, I pull on a pair of emerald-green shorts and a sherbet-red top, just to send a signal to Angosom's limbic cortex, a whiff of freshness, a subliminal vision of a pearl-studded watermelon, of mucus membranes, of a moist and inviting slit. Now I just need to catch him as he wakes up, to make the most of a rather undiscriminating morning erection. When I can no longer stand it and finally open his door, Angosom has vanished, and the whole day suddenly seems to have lost its color. I don't know why I even bothered getting all dressed up, and the depth of my disappointment tells me how unsatisfactory or even dangerous life can be.

For once, I decide not to honor my morning rendezvous with Arcady. Despite being raised by followers of free love, I feel that faithfulness is part of my nature. Not that I've stopped loving Arcady, but I can't quite see myself fucking my number one love when I'm thinking of the dazzling charms of my number two love. That would actually be the most infallible way to screw everything up, both the old idyll and the new one. To succeed, people like me need to devote themselves entirely to their enterprise, one target at a time. And that's something I'm good at: focus, precision, perseverance, long-term projects. But the unwritten rules at Liberty House, our tablets of the law engraved in the air and sand, enjoin us to do exactly the opposite: to flutter, not to get attached, not to seek to attach others, to flee constancy, commitment, and exclusive relationships. But that's the thing: what I really want, actually, is exclusivity. If I'm going to disappear, it might as well be for a good cause, absorbed by a foreign body, melted into it like snow on a fire—crackling, exalted, happy.

Rather than spending the day reading or hanging around, or spending hours in idle discussion with Daniel, I borrow his motorbike and zoom off to the nameless town, to try and find a remedy for my lovesickness—for why insist on calling such an imperious and absolute feeling desire? I love Angosom, and I can shout it into the warm wind on my madcap ride, sure that no one will hear me or pay any attention to me: Angosom, I love you! I get into town before I exhaust my jubilation. So much the better: that way I have enough left to wander the streets without being worn out by the heat or people's gazes flitting to me without the slightest spark of interest. To preserve myself from their indifference, I have all the fury of love, my personal and perpetual illumination.

On the beach, I join the bunches of tourists plastered with sunscreen—whose chemicals will settle straight onto the coral reefs, decimating seaweed and plankton on their way. For now, the water is still crystalline, and the wavy sand is clearly visible under the spangles of morning sunshine. I'd go for a swim if only I had my togs. That said, given the turn my anatomy has taken, I can probably get away with my boxer shorts. It would even be a good idea to try this out, here on this beach where only men allow themselves to go topless. Ha! In a flash I take off my top and join the swimmers, looking around at them cautiously, just to observe the effect produced by my new chest—i.e., two pecs just slightly more swollen than the average, a far cry from the udders that girls triumphantly squeeze into flowery bandeaus or diamanté-studded triangles. Since my boxers are loose enough to leave room for doubt about my genital architecture, I attract no surprised looks or malicious sniggers: my virility goes unquestioned. To get used to this idea, I swim away from the shore with a vigorous breaststroke, reach a slightly sticky yellow buoy, which I clasp for a moment in my newly strong arms, before heading beyond the safety perimeter, far from the warm, shimmering water by the beach. I dive down: maybe there are calming truths to be found in the deep, encounters less upsetting than those that occur on dry land.

On my return to the hot sand, I adopt a slightly rolling gait, get dressed with nonchalant gestures, and look around with a Stallone-like expression, something between unfeigned sullenness and veiled aggressiveness. I'd like to stop, but I can't help myself. I even almost swagger and whistle—although I hate people who whistle or sing to themselves. In other words, something seems to have happened while I was swimming weightlessly in that unreal space-time—an imperceptible flip, a secret and involuntary rallying of all my cells to this new agenda: being a boy. Except that I don't want anything to do with this new agenda: I've never liked any of the paraphernalia of masculine equipment, the complete range of sagging purplish genitalia, banging drums, bugle calls, never-ending and never-successful efforts to make the grade, a whole life of insecurity, no thanks! I prefer the conch shell enclosing its triumphs, victories with no singing, the grapes of my vines: my mother's castle, that well-administered kingdom, rather than my father's glory, always fragile and under threat.

As I walk along the beach towards Italy, my attention is caught by large black letters, painted straight onto the rocks: "no nation, no border, fight law and order." Born from someone who should not have made me, raised in the bosom of a sect of naturist illuminati, I was probably destined for some kind of intimate disorder, but that's just it, I've always aspired to law and order. It suits me just fine that there are nations and borders, even if it doesn't suit Angosom and all the other exiles. I feel like crawling underground or, if not, curling up inside Nelly's funeral urn, just to put an end to my story, which has been a mistake right from the start.

I sadly shoot a rock into the water, just as boys do, always and everywhere—except that this is new to me, this propensity to throw stones and pretend I'm pitching a ball, it's the sign that my metamorphosis is complete. Even though I aspire to retreat into the last remains of my femininity, I might as well resign myself, confirm the change, ask to be called Farrell, sign up for soccer, spit on the ground, screw girls. . . . Just as my mind grasps this last idea, to examine it more seriously and attentively than usual, a cheerful voice calls out to me, a hand falls onto my shoulder, I turn around, and it's Maureen, like a genie rubbed from my inner lamp. She now sports pretty pink locks, matching her fair complexion:

"Hey, Farah! Hi!"

"Hi."

"This is, like, so totally wild, finding you here: I've been thinking about you, like, so much! How are you?"

There are too many "like, sos" in this salutation, but I forgive her because of her gratifying enthusiasm—for it's a well-known fact that I'm not used to arousing any. Settling ourselves at an outdoor-café table looking out over the sea, we exchange the latest news—in other words, not much as far as I'm concerned, since my latest news is unmentionable: not only is my heart taken but I am now a boy—the kind of information that ought to make Maureen give up. In fact, it takes her only three sips of beer at the beach bar before she scrunches up her little nose—just a swelling below her velvety forehead:

"Shit, what's that guy smell, is that you?"

"Do you have a problem with that?"

"With what? With guys, or with smells?"

Without giving her an answer, I sit back in my chair, stretch my legs out, and look at the horizon with an air of determination.

"Why are you playing at being the manly man?"

How can I tell her that I'm not playing at anything? That it's actually me who is the plaything of obscure forces trying to turn me into a biological anomaly and an object of ridicule?

"Don't you like me anymore?"

She looks me over, her nose still scrunched up, trying to find the trap that I've set for her with my new boyish airs:

"I'll have to think about that."

"What do you like about me?"

"I dunno! I'm just, like, totally into you!"

It looks like Maureen is not the right person to talk to if I want to understand what my powers of attraction might be.

What is the deal with these people who don't know anything about anything and can't even penetrate the arcana of their own psyches?

"Oh, well, forget it."

Apparently forgetting it is not in her nature: despite my male odor and my swaggering poses, she slaps her hand down on my thigh. It seems my power over her has survived my sex change. Since that is precisely what I want to be sure of, I splatter the overheated sidewalk with a virile spurt of saliva. In vain: Maureen tightens her grip on my thigh.

"Shit, Maureen, make up your mind: are you gay or not? Can't you see I'm a guy?"

She takes back her hand as if it had been burned. A series of expressions cross her clear face at an almost comical speed: disgust, incomprehension, mistrust.

"Last time you told me you didn't have a phone and now you tell me you're a guy? Like, what will you think up next just to get rid of me?"

"You're calling me a liar?"

"Totally."

"Mor, I know this is super sketchy, but it's true: I'm turning into a guy!"

"Are you transsexual?"

"Um, I don't know."

"What do you mean, you don't know?"

"Well, trans people choose, right? But I didn't choose anything: I was a girl, a bit fugly, but still a girl, and now my breasts are shrinking and I'm growing balls!"

"I know heaps of girls who sort of have balls, I mean, like, you know, junk, hanging under their pussies. That doesn't make them guys!"

"Oh, really? You know them? And they have breasts?"

"Some do, some don't. You know, breasts come in all shapes and sizes."

Yes, I do know, thank you. Breasts are like testicles, I've had the opportunity to observe them all my life: my mother's, my grandmother's, Malika's, Jewell's, Dadah's.... I know what they look like, and I know what they turn into with age, for one of the benefits of nudism is to banish any illusions one might have about the ravages of time.

"Well, anyway, I don't know what goes on with other people, but I'm pretty sure not everyone changes sex at puberty."

On reflection, everybody does change sex at puberty, everybody sees their genitals being struck with a curse: smooth, warm, relatively odorless, and the source of innocent pleasures in childhood, they get covered in hair, take on pigment, start filling out, demand hygiene measures, get turned on, and fuel the most disturbing daydreams.

"Maybe you were a guy right from the start, and you can only see it now. I saw a TV program..."

As soon as you mention intersexuality, someone has always seen something on TV. You'd think that's the only thing there is on TV. Except that I don't have a TV, or internet, or anything, which means I'm all alone with my symptoms, and am not a transgender person, or a shemale, or a hermaphrodite, or a ladyboy, and even less a transsexual or a cross-dresser or who knows what. Yes, that's it, I'm all alone: nobody ever went through what I am going through. Maybe I'm a mutant? After all, I'm well aware that we're living in dangerous times, in an environmental situation that is playing havoc with the seasons, leading to all kinds of cancer, allergy cross-reactivity, menstruation at age eight, menopause at thirty, and infertility in between. In fact, who knows, maybe there are thousands of us powerless witnesses to our bodies' mutinies, as they get bombarded with electromagnetic radiation, endocrine disruptors, and other invisible pollutants. But then, let's just wait and see who's in charge, my body or me: testicles or pecs are not going to stop me from being a girl if that is what I'm aiming for. That's the gist of what I explain to Maureen, who supports me 100 percent:

"Yeah, you're totally right: it totally sucks to be a guy. They're, like, so totally stupid, I hate guys. But then, I'm actually not a fan of girls who are, like, totally girly, you know?"

Yes, I do know—but I really need to teach Maureen a more parsimonious use of adverbs, because it's starting to get annoying just listening to her. But actually, what Maureen is trying to tell me, is that she likes girls who look like guys. My grandmother, who is just as much of a dyke, prefers girls who are, like, totally girly, all the Malikas of this world, stinking of musk and anxiety, along with painful periods, spasmophilia attacks, a kind of fragility that is difficult to counter, a kind of sadness in need of constant consolation—in other words, exactly what my grandmother needs. Which goes to show that there are several ways of being homosexual and several ways of being a woman—and whatever the case may be, so many ways to love. . . . Mine would probably be rather like my grandmother's, protective and consoling, but since my love life until now has been only about Arcady, who protects and consoles himself just fine, I don't know what I might have to offer someone more vulnerable. As for Maureen, I can see that her emotional climate is all about power plays, fights, hassles—you can tell just by looking at her, her stubborn forehead, her ornery look, her leg jittering under the table, the way she turns purple. . . . She looks like she's constantly ready to jump up, to pounce, to lash out. Boorish butches do have their charms, which I can't say I'm not attracted to, but then again, I have enough problems to deal with without adding rough love with Maureen.

Under her beautiful puzzled eyes, I stand up, making an effort to be graceful and smooth. It's crazy, but now you're aware, just look at how boys and girls make their entrances and exits: jumping to their feet, clapping their hands, and banging their chair against the table, or almost tenderly and regretfully caressing its wicker back. It's a pity I'm not able to procreate, because I have a few ideas about raising children: as a mother of boys, I would teach them about tipping the velvet and discourage them from throwing stones—and especially from spitting on the ground. And my daughters would grow up like me, in the treetops and with the chickens: learning the basics of contouring on YouTube would be out of the question. So bye, Maureen, whether you believe it or not, I don't have a mobile phone or number to give you, but we will meet again someday, you, the girl who likes girls, and me, the girl on an anatomical journey with no destination. Because looking at it from all angles, what suits me best is this transitional stage, this whole mix and match that is neither male nor female, and which I want to make my own condition.

She catches up with me before I start up my motorbike and grabs my arm with an imploring and determined look:

"Whenever you're ready, Farah, I'm serious. You know where to find me. If I'm not here, I'll be at Les Tamaris or L'Arbor. Or in town: I work at Pulp, you know, the big bar with the green awning? Or at Longchamp Palace, there too. Near the covered market. I go there quite a bit. OK?"

"OK. I promise, I'll come find you."

26.

Border Incidents

As soon as I put away the motorbike, a first strike of the gong rings out, immediately followed by a second, then a third, which has the effect of mobilizing the entire household, Dadah trailing along last, but energized by this tocsin—which comes as a strange echo to my own intimate alarm. Arcady and Victor are on the terrace waiting for their flock, with preoccupied expressions that augur nothing good. For meals or discussions, one strike is enough. Last time there was a call to action stations, it was for the exorcism of the potager garden, but it won't take me long to find out that a new invasion has been detected that necessitates an equally savage purging ritual. Victor is the first to speak—for in exceptional circumstances he'll always be on deck, rolling his eyes, foaming at the mouth, leaning with both hands on the pommel of his cane:

"Fiorentina has an announcement to make!"

Fiorentina denies this pronouncement with an irritable gesture, but I know her well enough to detect that she is upset. Her cheeks, which are usually as placid and ivory white as a ball of burrata, are pink with emotion, and a lock of hair is escaping from its carapace of hairspray and corkscrewing down onto her forehead. Since she persists in remaining silent, Victor speaks for her:

"For a few weeks now, Fiorentina has noticed items missing from our reserves. I mean groceries: cookies, cheese, jars of mushrooms in vinegar, quince paste, chocolate, olives stuffed with peppers, wine . . ."

At the mention of quince paste and stuffed olives, I look over at Daniel, and the same smile rises to our lips, brought forth by the same memory of silvery triton thighs under the moonlight, a spellbinding abdomen, a black mop of heavy wet hair, eyelashes like a biblical menorah, but with more branches than required. Victor continues without noticing our signals of connivance or the beatific state into which our visions plunge us:

"This morning, when Fiorentina got up, she saw a man leaving the green room. You know, Charlie's room. I say that for those of you who knew him . . ."

He lets a moment of emotional silence pass as an homage to this lost resident, an apoplectic sexagenarian, converted too late to frugality: then, boom! He exploded under our very eyes during a hike under the giant fir trees of La Maïris, for which he had overestimated his strength—but then, no one had forced him to come along.

"The room shows all the signs of a recent occupation: the bed is not made, there is a basket of provisions under the bed, a water bottle on the nightstand—in other words, there is no room for doubt: we have a squatter!"

Victor's forehead immediately takes on an appropriately worried frown, as his eyes shoot daggers at us, trying to penetrate us with the gravity of the situation.

"According to Fiorentina, he is a man of color. In all probability, a migrant . . ."

A breeze of worry feebly agitates the predominantly white audience. Our only Black man was Epifanio, but in his desperate desire for integration, he managed the double exploit of depigmenting himself and giving birth to two red-haired children, which makes his ethnicity difficult to categorize.

The wind rises—a fickle libeccio, with burning squalls that might carry me away—but I hold on to the sight of Fiorentina's nervous fingers drumming on the railing, her wrathful grimace, her expression a thousand miles from any kind of pleasure, so far from my own bucolic fantasies that I come back to my senses. My coreligionists, the people I have known forever and who pretty much raised me, are bustling around me, waving their hands to be invited to speak, all furious exclamations and indignant protests:

"No, really!"

"What a joke. Liberty House is not a hotel as far as I know."

"Nor a reception center for migrants!"

"You start like this and then we'll end up in the jungle, just like in Calais!"

At the mention of "jungle," which they appear to take literally, the members of my community fall into a trance. Their vociferations are such that no one can hear anyone else—except that I unfortunately hear enough to be enlightened:

"Yes, you start with just one migrant, then two, then three, then, boom, all of a sudden there are hundreds of them!"

"Thousands, you mean!"

"Men, usually! Young, dirty, uneducated!"

"In Cologne they raped heaps of women on New Year's Eve!"

I might be wrong, but I seem to be perceiving something like a disruption in the tone of the clamor, an imperceptible rise in the high frequencies—enough to wonder whether their indignation is unmitigated, whether there isn't something like an unmentionable desire to be violated themselves.

"It's obvious! They're in such a state of sexual frustration that they jump on anything that moves! You have to understand them too!"

"No, no, frustration, sexual deprivation, and all that, that's no excuse: we're not animals!"

"In any case, we must do whatever it takes so we don't get invaded!"

"We need to lock up Charlie's room!"

"And put a padlock on the cellar door!"

And why not barbed wire, electric fences, broken glass on top of our walls, moats full of stagnant water, machicolations from which we can pour boiling oil on the maniacs threatening to assault us? I sense Djilali shuddering beside me with bellicose ardor and chivalric daydreams, but he has the excuse of being ten years old and having quite a bit of medieval reading under his belt. The sudden virulence of all these pacifist adults is what is more difficult to explain and forgive. Luckily, Arcady is not like them: if I know him, he will open his arms wide to Angosom and offer him room and board until the end of time, especially since he cannot fail to be affected by such majestic beauty, and this will no doubt end in a threesome in my leafy hollow—a possibility that didn't really turn me on with Daniel, but which suddenly becomes very enticing. And who knows, maybe we could extend this generosity to other refugees who have been deprived of love for months or even years? I have the sudden and incredibly clear vision of bodies intermingling in the clear moonlight, young migrants and old residents, dark skin and wilted flesh, a sudden irrigation, the parched desert earth growing green again, the elixir of youth—enough to save our house from its impending and predictable fall. What's the point of preparing for the end of the world if we come to grief in the meantime? Arcady raises his arms to calm us all: the yapping ceases and Victor takes a step backwards, keenly aware that a sovereign voice will rise up to mock his pompous and mean-spirited words. Liberty House may not be designed to provide accommodation for refugees, but tolerance and love are written into our regulations, and Arcady is the first one to promote all kinds of humanitarian aid.

"My friends . . ."

His clear eyes scan our stormy ranks, with an imperceptible shiver when he looks into mine. Yes, my love, I am here, I am listening. You haven't stopped being the master of my soul just because I love someone else. Arcady clears his throat with a little nervous giggle that is not like him at all:

"My friends, all I ask is that you take a moment to think about what life is like for all these people, about everything they go through, before they get here."

Bravo. I raise an appreciative thumb to show him my unconditional support for his speech and prepare myself to let it flow into me like sweet honey.

"Try not to judge them too quickly or too harshly. Start by asking yourselves what you would do in their place, right . . .? Wouldn't you try, by any means possible, to leave a war-torn country, a city being constantly bombed, where you no longer have a house, a job, a future for you and your children?"

"Well, for Syrians, you can understand that, but Guineans? Eritreans? What are the Eritreans doing in our country anyway? Is there a war on in Eritrea?"

A unanimous grumble greets this outraged intervention from the abominable Salo. If I had a smartphone and connection, I'd waste no time in finding this out, but it seems to me that Eritrea has not been spared armed conflict—not to mention the fact that Isaias Afwerki's regime is one of the worst dictatorships on the African continent. What would Salo say if his precious freedoms of movement, expression, and thought were constrained—even though, in his case, thought is reduced to an unceasing transit of idle recriminations and anxious ruminations? Again, Daniel's eyes seek mine and we exchange grimaces of exasperation. Arcady doesn't even bother to give a geopolitical correction to Salo the Scumbag's rhetorical questions. He continues, looking off into the distance, as if gazing at a mental horizon that was more open than his congregation's:

"Syrians, Afghanis, Eritreans, Sudanese, who cares. What you have to understand is that these people are not here on vacation, on a whim. You yourselves, who are listening to me today, are at Liberty House only because you abandoned your previous lives, left your homes and your families. Because if you had stayed, the only thing you could hope for—whether in the short or long term—was death!"

Everyone around me is gravely nodding: they all like this idea, it flatters them—this dramatic image of themselves as doughty voyagers, as adventurers who *in extremis* found a lost ark where they could lay down their neuroses, their syndromes, their permanent handicaps, their inability to create life. Poor people! I wouldn't even dream of interrupting Arcady with these sarcastic reflections, which I formulate *in pectore*; on the contrary, I display my approval once more with a silent clap, my hands joined like a conch shell, a smile from ear to ear. I know my mentor's rhetorical ruses all too well, his ability to soften hearts, open minds, get the best from us all. I'm waiting for what comes next: the injunction to remove our blinkers and give a warm welcome to all migrants, starting with Angosom the Magnificent. But what comes next seems to be slow in getting out: Arcady is prevaricating, finding excuses for everyone, for asylum seekers as well as for those who refuse them, and after a quarter of an hour of acrobatic ratiocinations and circumlocutions, he ends up coming down in favor of protectionism and citizens' vigilance:

"OK, so we'll padlock what needs to be padlocked: the empty rooms, the cellar, the attic. As for you, keep your eyes open. And if you come across any intruders, ask them kindly but firmly to leave the premises. If you have to, threaten them with calling the police."

What? What did I just hear? While Daniel, across from me, is desperately rummaging through his recently bleached hair, I let myself be submerged by indescribable disgust, a disappointment so strong it might kill me. My legs start shaking, my heart is pounding, my stomach rises. It seems that up until right now I haven't understood anything about anything, haven't grasped the rule of the mob: a mob always tightens ranks around its own interests in the end, to face off the common enemy—an already downed enemy, if possible. It's worth noting that the members of Liberty House have nothing against refugees or the right to asylum and so on and so forth, but it's just not imaginable for that right to be exercised here and for them to be the turkeys in the international farce from which they have prudently removed themselves. That this farce is first and foremost a tragedy doesn't completely escape them, but they are not charitable enough to go so far as to take pity on the real victims. Feeling the audience preparing to disperse, I hastily raise my hand to ask to speak.

"Couldn't we actually open an accommodation center for refugees instead? I mean right here. We have enough room. All we'd have to do is fix up the attic a bit, put beds in there. And we wouldn't take thousands and thousands of them, right, just a dozen or so. Give them enough time to recuperate and get their life admin sorted out. And we could even help them, I dunno, to apply for asylum, or family reunification, or whatever. And after they leave we would get new ones, there'd be a turnover."

I blaze with enthusiasm as I speak, and more ideas just come to me:

"And most of them are young: they could work on the property or in the house, they could help Titin and Fiorentina, chop wood, fix the stone walls. . . . And then we could have another greenhouse, for Marqui's flowers. And enlarge the vegetable garden, open a dairy, make cheese: we've been talking about that for a while, it would be amazing, wouldn't it? We help them, they help us, everybody wins!"

All around me the adults are silent. They're probably thinking about my proposals and realizing what precious manna all these young people wandering in the valley are—not to mention that all that new blood would revive our degenerate and dangerously declining tribe. Cautious little coughs, noncommittal whispers, the first reactions are difficult to interpret. All eyes turn towards Arcady—and I imagine all the brains doing the same thing inside their craniums: whish, they all complete the minute heliotropic rotation which will align them with the chief's decisions. In the end, that's what they pay him for, to be dispensed from the need to think and make decisions for themselves, to be discharged of their preoccupations and their burdensome responsibilities. But while everyone is looking at Arcady, Arcady is looking only at me, with a slightly pained and imperceptibly lost expression. He finally takes up his speech from a moment ago, a mixture of platitudes about where charity begins, the limits of hospitality, the danger to our community of uncontrollable foreigners, the delicate financial balance to be found between paying and nonpaying guests, but the more he talks the more it becomes clear to me how wrong I was—about him and, therefore, about everything

"You see, Farah, I share your feelings, right, don't go thinking that. . . . Those poor people, my heart bleeds. . . . They come from so far away, they cross the desert, the sea, at the peril of their lives, so, yes, OK, that affects me, of course it does. Especially since they are looking for a better world, right, just like us in fact. And so we see them everywhere, walking in flip-flops along the side of the road. . . . Of course, it's pitiful. And the situation is absurd, I grant you that, we send them back, they stay blocked at Ventimiglia. Or they get sent back, I dunno, to Genoa, or Bari . . . when of course . . . but then, you're young, and so obviously you think we have all this space here, these empty rooms, all the creature comforts, whereas they have nothing, they sleep outside, wherever they can . . . but you know, it's not that simple, right, you should always beware of simple solutions. And it's not our role to remedy the shortfall in the state's provisions . . . The solution for migrants first has to be political, right? There's not much we can do at our level, is there . . . ?"

He probably expects me to approve his pathetic little sermon, but the time for approval is over. I have statistics to counter all his "right, you know, dunno, but then," all those hesitant and doubtful statements: 7,495—that's the number of people who died on the path of exile, just last year, which makes a daily total of 20.5. And I'm talking only about the duly registered deaths, not those that go just as unnoticed as the lives they brought to an end. And don't try telling me that France or Italy are the end of the journey or the end of danger: they die even in our valley of delights, even though most of the time no one hears about it or could care less. I'm blazing again, but this time, it's from thinking about all those Black deaths that don't matter to anyone, from talking about all those endings to lives that were only beginning, those lives that were just as unique as anybody else's—and no doubt much more worthy of being lived than those of the members of my community, these abulic, fragile people, who are just biding their time here waiting for death. Suddenly, looking at the impassive face of Victor, Jewell, and Kinbote, I feel an urge for eugenics: what use is life if you don't do anything with it? Why don't they give it to those who know how to make something of it—and if they don't give it, let's take it from them: does anyone ask permission from brain-dead comatose patients before stealing their useless organs?

Arcady's eyes are no longer looking for mine—they lose focus, go all hazy or fix my lips, as if he was trying to read a hidden message there, one less virulent than the accusations they are now proffering. He's not used to being opposed in the bosom of what must be called his little sect—and even less used to that opposition coming from me, his most enamored and zealous disciple. When I triumphantly cross my arms to finish my diatribe, he looks up to the heavens, in a pantomime of what could be either a sign of irritation or the expectation of inspiration, a little nudge from the divine, something to bat down my impudent prattle.

"Now Farah, you're not telling us anything we didn't already know about the real tragedy of the migration crisis. Yes, of course, people die every day, drowned at sea, suffocated in trucks, or whatever. But just for your information . . ."

He pauses, checks that we are all hanging on to his next words, then waves a sententious and vengeful index finger in my direction:

"You should know that malaria killed 1,175.3 people per day in the same period! Yes, my little Farah, before getting up on your high horse, before accusing everyone of selfishness and insensitivity, give that some thought and put those deplorable and derisory deaths into context, for a female anopheles causes much more devastation than a Libyan embarkation or an Austrian refrigerated truck." He speaks with an engaging and emotional voice, his usual voice—and usually that voice makes me lose my mind, but this time I keep hold of it, it's all mine and capable of cold reasoning and lucid judgment.

Seized with horror, I take the three unsteady steps that separate me from my host family, my brothers and sisters in religion, this religion that I mistakenly took to be good news, an outpouring of love, a message of peace and tolerance. Up until now I hadn't understood that love and tolerance were only for bipolar and electromagnetic-hypersensitive white people: I thought our hearts were big enough to love everyone. Nope. Migrants can cross the Sinai and get tortured there, be turned into slaves, drown in the Mediterranean, die of cold in a reactor, get hit by a train, get swallowed up in the tumultuous waters of the Roya: the members of Liberty House will not raise a pinky to save them. They keep their solicitude for rabbits, cows, chickens, and minks. Meat is murder, but sixty-six Syrians can pile into a refrigerated truck and die there, and I have no idea which crime and which carcasses they will find more scandalous. Or actually, no, I do know, I know all too well how their emotions work, their shallow sentimentalism about our friends the animals, and their pragmatic cruelty towards our migrant brothers. They no longer eat meat and are afraid of the jungle, but they tolerate its law being practiced even within their sensitive little hearts.

On our terrace of blond stones and ironwork railings, the members disperse with clear consciences and the feeling of having done their duty. They will go back to their rooms or go about their business until another strike of the gong calls them to dinner. Fiorentina has made vegetable terrines and caciocavallo cannelloni: they will conscientiously stuff themselves before leaving the table, without the slightest remorse or the shadow of a thought for those people whose fate they have sealed once and for all. As for me, I'm going to skip tonight's dinner: it's out of the question for me to pig out in the company of all these traitors, all these deserters from the great idea of love. Because it was actually in that idea that I was raised, that gospel that I naively believed in. I was wrong, and I probably endured ten years' worth of inspired sermons and preaching for nothing. For what's the use of passionately extolling boundless altruism, flaming desire, infinite loving-kindness, goodness, and forgiveness, when you balk at the first obstacle, the first asylum seeker, the first penniless Black migrant?

Daniel comes to find me in the straight lines of the vegetable garden beds, where my father makes his own personal version of love and order reign. This place always calmed me down: I would crouch between the cabbages gone to seed and the parasols of the fennel plants, I would let the green smell of the tomato plants rise up to me, I would crumble the rich earth, I would think about my father, that simple heart—and mine would return to a normal rhythm after my mad dashes through the pine woods and my no less mad and equally agitating daydreams. But it looks like I've grown up, here, today, all of a sudden, because the vegetables have lost their soothing properties.

"What are we going to do?"

"We need to warn Angosom. He needs to be super careful! And not show up here again!"

"Oh, yeah? And how are we going to warn him? Do you know where he is?"

"We can catch him tonight, when he comes to have a swim."

All I can do is hope that the evening will find him again at the watering hole. Beside me, Daniel sighs like a soul in torment, in unison with my own intimate anguish and worried questions: how can we save Angosom? For I can see that the members of my community are waiting only for the signal to start the hunt—where does this sudden love for blood, the chase, the pack, the kill come from? Which lever was secretly pulled for them to forswear their placid kindness? *Omnia vincit amor*, my ass, it's exactly the opposite. . . . Love is weak, easily overcome, as quick to be extinguished as it is to be born. Hatred, on the other hand, prospers from nothing and never dies. It's like a cockroach or a jellyfish: take away its light, it doesn't care; deprive it of oxygen, it'll siphon off someone else's; chop it up, and a hundred different hatreds will be born from a single one of its pieces.

27.

What's the Point of Love?

Here we are again, staking out next to the pond, watching for Angosom's appearance, that moment when he will emerge from the faint line of the ash and willow trees, first similar to them, then his flesh detaching itself from theirs, advancing towards the pond glazed by the moonlight, to see his shadowy swanlike beauty reflected there. And it happens just like that, at least there's no disappointment there, he arrives with little steps and undresses in the same movement, intermittently sending us his warm, musky, male fragrance. Just to check whether I still smell like a girl at all, I discreetly poke my nose under my armpit: but there too my glands are definitely sowing more trouble and emitting perturbing signals. One is never betrayed so badly as by oneself—by oneself in general, and by one's body in particular.

On the edge of the pond, Angosom turns his back to us.

Is the moon fuller and brighter than the previous night? Are we closer? More attentive? More concerned not to miss anything of the spectacle we are seeing for the last time? In any case what jumps out at us tonight is the crisscross pattern of swollen scars on his back and shoulder blades. I hold back a hiccup of astonishment as my eyes seek Daniel's and we commune in the same horror and pity. My hands immediately want to escape me, to go press their smooth palms against that trellis of painful keloids, to infuse them with the antidote of my boundless desire and goodwill. My feet want to walk, to go meet his feet, whose light soles flash for a moment in the moonlight before he plunges into our water feature. My mouth would have liked to be involved too, and to meet his mouth between the mastic trees and water lilies. Too late, too bad, and anyway, he's coming to the surface again, his eyelids closed, his body dripping—an immaculate naiad, an odalisque with no painter to immortalize his perfection. As we leave the softly clicking reeds and advance towards him, he opens his eyes and offers us the wonderful and terrible spectacle of his smile, his dazzling teeth, the trust and gratitude in his eyes, everything that we are about to trample and destroy in a few seconds. Daniel is the one to take this on, in his bad English:

"You must go, Angosom, far away. People here no want you. If they see you, they call police."

At that last word, the wonderful smile flies away forever. Without asking for anything more, Angosom finds his sports bag hidden between some shrubs, pulls on a pair of threadbare gray underpants, jeans, a T-shirt. He doesn't even look at us anymore, he's elsewhere, concentrating on his fugitive's moves, tying his laces, checking the contents of his bag, moving away, already, into the cover of the trees, his hair still soaked and dripping all over the Barça T-shirt he always wears, a poignant image of an unimaginable, and no doubt unbearable, loneliness.

He's gone. We just had the time to go from fear to love, from the most shameful prejudices to the most devouring desire, before he is out of our lives, leaving us with all the contempt that our community of thoughtless and selfish adults now inspires in us. I didn't expect much from Victor, Palmyre, or Salo, but Arcady? How will I be able to continue loving Arcady after this disappointment, this betrayal of all our principles, this pollution that is so much worse than any of those we were escaping from, since it is poisoning my young mind?

Without conferring, Daniel and I take the path to the forest. It's not so much about following Angosom as getting out of sight of the pond, the gardens, and especially the house—that forbidden house of pleasure accepting no more clients. Our autarchic kingdom can handle a little cruelty between its walls very well—and can handle the reign of barbarity and servitude in the neighboring states even better. Arcady's herbivore speeches can no longer deceive me and hide the true nature of my home: a hunting lodge where only the stag's antlers are missing on the façade. Our freedom starts where everyone else's stops dead, at our awnings, our turrets, our blue slate roofs, our drystone walls, our *hortus conclusus*, our private Garden of Eden. Our freedom is forbidden to vagrants, reserved for people who have absolutely no idea what to do with it and abdicated from it to come live under Arcady's shepherd's crook—Arcady, that unconscious dictator, that cruel king of hearts, who is even crueler for being unaware of his own cruelty:

"Off with his head!"

Nobody has pronounced that sentence, but it is floating in the air, ever since Arcady decreed that there was no room at our place for people who are not like us. Off with their heads, all those travelers without luggage: that'll teach them to show up with empty hands. Off with their heads, and get it over with quickly: that will save them from months of aimless roaming and additional torture. Off with their heads, because, really, they're a stain on the landscape, they stand out, they mar the beauty of this wonderland. At Liberty House, you have the right to be old, ugly, sick, drugged, asocial, or unproductive, but apparently not young, poor, and Black.

As we push forward into the forest, it closes in around us, as if it was waiting only for our passage to squeeze its squamous trunks together and exhale its balsamic breath. As we pass, short squawks and coos sound here and there in the foliage, up in the vaults of the larch boughs weaving gothic arches between us and the sky. At any other time, we would probably have been moved and happy at the sight of so much beauty, but what's the use of beauty? What good are enchanted forests, valleys of delights, nirvana in a bubble, heaven on earth, under high surveillance? The overwhelming heat doesn't fade as the night progresses. Seated between the mossy roots of a large oak, we exchange disappointed comments and plans:

"Let's just get the fuck outa here."

"You want us to leave?"

"Yeah, I just can't stand what's going on anymore."

"Yeah, totally, me neither."

"I mean, like, what's the deal here? Are they for real with their padlocks, and the cops, and all that?"

"I'm sure it's Victor. Arcady would never have come up with the idea of calling the police on his own."

"You're just saying that coz he's your guy."

Daniel is quite right: I'm not quite ready to admit that

I've been in love with an impostor forever, and that I've been fucking him for months. He's right, but instead of ranting on about this, I draw him onto the terrain of practical decisions:

"But where will we go, if we leave?"

The idea crosses my mind to do what Angosom and his brothers do, to wander along the roadsides with my bagful of rags, sleep in camps, jump on trains. . . . Except that the border police wouldn't waste any time busting me, with my unusual looks, my mahogany cheeks, my thick black hair, and all the contradictory messages my body sends. Daniel's plan is not as half-assed as mine: he'll go to Palma de Mallorca, where Richard promised to find him a job.

"Oh, yeah? But you're not even eighteen!"

"No worries. Richard said I could work under the table for him until I'm legal."

He gives me an underhand look, something between satisfaction and worry about my reaction:

"I, um, had a bit of a thing with Richard, last winter . . ."

"What? But Richard's straight!"

"Well, maybe he's not so straight after all."

Although I grew up in a libertarian confraternity, I still noticed that despite their vehement assertions, my brothers and sisters of the free spirit were oriented towards one gender or the other since childhood. Apart from Arcady, of course: but Arcady, as disappointing as he is, remains that erotic prodigy, that fountain-man generously dispensing his seed—but also his time, his energy, his attention, his desire, his pleasure. I am only sixteen years old and at the start of my sexual life, but I already know that I will meet few partners as gifted as he is at physical love. Daniel, who also got a taste of Arcady's indefatigable cock, once told me:

"Arcady missed his vocation: he should have been a hardcore porn star. I've never seen anything like it: for fuck's sake, he's always hard, he always wants it, everything turns him on! Even shit!"

"What?"

"Shit! What I mean is, even in shitty situations, he can still get it up. And I know what I'm talking about, since we've been in a couple of shitty situations, the two of us."

"Like what?"

"Like, four in the morning, everyone wasted, Dadah needing to empty her ileo-anal pouch, and Victor having a full paranoid attack. You have no idea . . ."

Despite our fundamentalist vegetarianism and our detox regulations, we gave alcohol consumption a protected status: at Liberty House, everyone drinks, except for Fiorentina, who must have an extra chromosome, or a missing enzyme, or some kind of gene that allows her to navigate serenely among winos without being tempted herself. It just goes to show our personal development has not yet reached the optimal level. That said, Arcady doesn't drink much. And even when he does drink, he doesn't fall into any of the variously annoying patterns of most drinkers: ecumenical love, waves of paranoia, bitter aggressiveness, self-pity, and so forth. He stays deliciously himself and perfectly serene. But I don't want to reconcile myself with my impression of Arcady: it's all very well his being a good lover and able to hold his liquor, he still needs to act in keeping with his own teachings.

Daniel cuddles up to me and we spend the hours until daylight sleeping fitfully and talking dreamily of our future far from here. Which goes to show that growing up on a radiant hillside, almost without assigned parents, with the only instruction being to love and take pleasure where you find it, doesn't stop anyone from becoming a tortured adolescent or an escape artist.

28.

The Long Goodbye

At dawn, without conferring, we set out hand in hand for a tour of the property, a final inspection before our escape. We leave the forest by its northernmost edge and find ourselves in the meadows, facing the cows who are heavily stamping their hooves in our direction, as if to bid us farewell. They recognize me now? After all those years turning their backs on me, or even crowding at the opposite edge of the paddock, horrified even by my presence? Now that it is too late to make friends, here they are pressing up against the fence, offering us their pink muzzles, and snorting as a sign of goodwill as we pass. Idiots. . . .

Leaving the pastures behind us, we take the pathway around the boundary of the property, between collapsed low walls, shrines decorated with flowers by unknown hands, silvery trunks, hillocks, and hollows carpeted with long grass. We soon come to my green hideaway, still tender and engaging, still boasting its fringed canopy, whose pink color is a little faded after a whole summer of loving. Daniel gives me a good pinch on my cheek:

"Arcady really hizzit the skizzins with you, didn't he?"

"Try talking to me in a real language if you want me to understand what you're saying."

"He really screwed you good in your little hidey-hole, didn't he?"

"Why are you asking, if you know anyway?"

"I had sex here too, by the way."

"You asshole, this is my hideout! I never gave you permission . . ."

"It was with a guy from school too."

"No way! How could you?"

"Like I would give a shit!"

At the same time, the idea is one I don't completely hate: why shouldn't everyone get their rocks off on my grassy canopied bed? In any case, I have nothing to worry about, no one will have had as much pleasure as I had under my first love's passionate tongue.

The pale mass of Liberty House soon comes into view between the pines, and we pause for a moment to admire its majesty and harmonious proportions. Rosy daylight is vibrating on the horizon, hastening to spread its shimmering veils over the afflicted countryside, just as we sneak into the monumental entrance hall. Nobody there. Just as well. I drag Daniel into the library, where the stained-glass rose windows, the Savonnerie carpets, the rich leather of the bindings, and the worn velvet of the armchairs all rend sighs of anticipated regret from me. We then climb the main staircase, with its polished marble steps and softly worn handrail. As usual, I have an LGBTQ flash as my hand strokes the polished wood. It gives me an idea, in fact. But before I can think it over, I content myself with registering my usual visions of girls straddling their dark oak mount, their firm thighs, the white cotton of their underwear, their escutcheoned blazers, their braids thrown back over their shoulders, and their laughter fading into the stairwell.

Once I get to my room, I gather up my stuff, mostly books and a few things I can wear without looking like a scarecrow: I leave my grandmother's hand-me-downs on their hangers—the jackets with epaulets, the fringed tops, the ponchos, and the devoré-velvet harem pants. And since I don't have any photographs of my parents, I slip the ones of Farrah Fawcett and Sylvester Stallone into my wallet. With my bent index finger, I send a little coded message of adieu to the Turkish child in my funerary jar: goodbye, my friend, I loved you well, but you would be a burden on my road to freedom.

Daniel gets there very quickly, with his own bundles: a whole bunch of bags stuffed to bursting. He has an expression I've never seen on his face before, a look of happy impatience. Maybe I never realized how hard it was for him to grow up in the House of Pleasure. One of our foundational anecdotes is that Arcady and Victor had long arguments about what name to give their self-managed utopia—Arcady obviously pitching for Paul Gauguin's expression, whereas Victor strove for the triumph of the Hugolian agenda.

I close the door of my room with infinite care, so as not to wake Fiorentina. Seeing her show up in her quilted dressing gown is the last thing I need. And Fiorentina is always the first one up, insensitive as she is to the Dionysian injunction. Take pleasure where you find it? For her, not so much. Daniel pulls me away, down the stairs four at a time.

"Let's take a selfie. Before we go. Which is your favorite room in the house?"

"The kitchen."

"Me too. Come on."

Here we are in our beloved sorceress's lair, bewitched by the same delicious apprehension, the frisson our audacity inspires in us: being here in her absence and without her permission. I breathe in the inimitable scent of the place one last time: basil has come to impregnate the walls, having been stripped and chopped for days on end, but is layered with aniseed from Buccellato, the green smell of the last tomatoes, and the insistent aroma of Menton lemons.

Daniel is brandishing his Samsung, so I strike a pose by his side, and my forced smile ricochets off the copper pots and pans, polished by the mistress of the place.

"What are you going to do with it?"

"Nothing. It's just a memento: I'll look at it whenever I miss you. And take a note of my number, it might come in handy. You'll have to get a cell phone sooner or later anyway."

We finish our farewell tour with the outbuildings and kitchen gardens, the chicken coop, the potager, the greenhouses, with a pause to smoke a joint in my father's *hortus conclusus*. The day takes this opportunity to rise, and Fiorentina to make her first morning appearance. Already dressed from head to foot, she sits down on a little wooden bench set against the wall and exposed to the first rays of the sun. She is soon joined by a hobbling figure, which slumps down beside her with a sigh of relief: it's Titin—about whom I realize I haven't said a thing, even though he is an integral part of the life I am just about to leave behind. Once a farm laborer, Augustin Pesce is part of the furniture here, even though he tends to be an outdoor man.

At eighty-something, he spends most of his time chopping wood, trimming hedges, cleaning the water features, harvesting walnuts with a pole, or picking mushrooms and blueberries. Before Liberty House adopted a meat-free regime, he used to poach quite a bit, and I wouldn't swear he completely stopped laying traps, but if any offenses are ever committed, those two oldies will carry the secret of their medianoches to the grave— *vitello tonnato*, *fritto misto*, or *carne cruda* gulped down in the secret of the kitchen and the polished luster of the moon on the copper basins and glass preserving jars.

Every morning, rain or shine, Titin and Fiorentina have coffee on the bench, while exchanging passionate whispers. Nothing ever filters out from this ardent conversation, which continues day after day, so we are reduced to mere conjectures. Titin communicates only with Fiorentina anyway: half-blind and completely deaf, he puts his cupped hand to his ear as soon as anyone tries to talk to him, as a way of showing that it's no use. As a result, he leads a quiet life, indifferent to any instructions, advice, or remarks. And since he does the work of four people, Arcady and Victor leave him in heavenly peace. Farewell, Titin, I will now never solve the mystery of your little bucolic existence. But maybe there was no secret? Or maybe that is the secret: not to have one. I hang on to this idea to explore it later, this possibility of a life with no dark hidden corners it would be fearful to expose.

Moving under the cover of the lavender bushes and exuberant masses of asters, we reach the main path without being spotted by Metallica's implacable eye. In front of the heraldic symbol with which Victor saw fit to decorate the main gates, we pause for a rather emotional moment, which is soon interrupted by the noise of footsteps rushing up behind us. It's

Arcady. Contrary to Fiorentina, who is impeccably dressed no matter what the hour, he has just pulled on an old shirt from some bygone era, under which the familiar protuberance of his genitalia can be seen. He stands there, in front of us, one hand on his ribs to catch his breath from his headlong sprint—or from sadness. For he scans the scene with a tragic eye, as if he had immediately perceived its definitive and irreversible nature:

"You're leaving? Just like that? Without saying goodbye?"

We both protest together, but with no hope of convincing him:

"Well, we didn't want to disturb everyone. And it's not forever, is it . . . ?"

"Yeah, we're just . . . going for a wander."

Suddenly hard, his eyes seek out mine, those eyes that always looked at me with so much love and confidence, those eyes that so often saw me swoon with pleasure, no later than the day before yesterday, in fact—but the day before yesterday is farther away than India or China, the day before yesterday is a green paradise ransacked by betrayal.

"Don't talk nonsense to me, Farah. Not you. And not to me."

Excluding Daniel from this exchange, brutally locking me and himself up in the uncommunicable memory of our relationship, is probably a good way to cut me off at the knees, to stop me in my tracks and enforce the law and order of love. I spent all summer loving Arcady, running as fast as my legs could carry me to the makeshift canopy; all summer discovering my body and his, in the endless languor of pleasures and days. I say *summer* to make it simple, but, in fact, my love for Arcady goes back to the beginning of my sentient life, which I always organized around him: as far back as I can remember,

I have always blindly venerated and desperately desired him. I have just lived through the best weeks of my young existence, but also the miraculous fulfillment of my maddest wishes. And now here he is before me, telling me with his eyes not to leave him, throwing the considerable weight of those years of adoration and a whole season of erotic frenzy—my season of pleasure—into the balance. Under the gusts of the libeccio, the flaps of his shirt are beating against his powerful thighs, and just imagining the grip of those thighs, as they locked me in a vise around my waist so many times, I feel my resolve weakening, my hand gripping the gate rather than slamming it behind us. But only desire is there: trust, respect, and admiration have disappeared. I'm even pretty close to pitying Arcady, because I am about to plunge into the whirlwind of life whereas he will stay stuck here, preaching his inapplicable gospel to a motley bunch of melancholic, sick, impotent old fogies and social misfits.

"Farah..."

He always pronounced my name in an incredibly sexy way, but for the first time, the magic isn't working. I remain cold to those two syllables, as they fall from his fleshy lips, a little purplish in the harsh morning light and so much less seductive since I saw them declare a state of siege, instead of uttering the welcoming words I expected. The memory of Angosom being summarily expelled from our artificial paradise sweeps away my last hesitation and vague hopes of compassion: if I must feel compassion, it might as well be for the truly needy, and not for charismatic fifty-somethings who profess universal love only to be able to fuck fresh young things.

From the vibrations of the gate in my hand, I realize how tense I am in this moment of cruel truth. What I am feeling, right here, right now, faced with this man, who is also my spiritual director, my mentor, and my first love, is that I am actually sixteen years old. I may be physically strange and impossible to assign to any kind of gender, but I'm still completely normal psychologically, and the natural order of things is for me to leave my host family and valetudinarian confraternity and go out into the world. I don't even need to look at Daniel to know that he is shaking with the same rage to get it over and done with. Our youth, our energy, is too much for Liberty House and its inhabitants. If we stay, we leave them with no other choice but to devour us, and I have no doubt that they will do it their way: more slow suction and silent manducation than honest bites. It's us or them, that's what I tell myself so I don't feel like crying, but I cry anyway, because love never dies.

29.

Far from Heaven

If it wasn't for Maureen, my reintegration would be problematic: although the children of Liberty House go to school on the outside, they still don't know the basics they need to be completely at home here. Luckily she is here to give me the keys to a world subject to unimaginable laws and to facilitate my first steps outside my space station. That exit was something I had to negotiate: it was all very well to leave with my backpack and slam the gate, but I'm not yet old enough to make a living. If I don't want to freeload off my little lover, I need to get a subsidy from my confraternity, and it must be said to their credit that they didn't haggle about either my liberty or their logistical support. All it took was a phone call, made from my brand-new smartphone. Thanks to Nelly, I will be the recipient of a generous monthly allowance, about which Maureen is both flabbergasted and suspicious. In her view, everything has to be earned or paid for and I would do well to ask myself about the real motivations behind this munificence.

How can I explain to her that I've already paid for it? For years and years, all those old people warmed themselves at my vitality and innocence; for years and years, they were paid in kind and will now always be in my debt. With me gone, they will continue to take their tithe of young flesh from Dolores, Teresa, and Djilali, or from any other child joining the community. That's the way it goes at Liberty House—and I'm not at all certain that the outside world works any differently. In the meantime, here I am, and every day wallops me with another load of overstimulating discoveries—for overstimulation is the climate in which I'm evolving at the moment, far from the four peaceful seasons that set the rhythm of my former life. One of my other discoveries is realizing how badly prepared I am for this erotic effervescence and permanent tension. I was raised with the idea that love was the most important thing in life, but I was never told about seduction. At Liberty House, there is no need for strategies or preliminary maneuvers to find a partner: by joining the community, all the members commit to having sex with each other. It's out of the question that anyone should stay on the sidelines because of infirmity or senility. Arcady keeps an eye out for this: if he has to, he offers himself up so that everybody gets their fill of sexual pleasure, or at least of carnal exchange: in the House of Pleasure, taking pleasure is not compulsory, but contact, caresses, and goodwill are. And so, my coreligionists make absolutely no efforts to please. With the innocence of macaque monkeys, they do nothing more than exhibit their genitals, and, presto, the trick is done! No, I'm going too far. On the one hand, some of them do take care to remain desirable, and on the other hand it's actually harder than it looks. Dadah, who has not become less libidinous with age, often takes the opportunity of our weekly assemblies to complain that her advances have been rejected. Our house rules do not include sanctions, but a unanimous censure falls on the unhappy offender. After all, she's not asking for much, especially since Dadah is one of the few residents who maintain a certain level of sartorial elegance—for which she considers herself very poorly rewarded. But then, for Dadah, who does her hair and makeup, wears a different dress every day, and douses herself with musk, we also get Palmyre with her sweatpants, Jewell with her scruffy polar fleeces, Titin's cargo pants, and the careless nudity of Salo, Vadim, or Orlando, who mince about in their mules or their espadrilles, sparing us nothing of their flaccid physiques.

All this to say that the nameless town, with its shopping streets, its packed sidewalk cafés, and its crowded beaches, offers so many possibilities of enticing outfits, seductive smiles, clinking jewels, varnished mouths, tight skins, and bodies exposed to the eyes and offered to desire. The first days, I come home punch-drunk and shattered, and can do nothing more than collapse on Maureen's fold-out couch, even though she offered me her bed, her arms, and her heart. I won't say no, but first I have to get over the shock and calm the tempest in my skull: all these solicitations are too much for me, my brain is overloaded, my neuronal connections can't keep up, and my pussy is throbbing more than is entirely reasonable.

High school starts again, but I couldn't care less about it because life is elsewhere, the *vita nuova* I was wishing for without even imagining how much it would fulfill those wishes. I go to class, hand in the homework I'm asked to do, and just about get by under the radar. In any case, I quickly discouraged any curiosity and rebuffed anyone asking whether I was a girl or a boy. I don't know what I am, but I don't intend to make it a topic of conversation.

With my reconditioned iPhone, I send Daniel my first text message, to which he answers with a laughing selfie with the Mallorca sea and sunshine in the background. But there's plenty of sunshine here anyway and I never go to the beach: I have too much to do, and I keep my diving sessions for the world of the night. For if there is a space-time in which my intersexuality raises no questions or reserve, it sure is that one. My evenings in clubs with Daniel had given me only a weak foretaste of it, and I must say that Maureen is a better-equipped and much more informed guide to introduce me to the heat of the night than poor Nello. But he seems to be having just as amazing experiences in Mallorca as I am here, if I'm to judge from the obscene snaps he sends me at dawn, when both of us are going home from our queer nights out. I miss him and I can't wait to see him again, but I have no more time for regrets than I do for the beach and other diurnal distractions. The night keeps me busy, even during the daytime—which I spend getting over my excesses or daydreaming about my encounters at Panic Attack or L'Arbor.

I don't have sex with anyone, but in fact, I don't really need to: drinking, smoking, dancing, getting groped in the crowd of bodies, a face-suck now and then, that's enough to keep me happy and to humor Maureen, who has clearly positioned herself as my official lover and is biding her time until the miraculous spark, the lightbulb moment that will make me open my eyes to her. In fact, my eyes are already wide open: Maureen is generous, honest, curious, keen, and ten times prettier than I will ever be; she inspires me with gratitude, respect, affection, and desire, but the sum of all those sentiments will never be called love.

Love was running through the dew to meet Arcady, it was having his name on my lips when I woke and when I fell asleep at night; it was giving him the starring role not just in all my erotic scenarios but also in all the moments of a life that I could not even imagine without him. Love was the unexpected apparitions of Angosom, the painful desire to melt into his perfect body—or at least to be a watermelon so that he could penetrate its juicy innards, a peach pit so he could spit it out. Just as I can recognize love when I see it, I can accept its inexplicable absence. I would love to love Maureen, but neither she nor I know the alchemy that transforms sluggish tenderness into incandescent gold.

"Don't you find me attractive?"

"Of course I do."

"Do you think I'm too fat?"

"Stop it, you're gorgeous: don't go fishing for compliments."

"Is it because I'm a woman?"

"For fuck's sake, we've talked about this a hundred times, you're such a pain."

"You're straight, is that it?"

"Stop it, OK? How can I be straight? To be straight, you basically have to be something. And I'm nothing."

"You're not nothing. No one is nothing. You're totally a guy, or you're totally a woman, or you're a trans guy, or you're a trans woman."

At this stage of the conversation, I let her lose herself in sterile reflection and idle distinctions—or I shut her up by forcefully kissing her. I may be nothing and no longer love anyone, but my arousal threshold remains very low. Seeing her standing there before me with her blond and pink locks, her plump cheeks, and her wrestler's shoulders, I feel myself melt, and really want her, want to brutally undress her, to bury my nose, my mouth, in the gelatinous mass of her stomach, want to hold her by the hips and make her big white breasts jiggle, want to thrust my hard fist inside her. She would so love to be hard herself, but she is all elastic curves and irritable flesh. It's even comical, that contrast between Maureen's pretensions to strength, her affectation of brutality, and that smooth body that is all pallor, softness, and roundness, that body she hates and says she is ready to hack up:

"Well, not anymore, right, but when I was, like, fourteen or fifteen, and it all happened, you know, boobs, belly, like, when it all settled—because at the start I hoped that it would go away if I ate less and got more exercise—so like, when I finally understood that this was my body, I swear I wanted to go under the knife, to cut slices out of it! Look at this!"

With both hands, she grabs the wobbly flab surrounding her navel and flowing lazily over her hips before going up to her back in a adipose flap, a thousand miles from my own anatomy—and that's probably another comic contrast offered by our two bodies jumbled together on the fold-out, the dry slenderness of my thighs, my ephebe's chest, my tanned hands on the mauve efflorescence of her nipples. As it turns out, Maureen's body betrayed her just as ignominiously as mine did me, and puberty played the same trick on her as it did on me, transforming her into a little fatty with big boobs while it turned me into an androgynous creature. All I can do is inculcate her with one of the rare chapters of Arcady's teachings that I didn't throw in the garbage along with his anti-speciesist claptrap and his dime-store libertine gospel:

"All bodies are part of nature, Mor."

Just repeating my mentor's motto, I feel myself weakening. I hear the familiar inflections of his voice, I see myself lounging by his side, inhaling the smell of bark, crushed grass, our mixed juices, his sweat, his seminal liquor, the heady amber of his cologne, the fresh yeast of my wetness—all that happiness from before the Fall. As I try to tell my little lover that desire never waits for perfection in a body and never depends on beauty in a face, I sink into melancholia, but to back up my words with deeds, I end up fucking her. Fucking always made my morale rise like a rocket. It doesn't stop melancholia, but it does relegate memories to the background—and regrets too. And anyway, what is there to regret? The Garden of Eden? I grew up there and was as happy as could be, but the time for innocence is well and truly over, so I might as well get used to the city, the crowds, electromagnetic pollution, phthalates, McDonald's, fine particles, music playing all the time, images everywhere, networked living, permanent connectivity, ambient overstimulation, and Maureen's possessive love. For the change in regime is radical there too: Arcady loved me without wanting to own me, and I never dared to admit that I wished he might. Then Angosom arrived, turning everything I thought I knew upside down, sweeping away my imagined constancy and pretensions to fidelity, sweeping away all the rest as well, pulverizing my castle in the air and the deceitful shimmering of its cupolas. He was my exterminating angel, but far from holding it against him, I can't stop looking for him on the roads in the valley or on the streets of Ventimiglia when Mor and I go shopping there. All it takes is a profile, a brown face, the bounce of a cheekbone under fuliginous eyelashes, for my heart to skip a beat, but it is never him. And even if it was, I would have nothing to say and nothing to offer him except my goodwill and my desire to repair what never can be repaired: endemic poverty, conscription, torture, trafficking, shipwrecks, endless roaming, expulsion from paradise, lifelong banishment, just two steps away from our plethoric El Dorados. There's no point trying to explain this to Maureen, all she can see is a threat hovering over our love. The only time I told her about Angosom's archangelic apparitions, she pelted me with questions:

"So who is this guy? Do you like him? How do you like him? Do you wanna do him? You see, you are straight!"

"Mor, you're a pain in the ass, you know, a real pain in the ass!"

"For fuck's sake, you're the one who's a pain in the ass! We can't go anywhere without you staring at everything on two legs! You think I don't see what's going down? Can't you just calm your cooch?"

With Maureen, conversations can very quickly get out of hand or reach summits of explosive and vulgar fury. Is she unwell? That's the question I cautiously asked her after three months living together, her tempestuous moods being so inexplicable to me otherwise, except by an overactive thyroid or a brain tumor. I've lived most of my life among placid adults, who avoided conflict and loved nothing more than easy consensus, and so this bull-like irascibility and these attacks of jealousy were hard to come to terms with. But no, in fact, she is not unwell and has never even imagined a relationship to be anything but passionate disagreements, fights, and reconciliations. Are we in a relationship? That's the other question I ask myself, but take care not to express out loud, for fear of setting off another Egyptian drama. I keep all my doubts to myself and reserve my passion for the New World, for my discovery of all these unknown lands that are Instagram and Snapchat, Netflix and YouTube, Google Maps and Uber Eats. In this New World, Mor is my guide and my simultaneous interpreter: I would be showing rare ingratitude if I revealed the substance of my thoughts to her. And then, even though I don't love her in the way she expects me to, I do like living with her, because when she's not in a foul mood, she can be attentive, affectionate, energetic, and cheerful.

More than anything, I love sleeping with her—I always knew I would like sharing someone's bed. Knowing Arcady, it might seem strange that he didn't institute collective sleeping practices, but all our members had their own rooms, their little bastion of privacy in a house where privacy was reviled. Even the children. Snuggling next to Maureen at bedtime, waking up in the middle of the night with her warm breath on my neck or her heavy arm on my thigh, hearing her moan or breathe in the intimate darkness of her room, is overwhelming and feels like an incredible luxury to me. I have no explanation for this feeling, other than, perhaps, the memory of my first morning at Liberty House: the whitewashed alcove, the matrimonial bed, the starched sheets, the bodies of Marqui and Birdie, relaxed at last, and me in the middle, blissful, keenly aware of the sounds and the first light of dawn, the first birdsong, the first insects' buzzing. I say very little about my kingdom, for as little as I talk about it, Maureen still finds it upsetting. Our way of life scandalizes her, and she doesn't have strong enough words to vilify both the technological desert and the sexual promiscuity in which I grew up.

"What? You were having sex with that guy, who was, like, your guru? That's just gross!"

"I didn't have to, OK? I was the one who wanted it."

"Sure you did. They have brainwashing techniques in sects:

you thought you were consenting, but in fact you were just under his influence, you didn't have a choice."

I keep quiet. What's the use of explaining to her that I loved Arcady as you love only one person your whole life—in other words, absolutely and probably forever? For although I know he isn't the man I thought he was, I still love him and might die from missing him if I wasn't so busy. Except that Maureen isn't buying it: according to her, I'm far too nice about the members of my former community, all those pedophile pigs she encourages me to expose pronto in my own "Me Too" accusation.

"They abused you, Farah!"

"Who do you mean by 'they'?"

"Arcady, Victor, Kinbote, Richard, all those old guys you told me about! And your parents were an epic fail, for fuck's sake! They should have got the hell outa the cult when they saw that the guru had his eyes on you!"

"Stop calling it a 'cult,' it's not a cult! And Arcady waited for me to be over fifteen, remember? He was the one who didn't want to have sex earlier: I was ready! Even at thirteen, I was totally ready! It was actually me who was harassing him!"

"That doesn't change a thing! You thought of him as your spiritual father, you said! So it's totally, like, incest! It's disgusting!"

If, from the outside, my relationship with Arcady looks like the abuse of a minor by a person in a position of authority, I'm very sorry, and that will teach me not to talk about it with people who have no way of understanding it or even admitting it as a possibility. From now on, I'll keep the story of my unusual childhood in a confraternity of the free spirit to myself. I'm even going to think about that childhood as little as possible. I'm seventeen: adulthood is now.

30.
Here but I'm Gone

Before anything else, I had to get used to a different daily rhythm, a disconcerting temporality, an alternation of lifeless stretches and elusive instants. Nothing like my rich hours of idleness and contemplation under the unsettled skies, with only the trees and birds for company. Nothing like our communal rituals, the meals in the dining room, Arcady's sermons, exorcisms, great outpourings, or shamanic-trance sessions to purge sadness. My life outside the walls gives me few opportunities to be myself: rather, I have the impression of being a force-fed goose, an organism saturated with strong sensations, too many images and too much music—but that's just as well, since I love music more than anything. At Liberty House it was reserved for parties and forbidden to children. We had neither a radio nor a TV: there was only one archaic hi-fi system on which members of the confraternity could listen to their chosen pieces—Epifanio's salsa, Richard's techno, or Victor's arias. Before going clubbing with Daniel, I had danced only on special occasions: New Year's Eve, birthday parties. Now silence has deserted my existence and music is my constant companion. Thanks to Nelly's money, I've bought headphones and a subscription to Spotify. Daniel and I exchange playlists and ecstatic comments, both of us equally enthralled by this constant immersion in sound, which allows us to be alone in a crowd while being connected to something like a worldwide party, a galvanizing collective vibration. In some ways, I'm now closer to Daniel than when we lived under the same roof. A thousand miles apart, we are living through the same technological and sociological deflowering, we are reeling from the same sensory and communication overload with the same euphoria—although, of course, he was always a couple of lengths ahead of me with his smartphone and his addiction to George Michael. But anyway, deflowering doesn't take long: I'm very quickly up to date with what to listen to and what to watch.

Since Maureen goes to sleep with her laptop on her stomach, in the blinking blue light of her favorite series, I've even caught up on *Game of Thrones*, *Atypical*, *Riverdale*, *Vikings*, *Narcos*, and *Gomorrah*, first a little taken aback by the threshold of her tolerance for violence, then hanging on like her to the hypnotizing opening credits, the rising crenelated towers, the black dragons, and the archive images of Pablo Escobar. One night, while I'm sleeping off my rum and orange juice on her shoulder, I'm awoken by gurgles and groans, no doubt from someone being strangled and trying to catch their last breath. I open one eye onto a decomposing face, excavated eye sockets, rotting gums, matted hair.

"Yuck! What is that shit?"

"*The Walking Dead*, for fuck's sake, you're the only person in the world who wouldn't recognize it."

Yes, it's true, she's already tried a hundred times to get me hooked on her living corpses, her all-time favorite series—well, at least until season four, because afterwards, apparently, it just repeats itself, goes round in circles, and even she was sick of it and moved on to something else, like Neapolitan mafiosi or narcotics traffickers. It doesn't stop her from rewatching old episodes from time to time, for the pleasure of seeing her zombies again. Settling myself more comfortably against her, into her warm body and reassuring reality, I get ready to watch an abominable scene of evisceration: apparently, disguising oneself as a stinking carcass allows the living to go unnoticed among the vampires.

"Not vampires: the living dead!"

"Well, yeah, but aren't vampires also living dead?"

"Yeah, but it's not the same thing. If you want vampires, I'll show you *True Blood*. It's even a crypto-gay series. It's so cool."

"No, gimme a break! Don't you have a series where everyone is actually alive, healthy, not too cray-cray, and not delinquent either?"

"Well, there's me: actually alive, healthy, not too cray-cray, and totally not delinquent. Or is my normal not interesting?"

"Of course it is."

"Well, then, make the most of it! Here you are: I'm all yours!"

Just as I am about to melt onto her healthy cheeks, her quivering stomach, her wonderful smell of slightly tipsy girl, an image stops me in my tracks, one of dark bodies crowded against a barbed-wire fence.

"I didn't get the subtitles on the right setting."

I couldn't care less about the subtitles or the dialogue: what I see is a besieged citadel, a building defended by armed individuals, an autarchic way of life, with its plowed fields and blue-eyed children—while on the other side of the fence there are lost, haggard drifters in tatters; what I see is my previous existence, its organization and focus on self-preservation with no concern for other people's lives and the misery of the world—my lost members-only paradise. Blessed are the rich, for not only are they rich but they have the right to enjoy the enchanted kingdom before everyone else. Unhappy the others, the exiles, the refugees, the poor! I think about them, of course, but what's the use of thinking, when what we should be doing is opening the doors wide, breaking down the fences, raising the siege, sharing the harvest, handing over the fortress. How can I make Maureen understand that *The Walking Dead* is the story of my life, and that letting Angosom return to the cohort of zombies is something for which I will never forgive myself. She can tease me all she likes, ask me why I'm in a bad mood, shut down the laptop and turn to me, but I don't have the strength for love tonight: I have just enough left to keep quiet about the reason I'm upset and tell her I want to go to sleep, with no nightmares if possible, no corpses perambulating through the fields looking for shelter. Maureen turns her back on me with a little sign of contrition. There's no point wishing her a peaceful night: she sleeps like a log and says she never dreams. My morning accounts leave her stunned:

"So how come you have dreams every night?"

"Everybody has dreams every night, even you do: you just don't remember them."

"Well, that's the same thing as not having them. So how come you remember yours?"

Maybe dreaming is something you learn just like everything else. I grew up in a community where visions, phantasmagorias, and premonitions played a big role. The interpretation of dreams was part of my education, along with drawing, paper cutting, botany, and reading, all those nineteenth-century pastimes that are completely foreign to my little lover, and impress her as if they were superpowers. What Maureen calls her library is all of three cheap dog-eared paperbacks: *Bel-Ami*, *Candide*, and *The Game of Love and Chance*. She never managed to finish *Candide*, thinks that Georges Duroy is awesome because he got the best girl, and that there might have been chimpanzees in Marivaux's play, where I remember only a laborious game of deception. Her French teacher probably showed her a contemporary interpretation—or else she's confusing it with *Planet of the Apes*, which would not be the most glaring or surprising of her confusions, since she talks openly about Johnny Hallydepp or Barack Obahamas.

"Well, yeah, Johnny Hallydepp, ya know, the one who died!"

"Oh, wow, you just scared me, I thought you were talking about Johnny Hallydepp, the one who was in *Charlie and the Chocolate Factory*, and is Vanessa Paradis's ex!"

She looks at me, her eyes shrinking with suspicion—am I making fun of her?

"That's not the same guy. The *Charlie and the Chocolate Factory* one is still alive! He even played in *Pirates of the Caribbean*! And they don't even look alike!"

As for the forty-fourth president of the United States, I don't insist: he was born in Hawaii after all, so from one archipelago to another, I can completely understand how Mor doesn't have a clue.

Despite my partner's illiteracy, I continue to read for pleasure—but when it's information I need, I'm grateful for the internet so I can avoid hours of research on dusty shelves. Just thinking about it, I can still see Victor's cane dislodging the books and letting them fall one by one onto the carpet, while he rattled off the titles and his advice:

"Here, read *War and Peace*! Read *The Sound and the Fury*, read *The Flowers of Evil* . . ."

I scrupulously followed all his reading recommendations, but now to complete my great study of sexual identity, I'm going straight to the source, onto websites intended for people like me. As I suspected, there are thousands of us who are sure of nothing, although I haven't found anyone who had the same thing happen to them as me: a completely unexpected sex change, one that was not actually wanted and, especially, not entirely completed. For as the months go by, it seems my condition has stabilized halfway between one sex and the other: I have a pussy but no uterus, balls but no penis, ovaries but no periods—to say nothing of my muscle mass and body hair, which are so unsettling that no one dares to hazard a decision anymore. As for my questionnaire, it still has no answers, or at least no satisfactory answers: as aware as intersex people are of their condition, others have no idea what they're all about. They may have less ambiguous genitalia than I do, but they still spend their whole life stumbling between their clear cisgender consciences and their nostalgia for fetal androgyny. Try this out: start asking the people around you, and you'll see that they have absolutely no idea what constitutes their femininity or masculinity. Nobody actually understands it at all, apart from the crazies opposing gay marriage. Maureen, whom I obviously asked in the first months we lived together, at least made the effort of thinking about it seriously and sparing me another cliché about the fragility of women or their generosity in love. One evening, as we're getting ready to go clubbing, with minimal preparations for both of us, no makeup or crazy clothes, she glances at our reflection in the living-room mirror—her round face, my horsey jaw, her blond hair gelled into a hard brush, my black mop slicked back—and gives me a solemn embrace:

"Femininity is the hyperawareness of being penetrable."

"But guys are penetrable too. Just because they have one less hole . . ."

"One less hole is a big deal! And excuse me, but the vagina isn't any old hole, you can't compare it with the anus or the mouth."

"Oh, yeah? How is it not comparable?"

"It's better lubricated: it's super easy to get in there."

"Better lubricated than the mouth? Hah! Don't make me laugh!"

"OK, a mouth is wet and everything, but if a guy tries to put his dick in there, you can bite it."

OK, so if I got this straight, the problem with the vagina is that there is too much moisture and not enough teeth. After this little conversation, we head to Le Fox, and for the whole evening, I feel like a fragile hunted animal, even though my appearance discourages even the pushiest guys. From time to time Mor and I make eye contact, and her smile tells me she is also thinking about all the moist orifices dancing all around us, accessible, vulnerable, so much easier to force than the barrier of teeth or the anal sphincter. Of course, I'm also thinking about my own vagina, my tight yet still penetrable cupule. Maureen enjoys filling it with her tongue, fingers, vegetables, various sex toys—she's tried her entire collection, dildos, vibes, and geisha balls. How can I tell her that I couldn't care less whether I'm penetrated or not? But she looks so happy with her strap-on, I let her busy herself in one hole or another, but I can cum without it. I can cum just from stroking her, I can cum when she licks me or fingers me—and with a little concentration and a cushion between my thighs, I can cum just thinking about it again, or thinking about my canopy between heaven and earth. For this is the problem in my new life: how my old life still invites itself into it. It doesn't take much, an awning flapping in the wind, the smell of cut grass, and bang, there I am, teleported back into Arcady's strong arms. A swampy odor? Then I'm back at the edge of the pond, crouched down behind a bunch of reeds, spying on my dusky object of desire, my Black angel, and the terrible apocalypse of his beauty. Everything would be almost OK if poor Maureen didn't have a seventh sense for virtual infidelity.

"Hey, what are you thinking about? Are you here with me, or what?"

She is perfectly right to ask the question, because I'm not, not at all. Instead of going for a walk with her in the nameless town, instead of lovingly squeezing her arm as she does mine, I can hear Arcady's admiring voice in my ears:

"Geez, you're a first-class bitch, Farah!"

Yes, it's true, and what a pity it is that my ardent initiator, the one who made me the bitch that I am, revealed himself to be only a phony preacher, a charlatan who failed to put his fine principles into action, a leader incapable of keeping his pack on the path of real love. All the same, would I have left if Arcady had kept his untenable promises—love for all and eternal life in our concrete utopia? You might say, and Maureen certainly does, that I was a fool to believe in it for a single moment. But you need to remember I was only six years old when I arrived in the community, and that I grew up surrounded by adults who were just as duped as I was by his exalting and reassuring gospel. Perhaps I am still too close, geographically speaking, of course, to all his works and all his pomps to completely escape his influence and the intermittent longing for everything I left behind me. Especially since in my eyes, the nameless town is a little small for me to live large in. The kind of city I'm dreaming of is at least Paris, Tokyo, Cape Town, LA, or New York, and I keep nagging Maureen to consider a new start and other latitudes.

"What, are you serious? What would we do in Paris? It's super cold in Paris. It rains all the time."

"Well New York then. Or Rio."

"I don't speak Brazilian."

"Portuguese."

"Yeah, but I have my job here, my family."

"You hate them."

"No, I don't. What makes you say that?"

I say that because Maureen's family is a nest of vipers that don't even wait to be stepped on before spitting out their venom, in little lethal statements, sniggers, and wholesale judgments. They never even tried to hide the horror I inspire in them, with my strange physique, my childhood in a libertine sect—to say nothing of my source of income, which is as enviable as it is mysterious.

"She's so ugly: what are you doing with such an ugly chick?"

"Well, chick, who knows? We thought you didn't like guys: you're a great disappointment to us."

You have to understand them too: they'd gotten used to their daughter, sister, or niece's homosexuality, had even made it a point of pride, a proof of their fine open minds and tolerance for the intolerable, and now I come along and turn this all upside down with my undecidable sex and my abnormal ugliness. Maureen defends me like a little devil, in public and in private, but I have no illusions about her family or my physique. What I can't understand is why she is hesitating to put nine thousand miles between herself and all those venomous creatures:

"OK, fine, you don't hate them. But you must admit you should."

"Gimme a break with my family. It's no worse than anyone else's."

Yes, it is. It's abominable. I much prefer my sect of social misfits, my extended family of damaged crazies. Despite their fragility, their selfishness, and especially their incapacity for putting their dogma into practice, they are still kind and benevolent. I was right to leave before I started loathing them: they will not have my hate. That's the substance of what I try to tell Maureen: when you love, it's time to leave. But when you don't love anymore, it's also time to leave, to save what can be saved: residual tenderness and infinite pity—in other words, the last stages before too much contempt and permanent bitterness set in.

"For fuck's sake, Maureen, we're not gonna spend our whole life in this hole!"

"Hang on, it's so, like, totally cool here! People pay money to come here, did you know that? We're, like, one of the top tourist destinations in France!"

"Yeah, we're even one of the top tourist destinations in the world: look, even the Syrians and Afghanis envy us! Even the Guineans want to come here!"

"Gimme a break with your migrants! You're just totally hot for Blacks, for real!"

"I'm not hot for anything, Maureen! But let me just remind you that migrants, as you call them, would love to come here, but they usually get caught at Garavan station or stopped at Breil."

"Well, yeah, so what? I'm bummed out about it too, like, I'd much rather they were let in and allowed to live here, but you know, it's not my decision or yours, and I don't see what this has got to do with the fact that you wanna get outa here!"

I don't see it either. I just know that my life cannot end where it started, in this tacky department stuck between Italy and France, between the mountains and the sea, between No Border activists and National Front sympathizers, between seniors retrenched into their electrified retirement homes and youths out on the road, sacrificed in the name of pragmatism, immolated on the altar of common sense and clear consciences—since the Riviera is not about to welcome all the misery of the world. But even if it did decide to do so, my decision is made: I want to live in a city, a real one, not this small town proud of its seashore and its lemon trees. Daniel, whom I informed about my departure plans, showed himself to be much more understanding than my stubborn little lover, but not quite understanding enough for my liking:

"Well, come here then! Come to Palma! You'll love it!"

"I dunno, I don't think islands are my thing. I want to see skyscrapers, to get lost in the streets, to take the metro . . ."

"You sure want weird things."

Consulted through Daniel's mediation, Richard recommends New York, Hong Kong, or Berlin, cities alive with youth and dripping in sensuality, according to him—in other words, exactly what I need. Shame that Maureen is digging her heels in.

"But we'll have to find a job! You don't even have your high school diploma!"

"I'm going to take the exams as a free candidate. And I'll get Nelly to give me some more dough. And you can work as a waitress, Mor, there are, like, zero issues here. The only issue is that you just don't want to move! But I'm warning you, I'm not staying here!"

"All right, OK, fine, I'll have a think about it. But you know you're being really pushy here!"

I am being pushy, indeed, but it's in everyone's interest, starting with mine. If I stay here, I'll go crazy, between the private beaches, the border posts, and the polished lemons. Especially since up in the hills, a few steps away, my ashram is still spread out over its acres of woods and meadows, its terraces and ponds, and its walls crumbling under the assaults of the clematis. Living here is living a few steps away from my wild childhood, a few steps away from my garden of delights, a few steps away from my master of souls. A few steps away is too far, or too close, far too close for me; I'm always at risk of falling into the temptation of going back to the best of all possible worlds—going back to my father's greenhouses, Fiorentina's *orecchiette*, the children's discussions on the drystone walls, and especially, let's be honest, my guru's squirts of sperm.

I'm in the midst of these considerations, mulling over my plans for the great replacement, the megapolis instead of the southern town, the novelty of the unknown instead of routine, when my father shows up at our place. Since my departure, my contact with my parents has been limited to the strict minimum, but I still make a few phone calls from time to time, for pointillist conversations and long silences that express their tender and awkward feelings. The fact that my father has found his way to Maureen's one-bedroom apartment can only mean there's been a catastrophe, the destruction of the property I was just thinking was too close, but which now seems unbearably far away, out of reach, impossible to save from the vandals, the looters, a horde of enraged migrants driven mad by our exorbitant privileges, our blossoming Theban retreat, our festivities up in the hills. By the time my father finds his words—and that can take him quite a while, as we know—my mind has created the worst possible scenarios, for advantage number three of growing up in a quiet zone is that it considerably develops your imagination.

"Did someone die? Is it Mom? Arcady?"

"Yes . . ."

"What do you mean, *yes*? Is it Mom or Arcady?"

He bursts into tears as I'm yelling at him, which is not the best way to make him talk, but also, he is just horrifyingly slow and incapable of producing an intelligible statement within a normal time frame.

"No, no . . ."

"What do you mean, *no no*? For fuck's sake, Dad!"

"It's Dadah."

I'm relieved, obviously, because some deaths are worse than others, but the relief doesn't last long, and I am instantly caught by sadness. Hesitating and sniffling, my father stays on the doorstep and refuses to come in despite Maureen's reticent invitation and my own adjurations. No, no, he's parked in a bad spot . . . the truck . . . he just came to tell me . . . he didn't want me to find out any other way . . . and the funeral will be in Nice, according to the last wishes of the deceased.

"Well, last wishes, we don't know. Her nephew claims . . . he's found a will. But which is dated, you know. It turns out, maybe . . ."

"It turns out what?"

"Maybe she wanted . . ."

"Yes?"

"For her ashes to be dispersed at Liberty House. She had spoken to Arcady about it. But then . . ."

"Then what?"

"There's nothing on paper, you see . . ."

Yes, I see, I can even see it very well. It already comes as a surprise that there even is a will at all, or any expressed last wishes, given that Dadah fiercely refused to consider the world without her. Although . . . I feel a sudden suspicion come to me:

"A nephew, you say? To whom she left all her money? Not him, I hope? Because from what I know, he's a real asshole. You better watch out, right, he might have forged it!"

"No, no, don't worry. I mean, he does inherit, of course, the nephew, but it's nothing compared to what she leaves to us. On that score, I think . . . um, everything is in order. Well, I mean, I don't really know, but Arcady . . ."

As usual, Arcady is the one who knows, the one who sorts it all out, the one who will defend the interests of the community, which is probably just as well for all concerned.

"Will you come? To the funeral."

"Yes. Just tell me where it is, and when, and stuff."

He goes away, leaving me with Maureen, who is circumspect, faced with a sadness whose immensity she cannot understand.

31.

The Black Dahlia

I'm well aware that it is in the order of things that people in their nineties end up dying, and that Dadah owed her survival to oxygen tanks and a colostomy pouch, but I still feel sad. I loved her. She was stupid, selfish, and nasty, but if we loved only people who deserve it, life would be a very boring prize-giving ceremony. And Dadah compensated for her countless flaws with some rare qualities, such as never complaining about her infirmities and always being a goer when pleasure was to be had: a fine meal, a party, a visit, a walk. Not to mention the fact that at ninety-six she had not lost hope of finding love, or at least a good fuck, and she kept herself in readiness for this eventuality: fine lingerie, spellbinding perfume, ebony chignon, Hollywood dentures, still plump cherry lips. I've always seen Dadah drag herself around with a reticule clacking with lipsticks, furiously smearing her mouth with crimson or coral, which could then be found in greasy smears all over the place, on glasses, teacups, and even our own cheeks, which she kissed just as furiously.

Having quickly exhausted her reserves of compassion, Maureen nags me about my intentions:

"Are you gonna go? To the funeral?"

"Of course."

"But, like, she's not there to see you anymore: what do you care?"

"The dead are never there to see who does or doesn't attend their funeral. But generally, when you loved someone, you stay with them to the end."

"Did you love her? That old Gaga? You never talked about her."

"Dadah."

"Yeah, Dadah, Dido, Gaga, same thing."

"Listen, I'm not asking you to be sad with me, but can you just accept that I am, OK?"

"OK, fine. Respect. Will the other guy be there too, your old pervert? The one who abused you?"

"Nobody abused me."

"But will he be there?"

"What's your problem? Of course he'll be there! Everyone will be there, if you must know! Liberty House is a family!"

"I'm your family now. And I would prefer it if you didn't go. It'll do you no good to see them again."

"Maybe, maybe not, but I'm going anyway. You can come with me if you like."

On the day, we all gather together to tramp behind a hearse weighed down with bouquets and wreaths—black lilies obviously, but also other exuberant floral creations. My father must have spent hours in the moist warmth of his greenhouses choosing and arranging poppies, sweet peas, fire-colored dahlias, boughs of greenery, fuchsias, and acanthus palms. It's as beautiful as fireworks, lively and petulant just as Dadah was, and my sadness deepens. With Maureen on my arm, I'm the last in the procession, which gives me the perspective to observe the members of my community in all their splendor—and unfortunately they are anything but splendid. I even get the impression they have aged twenty years in twenty months. My grandmother, Malika, and Victor are the only ones to have dressed elegantly for the occasion. The others have made an effort with their outfits too, but the result is appalling: embossed velvet pants, Spencer jackets, honeycomb sweatshirts, fringed vests, lamé blouses—nothing goes with anything and everything clashes with everything. Dadah's family has no trouble looking like paragons of elegance. The nephew is there—Lionel, his name comes back to me. He looks like he's around a hundred years old too, but as far as I know he's only seventy. His sons are by his side, stiff in their little suits. The two of them laboriously managed to have two children, built on the same disappointing model: modest height, haggard complexion, stringy hair, caper-colored eyes—why bother reproducing, I ask you? Dadah often told us about them, her great-nephews. I didn't see them once in eleven years at Liberty House, but she sometimes met up with them in Nice, Paris, or Courchevel, just so she could cover them with undeserved presents and then bring back all sorts of flattering anecdotes about them: successes at school or horse-riding trophies. Their names are Ralph and Lauren, which must be a rich person's joke, and they stand shivering next to each other and throw us frightened looks, which is completely understandable given the spectacle offered by my variegated little gang of freaks, the depigmented, the obese, the ex-junkies, the crazies with all sorts of tics. Even the twins look like they've come straight out of a Diane Arbus photograph, in their heavily starched old-fashioned pinafore dresses.

Dadah's coffin, a hideous box decorated with marquetry and probably lined with snowy silk, is lowered unceremoniously into a freshly dug grave. It seems that no one thought to personalize this inhumation with songs or prayers, as if they were in a hurry to get rid of her remains as quickly as possible. But then, of course, Arcady advances towards the graveside, looking inspired, his arms already stretched up to the low, heavy sky. Unfortunately, just as he is about to speak, Ralph and Lauren each throw a handful of earth onto the mahogany lid, with what seems like malignant concertation. The others follow suit with equally suspicious alacrity, and, plonk, plonk, the clumps of earth start falling onto the varnished wood, plonk, plonk, let's get this embarrassing ceremony over and done with, this bringing together of her biological and adoptive families—her chosen family, the family of her heart, the only one that counts of course, even if Lionel, Ralph, and Lauren will never see it that way. Resigned to be sidelined, the members of my confraternity, even though they are the last companions and dearest friends of the deceased, do no more than scatter purple petals to the four winds, before returning to their flotilla of tired vehicles, mostly vintage trucks covered in illuminations painted by Jewell's hand. Before I go, I give my mother a quick hug, and Arcady looks at me with eyes full of anxious hope that I will do the same with him. But that's impossible. First of all because I'm still too mad at him, and second because Maureen's fingers are digging into my triceps to contain any effusions and prevent a reunion. In the regional train taking us back to the city of lemons, she doesn't hold back from tearing the members of my community apart:

"They're all total losers! You say they're your family, but honestly, my family actually looks less crazy! What did you say the fat one was called? Victor? And the other one, the guy with the splotches all over his face, who's he? Ah, and then those two girls: what shitty luck to be so ginger! They're sisters? Poor things! And Arcady, well, he looks like a chimpanzee: how you ever had sex with him, I'll never understand!"

"Gimme a break!"

She continues sniggering stupidly throughout the whole trip, you'd think she'd never seen anything so funny as my grieving coreligionists. Although I know that the root of the problem is her pathological jealousy of Arcady, I'm still sickened by her inane remarks—to say nothing of her total indifference to my sadness, such that when we get back to the apartment, I explode:

"You know what? I'm outa here! I can't stand you anymore! You're just so annoying, talking all that shit! And what makes you think you can judge people like that, without even knowing them? Who are you, anyway? Are you better than everyone else, maybe? Do you ever look at yourself? Do you listen to yourself sometimes? You're just a fat bitch!"

Maureen's fist connects with my jaw, and my immediate reaction is to slam her against the wall while pressing on her trachea with my forearm. The advantage of being a guy is that I am stronger than she is: she can't get away, she panics, turns purple, and mutters strangled pleas. I let go of her suddenly, disgusted by the extremes we just reached—but I think she's now feeling the same disgust as I do, which means that we stand there for a while without saying a word or moving, as she just vaguely massages her neck before saying in a flat voice:

"You're bleeding like hell."

It's true: one of her Goth rings dug a deep hole in my chin and the blood is already soaking the front of my funeral shirt. Dadah would have approved: she loved red, passion, executions.

"You're gonna need stitches, I think. Come on, I'll take you to the ER."

There's nothing more miserable than our scooter ride to the hospital. I hold a rolled-up towel against my bleeding chin in one hand, and hang on as best I can to the seat with the other, trying to limit my contact with Maureen, although I sense she is contrite and repentant. The nurse who sews me up does it with such petulance that I have a good mind to lay into her as well, just to teach her a lesson about what it feels like to have your chin cut to the bone and then to have to put up with her little squinty eyes, her cheery comments, and her enthusiasm for pulling the needle. When we take our leave, she turns to Maureen with a last knowing pout:

"You hear about women getting beaten up all the time, but do you have any idea of the number of guys we see here messed up by their girlfriends? Your young man there is not the first one I've sewn up! Or the last, ha ha ha!"

She seems so happy to take me for a man and also a victim of domestic violence that neither Mor nor I have the heart to set her straight. Especially since the stitches make me look like I have a goatee, a young boy's little vanity, another secondary sexual characteristic to add to the confusion. Did I mention that as part of my great survey I had interviewed Dadah and heard her fervent confidences about her pure joy and boundless pride in being born in a woman's body? At the antipodes of my own doubts and torment, Dadah never had the slightest doubt about her sexual identity or orientation: she delightedly slid into the skin of a blazing brunette, a black dahlia, a Miss Pandora, all toxic lipsticks, smoky stockings, crimson silk camisoles, jet-black mane, and peppery perfume. It never crossed her mind that there might be other ways of being a woman—or even that there was anything else in life besides seduction. I can still hear her guttural voice and the painful wheezing of her emphysema-stricken lungs, as she did her best to convince me of the incredible luck we had, her and I:

"Yes, Farah, believe me, those poor men! They are really so pitiful! So weak! It's so easy to tyrannize them, to get them on their knees, to lead them by the end of their noses, and all the rest! A décolleté, a miniskirt, and you're done!"

"Oh, really?"

"Yes, well, of course, for you, it's going to be a bit trickier, don't take this the wrong way, OK, darling, but it's true you won't win any beauty contests . . . but even girls like you, if you make a bit of an effort . . . I mean, you have lovely legs, don't you?"

"Not really."

"You have legs."

"Everybody has legs."

"That's where you're wrong. Look at Nelly, hers are so short! Hideous! I would have killed myself if I was her."

Yep, even at ninety-something Dadah still thought she had a chance in some kind of grand international beauty contest and considered Nelly a competitor to be eliminated. And maybe she lived so long only for the dubious pleasure of prolonging that imaginary competition, seeing her rivals collapse, seeing them all get wrinkles, stoop and shrink until they disappeared. In any case she saw herself as an irresistible vamp right until the very end, and if that isn't the secret of longevity, then at least it was the secret of happiness for her.

I want to be happy too. But I know that I can't be happy in Dadah's way, which involves too much selfishness. I want to be happy, but if my path to happiness has to slalom between other people's woes and blind me to everything that is not in my own narrow interest, I prefer to set myself other goals. For now, I go to bed and turn my back on Maureen. Our reconciliation will have to wait until I know a bit more about my life plans. It's all very well to have opted for the third sex, but that doesn't resolve any of my existential questions.

Et in Arcadia ego

32.

Girls in Hawaii

"Dad? I passed my exams!"

"Ah, bravo. When are you coming back?"

"Never. With honors. And I wasn't far off high honors."

"Ah. . . . Do you want to speak to your mother?"

"No, but tell her I passed."

"OK. Do you want to speak to Arcady?"

"No."

"So when will we see you?"

"Well, if you want to see me, come on over. But come before the fifteenth because I'm leaving—with Maureen."

"Ah. Are you still with her?"

"Yes."

And that's it. If I was hoping for effusiveness, congratulations, a moving little speech about the importance of a good education for succeeding in life, I'd be disappointed. Luckily

I wasn't expecting anything. He didn't even ask where we were planning to go. I have to say my parents don't seem to understand my relationship, even though they express their disapproval less brutally than Maureen's family does:

"It's still weird, though . . ."

"What? That I stay with my girlfriend?"

"Well, yes. That's not how we raised you."

Indeed, I grew up in the Republic of Free Love, with the idea that monogamy led to the agony of the soul, and that the source of all the woes of the world was its hypocritical and restrictive sexual morality. Even though I've left my community, I still believe in its fundamental dogma—namely, that one should desire without fear, liberate one's explosive sexual powers, drown all creatures in a torrent of love, repair the living, and overcome collective trauma, so that everyone, including animals, can make a joyful leap forward, out of our technological rut, out of our evolutionary cul-de-sac, heave ho, me hearties! But the civilizational leap will have to wait until I've lived a bit and experienced something besides global love. For the time being, my plans are to travel with my girl and gently encourage her to share my libertarian views and my concrete utopias. The good thing about Maureen is that she is young, and under her mask of being a boorish butch, she is still capable of passionate infatuations, unexpected U-turns, and faith in sketchy plans. Ours is now to join a hackerspace somewhere in India or Silicon Valley, but I say nothing of this to my parents, of course, since the rise of tech as a tool for good has completely passed them by, and they would see it as a personal failure to discover that their daughter is a shameless geek.

Unlike my parents, Daniel greeted my exam grades with a salvo of hot snaps:

"Fuck, Nello, what is that thing? Is that your penis?"

"Didn't you recognize it?"

"What's on it?"

"A bird. You know, one of those paper things you stick on cocktail glasses, like a decoration: isn't it gorgeous? It's just to say that I'm sooo happy for you, you've totally aced it!"

"Well, thanks. But I would have preferred the bird all by itself. Not a gazillion snaps of your junk."

"Come on, don't be a bitch: I know you're hot for cocks."

In fact, I'm not particularly hot for them, but I do appreciate the fact that someone is happy and proud of my success. But then, Maureen and I also celebrated it fittingly at Le Fox, along with our imminent departure.

"How about Hawaii? What do you think?"

"Yeah. . . . But why are you talking about Hawaii? Is there a hackerspace in Hawaii?"

"Dunno. But we could get a job somewhere and go surfing."

"So you can surf now, can you?"

"No, but I like the idea of the two of us on a board."

All around us, everyone is boozing, ingesting, throbbing, and I feel my own euphoria rise, thanks to the Deutz Brut that Mor knows I like for its fine bubbles and lovely amber color. While my little lover grabs me by the scruff of the neck and sticks her tongue cooled by the champagne into my mouth, I can already see us a thousand miles away from Le Fox, which I really like, but which is nothing more than a moderately exciting girls' club, with its oriental divans, mismatched cushions, circular bar, and lit-up checkerboard dance floor. Perched across from me on an equally luminous barstool, like a jewel box for her blond beauty, Maureen went to the trouble of putting on a dress, a plain straight tunic, but still, a dress, which shows off her fleshy thighs and calves, which I've taught her not to be ashamed of. She is popular, but I am even more so, and not just in lesbian clubs. Given my unattractive physique, this comes as a surprise, but that's the way it is, and I can say this without boasting, just because truth always deserves to be established: Maureen has a dazzling complexion, fine features, voluptuous curves, but of the two of us, I'm always the one getting hit on, even harassed, in clubs, cafés, on the street, in buses, everywhere. Ever since I'm no longer a girl or a boy, everyone finds me attractive. Men, women, young, old, gay, straight, no one can resist my charms—except alpha males and tradwives, who seem to feel an insurmountable disgust for me, but then, alpha males and tradwives are 1 percent of the population, so I couldn't give a shit. In fact, it actually makes me laugh to see it, to observe their faces tense up with revulsion, incomprehension, and even the sacred terror of finally finding their master. Since they usually decamp shortly after my arrival, I'm not a problem for them any more than they are for me. The problem is rather with those who stay, and can't keep themselves from talking to me, touching me, trying to attract my attention. Everywhere I go, the atmosphere turns electric, and all I can do is observe this without understanding it. Maureen is probably the one who came closest to a convincing explanation:

"It has something to do with your gentleness."

"What do you mean?"

"Well, yeah, no one is gentle like you are. Look how aggressive people are! But you are always mega-calm and mega-attentive at the same time. There are people who never say anything, but that's just because they're total fuckwits and, like, don't have anything to say. It's way better if they keep their traps shut, right? But you have all kinds of stuff to say, since you're, like, super intellectual, but you're never in a hurry to speak, you always wait for the right moment, you're patient."

"I'm not super intellectual, don't talk crap."

"You read all kinds of books, you know a million facts, you're always thinking about shit, you're, like, such a nerd, for real. And I think that people can actually sense that."

"Yeah, right. All it takes to be attractive is to be calm, patient, and intelligent. Everyone knows that. Sure."

"OK, fine, but you're sexy too! Nerds aren't usually sexy at all. They're all fugly."

"Stop it, Mor, you can't say I'm really sexy. I'd like to be, right, but I know what I look like."

I know what I look like, but I also know the effect I can have on people, the space I can take up in their lives in no time at all, as if I was the incarnation of their intimate dreams and twisted fantasies—as if I was the ideal confidant too. Once they speak to me, people seem relieved, but as the depositary of their disturbing craziness, I don't share their relief or understand their persistence in trying to seduce me. Tonight at Le Fox, I'm generating the same excitement as usual, a dazed and joyful crowd, girls elbowing each other out of the way to get near me, or trying to attract me under Maureen's now unperturbed eyes. It seems that one of the effects of my gentleness is to evoke it in response from others, as if they were won over by my serenity and art of joy. Tonight, life is mellow like a Hawaiian sunset, all soft golds and frayed pink, all trade winds, sea spray, and alohas, the perfect setting for a new start with my little lover, who has finally come round to my idea of happiness.

33.

Pollice Verso

Just when we're all set, airline tickets, passports, ESTA forms, suitcases, I receive a news alert on my smartphone: "Billionaire's Nephew Sues Sect for Senior Abuse and Inheritance Misappropriation." The billionaire is Dadah, the nephew is Lionel, the sect is us. The rest is just a web of lies and calumny, and this is just the beginning of a media storm whose brutality might have surprised me, since I grew up among nonviolence experts, but no: I've had two years to get used to the bloodthirsty appetites of my fellow humans and their desire for ignominy and degradation. Next to those wolves, the inhabitants of Liberty House are lambs. I hated them for their selfishness and their arid hearts; I was mad at them, I'm still mad at them, not to have thrown our doors wide open to other refugees, but in matters of cruelty and stupidity, they are beaten out of the league by any old gossip columnist or internet commentator—by anyone at all actually, given that they haven't had the benefit of training in cruelty that people in the outside world receive.

As far as the public is concerned, Lionel's complaint might as well be a prison sentence, and I'm rapidly swamped by a flood of hateful hashtags and raised thumbs as signs of approval of the lynching of our community. We are all guilty of senior abuse, undue influence, and rapacious acquisitiveness—but Arcady, of course, is the worst among us, the one who planned this embezzlement for years, the one who instrumentalized Dalila Dahman's wishes, the one who broke her ties with her family, the one who arranged and profited from the flow of her largesse and her tax evasion.

Chosen with diabolical perversity, the photos provide supporting evidence for this damning portrayal: puffy, sinister-looking, with a twisted mouth and underhand look, Arcady looks nothing like the dazzling man who revealed the meaning of love and the meaning of life to me. Victor, Orlando, Kirsten, or my parents don't receive any better treatment: even my mother's exceptional beauty takes on a rather malevolent character in the chosen pictures. As for Dadah, if I wasn't overwhelmed by these events, I would burst out laughing at the sight of the photos of her that are circulating, showing only her great age and her infirmities. It's quite simple, she would have swallowed her priceless dentures—then moved heaven and earth to have the heads of those responsible, those ill-intentioned journalists and photographers, on a platter. Presenting her in page after page and tweet after tweet as an "elderly victim" is an insult to her memory, but also to truth. Dadah was never weak, or even old in fact: she thought that growing old was all very well for other people, but that she could just be—in the same way she had always been—just be and continue to be, with the same dazzling intensity at ninety as at nineteen. And it was true. Age is all in your head. Try this out: act as if you were thirty or twenty years younger, and people will adjust to the idea that you have of yourself: they will celebrate your triumphant morns, drink the wine of your vigor, and let themselves be contaminated by your imaginary youth.

From Palma de Mallorca, Daniel sends me a profusion of anxious and sympathetic messages, to say nothing of our Skype sessions at one in the morning:

"This is just bullshit!"

"Yeah, word is Arcady abused Dadah!"

"As if Dadah was the kind of woman to ever do anything she didn't want to do!"

"Yeah, right!"

"Fuck, don't they understand that Arcady couldn't give a shit about moolah? That he's not a gold digger?"

"They're the ones who have shit for brains!"

"It's that nephew, that Lionel!"

"He's the one who got them all wound up."

"And so what's the deal now? Are they, like, gonna throw Arcady in the cooler?"

"Of course not, there's no proof of anything! The will is rock solid, no worries, it'll go through just fine."

Go through just fine? Don't make me laugh, or cry for hours. Not only does the controversy not let up but it expands, turns into a soap opera, and people follow all its sordid plot twists: the investigation, the speculation about the millions Arcady was paid, all those eye-popping checks, the life-insurance policies, and the unencumbered possession of old masters' paintings.

A few days after the proceedings start, I get a phone call from my father. Needless to say, I gave up on Hawaii, my eternal summer, my new start between the golden sands and the vivifying sea spray. I will not leave until the honor of Liberty House is saved, Arcady's reputation restored, and justice done. I even called the house myself and told Fiorentina, the only one to pick up the phone during the crisis, that I was ready to fly to my confraternity's rescue.

"*Pronto?*"

"Fiorentina? It's Farah. Are you OK?"

"Of course not. What do you want?"

"Nothing. No. Yes. I'm here, right? If you need me."

"OK, I'll tell him."

Him, for her and for me, is Arcady, the man of her life and of mine, the man of all our lives, not only because he took them in hand but also because he made them all more beautiful. From the very start of the case, I forgot all my grudges, set aside all my doubts and reticence, and was ready to fly to the rescue and crush the baddies. Life is hard, but it is simple: there are the baddies and the others. You just have to choose your camp. I chose to be on the goodies' side a long time ago, but also on the side of all those who are made into scapegoats—illuminated preachers, strange fruit, Black lives, the wretched of the earth and the toilers at sea.

When my father finally calls me back, he's as evasive as usual, but the deal is that Arcady wishes to see me in a neutral place, not at Liberty House and not at Maureen's.

"You know Le Brazza? At Les Sablettes?"

If I know it? Of course I do. . . . Le Brazza is Arcady's favorite café, the one where he wanted to take me to celebrate my Rokitansky syndrome. And also the place where I had a beer with Maureen the day we met by chance on the beach.

Against all expectations, she doesn't have any objection to my getting together with Arcady again. She even seems to be just as alarmed as I am by the blows thrown at our little libertarian community, and I love her all the more for it.

"I'm standing by you, through all this, you know."

"Yeah, well, no, I didn't know. But thanks. I need your support. Coz it's going to be hard."

That same day, I meet Arcady at Le Brazza, where a bottle of prosecco is waiting for me in an ice bucket. Arcady is wearing his eternal orange quilted-velvet jacket and giving off the same heady scent as always: green palm, Levantine cedar, animal musk. What has changed is the way he looks at me, and I have to control myself not to rush towards him and hold him tight, just to get rid of that despairing look. Luckily he regains enough of his panache to make a toast and dreamily contemplate the sea's horizon through his flute of vintage San Simone.

"I'm not a fan of flutes for *spumante*. I prefer wine glasses."

"What are we drinking to?"

"Our reunion. I've missed you. How is your new life going?"

"Good. We're going to Hawaii soon, Maureen and me."

"Oh? That's great."

"I mean, not right away. I'll wait to see how things turn out here."

"You don't need to worry, you know. I have everything under control. It's just going to be tough for a little while."

"You're being investigated, you and Victor, you can't pretend it's not serious!"

"In eighty percent of investigations the charges are dropped. You'll see. When you know Dadah, I mean, if you knew her, it's so ridiculous . . ."

He pauses with a disillusioned wave of his hand.

"No, what's annoying is that there is going to be another court case. I prefer to tell you about this before you read it in the press. Djilali's father is back in the picture. All those accusations, all those lies gave him ideas."

"Djilali's father? The horrible one? The one who beat Malika? What does he want? To get Djilali back?"

"I think Djilali is the last of his concerns. No, he just wants cash, his share of the cake. He's thinking there's probably some way of getting something out of this whole clusterfuck. Well, actually, I don't know what he's thinking and I don't care, but in any case he laid charges of rape and sexual assault on a minor. And he's joined the proceedings as a civil claimant."

"But you never raped anyone! What does Djilali say?"

"Well, he says I raped him. And the twins do too."

"What? Dolores and Teresa? They're crazy! What about Epifanio? Does he believe them? Is he still at Liberty House?"

"He believes his daughters, of course. He even tried to beat me up. And no, they're gone. They got an apartment in Nice."

"I'll go see them, I'll talk to them and make them get over wanting to talk shit like that!"

"Yes, Farah, talk to them. They may listen to you. I tried, Victor and Fiorentina did too, but it's as if. . . . Anyway, I don't recognize them anymore, it's like they're not the same people. Dos, Tres, Epifanio, Djilali. Even Malika, you know, she believes me, but she's not entirely sure, I can feel it. She believes me now, but for how long? At the same time, I can understand it, when your twelve-year-old son looks you in the eye and tells you he's been raped, and not just once, right, he says it started as soon as he arrived at Liberty House, that I would trap him in the cellar, or track him through the woods, or take him into my room, I mean, everywhere."

"Fuck, I don't believe this! Why would he say that?"

"Because he wants to please his father, or he wants people to pay attention to him, I don't know, because he's still a little boy and he doesn't realize he's destroying me and everything I tried to build. Who cares about the reasons? The result is that the cops are going to interview everyone, including you! The result is that we're going to read all these lies and horrible things about us for months, and even if the case is dropped or I go to trial and I'm acquitted, we're screwed, everything is completely screwed!"

"But just now, you were saying, I mean, you sounded optimistic!"

"I'm trying, Victor and I are both trying, you know, to hold strong, to reassure everyone, and they support us, mostly—your parents, your grandmother, Jewell, Orlando, Kinbote, Vadim . . . but some of them left. Like Salo and Palmyre."

"But that's bullshit! I'm in a good position to know that you don't touch children!"

"I had sex with you. Epifanio told the cops about it."

"If you want, I can tell them it's not true."

"Farah, I will never ask you to say anything except the truth."

"What about Nelly? What does she think of all this? Is she saying you manipulated and raped her too?"

"No, Nelly's fine. But there's her family, her children, her sisters . . ."

"So? What about them?"

"So they are pestering her to leave the community. And as far as I know, they're going to file charges too. Senior abuse, just like Dadah. I almost think it would be better if Nelly left, for a while at least. That might calm them down."

"Don't worry about me whatever happens: I'll tell the pigs

that you never tried to pressure anyone, not me and not the other kids either. And that you never acted inappropriately, and there was never any sexual contact, or anything! And that it was me who seduced you! And that's true too!"

He laughs sullenly and turns the empty bottle upside down in the ice bucket before ordering another beer, which he sets about gulping down pronto, while staring at the horizon with tragic determination. We are drunk, and maybe it's just as well, because otherwise it would be too hard to see him again in such sordid circumstances, to see him so affected, so diminished, when all I've ever known is his insolent splendor. We are drunk, the sea is joyfully rolling, and the bar stereo is booming out "*Viens, je t'emmène.*" Michel Berger, Daniel Balavoine, and Jean-Jacques Goldman came along too late in my life for me to love them and understand the nostalgia that is the stock in trade of some radio stations, but go figure, France Gall singing "Come On, I'm Taking You Away" inspires me with the mad desire to take Arcady's hands and to tell him that I'm taking him away, far, far away, beyond the coral sea, to the home of the wind, to the country of fairies, anywhere as long as he escapes from this feeding frenzy and impending catastrophe.

"Come on."

"What?"

"Come on, I'm taking you away, let's go."

"Where do you think we can go, Farah Faucet?"

He's probably right, but since the radio is now playing "Just an Illusion," I feel like I can believe that there's another place, another time, magic in the air, hope for all of us, and a shelter somewhere, even for manipulative gurus and sexual predators. Not that I'm endorsing the terms in which Arcady is being hounded, but one might as well face the facts: the public is much less interested in reality than in titillating scenarios of perversion, especially if it's about sex crimes on children. Try this out: as soon as it's about children, there are no limits to public excitement. I didn't have to wait for this to happen to Arcady to know that most people hate children and want only the worst for them, including mutilation and sexual abuse: pedo-criminality only answers their unspeakable wishes. Children are born free, and everywhere are in chains; children are born pure, and everywhere their original innocence is ravaged, for children are bearable only when governed, tamed—in other words, grown up. I know this for a fact because, thanks to Arcady, my own childhood was free of governance and domestication. I count the absolute freedom with which my body developed as proof of this. As if he read my mind, and I know he can do this, Arcady glances at my chest in my tight top with suspenders.

"Didn't you used to have bigger breasts?"

"Totally!"

"You don't have any now."

"Well, you know, it's not like I ever had big tits, really."

"No, but you did have them. They were pretty. Promising. Two little crocuses. I liked them."

"Well, they're gone."

"But, of course, I like you as you are now too."

There you are, just as I said. How many other girls do you know who start puberty normally, with budding breasts and a swelling pubis, and then turn out to have a pair of balls and visible pecs under their T-shirt? And then there's the fact that my vulva, vagina, and ovaries are still there, even if they are atrophied. No one will be able to convince me that my intersexuality is not the result of my wild life among indifferent but well-meaning adults, placid cows, adventurous chickens, softly sloping meadows, and trees creaking under the assaults of the wind. I am the living proof that if you let children do as they please and find out what they like on their own, then anatomical programming fails or takes another pathway, anarchy spreads to the organs, and then, bingo, you're not a guy or a girl, but someone like me—in other words, a nobody. Having thought about it a bit, I think I can say that the third sex is the future of man. Instead of crying for the blood of places like Liberty House, it would be better to declare them a public service and to consider them as the incubators of our future Eve, the one who will put an end to six thousand years of patriarchy, war, and tragedy, because she will be queer and surely trans.

I look at Arcady, his slumped body, his gray stubbly cheeks, his slightly shaking fingers, all the signs he's showing of despondency and dismay, and I am thunderstruck with the startling joy of a revelation—a miracle, an apotheosis! After all these years when he guided me, supported me, helped me to take possession of myself, now it's up to me to protect and look after him. It's about time my energy found some good use for itself, and saving Arcady seems a worthy mission. Ha! I celebrate my new resolution with a gulp of *spumante*, I almost want to clink glasses, *l'chaim*, to life, and may it last a hundred years! I'm tipsy with that vision of myself as a righter of wrongs and with the radiant future that this vision opens out to me, when the radio decides to play Claude François, "*Toi et moi contre le monde entier*," like an ironic echo to my new life plan—"I am the shadow of your pain, the sorrow of your sorrow, I see you winning the war, and I'll be afraid no more . . ."

"Claude François, that's too much, we really need to get outa here!"

"It's true you're a little young to appreciate it . . ."

"It's not a question of age: it's just shit! Come on, let's go!"

He stands up, distractedly pays the bill, his eyes elsewhere, his hands still shaking, those hands I want to grasp and bring fervently to my lips, in memory of all those times they gave me pleasure, such pleasure as I have never found since: because as much as I like having sex with Maureen, and even love her more and more, since passivity is not in my nature, Arcady holds the key to my erotic life.

"I want you."

He smiles, a hesitant and brief smile, nothing to do with his former smile, which was magnificent, generous, and communicative, but it's better than nothing, and I try to see this as the beginning of the end of this shit storm. Arcady is not made for sadness and neither am I: we don't need much to recover our optimism and energy.

"'*Viens, je t'emmène*'. . . . Come on, I'm taking you away. . . ."

"I closed my eyes so tight, I dreamed so much, that I made it there . . ." There it is, the coral sea, shimmering in our eyes dazzled by the reflection. No need to go to Hawaii. No matter what Arcady says, I'll be more useful here than in Honolulu. But for now, I have only one desire, and that's to find a place to make love.

"Your car?"

"Are you sure? You really want to?"

"Of course I do, what are you talking about? And I'm an adult now! No one can break our asses about that anymore! And it's been a long time since I escaped from your authority and your destructive influence!"

"Destructive influence! Do you realize? I never wanted to influence anyone, never!"

I'm well placed to know that he actually did wield quite a lot of influence over us all, but that he never actually needed to do anything in particular to achieve that. His influence was the result of his charm and goodness, the inescapable effect of his convictions and determination. In a world where people have neither a rudder nor a grappling hook, anyone can pretend they're a captain and drag everyone's hearts along behind him. Individuals like Arcady are bound to find disciples looking for a master. I understand that completely since, after being a docile and unconditional groupie myself, I am now a group leader in my own right, an alpha individual of indeterminate gender but with an incontestable domination over fragile betas and gammas.

As Arcady parks the car in a quiet street and leans the seats back with the same serious expression, I feel my excitement rising. It's the first time that I've fucked in a car, but I'm thrilled by the idea and quickly unbuckle Arcady's belt to take him in my mouth. No sooner has his penis touched my palate than a shudder runs through me, an exquisite pleasure that is infinitely beyond me, a reality before which all others fade away. With the familiar sensation and taste of his penis in my mouth, my whole green paradise reveals itself to me, my pleasures and my days, in this cruel summer—my season of ecstasy, both the first spark of wonder and the beginning of terror; with the moisture and smell of his thighs, I rediscover my joy at being in the world, my impatience as I waited for him on our nuptial couch, with its crushed grass and canopy battered by the wind, my perpetual fairyland, my life filled with love, my life in his power, my life that seemed infinite to me. On this car seat so ill-suited to ecstasy, I am about to experience a new episode of mental disintegration that risks taking me far away from here, and it is only with a painful effort that I manage to concentrate on Arcady's flaccid flesh. And actually, why is his penis so desperately inert despite my vigorous suction movements all over it? I'm not used to inertness or passivity with Arcady. Seeing him like this, his head leaning back on the seat, eyes shut, without even the beginning of an erection, is just beyond comprehension, so I stop:

"Are you OK?"

"I'll never be OK again, my darling. But why do you ask?"

"Well, you're not hard . . ."

Grasping his penis between his index and middle finger, he seems to test its volume and firmness for a moment before letting it fall with a disillusioned gesture onto the metal teeth of his zipper.

"Well. . . . That's the way it is for me now, don't take it personally."

There's absolutely no question of my taking it personally, quite the opposite. . . . A world in which Arcady would no longer feel desire or energy is unthinkable, even unlivable—for life needs a radiant hearth from which to be nourished. Strong souls are of public use because they know how to communicate a little of that missing fire to weak souls. To those who might object that the strength of one's soul has nothing to do with sexual prowess, I would answer that they have no idea, and that both have always been inextricably linked together in Arcady.

"Does it happen with Victor?"

"Yes, with Victor too. Mind you, it suits him: I was always too much for him, with all my demands. He's not in great shape either these days."

Ah, yes, of course. The weak cope with others' failings very well, at least to begin with, because those failings reassure them about their own vegetative existence. They have no idea how much their own functioning owes to the exuberant beauty and inexhaustible strength of those who have chosen to plunge into the whirlpool of life. Arcady's limp dick is therefore a worldwide catastrophe, even if no one can measure its lethal consequences—except me, of course, which makes me try everything I can for fifteen minutes on Arcady's cock until I throw in the towel. At least I did my best: frenetic back-and-forth, tonguing, gulps, breathing, flows of saliva, acupressure, palming testicles, anal stimulation—all in vain, just a shudder, a shiver, then nothing.

I should have known, right then—there are telltale signs: that was the end, even though it was masked under the debonair airs of a little sexual incident. It was the end from the very beginning.

34.

Dschungel

We sought refuge at Liberty House because the catastrophe was imminent, because death dominated life and seeped into its every mechanism, with fine particles, electromagnetic radiation, heavy metals, GMOs, pesticides, toxic waste, acid rain, volatile organic compounds, space debris, and schist gases: the list of threats got longer every day, and my poor parents had lost all hope of ever leading a normal existence ever again. Theirs was a prolonged sentence of confinement, a series of mortifications of the flesh that didn't relieve them of any of their anxieties. Arcady himself never spoke of anything else except the end of the world. But whereas birds of ill omen do nothing more than announce catastrophes, he promised that we would be spared. I never really understood what secret bunker or prophylactic measures would allow us to survive the Apocalypse, but I trusted Arcady to provide us with a golden age and endless happiness.

Except that now I can feel it's my turn to save the world, my turn to defend my zone from the unjust attacks it is enduring, that rolling fire of calumny directed not only at Arcady but at our whole disconnected way of life. As the last nature reserve of endless desire and free pleasure, we are contravening the world's steady march into the technological abyss; as the last representatives of the human race, we don't fit in with the grand post-human parade. But let it not be said that I stood idly by while the house where I grew up was burning. As soon as I get home from my rendezvous with Arcady, I start preparing a battle plan, with the support of my little lover—who has been rallied to the cause of planetary love although she hasn't yet converted to degrowth. In any case, we will use the weapons of the enemy, create our own fake news, fake headlines, and striking hashtags: #freeArcady, #myheartisinfinite, #freedomiwriteyourname, #paradise4all, #sexisallweneed. . . . Daniel is here too, back in a flash from Palma to join our campaign committee, and I feel that the three of us are going to perform miracles—the miracle of love.

Daniel has changed. The tall lanky guy who looked like my brother has disappeared: he has lost his spectral pallor and developed a Hollywood tan, he has built himself a dream body, opted permanently for George Michael's bleached blow-dried hair, and become his perfect double, with his three-day beard and carnivorous jaw.

"Did you get stuff done?"

"What kind of stuff?"

"Dunno. Surgery? Your face looks different. Your teeth. . . ."

"Do you like it?"

"It's weird."

"You don't need to know if I got stuff done or not. It's me, Farah, it's still me, OK?"

"But I mean, George Michael, really? Are you serious?"

"Very serious. Why?"

"Well, you're like all those crazies, you know, those Angelina Jolie or Justin Bieber fans who get hacked up so they look like their idols."

"And if I prefer looking like George Michael to looking like myself, what's the problem with that?"

He's right, of course: if he really wants to take on the features of a dead singer and go around in satin hot pants from the eighties, that is not a problem at all. Someone will just have to explain to me someday why people torture themselves with their physical appearance instead of loving the one that nature endowed them with.

"It's just that we weren't raised that way, Nello. Arcady always said that we should accept ourselves as we are."

"I know. And I think it's great, really. It's just that it doesn't work for me. I accept myself a lot better since I changed a couple of things. But now, well, you know, I'm done. So don't worry about it!"

"And Richard?"

"What about Richard?"

"Why didn't he come home? He's been charged too, right?"

"Well, yeah, that's the thing. It's better if he stays in Palma."

I always loved Richard. Almost as much as I loved Arcady, whose irresistible charm and cheerfulness he shared—although not his honesty and constancy. And maybe I loved him precisely because of that unsettling charm and that inconstancy, for his way of coming home with his *amigas*, his music, his drugs—and of leaving straight away, leaving us in the blazing eddies of his wake.

A memory of one of our follies comes back to me. I'm eight,

maybe nine. It's very hot, as it always is in my memories, as if my life at Liberty House was spent during an endless summer. Our ornamental basin is not yet sumptuously enlarged and restored, but as it is, it constitutes a rallying point for the members of the community, a fresh green palm grove surrounded by the pulverulent landscape and the strident cries of the cicadas. Richard is sitting at the water's edge, and a speaker is pumping out the obsessive riffs he brought back from Ibiza or St. Barths. The adults who are present are clearly high, but at eight years old, I have no idea of the empathogenic effects of MDMA, and I'm happy enough just to notice that everybody is looking particularly cheerful and relaxed. Crouching on the edge of the pond, my father is rolling stick after stick of his aromatic herbs, whose plumes of smoke blend with the exhalations from the pond. As I'm paddling in the mud with Daniel and the twins, the adults silently slip into the water and Richard turns the volume up, before immersing himself as well. An electric-blue dragonfly, probably stoned too from the active principles in suspension, is flying in mad arabesques above the crumpled lily pads. Epifanio tucks a flaming flower into Dadah's loose hair, which she adjusts while simpering at him. As if obeying this signal, the bodies get closer, hands join, mouths find each other, and couples form: Epifanio with Dadah, Arcady with Victor, Coco with Vadim, Palmyre with Salo, Orlando with Jewell. . . . Off to one side, my mother wraps her legs around Richard and lets herself float on the water as her hair spreads out like a corolla. The sudden agitation in the water sends little foamy waves to the edge, and also tree frogs importuned in their own copulations, followed by all sorts of translucent creepy-crawlies, larvae, fingerlings, tadpoles—all trying to escape from this disruption of their biotope. That day in our Devil's Pool everyone is fucking, including the more impaired and graceless members of our community: legs wave under the transparent green water, while on the surface a convulsive trance melds arms, stomachs, breasts, and faces, a lacustrine version of pandemonium under our stupefied children's eyes.

If I have to be interviewed as part of a preliminary investigation, I'll be sure not to mention that episode, for fear that it will be held against Liberty House. How could I explain to a public prosecutor that you can see your parents have an orgy without it making you neurotic or traumatized? I learned at eight years old not only that there was no age limit for physical love but also that we are all beautiful enough to give and take pleasure: should I regret this? I saw Dadah offer herself to Epifanio with the flirtatiousness of a vahine; I saw Victor floating among the water lilies, lighter than a cork, passing from Arcady's to Salo's arms; I saw Richard slip between my mother's white thighs, and I saw my father putting his wet hand on them in a tender accompanying caress: should I throw stones at them all, when they were just trying to find pleasure with no obstacles and to build a better world, founded on free love and endless desire? I know this because I was there. I know this because my freedom is the daughter of their freedom, and my whole life will never be long enough to congratulate myself for having grown up in Arcadia.

"Daniel, do you remember that time when they all started making love in the pool?"

"Of course, how could I forget that! It was such a trip! They were all wasted! I don't know what they took: maybe it was E."

"I remember thinking it looked awesome to be an adult, coz you could do whatever you wanted."

"That's what you thought? That's funny, I did too! Or something like that... Anyway, I was watching Richard, he was doing it with your mom and dad and they were, like, so gorgeous, all three of them. I think that was when I started having a thing for Richard."

"But the others were super gorgeous too."

"Yeah. But still, Richard was just totally awesome."

"Fiorentina was the only one who wasn't happy."

"She was there?"

"Of course she was! First she rang the gong like a nutcase, then she came to tell us the meal was ready, that we had to come eat *subito*. And then she just stayed there and watched. Don't you remember?"

"Very vaguely. Was she really pissed?"

"You bet she was! Everyone stark naked in the pool while her polenta was getting cold!"

"Poor Metallica: I think she never really understood how anyone could prefer a good fuck to her risotto with cep mushrooms..."

"Who knows, maybe she didn't even know what a good fuck was."

"Don't you think there was something going on with Titin?"

"Of course, there was heaps going on with Titin, but I don't think it was anything sexual."

I'm lucky I can share my memories of that endangered world with Daniel, because otherwise they would soon take on the doubtful character of dreams. Even Maureen doesn't quite believe me when I talk about some aspects of our community life, like rotating partners, sex therapy, or erotic spirituality. Maureen has changed, but not to the point of accepting that love has nothing to do with possession.

In any case, now is not the time for nostalgia, it's time for direct action, a sudden inversion of all our roles, like a stroke of a sequined wand on my shoulders and Arcady's. I will save him, I will restore his honor, and our community's honor, I will avenge all insults. It is time for me to give back a hundredfold what I received as an inheritance, that free energy that might just ignite the whole world and put an end to the tragic misunderstanding that the human condition has become. I have it inside me, a sense of justice and a taste for impossible missions. I have it inside me: the sacred fire, the madness that comes from nymphs. That's the result of a childhood spent in the trees, far from screens and city lights. I have it inside me: absolute confidence in my own powers. I had good teachers: the lilies of the fields and the adventurous chickens, but also and especially Arcady, who taught me to fear nothing and to believe in my own skills of enchantment. That's all anyone ever wants. Try this out: speak to them loud and clear, with the irresistible ring of faith in your voice, with something like a luminous horizon in your eyes, and they will follow you to the gallows. I had no trouble galvanizing Daniel and Maureen, and I now feel capable of recruiting new followers, who are not yet committed to our cause—marriage for all, mystical weddings, infinite hearts. The more I talk, the more my plans take shape and the more I feel the giddiness of heights rise up inside me: not only will I save Arcady from the clutches of iniquitous justice but I will save him from himself too. When all this affair is over, I will easily convince him to turn Liberty House into an accommodation center for migrants, where we will all live happier for having our actions accord with our principles. I don't plan on stopping there either, and since Daniel and Maureen are hanging on my every word, I make the most of this to unveil my visionary hopes, my defiance of disaster:

"Once they recover and their situation is sorted out, boom, they get sent out again. But in the meantime, of course, we'll convert them and train them in planetary love, which means they will be our agents wherever they go. And in a flash, we'll see millions of people become activists for free love and voluntary frugality."

Daniel pensively whistles through his teeth.

"Yep, that's what we gotta do. Your plan is totally awesome!"

That's how you avert both the migration crisis and ecological collapse, but since you need to start at the beginning, I go along to the meeting with the public prosecutor, who wishes to interview me in advance of the Gharineyan case—Arcady's last name. A middle-aged woman greets me: tall, hefty, her hair a color invented by a hairdresser, between cappuccino and candied chestnuts. Her name is Mrs. Campo, and I really want to ask her if her sister is a gyno, but I don't think that would do anything for our cause—and, of course, last names are always precise down to the last letter, except in the third world where anything goes. After the preambles of protocol, Mrs. Campo attacks, with no more consideration than her sister who is not her sister:

"Did Mr. Gharineyan ever indecently assault you?"

"No, never."

"He never appeared before you naked?"

"Yes, often."

"How old were you when you first saw him naked?"

"Everybody was naked at Liberty House. I mean, those that wanted to."

"Even the children?"

"Obviously."

"Your parents?"

"Sometimes."

"What did it feel like to see your parents naked?"

"Fine. Nudity is natural. Clothes just get in our way. And in fact, I didn't have to wait to live in a community to see people naked: my first memory is of my grandmother's clitoris ring."

Her eyes remain expressionless under the artificial husk of her bangs, but a slight tension in her mouth reveals her annoyance at being diverted from her target:

"Did you take showers together?"

"All together? No, never."

"Don't play with words: did the children take showers with the adults, yes or no?"

"Our showers were communal and everyone took showers whenever they felt like it. But we weren't really into showers at Liberty House."

"What do you mean by that?"

"Washing too often is bad for your skin. And showers are wasteful."

Yep, there's a new fibrillation of the corner of her lips: she probably never imagined that anyone could forgo twice daily ablutions, and it's probably a lost cause to try to convince her of the health benefits of crud.

"Did the adults ever engage in inappropriate behavior in front of you?"

"Never."

"Did you ever see the adults of the sect masturbate or have sexual intercourse in your presence?"

"We are not a sect."

"Did you ever see the adults of your community masturbate or have sexual intercourse in your presence?"

"I never saw anyone masturbate. Not even me. I did it under the sheets."

She has another tic: she doesn't appreciate my sense of humor, either that or it's completely over her head.

"And sexual intercourse?"

"What?"

"Miss Marchesi, I can see that you are not approaching answering my questions with goodwill. Are you under any pressure at the moment?"

"None."

"Did you ever have sexual intercourse with Arcady Gharineyan?"

"Yes."

"You had sexual intercourse with a man thirty-five years older than you?"

"Yes. Is that a crime?"

"Rape is a crime."

"I consented."

"You were a minor, weren't you?"

"I was almost sixteen."

"He had authority over you: that's an aggravating circumstance."

"No one ever had any authority over me. I was free."

This time, the shudder reaches her marble forehead. Mrs. Campo doesn't believe for a single second that anyone can grow up freely, under the nonchalant watch of a few adults:

"For goodness' sake, you can't make me believe that you were left completely to your own devices!"

Yes, that's just it, we were, Daniel, Djilali, the twins, and I: wild children in the summer hills, little Mowglis running through an immemorial, grandiose, and majestic jungle book at their own rhythm. Our only servitude was voluntary—and as far as I was concerned, my servitude was dictated by love: I placed my life in Arcady's hands because I loved him more than anything and especially more than myself. But just try talking about love to a public prosecutor whose hair is the tint of a colorist's mahogany and whose nervous tics betray her rising anxiety and the irresistible desire to discipline and punish. She's worn down enough to let me go, but I'm not sure that I convinced her. I just hope I didn't score any own goals, with my harangues on naturism, Adamism, Tantrism, Sufism, libertarianism, anti-speciesism, all the isms and isthmuses of our little ideological territory. Just as I am getting ready to leave her office, Mrs. Campo stops me short in the doorway with one last perfidious question:

"Farah, by the way: are you a girl or a boy? Because according to your birth certificate, you're a girl, but, well, looking at you, it's not all that clear . . ."

Idiot. I am what you will never allow yourself to be: a girl with iron muscles, a boy who is not afraid of his fragility, a chimera endowed with ovaries and fancy-dress testicles, an unassignable entity, a free spirit, an intact human being.

35.

Apocalypse Now

Everything people say about life turns out to be true, eventually. Try this out: bellow out any old existential aphorism and it will be verified sooner or later. Life is beautiful, life is long, life is an impassive river that lets drunken boats or walnut shells or cruise liners go down it. It is eight in the morning. I slept with peace in my soul next to my little lover, in the soft lavender scent of our sheets. Daniel's voice comes to me from the living room, where he took up residence after his return from Palma:

"Farah!"

Without giving me time to answer him, he is here at my bedside, his cell phone in his hand, wearing only his two-tone shorts:

"Farah, they're dead!"

"Who? Who's dead?"

"They're all dead!"

He thrusts his cell phone under my nose so brutally that he nearly breaks it.

"'Sect: the bodies of sixteen followers discovered at the property.' And look, there's the photo! Fuck, Farah, it's them!"

Yes, it's the house, it's them, there is no room for doubt, but my mind can't let itself go into the crevasse of icy desolation that this notification has opened up in the world. Because if they really are dead, they take everything else with them, the summer dawns, the wind in the trees, the bursts of laughter, the caress of being alive. Life is horribly short and tragically devoid of meaning.

I get dressed, my hands shaking, but I don't cry. It's actually the infinite compassion in Maureen's eyes that affects me the most. The news alerts don't stop raining down on our phones, and with them come details that are just as unbearable as they are pointless. I don't need the media to tell me which members of the community chose not to survive the disaster. I don't need them to guess how the collective suicide took place either. They will have sat down under the pine trees, smoked some of my father's grass, and drunk *spumante* from our favorite glasses. Maybe they let the sun's rays play in the cut facets of their crystal bases, sending sparkling signals to each other, all will be well, clink, clink, no need to panic. They had even less reason to panic in that Arcady was there to ensure that death would be sweet. If I know Arcady, and who knows him better than I do, he will have surrounded them with his solicitude right up to the end, offered them his indefatigable love, and even made them laugh—for no one was more joyous or funny than he was. I am sure that in their last instants they were gently rocked by good cheer and the warm certainty that nothing bad could ever happen to them, since they were all together and Arcady was still watching over them.

I can imagine with great precision their last luncheon on the lawn. I can see Fiorentina busying herself over the white linen tablecloth and smoothing the central motif with her fingernail, a crowned heart of which she alone knows the meaning. I can see the upturned baskets, spilling out the fruit from our walled orchard. I can see the gold-rimmed plates, hear the clicking of cutlery, and the voices of Jewell, Victor, Orlando. I know they will have talked, waving their voluble hands in the great rays of sunlight the pines filtered towards them. I know they will have broken the crumbly aniseed-flavored bread that Fiorentina made every day of her life—the bread of the dead would have been fitting for the occasion, with its dark crumb, its raisins, and its whole hazelnuts and candied-citrus zest, but it is too early in the season; if I know them well, and who knows them better than I do, they will not have strayed far from their habits.

I hope they lay down to look up at the boughs and branches, saw them detach themselves from the blue sky, and drew comfort from the idea that these trees would survive them, with their twisted trunks, their balsamic scent, and the gray scales of their cones. I hope the cats and dogs came to claim the leftovers, with their imploring tongues and impertinent paws. Arcady always said you were one or the other: a dog who was crazy with gratitude at the least favor, or a cat persuaded that he was entitled to everything. Try this out with people you know and you'll see it works very well.

Maybe they mentioned their absent friends, raised their glasses to the memory of our dead, starting with Dadah, whose shade was no doubt still roaming nearby, delivered at last, finally released from her bionic wheelchair and her oxygen tanks. For us the dead are never really dead, and that is what gives me the conviction that my community took its last meal without fearing what was waiting for them. From the time of my arrival at Liberty House, I lived in the company of girls who died last century. I heard their high-pitched screams, I saw them quickly do up their braids again in front of the trumeau mirrors in the living room, I straddled the oak banister of the stairs behind them, polished by all their Amazonian thighs, I flicked the bean wildly while imagining them under the shower or their scratchy woolen blankets, in the big dormitory on the top floor: I know death is not the end of anything, and Arcady knew that too, but maybe he thought it best to remind them. Be not afraid. Those words were the first I heard him say, and my life was changed by them forever. I say "my life," but I never actually had a life that was all mine: it was always blended into others, my time given to theirs, our interests woven together. I know what it means to love, I learned that along with all the rest: how to identify a constellation, distinguish a cep from a boletus, climb to the top of a cedar, milk an unwilling cow, browse through a library—but also how to massage arthritic limbs, arrange thinning hair, push a wheelchair through muddy ruts, soap the hard body of a little boy, reassure an overly fragile mother, write letters for an illiterate father, inject a junkie between her toes, be of assistance to an inflexible governess in her kitchen, follow her ironclad instruction to the letter, then run through the wet grass to meet my lover and give myself to him. But even at the high point of passion and sexual dependency, when the thought of Arcady was a nuclear warhead in my brain and belly, I never lost sight of the fact that I owned nothing, not even the fervor of my own desire. I always belonged to the community and I still do: death changes nothing in that belonging.

My grandmother survived, of course. I didn't have to wait

for her call to know that she was not among the suicides of Liberty House. In the seconds of silence that follow our first exchange, our first awkward phrases, I catch my breath again, which the pain had taken away, just from hearing the sound of her voice, and in the background, Malika's and Djilali's.

"Why did they do that? Last time I saw Arcady, he was in a bad way, but not desperate."

I don't tell her that the last time I saw Arcady, we tried in vain to make love. I keep this astounding story to myself, it's so incredible when you know that Arcady's sex life had never known the slightest hiccup.

"We were being attacked on all fronts, you know, it was relentless. But the thing that, um, how shall I put this, precipitated their decision was the cell tower. We were no longer going to be in a quiet zone. In fact, quiet zones are done for: the government announced that there would be no more technological deserts in the whole country within two years."

"Oh, really? And what about electromagnetic-hypersensitive people? Where are they supposed to go?"

"They'll die like dogs in terrible suffering. That's why for Birdie's sake it's probably for the best in the end."

Her voice is strangled, but I know my grandmother well enough to realize that she doesn't find it completely abnormal to survive her daughter. And because she also knows me well, she quickly adds:

"It was Arcady who wanted us to go away, all three of us, with the boy. There was no question that Djilali should die, you understand . . ."

I understand perfectly. I even understand what she imagines is beyond my comprehension. I understand that she would have jumped ship anyway, because her loyalty was first and foremost to her own personal plans, her relationship with Malika and her hopes that could be realized only outside our confraternity. I will never hold it against my grandmother that she believed that happiness was still possible, but what is true for her is not true for me, and I should have been there for the last moments my nearest and dearest spent on earth. They would not have accepted that I die at twenty years old, but they would have let me do what I do best: smooth out their difficulties, help them avoid unnecessary suffering, be devoted to them right until the end, because devotion is in my nature and there is no shame in serving with love. I could have opened a last bottle of prosecco and poured in the poison my father had concocted—he had become an expert in toxicology, after all those years cultivating opiates in his secret garden. I could have cleared up the remains of the meal, shaken the tablecloth, shooed away the dogs, simulated normalcy so they could be at ease—especially Fiorentina, who was so pernickety about order and cleanliness. Above all, I could have told them that this ceremony was only a temporary goodbye. Yes, we will see each other again. We just have to wait for things to get worse, for civilization to implode, for Humanity to complete its mad enterprise of destroying everything—starting with itself, bingo, another big bang; we just have to wait for the end of technological colonization through smartphones, connected electricity meters, Wi-Fi and 4G, the dismantling of the network, the great unraveling of electromagnetic waves, the apocalypse, now.

Everything must disappear, except us, who never sought to harm anyone and were only guilty of trifles that have nothing in common with the atrocities perpetrated in the outside world. We deserve to be spared, and that is why I don't believe for a second that this life is the only modality of our existence.

One way or another, we will be there to see the postcolonial and post-apocalyptic golden age Arcady promised. Maureen, Daniel, and I, of course, but also our brothers and sisters who fell asleep in the hope of a resurrection. It will be in their company that I'll discover a world free of nuclear-power plants, industrial installations, road networks, fossil-fuel exploitation, and cell-phone towers; in their company that I will applaud the defeat of our other enemies: ionizing radiation, nanoparticles, dioxins, chlorinated cyclodienes, PCBs, radon, endocrine disruptors—all those invisible pathogenic agents that were the terrors of my youth.

Arcady was never very precise about the conditions of this nth massive extinction, the essential part being that a handful of chosen ones would be spared or come back to life, to start over from the beginning in a world purged of what made it intolerable—in other words, of human activity. I can still hear his voice booming in the dining room, vibrating with persuasion and unshakable conviction, explaining to us how we would leave the cave, with its familiar crannies, its rock formations, its flowering saltpeter, its cervids engraved on the walls, its paunchy horses, stylized in charcoal throughout the long nuclear winter, to make our entrance into suspended, immemorial, and found time.

First shaking and dazzled, we would soon be cheered by the great blue campanulas and the yellow broom flowers. We would walk through clearings covered in hardy wheat, and cross crystalline rivers, with their mossy stones, their puddles of sunlight, we would be caressed by fearless starlings, sniffed by friendly deer, marmots, or feral cats, a whole fauna that will have forgotten man and his predatory superpowers. Along the path, perhaps we would find the softened outlines of a city, with its foundations razed and buried under tender grass, which we would step on without the slightest regret for that old world—what's the point of regretting the violence of megapolises, of hideous rivieras covered in concrete, with their concentrations of intoxicated and diminished human beings? We would stop for a moment to gaze at the hills rising up in layers into the distance, the racing clouds, their fleeting shadows skimming the new earth, and look at each other with emotion, gratitude, and relief. After the long winter journey, we would have found a place to live. Our real story would begin there and never end.

36.

The Coming Insurrection

The golden age is all very well, but it's still too early for the apocalypse and the return in glory of the members of my confraternity. At a rough guess, I have a life expectancy of another sixty years—sixty years that will feel like a thousand without Arcady and far from paradise. Where did my enchanter, my mentor, my muse go, the only one who could turn my blackest hours into a sumptuous fairyland sparkling with promises? When I think that I doubted him and nearly stopped loving him on the pretext that he didn't want to open our doors to migrants and welcome them decently. . . . He was wrong of course, but since when is wrongdoing unforgivable? Since when does it constitute a good reason to abandon people, when to the contrary you should stand by them, to enlighten them, and be a good example? But that taught me a lesson, and I'll never do it again: I'm done with defection.

The fall of our House of Pleasure unchained a whole maelstrom of articles, overblown news reports, vengeful tweets, solemn comments, and outrageous testimony from people who said they had known us—all those betrayals were like as many thorns in my heart: Epifanio, Kinbote, Palmyre, and, quite unexpectedly, Jewell! Jewell not dead with the others, not lying down under the pine trees with them, but miraculously transformed into a survivor of hell, rehabilitated, unrecognizable, and telling one insane story after another. But even though all you have to do is look at Jewell to realize that she is not in possession of all her faculties, she was able to calumniate Liberty House with impunity for days on end, while my dispassionate testimony was of absolutely no interest to anyone.

It should be said that the finale of Liberty House, sensational though it was, left the pack hungry: with Arcady and Victor's death, the investigation was closed, along with its expected orgiastic and barbaric revelations, rapes of virgins, human sacrifices, neonaticides—all those ways humanity quenches its desire to exterminate beauty and put an end to itself. My letter to the world, if I ever write it, will start with these words: Dear world, it is high time you examined your conscience and drew all the necessary consequences. That letter is one I'm prepared to sign in my blood, which will not have flowed in vain if I obtain a truce in the great anthropophagic fury, the disarmament of the universal militia, and an opening of the Red Sea to the Promised Land, instead of the graveyard by the sea that it has become.

After weeks of police and media agitation, the corpses requisitioned for autopsy purposes reappeared. Coming out of the woods, the biological families claimed their rights, each leaving with their own assigned remains. For our part, we buried Birdie and Marqui with no fanfare, with Kirsten as mistress of ceremonies, draped in black and clutching Malika, who was tearful but even more flouncy than ever. My paternal grandparents were there too, and mechanically shook a few hands, including mine, without recognizing their granddaughter in the young man I had become. They must have come to Liberty House three times in fifteen years, and they never really understood what went on there, and so this collective and planned death left them more dazed than sad. My laborious identification was the last straw, the piece of information that left them with no idea what to say or do:

"Ah, Farah, you said?"

"Yes, Farah."

"Farah, you know . . ."

"Farah."

"Oh."

Their words dwindled away until there was nothing left between us except deathly silence, which fit the occasion, after all, and on which we parted ways. Farah, of course. . . . I could perfectly understand their awkwardness: the last time they saw me, I was thirteen and all hope of normalcy was not lost. I was just a chunky brunette with a little amphibian face under heavy bangs. They must have thought that at puberty I would become more womanly, even if I didn't become more graceful, but who would have thought that the exact opposite would occur? For grace is exactly what I gained by losing my gendered identity—a grace that doesn't prevent ugliness but moves through it without stopping. Grandma and Granddad probably went away wondering about their encounter with the third kind, but I doubt those questions lasted more than fifteen minutes among their senile anxieties about the return train trip and the digestion of their salmon sandwiches—and had they given me the time to do so, I could have given them a few dietary tips, including not to eat an animal whose life and death were as sad as a farmed salmon's.

I still don't know what I am, but my wish list is infinite—and my hate list is too. It's out of the question that I live like everyone else and spend most of my time filling myself with industrial foodstuffs, insane images, and soulless music. You always resign yourself too quickly to being a trash can. It amused me for a few months, just long enough to understand what it was all about and what other people's lives were like, but that's all over now too. I received love as an inheritance, and with it the duty to reveal its good news, like a trail of incandescent powder in a society that doesn't want love and especially not incandescence, a society that prefers to be an open garbage dump, a gigantic accommodation establishment for unhappy people who are cruelly dependent on what is killing them.

With Mor and Nello, I feel up to the task of founding a new community, which would learn from the mistakes of the old one and not reproduce its autarchic modus operandi, with its closed doors and jealous possession of happiness. The idea is to create a flying brigade, a nomadic intervention force traveling to the zones that need defending, as required, instead of operating from a manor house, a citadel comfortably nestled behind its walls. Liberty House was a paradise, but from now on we will lug paradise around inside us and try to establish it everywhere we go.

The good thing about the three of us is that we are not straight or cisgender. Of course, we are white, but that can be fixed: as soon as our first disciples are recruited among the refugees wandering in the valley, we will go for intersectional activism. Nothing will be able to withstand this convergence, this great pride parade, this migratory wave of a new kind, as fluid as it is colorful, as deviant as it is radical. My inheritance is there too, in the certainty that transgression should overrule normativity, in the conviction that life can only ever be irregular, and beauty, monstrous. I was born to abolish the Old Testament, which always left the world to those who already had everything, eternally perpetuating the same dynasties with their exorbitant privileges. The game of thrones did not take place, it was only a simulacrum, a game of musical chairs, a quid pro quo between elites, which always excluded the prisoners of want, the captives, the vanquished—and many others more.

The good thing about the three of us is that in less time than it takes to say it, there will be millions of us. It won't be a question of conquering but rather of submerging. In any case, I'm not interested in conquering anything, or even fighting. I get that from Arcady too, the knowledge that victory always carries too high a price. I've lived too long in peace to want war, and it's a well-known fact that the taste for blood is acquired in childhood. The good thing about a confraternity is that the toxic ferments are diluted, until they disappear—whereas family reunification favors ambition, jealousy, bitterness, and mortal combat. All of us together, Eritrean archangels, lanky hermaphrodites, those with Asperger or Rokitansky syndrome, Black Venuses, depigmented bipolars, exiles from paradise or refugees from war, we will form a critical mass, we will have the numbers. One could argue that revolutions contribute only to maintaining order, and that ours, our great pacifist and pathological uprising, is heading in the wrong direction right from the start. So much the better. The less we are taken seriously, the greater the effect of surprise. They won't see us coming, but the day will dawn when we will be indispensable, and we will be the ones that people come to in order to recharge their vitality and cure their rottenness.

But let me come back to the barbaric days that followed our final season, the inhumation of one, the cremation of another, earth and ashes on our childhood, since its witnesses were buried one after the other and even without informing us, as if the death of Victor or Fiorentina concerned only their biological families. As for the surviving witnesses, Jewell, Epifanio, Palmyre, they were capable only of burning what they had adored, offering their convulsed faces and hateful mouths to the crackling flashes of the cameras. It will come as no surprise that Arcady's corpse made the most of these difficult times to volatilize itself. Somewhere between the candlelit chapel and the cold storage room, the external examination and the forensic autopsy, he managed to disappear, performing a last magic trick and perhaps a prelude to a whole series of miracles, including his return among us.

I have never wanted anything more ardently than this, but my madness does not go so far as to believe in it: I know I will not see Arcady again in this life, but in the luminous pastoral eternity he promised us. The finality of death is all very well for most people, but a psychological architecture as sophisticated as his, such magnificently inventive generosity, and such a talent for joy are not meant to dissolve into the void—to say nothing of moldering in a sepulchre.

My letter to the world is already written: it is buried six feet under, in a gently sloping meadow where the cows graze to the tinkling of their bells, and it will pass through time as surely as a spatial probe; my letter to the world is made up of a few objects: a jay feather, some seashells, the resinous scent of Arcady's cologne, a Bakelite cicada, and a slightly dimpled peach stone that enfolds the germ of a whole endless summer; my letter to the world needs only a few words, which my human brothers will have no trouble translating, no matter what happens to language in the time that separates us from its exhumation: love exists.

◙   ◙   ◙

This book includes quotations, sometimes slightly modified or in translation, by: Jean Anouilh, Louis Aragon, Christine Arnothy, Antonin Artaud, Charles Baudelaire, Samuel Beckett, René Belletto, Hélène Bessette, Ernst Bloch, Enid Blyton, Jacques Brel, André Breton, Judith Butler, Lewis Carroll, Blaise Cendrars, Aimé Césaire, Raymond Chandler, Anton Chekhov, Paul Claudel, Dante, Charles Dickens, Emily Dickinson, James Ellroy, Paul Éluard, Gustave Flaubert, Michel Foucault, André Gide, Jean Giraudoux, Kenneth Grahame, Victor Hugo, the Invisible Committee, James Joyce, Maylis de Kerangal, Rudyard Kipling, Milan Kundera, Marie-Ève Lacasse, Jean de la Fontaine, Patrick Lapeyre, Antoine Leiris, René Leriche, Mathieu Lindon, Curzio Malaparte, Stéphane Mallarmé, Louis Malle, Guy de Maupassant, Daphne du Maurier, Curtis Mayfield, Henri Michaux, Octave Mirbeau, Michel de Montaigne, Robert Musil, Alfred de Musset, Vladimir Nabokov, Marcel Pagnol, Cesare Pavese, Marguerite Porète, Eugène Pottier,

Marcel Proust, Jean Racine, Atiq Rahimi, Rainer Maria Rilke, Arthur Rimbaud, Jean-Jacques Rousseau, Goliarda Sapienza, Sophocles, Paul Valéry, Paul Verlaine, François Villon, Voltaire, Sarah Waters, Oscar Wilde, and Virginia Woolf.

About the Author

EMMANUELLE BAYAMACK-TAM was born in 1966 in Marseille. She has published twelve novels and two plays with P.O.L Editeur, three, under the pseudonym Rebecca Lighieri. She is a founding member of the interdisciplinary association Autres et Pareils and co-director of Éditions Contre-Pied. *Arcadia*, her first book in translation, won the Prix du Livre Inter; was shortlisted for the Prix Femina, Prix Médicis, and Prix de Flore; and longlisted for the Prix France-Culture and Prix Wepler. She lives in Paris.

About the Translator

RUTH DIVER has translated works by several of France's leading contemporary novelists, including *The Little Girl on the Ice Floe* by Adélaïde Bon, *The Revolt* by Clara Dupont-Monod, and *A Respectable Occupation* by Julia Kerninon. Her translation of *Maraudes* by Sophie Pujas won the 2016 *Asymptote* Close Approximations Fiction Prize.

About Seven Stories Press

SEVEN STORIES PRESS is an independent book publisher based in New York City. We publish works of the imagination by such writers as Nelson Algren, Russell Banks, Octavia E. Butler, Ani DiFranco, Assia Djebar, Ariel Dorfman, Coco Fusco, Barry Gifford, Martha Long, Luis Negrón, Peter Plate, Hwang Sok-yong, Lee Stringer, and Kurt Vonnegut, to name a few, together with political titles by voices of conscience, including Subhankar Banerjee, the Boston Women's Health Collective, Noam Chomsky, Angela Y. Davis, Human Rights Watch, Derrick Jensen, Ralph Nader, Loretta Napoleoni, Gary Null, Greg Palast, Project Censored, Barbara Seaman, Alice Walker, Gary Webb, and Howard Zinn, among many others. Seven Stories Press believes publishers have a special responsibility to defend free speech and human rights, and to celebrate the gifts of the human imagination, wherever we can. In 2012 we launched Triangle Square Books for Young Readers with strong social justice and narrative components, telling personal stories of courage and commitment. For additional information, visit www.sevenstories.com.